BETWIXT *the* STIRRUP *and the* GROUND

BETWIXT *the* STIRRUP *and the* GROUND

a novel

Karen McGoldrick

Deeds Publishing | Athens

Published by Deeds Publishing in Athens, GA
www.deedspublishing.com

Printed in The United States of America

Cover photo courtesy of Roger Fetlock

Cover and interior design by Deeds Publishing

ISBN 978-1-961505-05-6

Books are available in quantity for promotional or premium use. For
information, email info@deedspublishing.com.

First Edition, 2023

10 9 8 7 6 5 4 3 2 1

This book is dedicated to my late mother and father, Harry and Marjorie Jaffa, both "extreme" readers. My father gave me a love of history and was a celebrated Lincoln scholar. My mother did an amazing amount of accurate genealogy research long before the days of the internet. And she was, and therefore I am, a Robertson through her maternal line.

Betwixt the stirrup and the ground,
mercy I asked and mercy I found.

—William Camden

1

Eloise Robertson felt that being an early riser gave her an edge. It gave her margin, white space, time to think, to be prepared. Sunrise rarely caught her sleeping. Still, life had a way of laying traps. Like today when she pulled into the vet clinic to start her normal workday as a kennel-maid.

She had just gotten out of her car, grabbed her back-pack, and was slightly turned to hit the "lock" button on her key fob, when she was nearly spun around in her shoes. A black form coming out of nowhere, side-swiped her legs, and blew past her. Her moment of panic passed as she watched a large black hairy dog bounce up the front steps.

There did not appear to be anyone with him.

The dog made eye contact with her, bouncing from paw to paw, and then looking at the door.

He looked like a dog who needed to go out. But he *was* out. This was a dog on the outside who wanted *in*.

Maybe it was from relief, but Eloise began to laugh, shaking her head.

"Good grief! Well, okay then."

She reached out to give him a rub on the top of his head and ran her hand over filthy matted hair. The dog stank, a cloud of "rolled in dead animal" vapor wafting through the morning air. A big fat tick had latched on behind his ear.

Eloise unlocked the front door of the clinic and the dog bounded in. She shook her head, amused. "Okay; after you."

The building was narrow but tall. The kennels were in the daylight basement. Cat housing was on the second story along with the vet's office, while the main floor included the reception area, exam rooms, a lounge, and a restroom.

Although the stray startled her, no harm, no foul. His appearance out of nowhere was a puzzle though. A vague story niggled at the back of her brain.

In fact, the dog would make a good subject for a shaggy-dog story; he was a shaggy dog, after all, and there was nothing Eloise liked better than a good story. But she reprimanded herself. The last thing she needed to do was tell more stories.

The dog was studying her face intently and he gave a bark that disrupted her thoughts. The basement full of dogs erupted in reply, calling her back to duty.

The shaggy dog tipped his head and froze at the sound of the barking.

"Care to join the pack for breakfast?"

As soon as Eloise opened the door to the basement, her new friend bounded down the stairs. One of the runs was empty, so Eloise filled one stainless steel bowl with kibble, and another with water, and her friend followed her into the run.

"That will keep you for now." The dog then put his attention on eating.

Time to put on a smock and get to work. Eloise had to feed the resident animals and clean the public areas. Then she would walk dogs and clean cages, help Pinky (the groomer) and Susie (the tech), by running dogs and cats up and down the three levels of the clinic.

Eloise could go through her morning routine detached from her body but alive in her mind. Since she was the only one there, it was her time to reflect on her latest read or listen to an audio book. Routines anchored Eloise. Routines gave her purpose, and the physical activity reduced her anxiety. But books, books made her more than she was. In a book you could leave yourself behind and rest in someone else's story. Eloise put in her earbuds.

She filled her rolling bucket with warm water and green disinfectant. Then she began to mop. When she got to the front reception area, she stopped and hit the pause button on her audiobook.

The bulletin board was covered with photos and fliers. Pinky and Doc were volunteers with "The Good Steward" animal rescue, and they helped place the latest "Adoptables."

Eloise smiled thinking of the rank and vermin-covered "rescue" she had waiting for Pinky. She knew that Pinky loved that sort of challenge and would take a "before" and "after" photo to go on the bulletin board.

But, for several months, one flier had held Eloise's eye. It was not one of the Adoptables. She had told herself many a story about that one. Not the dog. The man in the photo. He was dark-haired with soulful eyes who looked right into her, or rather the camera, standing next to a dog.

3

My God, he was handsome. Underneath the photo was the sad story of how the dog had somehow gotten out of his crate at the Atlanta Airport and gone missing. There was a reward for his safe return. The dog's face was hard to see (maybe a Bouvier or a Giant Schnauzer). But it was the man, "Joe" (his name was on the flier with a phone number) who made her insides go squishy and her head float off her shoulders if she gazed at him for more than a moment. And she had.

Today, when she squeezed out the mop to have her private moment with "Joe," the flier was gone, replaced with a new selection of "Adoptables" from The Good Steward Rescue.

Joe was gone. An unpleasant but familiar rush of dizziness came and went. But when she slowly emptied the trash cans (pretending that she wasn't searching for the flier), why, there he was! She neatly folded it up and slipped it into her backpack. "Joe" was a keeper. It was no one's business if she had a harmless crush on Joe.

Eloise retreated into the lounge and started the coffee. She could hear Janet's high heels come clicking down the hall. Janet ran the front desk. She nodded toward Eloise and poured herself a cup, and Eloise returned the greeting.

Doc arrived next, a flat of donuts in hand.

"Eloise, I got your favorites in here."

"Uh, Doc, weirdest thing happened this morning."

He raised his eyebrows, ready, and then turned to fill his mug.

"When I got here, a dog showed up—like he was waiting for me. I don't think I've ever seen him before though."

"Emergency?"

Eloise shook her head. "Just stinky, filthy, and covered in fleas and ticks."

"Well, as long as it's not an emergency, I can have a look after morning exams. Strays sometimes are drawn to us; they hear the dogs in the kennels. Tell Pinky I won't stop her from cleaning it up first." He winked at Eloise.

Eloise wrapped her donut in a paper towel, grabbed her coffee, and headed down to the basement. She preferred the basement once the workday started in earnest. This was her territory, hers and Pinky's.

Soon, Pinky arrived toting a large paper bag full of canine beauty supplies, which included bows, kerchiefs, and hair clips. Pinky was a vision, as curvy as Eloise was straight, with blonde hair dyed pink from her chin to the tips that fell below her shoulders. Today she had one strip of hair tightly braided with multi-colored beads.

"Morning Eloise. Did you get a donut? I stashed a couple in my bag just in case the vultures above tried to grab your old-fashioneds."

"Thanks, Pinky. Got one. Hey, I have a strange customer for you. Practically mugged me when I arrived. Check him out, in the last run."

Pinky set down her bag on one of the grooming tables by the elevated bathtub, her command central, and strolled back to the runs which erupted in barks and whines. She wrinkled her nose before she even got to him.

"God awful stench, I mean beyond the normal dog poop God-awful stench."

"It's him."

"Okay, that we gotta' fix or I'm going to upchuck my donut."

Eloise smiled. Pinky would never upchuck at anything. Pinky was a front-line warrior in the fight for all wounded and abandoned creatures. Pinky was also unlike anyone Eloise had ever known. Beautiful yet unencumbered by self-consciousness. A "bird of rare plumage."

Eloise pulled one leash off the overloaded hook for Pinky and one for herself. It was time for Eloise to walk and clean—clean and walk.

The first step was to prepare a clean cage or kennel. You take out a dog, walk it, and put it back into a clean space. Then you clean the dirty cage.

Eloise tried never to rush any of her "patients." The hospitalized dogs spent most of the day and night confined. This was a time for them to relieve themselves, of course, but also to feel the grass under their feet and smell all the smells that needed to be smelled. So, Eloise crooned to them as they meandered, delivering emotional support. Dogs, like people, counted on that intangible thing called love.

Eloise strolled slowly with an old Irish Setter, "Now Gypsy, no need to be depressed. Your exit exam is this afternoon."

Gypsy had recurring bladder stones. Her face was gray, her eyes cloudy, but Eloise thought she was beautiful. Pinky had her on her list for a bath. Eloise knew she would be sporting a kerchief printed with bright sunflowers before her exit appointment. She had seen them in the new batch Pinky had brought in this morning. It would look good on Gypsy.

When Eloise returned, the big shaggy dog was in the tub, covered in soapy bubbles with Pinky putting her back into it. His mouth hung open in what looked like a grin, his tongue hanging out of the side. When he looked at Eloise, his long tail began to wag, slinging soap and water off the long hair.

"You get the before picture, Pinky?"

Pinky nodded. "I think he looks absurdly happy."

Pinky kept scrubbing then added, "Picked off a bunch of ticks and he's crawling with fleas. I soaked him first with flea spray."

Eloise tipped her head. "How you suppose he ended up waiting outside. Someone dump him?"

Pinky pulled the retractable sprayer out and began to rinse. "Beats me. He's not neutered, so I doubt he's chipped. I'll call and let them know at "Good Stewards." I'm guessing he'll end up on our "Adoptables" list. Doesn't look like anyone has been taking care of him in a long time."

Eloise nodded. "Look at all that hair." Eloise had a strange feeling looking at the dog standing in the tub, his coat wet and flat; he looked like a different dog. She said, "I hope you don't shave it off. I like it long and fluffy."

"Not today. Too many dogs in the queue to do a freebie. I *am* springing for the expensive de-tangler, so the mats will be easier to get out. You think you can do the brush-out?"

Eloise gave him another pat on the head while his tail slung more water around the room. "I'd love to." She turned to Pinky. "You going to name him?"

"You do the honors. You found him."

"I didn't. Not really. He basically mugged me."

The dog put a paw on Eloise's chest, leaving a giant sloppy print.

When Eloise and Pinky laughed, he barked, as if laughing along with them.

Eloise removed his paw from her chest and placed it back into the tub.

Pinky said, "Mugged you? Or chose you? So, c'mon, what IS his name?"

Eloise and the dog locked eyes, and she felt a flutter of unease. "I'll wait and let him tell me."

Just then the intercom buzzed, making the dog tip his head quizzically.

At the base of the stairs was an intercom, with the volume set on high. Susie, the tech, was asking for Peaches to be brought up for Doc to examine. Janet buzzed in right behind to say that Pinky had her first grooming client waiting in the reception area.

Eloise pulled off her wet smock, threw it on top of the washer and grabbed a fresh one off the shelf, tying it off around her waist, "I need to take Peaches to Doc, can you fetch your grooming job?"

Pinky nodded.

While Eloise worked on getting Peaches, Pinky used her hands to wring off excess water on the hairy dog, rubbed him with a towel and then put the dog into the largest cage and turned on the cage dryer.

Peaches was a champagne-colored tea-cup poodle who had the habit of biting everyone at the hospital, except Eloise. Eloise opened her cage door and commenced her baby talk. "Miss Peaches, Doc wants to check your eye this morning."

Peaches had been hiding in the back of the cage in the folds of a blue blanket. Hearing Eloise, she flattened herself against the floor, ears pinned back, mouth pulled tight, shaking all over. Anyone who dared reach for her now would regret it. Peaches slowly belly-crawled her way to the front, shoulders hunched, blinking, and curling her lip. Eloise raised her voice to a high pitch, "Come to me baby girl, c'mon baby girl."

Eloise made a loop at the end of her leash and slowly lassoed her tiny charge, pulling Peaches gently into her arms, scooping her bottom up with the palm of her hand and cradling the tiny dog against her chest. She knew that once she got Peaches to this point, all would be well. Peaches began to wag her tail tentatively, then to reach up and lick Eloise on her chin.

Peaches spent most of her life in just this position with her owner, cradled against a warm bosom (a much more voluptuous one than Eloise's). Peaches' painted toenails rarely touched the ground when her mistress was around. But Peaches had a stubborn eye infection that had been worsening under her owner's care. Today, Peaches was to be released. If Doc gave the green light, Pinky would be giving her a lavender scented bath, applying a fresh coat of nail polish and a brand-new tiny hair bow to the pom-pom puff atop her head, all with the aid of the world's tiniest muzzle.

At the top of the stairs, Eloise put Peaches down and watched the tiny dog give a whole-body shake and then prance all the way to the exam room.

Eloise believed that Peaches and Gypsy and the big shaggy dog, they needed her, and she could help. That was something. She realized it was a small peg on which to hang her new sense of self. But for now, it was okay. She was okay.

Doc was leaning against the counter, engaged in telling one of his countless stories to Susie.

He said, "Turned out, those cows were feral. I had to jump up on the stall wall to keep from being trampled, straddled it, as they came charging down the barn aisle. I had the good luck to have a shovel in my hand. Turned that cow into the stall with a shovel and slammed that door shut." Doc swung an imaginary shovel through the air.

Doc was blessed with a surplus of charm, which made him a favorite with the more anxious clients. For Doc, having grown up on a horse farm in Kansas, an equine practice had been a natural choice. But he had given it up for a "cat and dog" clinic because his body got too "beat up" and his clients were taking longer and longer to settle their accounts. It did not mean he did not miss the horses, although they were now in the distant past.

Eloise learned about Doc's love of horses through his stories. Back in the day, his Grandpa had trained "remounts" for the cavalry at Ft. Riley. The cavalry school closed in 1947, but his grandpa and his dad continued to train horses and even mules.

Doc had told her, "Dad was a genius with horses. He'd put me up with only a rope or baling wire around the neck to hang on to, no saddle or bridle. We put on a show. Dad and I sold a lot of horses. Grandpa and Dad thought I would carry on the family tradition. But Mom sure was glad when I got into vet school."

Eloise, perhaps more than anyone else at the clinic, appreciated his stories, especially his horse stories. Word had gotten out in the clinic that both loved horses although neither had ridden in years. Doc's stories nourished Eloise. But they also made her feel nostalgic. They were both, in a way, expatriates from the horse world.

Eloise waited for Doc to finish his story before putting Peaches on the exam table.

She had the job of slipping the muzzle on Peaches and then handing the job over. Peaches was stiff legged with fear. The eye treatment couldn't possibly hurt at this point, but Peaches was braced for the worst. Eloise left the room while Peaches followed her with her eyes.

Pinky got her dogs bathed, while Eloise had everyone fed and walked, litter boxes cleaned, and had run the in-house dogs and cats up and down the stairs for morning check-ups.

Eloise began the slow job of working out the mats on the stray dog. Doc called Eloise on the intercom and asked her to bring him up as soon as she was ready. Doc would squeeze him in between appointments.

When she finally came upstairs with the dog, Doc said, "My God, that's a beast!" At which point the dog sat down, stared up into Doc's face, and held up a paw, panting cheerfully.

Doc took the proffered paw, "Pleased to make your acquaintance."

Eloise said, "I don't think he's one of our clients. Is he?"

Doc drew his eyebrows together and frowned, then shook his head. He put his hand on the exam table and before Eloise could do anything, the big dog hopped right up like it was nothing.

Doc said, "At least he's agreeable."

Eloise nodded. "Pinky told me to name him. You called him a beast, and that made me think, he's not. I mean, he's a big guy, but he's very well-mannered."

"Why don't we call him Prince then? The beast in the fairytale was a Prince, under all that hair that is."

"Oh, I love that. That beast just needed to fall in love to break the spell. What say you, big guy? You ready to fall in love?"

Incredibly, the big hairy "beast" barked in reply.

"There's your answer."

"I wonder who his one true love will be?"

Doc winked, then pulled his reading glasses down off his head and peered through them, "Let's have a look at you." He ran his hands over the dog and observed, "Hasn't been neutered."

Doc pulled at his stethoscope and listened intently. Then he looked in the ears with the Otoscope and said matter-of-factly, "mites." He got out the scope he used to examine the eyes and shone it in each eye. Next, the dog agreeably opened his jaws so Doc could examine his teeth. "Adult dog, but young."

He called for Susie. "Let's pull blood, scan for a chip, do a fecal for parasites and treat him for ear-mites. Go ahead and draw up vaccines while you're at it."

He nodded at Eloise. "Looks like another rescue. You

can leave him. I'll send Prince back down to you in a few. I've got a patient waiting."

Eloise stopped at the door, "Prince. I love the name. Of course, I loved the fairy tale, even before the movie."

Doc smiled, "I'll tell Janet to start a file on Prince."

Pinky and Eloise had taken their lunches to the lounge. Eloise brought Peaches and fed her tiny bits from samples of soft dog treats. Eloise chatted a bit, but then retreated to her audio book as Peaches climbed into her lap and curled into a little ball. Pinky listened to music and often used the time to do her nails.

Eloise resisted the urge to pull the flier of Joe out of her purse. But she could summon his face in her mind while she listened and rested her hand on the warm little dog in her lap. She found that small white space, that bit of margin. She had the afternoon ahead of her before going back to the empty townhome.

After lunch, Pinky headed upstairs, where she did all the cat grooming jobs. She had a regular weekly customer. Betsy's Persian cat, Marilyn. Marilyn always stood stock still in the sink to be bathed, without any restraint, and seemed to enjoy the blow dry and brushing. Not something that could be said of most cats.

Eloise went up the stairs to do her second run through the litter boxes, refill feeders and put down fresh water, and frankly, to shoot the breeze.

Pinky was finishing blowing and brushing, cat hair floating everywhere around her. "Hey Eloise, look at Marilyn! I used a new whitening product."

The Persian's eyes were half closed. She purred loudly and kneaded the rubber matting. The cat looked like a snow-white fright wig.

Pinky had stopped brushing and Marilyn gave her hand a head butt, to which Pinky replied. "You're welcome." Then she turned to Eloise. "Buzz called and said we're going to Moon Dogs on Tuesday night. We wouldn't stay out real late, but his sous-chef is the nicest guy, and I was thinking, we could make it a foursome. They have karaoke and other cool stuff to do there."

Eloise shook her head "no."

"What? Washing your hair?"

The intercom lit up. Susie's said, "Prince is ready."

Eloise said, "Gotta go. I have a dark handsome Prince waiting."

"You want to date the dog? I'm sure it could be arranged. Matter of fact, I think he'd be happy to go home with you, but you two just met. It's kinda' rushing things, don't you think?"

"He *is* trying to pick me up. And I don't even know his real name."

Pinky laughed, "Yeah, and now he's pretending to be royalty."

Pinky added, "Okay, so no foursome for Moon Dogs Tuesday night. But no squirming out of Doc's field trip on Saturday. You and I, we *are* going. No excuses."

Pinky wagged a finger at Eloise, cat hair hanging from the fingertip. Eloise drew in a breath and nodded back.

Susie was standing at the bottom of the stairs with the dog, her hand holding the leash away from her body. Susie was aiming for vet school. She had just gotten back her scores on her MCAT. They had been good. Susie was an example of someone with a plan, upwardly mobile and serious. Eloise was pretty sure that Susie disapproved of her, especially when Eloise baby-talked to the animals, which she often did.

Eloise asked, "Did he test negative for heart worm?"

She answered brusquely, "Yes, negative. Had internal parasites and we treated him. Dog's got a chip too, so don't go giving him away. Just have to run a search through the registries."

Prince was looking up at Eloise through a bouffant hairdo. The blow dry and brush really had made his size impressive. Eloise took the leash and stroked the dog on the head. He was soft to the touch and grinning, wagging his tail with enthusiasm.

She said to Susie, "He's an enchanted dog you know. A real Prince, and he's on a quest is all. He came to our door with a purpose, looking for his one true love."

Susie exhaled dramatically, "You're such a dork, Eloise."

Eloise was taking a perverse pride in her dorkiness. "Well, with that attitude, we can rule you out as the one!"

Eloise took him down the stairs and out the basement door for a walk, feeling happy. "Go on, magical or not, have a sniff; be a dog." She pointed to the bushes, and he followed her point, doing his best impression of a vacuum cleaner.

Eloise's day was coming to an end. Patients began arriving to pick up their pets.

Eloise made sure she was the one to bring Marilyn to Betsy. Betsy was her favorite client. They never used a carrier for Marilyn, but before taking her down, they put her in her pink leather harness studded with two layers of rhinestones—all attached to a pink leash. Betsy claimed this was a nod to Marilyn Monroe's movie, "Diamonds are a Girl's Best Friend." Betsy was both a dedicated reader like Eloise, and a movie buff.

Betsy was standing at the counter when Eloise said her name. She spun around to reach for her cat, who was purring loudly. Betsy was a retired schoolteacher, short and wiry with silver hair cut in a bob.

Eloise said, "Marilyn Monroe is ready for her close up!"

Betsy answered in her Atlanta drawl, "That was Gloria Swanson."

"Oops. Well, I'm not good at movie trivia I guess."

"No matter. But I wanted to speak with you. I'm starting a new study group on Extreme Reader. You've turned me down before, but I think you should reconsider this one."

Eloise ended up walking with Betsy to her car to hear more about it.

Before Eloise left for the day, she said good-bye to Prince, who answered her with a wag and a happy spin. Eloise felt a strange pain in her chest as she turned and headed up the basement stairs. She didn't want to look back because she just knew he was indeed courting her. She imagined him drooping with disappointment as she left. Was he? Could it be that she was his one true love? Silly.

Eloise would have loved to be his "foster." But it made no sense for her to foster because it was just too hard to let them go. She'd already been forced to let go of way too much. And she could not have a dog. She couldn't. A dog would tie you down. She could not get tied down. Besides, he was micro-chipped. He could be going home tomorrow.

2

Eloise was sitting on the upholstered bench in her mother's closet. She found it a good spot to read, surrounded by her mother's clothes and shoes and such. She was absorbed in a story about Teddy Roosevelt when she was startled by a persistent knocking at her front door.

Eloise jumped up, feeling annoyed, and answered the door in her bare feet. Eloise's first thought was, 'What was Pinky doing here?' Then she remembered. Looked at her watch to see it was indeed Saturday and exhaled. "Sorry."

Pinky crossed her arms and shook her head. "C'mon, stop dawdling and shake your tail feathers. Doc's waiting in the car."

"That Extreme Reader site that Betsy got me into? Totally hooked in this read. Sorry."

Pinky shook her head, "You're blaming Betsy?" She followed Eloise through the foyer and back through a hall into her bedroom. They walked into the closet.

Pinky's mouth fell open, "Now this is a closet! Arranged by color? Oh, man, the shoes."

Pinky sighed and looked back at Eloise. "You're moving in slow motion—minus the motion. Get moving."

Eloise looked at Pinky, "Where are we going? What should I wear?"

"Can't tell what I don't know. Doc said you're going to love it. It's your birthday surprise. Twenty-one is a biggie. He did say we're gonna' be walking in grass so don't wear your stilettos. Okay?"

"Very funny."

Pinky lightly ran her fingers across a row of high heeled shoes. Then Pinky raised her eyes to see the handbags above. She gave a low whistle. She said, "That leather satchel's a beautiful color. Looks like it would be soft to the touch."

Eloise glanced over at Pinky's footwear and noticed she was wearing old fashioned high-top sneakers that were bright blue.

Eloise pointed at them, drawing Pinky's attention away from the contents of the closet. "Those will get wet in grass. I'm getting my muckers out. I can't imagine why Doc is dragging us out into a field."

"Eloise, all this stuff, is it yours?"

"My Mom's stuff. What's left of it. We did a lot of, y'know, down-sizing."

Pinky raised her eyebrows. "Oh. Okay. This is your mom's house?"

"Well, it was. She died."

"Oh. I'm sorry."

Doc did a "toot-toot" on his horn.

Pinky said, "Whatever Doc has up his sleeve, act excited, okay. This is so above and beyond."

Pinky picked up an ornate disc of metal, leaves entwined in the shape of an R. "This is cool. What in the world is it?"

"Harness Brass. From my father's family, 'R' for Robertson." Eloise pointed at it, and Pinky set it back down.

Eloise was holding a pair of short green rubber boots in her hand. They were covered in dust. She grabbed a dirty sock off the floor and gave them a wipe, then pulled them on. "Okay, I'm good."

Eloise grabbed her backpack and followed Pinky out. Pinky opened the back door of Doc's car and noticed that Eloise had forgotten to brush her hair. She said, "Hey, I've got a hairbrush in my bag you can borrow. I might even have a scrunchie."

Eloise sat in the back seat, quickly brushed her hair, and pulled the scrunchie around her ponytail, tossing the curly brown mass over her shoulder and handing Pinky back her brush over the car seat with a "thanks." She had a strange feeling that she was a child again. In the front seat, Doc and Pinky chatted amicably about work. Pinky was being teased by Doc about her latest effort to groom a Bichon Frise into the shape of a cube. The client had seen it on a YouTube video. Evidently cubed shaped dogs were all the rage in China. Pinky had taken it as a challenge. She got a big tip for it too.

Eloise was silent as they drove along the interstate, coming to a crawl to get around the ever-present road work. Her mind wandered to her online group, called Extreme Readers. She was in a group studying Teddy Roosevelt. Roosevelt had a mother and a father who took a year off to take young Teddy around the world. Just to travel. Of course, it was the "Gilded Age." Such wealth. But, also, such devotion to their son. She could pretend for a moment that it was her mother and father in the front seat, and they were going somewhere exciting, just the three of them. She relaxed as she wove herself a tale that included the Nile River.

They exited on I-20 East, and the story vanished. Eloise wondered if they were headed to Six Flags, but that didn't make any sense. She would hate Six Flags and Doc knew her better than that. But they didn't stay on I-20 but got off at the first exit. They were out in the middle of nowhere—an industrial park.

Eloise knew this path. She tensed in her seat; Teddy Roosevelt forgotten. Was this a cruel joke? What was Doc thinking? So many times, she had been here, a horse trailer in tow. But Doc didn't know that. Doc was many things, but not cruel, not ever.

Eloise felt that old familiar dread and thrill. This was the way to rows of stables, fields as far as the eye could see, dotted with cross-country jumps, and show arenas. It was all from another life; a life Doc and Pinky knew nothing about. She leaned forward a bit in her seat.

Pinky said to Doc. "Are we going to learn to drive tractor-trailers? I hear it pays pretty good."

He turned to look at Pinky, then briefly over the seat back at Eloise, his eyes crinkling in the corners as he flashed a smile. "Patience, patience. It gets better soon."

On and on they drove, and Eloise didn't remember this part of the drive being so far. But she leaned her head against the glass as they passed the Texaco station. Yes, not far now.

Soon they passed a small directional sign with the single word "Event" on it. A flight of butterflies was set aloft in Eloise's stomach and a wave of dizziness swept over her.

Pinky said, "Event? What the heck?"

Doc explained. "It's an equestrian thing. I used to work these when I was doing equine medicine. An old friend's daughter, Emily, is competing today at Prelim. Lots of horses to watch—and shopping too. Besides, the sun is shining, a rare thing for cross country day. Always seemed to rain on the day the horses had to gallop and jump. Eloise loves horses. I love horses. Pinky, well, you're generally game. But, anyway, happy birthday, Eloise."

Pinky squealed, "Happy Birthday, Eloise!"

"Wow. Thank you." She *had* been surprised. Doc had been creative. Pinky had indeed been game. That Eloise was anxious, she'd keep that to herself.

Pinky added, "This is going to be so cool."

Doc said, "I can always count on your enthusiasm."

Doc pulled up a dirt road that wound through the pines, then crested a hill. A green panorama opened before them; hills dotted with cross country jumps. A majestic stable alongside the road featured a large sculpture of a horse. They drove past the main barn and followed the signs to spectator parking. They parked near the concessions stand, horses and riders names and numbers blaring over the loudspeakers, announcing the jump that had been cleared. Such-and-such was over the bank and ditch and headed to the water complex. So-and-so was clear over the final jump and galloping home.

Pinky was impressed. "Doc, that was some barn we drove past."

Doc grinned.

Eloise's insides were trembling. As they got out and followed Doc toward one of the stables, a sweaty horse was being led past them. Its nostrils were flared, a glimpse of pink membrane visible deep inside. Veins stood out on the horse's neck. A rider and coach followed, the rider's cheeks were flushed, and she was out of breath.

Pinky grabbed Eloise by the arm. "Look at that animal. I've never been so close to a racehorse before."

Eloise said, "Not a racehorse."

Pinky tipped her head. "Whatever. It's beautiful."

They caught up to Doc, "Barn five, stall fifteen. This is it."

A tall man strode out to greet them. "Ah, Doc! You made it."

Hugs were exchanged and then introductions made. But the man led them away from the stables, stage whispering. "I don't speak unless I am spoken to until she comes off cross-country. Emily is as nervous as a long-tailed cat in a room full of rockers."

"Still, after all these years?"

"Yes, and so am I. I never forget she could die out there." He moaned, "Why couldn't she just do dressage? Well, let's get coffee and I'll explain it a bit to your friends here. Then we can find a good spot to watch the action."

Eloise stood on the rise of the hill with the others, gripping her coffee, watching horses and riders. Her insides were still quaking. She had forgotten. Or maybe she hadn't forgotten, but just buried the desire. Desire made her miserable. Desire needed to stay buried. But there it was trying to claw its way back to the surface. She missed looking out between a set of alert ears. She saw in her mind's eye…bright chestnut ears, large, loose, ready to speak to Eloise with a swivel or a point or a relaxed flop. A million moods all expressed to the rider from the view behind.

Eloise took one last sip of her coffee. She didn't need the caffeine. She tossed it. Eloise was no longer a rider. She was firmly on the ground. A pedestrian. But in this moment, the desire to be back in the saddle gnawed at her gut. God damn desire needed to crawl back into the hole and leave her in peace. She was standing where she had sworn she would never be again. Someone was bound to recognize her. But maybe that was not true. Maybe she was gone, invisible. Forgotten.

She walked back over to stand next to Pinky.

Doc's friend was trying his best to give them a tutorial. He had a program in his hand with the order of the day, the page opened to the Preliminary division that was running right now. They had a view that included half a dozen fences as well as the start box. Just watching the starter count down, 10, 9, 8, 7, 6, 5, 4, 3, 2, 1, GO, had Eloise feeling light-headed.

She could not stop her mind, mentally she was back in the tack, trying her best to ignore the count, walking her horse in a circle on loose reins, instilling calm but steely resolve in herself and her mount. Her heartbeat would be drumming, her breathing faster than necessary, hence the light-headedness that she had to fight as long as she could remember. But then they would indeed go into the box, she would gather up her reins and "go!" Her horse would start out too fast, too eager. She had to find the right speed and settle into a steady pace, or risk burning out on course. She remembered that power, the bunching, and release of muscles, the punch of the hind legs, the reach of the front legs seeking purchase against the ground, the wind in her face. She could not forget.

Eloise was snapped back to the present by the sight of a different pair in the warm-up arena.

She realized she knew that horse. She knew that rider, could recognize her style in the saddle. She had been just a kid. They had been advancing, growing in the sport. Still in the game. The horse had a good ground covering stride. It had a tidy jumping style, not flamboyant, but economical and safe. The pair came out of warm-up, took their turn in the starting box, and then set out on course. Eloise rode each stride with them in her mind, rating the horse, trying to find that 520 meters per minute pace. She found herself absorbed and felt her focus, from afar, helping that rider and horse find a good take off spot for every jump.

"Eloise, what are you doing?" Eloise pulled her gaze from the horse and rider.

Doc said, "Pinky, I told you Eloise would enjoy this."

"You mean enjoy in her own special Eloise kind of way?"

"What? I'm watching, same as you guys."

Pinky shook her head, "No, you're leaning forward and doing weird things with your hands."

Eloise looked down at her hands, yup, they were holding invisible reins, and an invisible stick. She awkwardly tried to make a joke, "Walmart's fifty-cents a ride. I'm riding free of charge."

Pinky said, "Walmart horses are the right size and speed for me. What those horses are doing scares the bejeezus out of me."

Doc spoke up. "Hey, there's Emily and 'Bumptious' heading into the box."

They stopped talking to watch the countdown. The pair smoothly accelerated out of the box. Bumptious, appeared to be all business. Despite it being their Preliminary debut, they looked ready. Prelim. was a huge milestone in an Eventer's career. Eloise remembered the day. Her day. It had been scary, but good.

At Prelim. speeds were faster, the jumps substantial. Being there meant you had qualified to move up—although there were still Intermediate and then Advanced levels ahead of you. Emily and Bumptious' dressage score had them in the middle of the pack, but she could tell this phase was their strong suit. Bumptious was clearly a thoroughbred, likely purchased off the track, with the classic ground-eating gallop that was the hallmark of the breed. The long and low stride of a Thoroughbred didn't have the relaxation and swing over the back, the springy suspended trot stride, that scored well in a dressage phase, but no matter. The guts of the sport were here, out on cross country, where that long and low gallop stride ate up the turf, and the tension that spoiled the dressage test was released into catlike reflexes negotiating the obstacles and uneven terrain.

Once Emily and Bumptious were out of sight, Doc suggested they move where they could see the finish. Even though they couldn't see the pair, the announcer kept spectators apprised of where the riders were on course and what jumps had been cleared. They stood and watched a horse and rider come "home" and then another, and then it was time for Emily. The air grew still, her father and groom and coach looked anxious as they waited to sight them coming over the last fence. But then, Bumptious smoothly cleared the last jump to whoops of joy from "team Bumptious" as they galloped in.

Eloise caught Pinky staring at her, a smile on her face, a brow lifted. Pinky had been watching Eloise as much as watching Bumptious. Eloise had relaxed; her hands were open.

Emily, well past the finish line, pulled up, jumped off, ran up her stirrups and loosened the girth as the groom kept the horse walking, because with heart rates and adrenaline levels that high, you bring them down carefully. Emily's coach was patting her on the back. There was a clear sense of exhilaration, the adrenaline still coursing through veins, both human and equine.

Eloise knew it was the best feeling in the world. But the event was not over. Tonight, would be about keeping the horse loose, the muscles warm, the legs cold with ice packs, because tomorrow would be the vet check to determine if you could proceed to the third and final phase of the event, show jumping. And no effort was too much when it came to caring for that horse, the one who just galloped and jumped its heart out for you.

Doc said, "I'm going to go give Emily a hug. You two want to come? Or would you prefer shopping?"

Pinky said brightly, "Shopping? You did mention shopping."

Doc pointed toward an area of tents set up along both sides of a walkway.

Eloise was shaking her head no. So far, no one had recognized her. But there were too many people up around the shops.

Pinky was determined. "C'mon. I've always thought the outfits were cool."

Doc said, "I'll come find you two in a bit, and then we'll get something to eat."

Eloise was anxiously scanning the area but saw no one she recognized as she trailed behind Pinky. Pinky was drawn to a table of brow bands and dog collars, and what-nots.

"Oh my God. I love this." Pinky picked up a topaz and pearl studded brow band. "I don't know what it is, but I just love it."

Eloise pulled her toward the boot vendor where Pinky continued to "ooh and aah."

Eloise picked up a pair of black dressage boots, the shaft a shiny patent leather. She put it down and moved over to admire a pair of butter yellow with laces down the front. Her fingers lingered over them before moving to the next pair with Spanish tops with cut-out patent leather designs. Eloise reminded herself that boots were just things. No pair of boots made you a rider.

Pinky said, "Wow, what do you think these run?"

Just then a voice said, "Lulu?" Eloise silently mouthed

"shit" and then opened the brochure on the table and pretended to be absorbed.

Pinky wouldn't let her, up went that one eyebrow as she said, "Uh, Lulu?"

A woman dressed in boots and breeches, likely around forty or fifty, was striding toward them.

"Lulu, it is you! I told Margie, that looks like Lulu Robertson over there, and she said, don't be ridiculous, she's in Ireland. But here you are!"

Eloise was struck dumb for a moment.

"Yup, here I am."

"Weird thing, Margie and I were down in Ocala horse shopping, and who should we see, but your 'Brighty!' Loveliest family has her. She's taken three of the kids through Training level, and there's one more kid waiting for a turn. What a great match that was."

Eloise had a lump forming in her throat, but she nodded and said, "That's good to hear."

"How's your dad? That old daredevil still leaping tall buildings?"

Eloise nodded, her mouth going dry her head swimming.

"We sure miss him. Of course, your dear, dear, mom too. I still can't believe she is gone. But what fun we had."

Eloise's tongue now felt too big for her mouth.

"If you're truly back, you know I've got more horses than I can ride. I keep rescuing and reselling track horses. They could use an experienced rider."

Eloise unstuck her tongue from the back of her teeth, "Thanks."

"You ship your horse back?"

Eloise shook her head.

The woman looked over her shoulder. She clearly needed to get back to her students.

She turned back to Eloise, "Retraining track horses might be too boring for you now. What with all the action "across the pond" you've likely been seeing."

"I was never bored re-schooling track horses."

"Well, if you decide to stick around, you know how to find me."

"Thanks."

There was a long beat of silence where the woman reached out and placed a hand on Eloise's arm. There was a painful amount of sympathy in her voice when she said, "Darling Lulu, It's so good to see you back home again. I've got to get back to work. You take care."

Eloise had no ill feelings toward their former client and family friend, yet her stomach clenched as she said, "Thanks."

Pinky had moved away. Eloise took a moment to unclench her belly and breathe deeply. Then she located Pinky on the other side of a rack of shirts. As she approached, Pinky slid shirts along the rod, glancing at price tags.

When Eloise got to her, she said, "Blimey, look at these prices."

Eloise laughed, "Blimey?"

"I guess that's English, not Irish. What would you say over there?"

"I don't know. I've never been. My Dad lives there though."

Pinky looked hard into Eloise's eyes. "That woman thought you lived in Ireland."

"Long story."

Pinky lifted that eyebrow again, "So, Lulu, I've got nothing but time."

Eloise shrugged. "I like the name Eloise much better."

Pinky seemed to accept the deflection. "Sorry. I guess Brighty was your horse?"

"My first event horse. She was what is called "a packer.""

"A packer?"

"No skill required; she packed me around."

"Funny. You're being too modest. That lady she said ..."

Eloise shook her head. "I had another one after Brighty. She was not a packer. She was named Whiplash."

"Whiplash? Blimey!"

Eloise's mouth curled up in a smile that looked more sad than joyful. "Yup."

Eloise could see that Pinky wanted more. She leaned toward Pinky and lowered her voice as if she were imparting an important secret.

"Don't say anything to Doc. I really have enjoyed seeing the horses after being away from it. But I can't be part of this anymore. I really can't. Let's let him be our one-and-only expert."

Pinky said, "Hmmm. Newsflash. Expertise doesn't work that way. Anybody with eyes had to see you were into it. But maybe not that you were 'into it' into it, you know what I mean? But okay, sure," Pinky drew a finger over her lips, sealed.

"Thanks."

Pinky added, "I won't tell. But it doesn't mean I won't squeeze all the details out of you later. I'm as persistent as a Jack Russell Terrier. Can't help myself."

Pinky pivoted, "I'm starved. Watching horses galloping and leaping sure has whipped up my appetite.

3

Eloise sat on the upholstered bench in her mom's closet to take off her muckers. The first one popped right off but the second one got stuck. She stood back up and stood on the heel of the rubber boot with the heel of her socked foot. When she got her heel lifted a few inches inside the boot, she sat back down and pulled. And pulled.

As the suction increased inside the boot, she found herself yelling, "Damn! Damn! Let go, damn it!" Eloise felt sweat bloom on her forehead. The boot released with a sucking sound. Eloise hurled the boot at the closet wall next to the mirror. It hit so hard that the mirror shook in its frame.

Where was her e-reader? She was ready for this day to be over. She was going to go somewhere else, sometime else. She was going to listen to voices, long gone, speak to her from beyond the grave. She was going to read.

It was still her birthday—her 21st birthday. If it weren't for Doc and Pinky, the whole day would have slid by unnoted. Maybe that would have been better, but Doc had chosen the event for a couple reasons; his friend was there, and he knew Eloise loved horses. He also knew it was her birthday. She needed to calm down. They were just being nice. After they left the event, they had taken her out to eat, given her funny cards, and Doc had given her a bonus check.

Her mother always made a fuss over the day. Each year her mom told Eloise how much she had looked forward to meeting the person face-to-face who had kicked and wiggled and given her the worst indigestion of her life. She said Eloise had arrived with a full head of curly black hair and huge eyes. Her mom said they had stared deeply into each other's eyes for the longest time. And each year her dad, Jock, said it was because newborns can't focus. Mom corrected him. It was not blindness; it was the bliss of experiencing each other face to face. That was something Eloise would never experience again.

Jock, it appeared had forgotten her birthday. Handsome, dashing, talented—reliably unreliable, Jock. Her dad. Eloise wondered when she would see her dad again. Did she want to? Emphatically, no.

It was not an honest answer. Anger washed over her, then receded. She had no more boots to throw against a wall.

It was time to let go. She did so every time she opened a book. The balm of story always soothed her. She read until her eyes burned and begged to be allowed to close. She felt compelled to finish. She read on—and on—swept along in the rising tension, jubilant in the victorious finish, where she turned off her e-reader and earned a dreamless sleep.

She woke up early, as usual. Her eyes felt pasted together—the all-too-familiar book-hangover. It was Sunday, her day off. She made coffee, catching a mug full as soon as it began to brew. She turned on her computer, and hugging her cup of coffee, went straight to the site called Extreme Readers. Betsy, the client who owned the Persian cat, Marilyn, had convinced her to join. She had perused the different groups and joined one studying Teddy Roosevelt. Betsy led a different group. It was not a book club for casual readers, hence the name. She found her study group and began to paint a picture in words about the read she had just pushed to finish. She had strong opinions. She painted in bold colors only! Then she saw that someone had posted comments about her earlier posts.

She was artless and pretentious and there was something about being sophomoric in there too.

Eloise was about to take issue—but then realized she was just as likely to add "thin-skinned" to artless and pretentious, etc. She re-read more of that person's posts, and then some others that now took on a new and different light.

It was time to find a new group and Betsy had just invited her to join her new one she was forming.

Eloise was on her second cup of coffee, still in her pajamas. Eloise hadn't been interested in joining her earlier group as they had been reading books that start with the letter "D" (as in dry-as-dust).

It took a bit of searching, but Eloise found Betsy's new group. After reading some of the discussion threads from Betsy's last group, Eloise noticed that Betsy was always in control. Betsy led her group the way Eloise assumed she led her classroom. Professionally.

Betsy's new group was to be a study of Thomas Jefferson. Eloise hadn't been exactly drawn to the topic—although she did have a passing knowledge of Jefferson (enough to pass a college course on the American Revolution). There was a cottage industry of works about Jefferson, but Betsy's group was focused on the newer books that examined his life at Monticello, his mountaintop home, and his extended slave "family"—especially books about his slave Sally Hemings. There was now DNA evidence that connected the descendants of her offspring to Jefferson. It still had the potential to be dry. The tipping point was that Betsy was including fiction as well as non-fiction.

Eloise clicked the button and asked to join the group. She downloaded the current book to her e-reader. But Eloise needed to take a shower and dress.

There had been a time Eloise had shut herself in her house and skipped showering and dressing. She had taken a metaphoric fall where it seemed like it took forever to hit the ground. Getting back up started with taking a shower and dressing. She learned that simple routines, even when accomplished in a zombie state, are a sort of sustenance.

Eloise showered, dressed, and gathered up her laundry. She carried her basket to the laundry room and dumped it on the floor, separating lights from dark. When she realized it wasn't a lot of stuff to wash, she put it all in the washer together.

Once she had the load going, she let her eyes rest on her tack set up along the back wall of the laundry room. Yesterday had stirred things up. It was all there hanging neatly on racks, her jumping saddle and her dressage saddle—and two bridles, girths, side-reins, and martingales. Her boots standing tall with boot trees in them. Everything was covered in dust. It had been about three years since she brought all her tack here, setting up this makeshift tack room, waiting for the day to pack it all up for the big move to Ireland that never came. Dad, Jock, had let her down.

Eloise went out to the garage and lifted the lid on her tack trunk. She found her tack cleaning materials, a tin of metal polish, a tub of leather cleaner, and a tub of conditioner. Eloise unscrewed the lid, gave it a smell. It wasn't rancid, although it was dried out. She fished around for sponges and found one that had been greasy with leather balm at some distant time. She gave it a squeeze and it crumbled in her hand. Eloise brushed her hands free of sponge bits. The brushes needed to be washed and disinfected but held the smell of horsehair and dander and sweat. Those smells triggered emotions. They were indescribable, but strong. Not sad, but not joyous either. The closest word for the feeling was unsettling.

Eloise let the lid fall shut with a thunk. She carried the cleaner and conditioner and metal polish inside. She would choose one item, just one, and thoroughly clean and condition it: doable.

She started with a bridle. Eloise tried to unbuckle the reins from the bit. They felt like iron, welded shut. Eloise cursed. Hook-and-stud buckles were the devil to undo once they got stiff. She had to fetch a screwdriver to pry the loose end of the leather out from under the keeper. Then she pushed the leather that went around the bit ring with the butt of her palm, toward the loose end, to get it to pop off the stud. By alternating pushing and pulling, the leather came free, and Eloise could finally get the rein off the bit. Eloise rubbed her red and aching palm on her jeans. With diligence and determination, the bridle was soon in pieces, though she had broken a nail, and her hands ached. She gathered the pieces off the floor and dumped them in the utility sink. Eloise hosed all of it down with the sprayer, and then grabbed a rag and sat back down on the floor with all the wet pieces on an old towel.

First, she used the leather cleaner and a washcloth to clean each piece, then she set them on the towel to dry. While the leather dried, she used the metal polish on the bit. She washed off the polish with dish soap then rubbed the bit to a high shine. Now it was time to condition the leather. It was top quality leather and once-upon-a-time, lovingly cared for. As Eloise rubbed and flexed the leather, she felt it come back to life. Eloise examined the stitching. Still good. She put the bridle back together, and this time the hook and stud closure slid into place. She gave the nose band one last rub from her greasy hand, and hung the bridle on its rack, looping the reins through the throat latch, fastening the nose band around the cheek pieces, neat and professional. It was ready for use.

Eloise was startled by the timer going off on the dryer. How had the time passed so quickly? Her clothes needed to come out and be folded and put away. She filled her basket, leaving the tack cleaning supplies on the floor.

She closed the door on her way out, feeling better.

Eloise made herself fried eggs for dinner, did a Sudoku

puzzle, and then once again settled herself in bed with her read and a bowl of mandarin oranges.

It was time to become reacquainted with Thomas Jefferson…to travel to Albemarle County, Charlottesville, Virginia…to get the "lay of the land" of his mountaintop home. It was a home that took him most of his adult life to build. Jefferson wrote, "Architecture is my delight, and putting up, and pulling down, one of my favorite amusements."

Creation and destruction. Like a God, playing with the mortals. He had helped create a new country, was a revolutionary, but lost so much in his lifetime. And yet, building a structure, then pulling it down, that was amusement? Maybe you just destroy it yourself before fate did the job for you. Maybe this would not be dry-as-dust reading, after all.

Eloise knew the image of Monticello. All you had to do was look at the back of a nickel. The image was more deeply iconic than Washington's Mt. Vernon. Monticello became a symbol of Jefferson's life and mind. Eloise was stunned to learn the amount of land that Jefferson would own. It was hard to grasp by today's standards. From his father he inherited five thousand acres. The acreage included the little mountain, but extended over other farms, often called his "quarter-farms" and his childhood home, (that had unfortunately burned down) and other farms where his extended family resided.

But Thomas Jefferson's vast holdings included people. The black American occupants of his acreage vastly outnumbered the whites. He could never have built Monticello and lived the life of a mountaintop patriarch without those "who labor for my happiness." But what of their pursuit of their own happiness?

Thomas Jefferson lived with one foot in an idealized future, a bold experiment, and one foot firmly rooted in a slave-based economy that had made him, and those before him, privileged and wealthy. In addition to the five thousand acres of land and slaves Jefferson inherited at the age of twenty-one, he inherited almost five thousand more acres after Martha's father died. At that time, Jefferson also inherited more human beings, some who were half-siblings to his wife. He also inherited debt.

Eloise got a notification "ping." It was from Extreme Readers. She had been accepted into the group.

Betsy posted each profile so Eloise could be "introduced" to everyone. And then Eloise posted her profile. Of the six members of the present group, only one was male.

The sole male's profile photo was intriguing. He was pictured riding a horse. And one thing was obvious, as he tidily cleared a timber fence in classic form. He knew what he was doing. Lots of people *think* they ride, but talk is cheap. But this group was not about horses.

Eloise read over his profile multiple times. He lived near Monticello and had a special interest in Jefferson. His ancestors had been early settlers to the area, and he still resided in his family's farmhouse where most of the building dated back to the American Revolution. He had the odd name of "Dabs." Eloise squinted at the small photo. Well, it was a fine-looking horse.

What did Eloise's profile photo show? Pinky had taken

it at the vet clinic. Eloise was wearing a smock, looking like a dental hygienist. Her brown hair was pulled back in a ponytail, but short bits had come loose and hung like fringe around her face. She was smiling. Eloise liked the photo. She thought she looked lean and long legged, although she was only 5'6". But there was something else that she liked about the photo. She looked happy.

The next time that Eloise checked the site everyone had welcomed her. Betsy had written a short paragraph on how she had met Eloise, and that she and Eloise had often discussed books while Betsy dropped off or picked up her cat.

Betsy posted a question for discussion, sounding just like the high school teacher she had been.

"What do we know about the physical appearance of Thomas Jefferson? We have the official portraits of course, but they rarely capture the man in the flesh. I believe Jefferson's daughter remarked that one of them looked nothing like her father. How do we make men into Gods? By depicting them in heroic oil paintings or sculpting them into pale marble busts that turn them into philosophers of ancient Rome and Greece. But historians seek the real man, not a God. We start with the physical, complexion, hair color, voice, posture. If you have insight on the topic, please share."

Dabs posted, "I read his hair was sandy red. There are disagreements about his eye color, which was pale. Whether it was blue or gray or even brown, there seems to be no consensus. He stood 6 foot 2 1/2 inches tall. His stance was described as upright, even stiff. Of course, in the saddle, this must have looked commanding. He was described as broad in the shoulders, always thin, and looked younger than he was. Somewhere I read (but cannot remember where) that he was freckled and often sunburned. This makes sense for a redhead who grew up in the heat of Virginia summers and reportedly spent hours each day riding. I read one of his slave's accounts that he was always singing or humming when he rode. He played the violin, and Martha played the pianoforte. There is a story of two suitors to Martha (before she married Jefferson) turning back on the pathway to her door—because they heard music and two voices harmonizing. The two men agreed; they had no chance of winning her affections."

Eloise posted, "Hard to imagine him singing. I just read Jefferson did not have a strong voice, rarely spoke at the Continental Congress, and when he did speak, was difficult to hear. Both his first and second Inaugural addresses were nearly inaudible. He gave up public speaking and started a tradition of sending his addresses in writing!"

Dabs replied, "Was it due to a weak voice, or a fear of public speaking? My guess is fear of public speaking. Regardless, the entire world heard his written words."

Betsy posted, "You two have clearly read up on Jefferson! No worries, the number of new books on Jefferson is staggering. Keep reading and sharing with us about this important man."

Before turning off the light, Eloise grimaced and sighed. Maybe she *was* artless, pretentious, and sophomoric. She had wanted to show this Dabs person that she knew more about Jefferson than he did. What was wrong with her? She wasn't an expert on Jefferson. And this Dabs guy could really ride. She found that both intrigued her and bothered her. She couldn't help herself, somewhere deep in her brain, the competition was on.

* * *

Everyone called Eloise's Dad "Jock." His real name was not Jock. Jock was a shortened version of Jockey. He had earned that moniker as a boy. Jock was too tall to be a real jockey but fell in love with Thoroughbred horses and the speed they offered at a young age. Jock became an excellent rider, a popular trainer, and a coach for the sport of eventing. Jock was good at making decisions at speed. Most of the time, those horses of his were not only fast but gutsy and handy. They ran and jumped their hearts out for him. But anyone who jumps horses has their share of crashes. Jock's were usually at competitions on cross country. If he was going to make a mistake, it was going to be spectacular.

Eloise had his number in her contacts list: "Jock"—not "Dad."

When "Jock" came up on her phone screen, it made her heart pound. She wished she could stop being angry, it put her at a disadvantage. She would let him leave a message. It was early in the morning. At least for Eloise. It was six am. But in Ireland it was five hours later. Jock would have already ridden a couple of horses and likely was calling during a coffee break. Eloise would always be an early riser. Habits formed early are ingrained for life.

Eloise was heading out to her car to drive to work when she decided she was ready to play Jock's message. She got buckled in, started her engine, and then hit the play button on her messages as she backed out of her garage. She expected to hear Jock's low but always upbeat voice. But was surprised when it wasn't Jock. It was a woman.

"Hello, Miss Robertson. I'm calling from Mr. Jameson's office at Atlanta Bank and Trust. Please give him a call at your earliest convenience. Oh, and he wanted me to wish you a happy birthday."

"What the hell?" The next message began to play.

"Happy birthday, Lulu. Your old man didn't forget. I was teaching a clinic in Spain. Those Spaniards like to party. I can barely move today. I'm back in Ireland and thinking of my Lulu. I may be lining up a clinic your way soon. I'll keep you posted. I promise to make it up to you then baby-gi."

The beep cut him off before he finished the word "girl." Was that her phone or did he do that on purpose? She was too cynical. If she had picked up in the first place they would have spoken.

She was almost to the vet clinic. It was time to go to work.

4

Eloise walked through her front door, kicked off her clogs, and looked around the townhome that would never be home.

Moments like this one kick-started a negative feedback loop of discontent in her head, immobilizing her.

Before they had moved in, her mother had the hardwood floors refinished—all done so that they could highlight their oriental rugs. Those old rugs were poignant remnants of her past life. But she scolded herself. A rug was just a rug. The townhome was okay. The kitchen and bathrooms could have used an update, but it wasn't in the new budget.

Her mother's greatest weakness, as she liked to remind Eloise, had been horses—and her second greatest weakness had been men who liked horses.

Both were ferociously expensive.

And gone.

The farm, well, *that* was home. But without Jock there training and selling horses, the farm was an expense they could no longer afford. It sold fast. For a lot. It had been converted into a nest egg.

Land with horses and husbands turned out to be profitable—once rid of the horses and husband.

Eloise's mother insisted Eloise stay and finish college.

Jock had agreed to take care of her horse in Ireland. Or as it turned out, take her horse for good. When the family dog passed away, her mom asked they not replace him. There was too much going on.

The stuff going on had never been fully explained. Not the divorce, and not her mom's illness. Not until the very end when the truth, finally delivered, felt like a punch to the gut. Eloise would have sold her soul to the devil if she could have done something, anything, to help.

There was nothing she could do.

Finally able to leave her private pity-party, Eloise grabbed her tablet off her bedside table, walked into her mom's closet and sat on the bench to read.

Eloise's phone pinged. A message. It was the bank asking her to call. When she did, she was asked to make an appointment. She did. And then she worried.

It had to be bad news. That's what unexpected phone calls were. Bad news. She was now dizzy as-all-get-out. All too familiar a response. Jock could always calm her down. She could hear his voice in her head, "Lulu, you know what to do, breathe slowly and deeply, let the air go all the way down to your belly."

Jock had been more than a parent; he had been her coach. His directives were embedded like an ear worm she could never shake. She obeyed him. Even when his voice was only a damn echo from her memory. How many times had Eloise imagined disasters, and then experienced success because of his simple words?

"Deep breaths. Belly-breathe. Slow the heart rate."

Eloise logged into Extreme Readers as a diversion. Betsy was on. So was Dabs. So were some of the other members. Good.

They were discussing Jefferson and his earliest memory, which was of being lifted on a horse, onto a pillow, to sit in front of a slave as the family traveled from their home, Shadwell, to the Randolph home, Tuckahoe.

Betsy said, "Imagine that. Your earliest memory includes a slave. We have such a hard time grasping the normality of that."

Dabs typed, "Wealthy planters often assigned a slave to grow up alongside each child. Jefferson's slave was Jupiter. Jupiter was born the same year as Jefferson. The other children had their own slaves too. There was a sad situation where Thomas' thirty-year-old 'feeble-minded' sister drowned in the Rivanna river in a flash flood, and her slave companion drowned with her."

Eloise joined in, finding herself now calm and focused, "Creepy! Not just the two women drowning together, either. Imagine, all your life you have connected to you a person chosen by your family to be subservient to you. Imagine being Jupiter, knowing all your life you must accept this person, the very same age as yourself, as your superior. What if you didn't even like each other?"

Betsy wrote, "At the same time, the slave knows where the bodies are buried, so to speak."

Dabs responded, "I'm sure they did. At Monticello Jefferson took great pains to keep slaves out of the dining room during meals. But what could they do with the information? They had no power to use it. Not without great risk. A slave could be sold."

Eloise added, "Or physically harmed. Or sexually molested."

Dabs wrote, "True. But someone who is your own age, who is the playmate of your youth, well, it would be hard to imagine that fondness, or love, would not develop."

Eloise wrote, "I can't let go of the creepy factor. Having a slave attached to you by your parents, must have felt for slave and master like an injustice to both."

Dabs instantly added, "There's a quote somewhere from Jefferson where he says something about the child imitating his parents in cruel tyranny over the slave, and the slave child learning both subservience and subtle resistance."

Eloise wrote, "But he freed so few of his slaves, and even went after runaways. He wrote about the race as inferior."

Dabs came to Jefferson's defense first. "You have to consider where and when he lived and the wrong-headed ideas that were accepted as truths. He was of course deeply flawed, and sometimes detached, cool, removed. I think that's misread as unfeeling, when in fact, he felt so deeply he nearly lost his mind, tore up his stomach, and suffered debilitating migraines."

Betsy wrote, "Only one of seven children, survived him. And what about that gut-wrenching account of his wife dying?"

Dabs wrote, "Imagine his guilt over the repeated pregnancies that destroyed her health. The last childbearing clearly killed her. That newborn weighed fifteen pounds at birth. Can you imagine?"

Eloise typed, "That doesn't seem possible."

Betsy wrote, "Gestational Diabetes. I presume no one at that time knew about the condition. But they certainly knew that Martha's repeated pregnancies had put her at higher and higher risk."

There was a lull in the thread. Some other comments came in, but Eloise was focused on the statements from Betsy and Dabs and reread them a couple times.

Dabs wanted to know from Betsy which book in the list should be read next.

Betsy provided the title, and then added, "Dabs, I think you read faster than even Eloise."

"It's been raining here. Pastures need bush hogging, but since I can't…"

Eloise added, "I used to help with that."

Dabs asked, "You retired from bush hogging?"

Betsy wrote, "My goodness Dabs, are you a Virginia planter like our Mr. Jefferson?"

"My only crop nowadays is hay. The house requires a lot of work too. I'm living in a decrepit remnant of what must have been impressive in its day. But I do have some beautiful fields and gently rolling hills outside my door, and I still have a few horses."

"Eloise, did you catch that? Eloise loves horses."

Dabs changed course, "Sorry to get off topic. We were talking about how slavery was Jefferson's normal. The home he grew up in, Shadwell, well there were eight Jefferson children. And with each of those children, there was a slave child. Then there was his father's man, Sawney, and his mother would have had a slave-woman. Then the cook and housemaid, and who knows who else. Add to that the slaves that worked the crops and cared for the animals and drove the coach, I read it was around sixty slaves. Sixty slaves to eight children and a mother and father. Slaves outnumbered their masters, by a large margin. It's hard to imagine."

Betsy brought the session to a close. "All foreign and fascinating. Keep reading! Before I sign off. I forgot to wish Eloise a happy birthday! Eloise turned twenty-one this past weekend."

And then multiple keyboards tapped out, "Happy Birthday!"

Eloise replied, "Thank You!" and signed off.

Eloise got a notification "ping" that she had a message. It was from Dabs.

"Hi Eloise. I've really enjoyed your posts. Seems you've read quite a bit about Jefferson. Anyway, twenty-one is an important birthday. It has been a few years since I came into my majority, but it was the day that this farm, in all its decay, became mine 'free-and-clear.' It's been my obsession ever since. I am still discovering things here every day, and you are clearly of the same historical bent as I am, and you love horses too. You might like to see a copy of what I have found here. If so, send me your email address and I'll send it along. If not, well, I understand, the internet, and all that."

-Dabs

Eloise asked, "Is that really you, riding in your profile photo?"

"That's me."

"And that's really your horse? You own him?"

"Cross my heart. Dude is likely looking over the gate in the pasture not far from my back door wondering when I'm coming out to feed him."

"You event?"

"Used to. And you?"

"Once upon a time."

Dabs persisted, "Email?"

"Okay. But what are you sending me?"

"Something I found digging around this old house. I'm dying to share it with someone.

* * *

Eloise ate her bowl of cereal. Dabs appeared to know a lot about Jefferson. The way he said "came into my majority" indicated that he was old. Eloise decided he was likely old and lonely.

Who says stuff like that? But she had indeed, "come into her majority." Was she inheriting something? Maybe the call wasn't about bad news.

* * *

Eloise felt the urge to finish cleaning her tack in the laundry room. She placed her cleaning supplies in the sink and pulled the cover from her dressage saddle. It had been custom made for her. A brass tag on the cantle said, "Lulu Robertson."

Eloise had a burst of energy and didn't stop until every bit was clean, conditioned, and placed back into tidiness. She should have felt satisfaction.

But without a horse to wear this beautiful collection, it was just another poignant reminder of what had been lost. Not so different from the oriental rugs.

Eloise backed out of the laundry room, and quietly closed the door.

She still felt restless but had reading she could do. She dove into a novel that told the story of Thomas Jefferson and his slave Sally Hemings.

And it was good. She stayed up late and woke up tired. But she put herself into high gear. She felt a pang imagining the big black dog in the run, waiting. Was he anxious? She rushed to get to work.

She fed Prince, but before he would eat, he sat down and looked at his bowl, then looked at Eloise.

"Yes, it's for you, go ahead and enjoy." He replied with a soft, "Woof!" stood up, and eagerly chowed down, tail wagging.

Eloise paused a moment in awe.

After the dogs were fed, she went upstairs and opened stinky little tins of cat food, receiving head bumps and chin rubs. She swept and mopped, made coffee, then plopped down on the old brown sofa in the lounge for her break.

That's when she unzipped her backpack and pulled out the flier. Eloise communed with the handsome "Joe." His gaze gave her a lovely squishy-tummy moment. Eloise kissed her finger, then placed it on the lips of "Joe." She carefully refolded it, print side out, so that the man's face and torso were centered, leaving the dog and the text hidden behind the folds. As Pinky walked in, Eloise stuffed it back into the zippered compartment.

Pinky said, "Morning Eloise. God, coffee smells like heaven."

Pinky took her first sip and leaned against the counter, looking at Eloise. Her eyebrow went up, "You look a little rough. Stay up partying again?"

"Yeah, you know me. Swinging from the chandeliers and hooting like a monkey all night long."

"Reading a hot novel?"

"Something like that."

Pinky nodded, "You think you can give your latest read a rest and come have dinner at my house tonight? I'm not giving up asking y'know, so you might as well cave."

"Is Buzz cooking?"

Pinky laughed. Buzz was a chef at one of the toney restaurants in Buckhead, whereas Pinky was usually covered with dog hair, and not allowed near Buzz' kitchen.

"Eloise, I could cut your hair, but I promise never to cook for you."

"Can we make it kind of early? I'll still read tonight after I get home."

"Good grief it must be a juicy one. Okay, I'll tell Buzz to do his "early bird special" like they do for the blue hairs that come to his restaurant from those "mature" condominiums."

"Can I bring someone?"

"A date? You are full of surprises these days."

"Betsy. I thought it would be cool to have Betsy join us."

"Oh, Betsy? Sure. Just don't talk all night about people who don't exist, okay?"

Eloise looked puzzled.

"Characters in your books. News flash, they're not real."

"They are so!"

Pinky smiled, but in the way that a parent smiles to placate a fussy child. "You two get that faraway look in your eyes, and down the rabbit-hole you go."

"Pinky, you just made a literary allusion to make your point."

"I have no idea what you mean."

"Rabbit holes, *Alice in Wonderland*?"

Pinky wagged her finger at Eloise. "See, you're doing it again."

Eloise liked Pinky, but had resisted her efforts to socialize because, really, they had nothing in common. This was more proof.

Eloise finished her coffee and headed down to the basement to start her walks and kennels. Pinky followed her.

Eloise fetched Prince from a run and took him out for a walk. She decided then and there that Pinky should foster him. Pinky did foster from time to time, even though she already had "Ying" and "Yang"—her two little Shi-Tzu's. Eloise's townhome was no life for a dog—shut up all day. But Buzz was home during the day, and the little dogs would be company.

When Eloise lived on a farm, her dog was always free to roam, and someone was always there. It had been a great life for a dog. The best. This dog deserved something like that life. But for now, Pinky would do.

This dog bouncing at her side, well, he kept looking up at her like he had a crush on her. She was flattered. Sometimes his gaze wasn't so different from the way the guy in the poster was looking at her. Except of course, the guy in the poster wasn't really looking at her. But, this dog, this dog was. She reluctantly put him back in the run. Duty called.

Janet began shouting out names of dogs over the intercom that needed to be fetched from the waiting room. Pinky soon had a dog in the tub and her cage dryers going. It was almost lunch time before Eloise thought to ask Doc about the micro-chip on Prince.

He said, "Darndest thing. That dog's number didn't come up on any of the registries. I don't want to neuter him or put him up for adoption yet."

Eloise blurted out, "Pinky would foster him."

"Well, that's kind of her." Doc winked at her. "Tell Pinky if she's willing to foster him, I'm fine with that. I'll send an email update to 'Good Stewards.'"

When Eloise was back in the basement, she told Pinky, "Doc says you can foster this one."

Pinky was elbow deep in soap bubbles bathing a Collie. She blew hair from her eyes, raised her eyebrows, and said, "Huh? Buzz will be thrilled, but okay."

After work, Eloise headed directly home to shower and change so she could turn right back around to make her way to Pinky and Buzz' house. After climbing out of the shower, she dipped back into her book and set the alarm on the microwave for twenty minutes.

The alarm sounded in a spot that surely was near the end of the chapter. Eloise got up and set it for ten more minutes. When she got to the end of the chapter, she was regretting accepting Pinky's invitation, but she couldn't back out now.

Eloise made the short drive, and walked up to the small brick bungalow, but never got a chance to knock because her arrival had been announced by a storm of barking. It wasn't just the yap-yap-yap of Ying and Yang. Eloise was thrilled to hear a deep chested "woof-woof-woof-woof" as well. Pinky also had music playing at high volume. A happy sort of chaos reigned. Pinky waved Eloise in.

Eloise had to yell, "You did it! You're his new foster-mom."

"I told Doc I'd foster him only until you were ready to adopt him."

Eloise heard Jock's voice again, intruding on her joy. He said, "Sly fox. What's your game?" She ignored him.

Ying and Yang were tucking their butts and scooting around the sofa, the big dog grinning and bouncing before plopping his butt down on top of Eloise's feet and staring into her eyes. Eloise felt a happy rush as she locked eyes with Prince.

The moment was not lost on Pinky, "Unless I'm misreading the tea leaves, the heavens-above sent you a dog as a birthday gift."

Pinky turned the volume down a couple notches and called over her shoulder toward the kitchen, "Buzz, look, we did it. We got Eloise to put her book down long enough to come eat."

Pinky took Eloise's backpack off her shoulder, placed it on the hall table, and gave her a gentle push toward the kitchen. Prince removed himself from her feet, and the dogs followed them, creating a traffic jam at the kitchen door.

Eloise walked into the tiny kitchen where Buzz was making things sizzle on the stove. It smelled wonderful but the counter tops were cluttered and the sink full of pots and bowls. Buzz greeted her like a long-lost friend.

"Come and give me a hug... hands are covered in batter so forgive me that I can't hug back."

Eloise did as she was told, careful not to bump into anything in the tight space. She was smiling at Buzz with his shaved head and soul patch. He sported a stud earring in one ear. She thought he looked like a hip young chef should look—and if not a chef, then maybe a pirate.

The dogs crowded into the kitchen. Pinky said, "I'm pouring the wine and then clearing this gang out so that Buzz has some elbow room." Eloise backed out carefully, and the dogs followed.

Pinky handed a stemmed wine glass to Eloise, and they moved to the living room. As soon as they sat down on the sofa, the puffballs settled on either side of Pinky, while Prince crammed himself into the space between the sofa and the table, stretching out and again looking up at Eloise. His shaggy beard was wet, so Eloise stroked him on the top of his head, scratching occasionally behind his folded over ears.

"His coat feels great. It's fine and soft to the touch."

Pinky nodded, "Conditioner and your good brushing. Every time he gets a drink though, his beard becomes a wet mop. I don't want to cut it off though. That would look weird. He and Ying and Yang hit it off right away. He can go to a home with other dogs. We need to test him with cats and kids next; widen his options for a forever home, that is, if you still have a heart of stone."

Eloise added, "We still may find his owner."

"The chip wasn't registered; I'm thinking it's a long shot."

The dogs leapt up and ran to the door, creating a deafening chorus of barking. Eloise shot a glance at Pinky, and said, "Don't let him knock over Betsy."

Eloise began to get up, but Pinky raised a finger, and said in a stern voice, "Sit" and then "Stay." Pinky was speaking to Eloise, but Prince obeyed too.

As Pinky walked behind the sofa to get the door, she stopped and looked down at Eloise.

"Good God, there's a metal clip stuck on the back of your head."

"Oh."

Eloise had clipped up her ponytail for her shower. The ponytail had come out, but the clip had not. She reached up, feeling for it, and pulled it out as Pinky got the door. It was one of those aluminum clips, like they use at the hair salon. Eloise now had it in her hand, with nowhere to put it. Reflexively, she stuffed it down between the cushions of Pinky's sofa.

Pinky ushered in Betsy, who had dressed up for the occasion. She might have been over sixty, but Betsy had an impish youthfulness about her. She had long silver bangs that hung over piercing blue eyes. Those eyes were always direct. Because Betsy had long been used to corralling and controlling a room full of teenagers, she automatically controlled every room she entered, led every conversation, but was never dull or self-absorbed.

Betsy held up a six pack of beer. "I'm told we are having Korean barbecue, so I brought Korean beer. It's nice and cold, although beyond that I have no clue if it's any good."

Pinky took the beer from her hand, "Brilliant idea, Betsy." Then warned, "Don't trip over Prince."

Prince had obediently remained in a down-stay, although he was panting heavily and looking first to Eloise and then to Betsy and then to Pinky, and then back to Eloise, waiting for a release word.

Pinky said, "Okay." And he jumped up and turned a circle, nearly whacking into Betsy.

Betsy narrowed her eyes at him, and he wilted in apology.

Which made everyone laugh. Betsy sat down opposite Eloise in a club chair. Pinky went into the kitchen with the beer, returning with a glass of wine for Betsy. When she sat down, they made a companionable circle, Ying and Yang adding themselves to the sofa and Prince crammed into the space on the floor between the sofa and the coffee table.

The wine was aromatic and light and not too sweet. Buzz came back through the room to say there was time for one more glass.

Betsy and Eloise could have tried harder to stay away from discussing books but wandered there regardless as they critiqued television series based upon novels.

All was calm until Buzz called the party to the table. Prince popped up suddenly, long tail wagging, and with one great sweep across the glass-topped table his tail took out both Eloise's and Betsy's wine glasses.

Betsy showed extraordinary reflexes, catching one glass nearly mid-air, but tipping the contents into her lap.

Eloise's glass simply emptied on the table—as it broke.

5

Pinky said, "Oh for Gawd's sake." Then, "Your dress!" Pinky covered her mouth for a moment, "I'll get towels."

"No worries, dear, white wine doesn't stain." Then, "There are clearly hazards to having a dog that size."

Eloise added, "Maybe, or maybe Pinky and Buzz just need taller tables."

Betsy nodded, "Bar stools would do the trick."

Pinky rushed back into the room and handed them towels. The guilty party watched with zero remorse.

Both the mishap and the wine had loosened things up.

Dinner began with battered and fried asparagus with a chipotle dipping sauce. Then came Korean barbecue and coleslaw with jasmine rice. The ice-cold beer made the perfect pairing with the spicy barbecue.

Buzz had even ornamented the plates with orchid blossoms. They applauded Buzz before tucking in.

Prince's big head appeared on Eloise's leg, his wet whiskers soaking through her pants. She looked down at him and his long tail began to sway slowly as he coyly made eye contact.

"No Korean barbecue for you, big guy."

Prince sighed deeply, turned, and walked sadly out of the room. Pinky and Buzz exchanged amused looks, with Pinky lifting one eyebrow.

Buzz said, "That dog looks you straight in the eye like a person, and you can see he's trying to work out what you're saying. The scary thing is most of the time, he seems to get what you said."

Prince chose that moment to walk a few feet back into the room and sit down, staring at them. All conversation stopped.

Buzz said, "See, he's doing it again. He knows we were talking about him." Then, "Pinky, you think he needs to go out?"

"Ignore him, Buzz. He's just bored."

Prince once again left the room, looking forlorn.

Betsy laughed and said, "I recognize that look. He's like so many of my students. They come to class expecting, oh, I don't know, something more stimulating."

Eloise defended Betsy, "I don't believe that for a moment. You are the best leader on Extreme Readers. The best!"

Betsy said, "Let's be frank, teenagers and dogs have much in common. But, while the large dog has become restless, the little dogs have simply nodded off."

Betsy's comment had them all peeking under the table. Indeed, Ying and Yang were snoring away.

That elicited giggles from all. As Pinky pulled her chair back to get a better look, one of the puffballs lifted its head groggily and yawned.

Prince had reappeared in the room and awkwardly

crawled under the table to join the slumber party. He took up a lot of leg room. Pinky was about to move him, but he flattened himself down, pleading eyes staring at her under shaggy brows.

Buzz said, "He's been on the street. Cut the guy some slack."

Pinky shrugged, "Buzz has a tender heart. I guess the dog reminds him of a few guys he's hired."

Buzz offered second helpings.

The barbeque had been delicious, but Eloise's mouth was on fire from the hot peppers.

Buzz and Pinky cleared, and then offered Gelato which cooled the fire in Eloise's mouth. They were well into a generous helping when Eloise felt a gentle tug at her napkin.

Prince emerged from under the table, his new pals Ying and Yang along as sidekicks. He had all four napkins, stealthily removed from the laps of the diners, wadded up, one dangling from his mouth.

Just in case no one noticed, he stopped and gazed over his shoulder before he trotted off to the living room.

Buzz jumped out of his chair, "Hey! Those are good linen napkins!" and was in pursuit.

Pinky called after him, "Buzz, you're playing his game. Let it go, I'll grab some paper napkins and get those later."

Play growling and yipping from Ying and Yang came from the next room. Prince had baited Buzz and now had a tug of war game going. Buzz walked into the dining room dragging Prince by a wad of linen napkins while making a mock-angry face at Pinky.

Eloise, still sitting in her chair looked straight at Prince and commanded, "DROP!"

Prince spit the napkins out, looking at Eloise and emitting what sounded like an apologetic "woof."

Pinky snatched the napkins off the floor and gave Prince a withering glare that sent him slinking out of the room. The puffballs who had enjoyed the kerfuffle looked up at Pinky expectantly, as if they had rescued the napkins themselves and now a treat would be forthcoming.

"Not a chance, guys." They too, turned in disappointment and headed back to the living room, their long grey and white hair trailing behind them like trains on evening gowns.

Eloise took her slightly damp and wrinkled napkin and placed it back in her lap, making a note to herself not to wipe her mouth.

Buzz said, "Why am I sensing that dog is smarter than me?"

Pinky said, "Would anyone like more gelato?"

All demurred. Betsy and Eloise turned down after-dinner drinks and Pinky offered hot coffee instead.

Just as the conversation began to lag, Prince strolled slowly back into the room. This time he had Eloise's backpack in his mouth, his head and tail held high, picking his front feet up like a fashion model on a catwalk.

All four diners practically fell out of their chairs laughing as Eloise said, "Okay, message received. Of course, you're right Prince. Time to go home."

Buzz protested. "It's my house damn it, and you can stay all night if you want."

Betsy rose too. "No, Buzz, that was a delicious and delightful dinner, but the dog's timing is good. We really should be going. Buzz, that dog's intelligence is off the charts. You may want to sign him up for college. You know how it is on the internet. No one will ever know he's a dog."

That comment earned a few others, and a good laugh all-around.

Eloise went home feeling lighter, looser, time having slowed down. The evening had been joyful, companionable. She had turned down many an invitation from Pinky. Why? And Betsy had again asked her to meet for pancakes. Pinky and Betsy had persisted until she had said yes.

She settled back down with her book. But she had trouble concentrating. She couldn't stop thinking about Prince. He had been a lost dog. Or a runaway? With all his training, a dog like that had surely been the center of someone's world. But Eloise knew that could change, did change all the damn time.

* * *

After work Monday, Eloise dutifully arrived at the bank. She felt like she was back in high school and had been called to the counselor's office to review her many absences. Why should she feel like she was in trouble?

This was Mr. Jameson? He looked faintly familiar, but she couldn't place him.

"Can I get you coffee?"

"No, thank you."

"Soda? Tea? Water?"

"I'm fine."

"Do you like jellybeans? Frankly, I'm addicted. The one thing Ronald Reagan and I had in common. Here, try these, watermelon flavor. My dentist would like me to give them up, but really, can't one have one harmless addiction?"

Eloise reached into the small crystal bowl that had been pushed her way and picked up a single jellybean. Popping it into her mouth, she thought to herself, "Watermelon. Clearly. But, also odd."

"Is any addiction harmless?"

"My dentist said I would end up with a crown, and I said I would prefer a tiara."

Mr. Jameson tittered. Yes, he tittered. Eloise had seen that term used in literature many times but would have never used it herself—until now.

Eloise laughed at his dumb joke.

Mr. Jameson placed his hand on his chest and exclaimed, "You sound just like your mother when you laugh. Lovely. I knew her, you know, though we went years without seeing each other. Once Jock was in the picture, well. But she tracked me down, asked my help, and we spent a lot of time together that last year. She spoke of you all the time. Well, here you are, all grown up. Of course, you and I spoke at the memorial service, but it was brief."

He then observed, "Watermelon isn't your flavor. Cinnamon? Your mother loved the cinnamon."

He left the room and came back with an empty crystal bowl. This one was mounted on a wooden base with an inscribed brass tag. He grabbed a bag of jellybeans out of a desk drawer, and cut off the top, pouring the candy into the bowl.

"Forgot about that bowl. Read it."

"Atlanta Classic, Open Working Hunter Champion."

"When your mom was cleaning and sorting, she gave that to me. Seems fitting that I return it to you, with her favorite flavor."

Eloise took a jellybean. It was peppery and sharp on the first chew, then sweet on the second. The faint aroma of cinnamon was a confirmation, this guy did know her mom.

Eloise cleared her throat and said, "Thank you for the bowl. It sat with a lot of others in our movie room. Most of that stuff had to go with the move."

"Must have been a big job."

"We managed." Eloise felt a lump forming in her throat. She could not afford to let down her guard, not here. She said, "You didn't call me in to feed me jellybeans."

"You're right. I called you in because we have business to conduct. It's been my job to see you get your monthly disbursements, as well as other important things. I've been your trust officer."

"I guess that beats a probation officer."

"By a mile. I know you've gotten your monthly statements, and other information about our services, the portal, and all that sort of thing."

"I never open them. So, Officer Jameson, am I in trouble?"

"Please, call me Ralph. I called you in because you are not obligated to continue with my services. You are legally an adult. But I hope you will allow me to continue as your financial advisor. I promised your mother to do my best by you, to offer financial guidance, so to speak."

"Guide me? Guide me where?"

"I suppose that all depends on where you would like to go."

He turned his large desktop computer screen toward Eloise. "This is your investment portfolio, and here are how your investment funds are allocated."

Eloise noted the number at the bottom and pushed back her chair. She had expected her funds to be close to nil. Her mom had been stressed out about the drain the farm, the horses, and frankly, Jock, had created. She had called it unsustainable. But the number Eloise saw on the bottom of the screen, well it seemed like a lot of money. For some reason, Eloise felt a flush of anger. But also, guilt. This was her mom's money. Not hers. She felt like she was spying.

"I don't really need to know all this, do I?"

Eloise's reaction seemed to trouble the banker. He turned the screen away from Eloise, and took a small handful of jellybeans, chewing thoughtfully before answering.

"Eloise, I know these past few years have been difficult. You've experienced so much loss, and you needed time to heal. Your mother wanted you to have a chance to grow up, get an education, launch a career, before having to be involved in more weighty burdens. She thought though, that at reaching twenty-one you would want to take control of your finances. But no matter. I am happy to continue as we have been doing if that is what you want. If you agree, I can continue to pull your annual fee from your accounts. You'll simply have to sign our client agreement. But tell me, what do you see yourself doing in, oh, five years?"

Eloise sat back in her chair and re-crossed her legs, shrugging. Eloise was internally fighting the instinct to get up and walk, no run, out of there. She had no way to tell this jellybean freak what she had not been able to tell herself. She was waiting for a phone call that was never going to come. She was waiting for some magical external event that would restore to her what had been lost. That for now, she just needed to hunker down and wait.

Mr. Jameson took a deep breath, furrowed his brow, and then continued. "I understand you work at a veterinarian's office?"

"Yes."

"You like it?"

"Yes."

"Would you like to become a veterinarian?"

"I'm not interested in medicine."

"You're more front office? Or back-office?"

"Nope."

"What is it that you do there?"

"Clean kennels, litter boxes, walk dogs, mop the floors, stuff like that."

At this he finally raised his perfectly formed eyebrows.

"I expect you are the most overqualified kennel cleaner they've ever employed. You just recently received a degree in English if I'm not mistaken."

"I use it too."

"At the vet office?"

"Not there. I read a lot. I write about what I read on-line."

Ralph nodded, "Reading, writing, speaking well, those are critically important skills. But tell me why you work at a vet's office."

"I miss animals."

Ralph nodded, "Ah. I suppose working around all those animals is lovely. I adore my little Scottish terrier."

"Horses and riding were my life."

"Yes, the horses. Horses are a different sort of addiction than jellybeans, aren't they? Your mother was passionate about them, even in high school. But I would hate for you to burn through your money, you know, history repeating itself.

"History repeating itself?"

"I mean no disrespect. Your mother was by nature care-ful with money."

"But not Jock. Jock spent it all."

"Not all, or there'd be no use for me. No, your mother looked out for you better than she did for herself. That's what good mothers do."

Eloise felt that lump forming again, her throat began to ache. The need to leave was feeling more urgent by the moment.

Mr. Jameson. took another handful of jellybeans. Eloise thought by now his tongue must be bright red.

"Eloise, how about we meet again in a few weeks? Give you some time to think, think about what it is you do want."

Eloise exhaled loudly and got to her feet, immensely re-lieved. She must look stupid. She had not been able to articulate any of her thoughts. She hadn't even liked Ralph's jellybeans.

* * *

Dear Eloise,

Thank you for sharing your email address.

I have made quite a discovery in this old house of mine. I am dying to share the news with someone who would appreciate it. I sense that you might. I ask that you keep this private until I have transcribed it in full and gleaned from it what I wish. Perhaps I may publish it one day.

I was cleaning out the cluttered garret room. I wanted to move an old dresser to a bedroom below but finding it unnaturally heavy decided to remove all the drawers before trying. Strangely, even with the drawers removed, it was still heavy, and the load felt unstable, as if there were contents shifting about. As it turns out, behind the toe-molding was a hidden shelf. I found that a peg pulled out and the toe-molding swung open to reveal bound books. I opened the top one to find elegant handwriting. Some were dated, and to my shock and excitement they appear to begin in the year 1779.

Handling them is a huge responsibility. I have started the process of transcribing a page at a time. Frankly, the process is painstaking. The paper is fragile, the ink uneven, some bold, some faded, some pages are damaged. Would you like to see my transcriptions and share your thoughts as to their historical significance? I have no one else I wish to share them with at present.

I attach the first I have copied. If nothing else, they make a unique birthday gift for an Extreme Reader.

Dabs

Eloise was feeling like an idiot. She had blithely given this guy her email address and although they had just "met" he was sending her something privately? He was probably now going to be her stalker. Who was this guy? He knew a lot about Thomas Jefferson. But the way he wrote made him sound ancient. Nearly as old as TJ himself! Well, that happened sometimes when you read a lot from a distinctive era. Should she feel flattered? What she felt was uneasy. But not so uneasy that she didn't immediately read the attached document, and when finished, read it once again.

Friday May 7th, 1779

Bud and I were riding down the lane toward the front gates when we saw the clump of men, hats in hands huddled together. I put up my hand to tell Bud to stop. Bud is not always an obedient servant, being but a child, but this time he complied without sass.

I expected Beast to bark, but instead he froze, tail held high, legs stiffened in a pose of alert concern.

Our horses were tired enough to come to a halt, but

eager to return to their stable, so I kept back a good distance. Beauty was perfectly still of course, but Fanny tossed her head and fidgeted, while Bud scolded her. I turned in my saddle and put my finger to my lips. Bud finally realized what our stop was about. I noticed both child and horse quieted instantly as their attention was drawn to the men.

These rituals had been frequent of late, though I had not witnessed it as I did today. It had been a harsh winter, then the snow had melted away leaving sticky red mud, then the spring rains had added more. Once that mud warmed from the sunshine it created a warm but sickly miasma. And so, these men, unseasoned as they were, began to sicken and some, to die. And here, near the gates of our farm, they chose to bury their dead.

Beast had unlocked from his position and began to wander toward the men. I hissed his name, and ordinarily he would mind me. But not today, though he glanced over his shoulder, hesitated, and then made his way to the men. I watched as he joined the circle and sat down without a sound. The man standing beside him placed his hand upon the head of my dog.

Hats were placed back on heads and the men filed past the piled-up soil. My dog, stayed at the heels of his new friend, and this man too paid his respects.

Bud whispered, "Must have been a kind man they burying for Beast to not make a sound."

The line proceeded past us on the lane, some soldiers nodding to us, a few murmuring a "ma'am" at me in passing. The grave diggers remained, waiting politely to finish their jobs out of the sight and hearing of the men.

The last to pass was Beast's new friend. It was a man I had noted before. Well, I must say admired. Mostly for his form, truth be told. He was an officer. He had to have been, as he was the best and most cleanly dressed, and sported a trimly groomed mustache, but then the Hessian soldiers all seemed fond of facial hair. He stopped by Beauty's head and addressed me by name. "Miss Roberts."

I did not mean to be impertinent, but fear I sounded that way. I said, "And who might you be?"

"Major Johann Schmidt, at your service."

As he had been kindly toward my intrusive dog, I said, "I am sorry Beast failed to come when called. He is an intelligent dog, but equally willful. Thank you for bearing his presence."

He said, "Such a fine animal. As are your horses. It is a balm to the soul to have good animals about. Reminds us of our homes."

I felt I had been remiss in offering condolences, so I said, "I am sorry for your loss and the hardships you have endured this long winter."

He nodded sternly, and just then I could see my sympathy had distressed him.

I asked, "Major Schmidt, are men still falling ill?"

"No Miss Roberts, thankfully not this week. But the men who had fever are weak as kittens and stay that way for a month it appears."

I noticed then, how red his eyes, though large and thickly lashed, how dark beneath, how simply exhausted he appeared in both face and stance.

I tried not to be too tender when I stated, "You knew this man."

His mouth drew tight. "It is my job to write his family. He was from my homeland and only twenty-one."

I thought of myself. I admit it. I suddenly felt sad, not for the dead man, who no longer needed my sympathy. Stupidly, I was sad for myself, as if twenty-one was to be my limit as well. That idea was frightening. Because I knew my life was barely lived. At least I hoped there was much to come, never mind that I had no vision of what that was or should be.

My feelings evidently showed on my face. "I expect you and your family are in no danger, Miss. It appears those who grew up in these climes are immune."

I could see the grave diggers leaning on their shovels and cutting eyes at each other. I believe they had their orders to wait until the soldiers had gone. Bud was making small huffing noises behind me, which I ignored, but noted. Beast had stretched out on the ground, though he rested on his elbows, mouth agape, seemingly taking in the conversation.

I said as a way of parting, "Please extend my condolences to the other men. My Aunt Bess recommends boiling water for purification of a sick room. One must use boiling water on all the surfaces and boil the linens.

*It has a double advantage of killing the creepy-crawl-
ies."*

That last line produced a thin smile.
*"Creepy-crawlies? I do not know the term, but I think
I understand. With the thaw the men and all the barracks are crawling with vermin. Your Aunt is a wise
woman."*

*That made me smile. "Major Schmidt, you don't
know how right you are." At that I gathered my reins
and put my leg to Beauty and our party left the grave
diggers to their duty.*

Eloise did not know what to think of the journal entry.
Sure, it could be fake. Maybe Dabs sent this well-com-
posed entry to every geek-girl he could snag on the internet looking for romance. This sort of thing was catnip for
an avid reader of history like Eloise.

It *was* tantalizing stuff. And that horsey profile picture
could be part of his schtick, because that photo too had
been good, and heck, lots of women were nuts about horses.

If it was a schtick, it was a good one. Then there was his
courtly Virginia-gentleman language. And Dabs knew his
Jefferson, too, which was impressive.

But "If it's too good to be true, it's not true."

Eloise exhaled, what a weird day it had been.

There was Dabs sending her this, and then there was
the jellybean banker—Ralph Jameson. Oddballs, both of
them.

Jellybean Ralph had just told her she had assets. She

couldn't remember the number on the bottom of the computer screen. But she remembered it had a lot of digits. But now that everything she knew was gone, did it even matter? What was she supposed to do?

Her gut was telling her to wait. But for what?

Ralph expected her to come back again in a few weeks and tell him something. Eloise had nothing to tell. Nothing to want. What did she want?

Well, maybe to escape. But to where?

1779 Virginia seemed alluring at the moment. Eloise reread the entry a third time. This time she had an eerie feeling that she was more than a distant reader, but part of it. It was a scene at a funeral, a similar scene still fresh and painful in her memory. And the heavily lashed dark-eyed Major with the mustache, she felt she knew him, could see him. He understood that animals were a balm to the soul. He would understand her.

6

Eloise was grumpy returning home after work on Wednesday. The short commute felt perilous as she slogged through another Atlanta afternoon thunder-boomer. That's what happened when the weather turned sultry. Walking dogs had been a hot and sticky affair. Re-entering the chilled basement made the hair stand up on her arms. When Eloise left in the afternoon, the sky was roiling with clouds, grey on the top, black on the bottom, and soon enough they began to dump their load. Her car was buffeted on the road, and periodically it seemed like buckets of water were thrown against her windshield, but she made it home, pulled into the garage and shut the door. She pulled her flashlight from the closet and set it on the kitchen table. Power outages were routine during storms. The important thing was that her e-reader was fully charged, along with a power stick as backup. She also had stuff in the fridge. With a good book and food, she should feel at peace. But she felt as if she had brought her own black cloud inside.

Eloise threw her backpack in a chair and opened the fridge. None of it appealed. She looked back out at the rain pounding down and noticed the gutter was overflowing. Eloise went and found a pad of lined paper and wrote across the top:

1. Get Gutters cleaned.
Then she wrote,
2.

She tore the page off and left it on the counter. Eloise grabbed a cold drink, shut the fridge, went to the pantry, and found a bag of chips.

She ripped open the bag of chips and opened her drink, pulled the notepad over and began to write:

Jellybean Ralph wants to know what I want. I know what I don't want. I don't want anyone feeling sorry for me. I don't want to worry about money, or this house, or anyone else.

The rain, so hard and loud, stopped as if a valve had been shut off. The sun came out. Eloise looked out the window. Steam rose from the asphalt. She opened the front door and stepped out, then sat down on her stoop. The overhang had kept it dry. The air had cooled, although she knew it wouldn't last. She drew in a deep breath.

Her thoughts turned to Dabs, and the writing he had sent her. The supposed journal entry was too polished, the spelling too modern, too educated for a woman of that time and place. She had to give him credit for the bit about the hidden drawer. But why perpetrate a fraud on her? Maybe it was just the sort of cosmic come-uppance she deserved. But that was absurd. Maybe it was Dab's way of getting someone to read his writing, critique it so to speak, without calling it his own. Sly. Could be.

And what did she think of the writing? It wasn't bad. The popular novels of the time were awful. "Pamela" by

Richardson was so bad that Fielding wrote a parody called "Shamala." Those books were written as letters, and this was in the form of journal entries, which was sort of the same thing. Eloise supposed what Dabs had sent her could be authentic. Likely not, though.

The real question was what to say to Dabs. Eloise went back inside, picked up the bag of chips with a twinge of guilt. She shouldn't eat crap. She shouldn't be cruel to this Dabs character either. He was just one of the many reading-geeks out there like her, an Extreme Reader. If Dabs had reached out to her to share a bit of unpublished fiction, at least it was of the same time and place as Jefferson and added color to their study. She reminded herself she had chosen the group because it included fiction. Give the geek a break. Eloise would go along for the ride. She badly needed an escape and would take it, fictional or factual.

Eloise listened to her "better angels" which really meant the voice of her mother. She made a healthy plate and grabbed a bottle of chilled water. Mom always was pushing the water. She sat down in her chair and opened her e-reader. A new wave of rain hit, accompanied by a crash of thunder. Then the lights went out. The darkened house made a cushion. The rain, a veil. It was soft and private, and her book became a keyhole to peek through into another world. The lights stayed off for a long time.

* * *

The lights came back on like the ending of a movie. Time to get up from her chair. The reading had done its magic.

She had relaxed and lost her funk. She had thoughts about the book that she wanted to share online. But not yet. She wanted to mull over things.

Eloise stepped into the laundry room to toss her bottle into the recycle bin. She looked at her tack, now clean, the bridles hanging neatly on the wall, the saddles perfectly aligned, girths hung neatly over the seats. The clean bridle leather demanded her touch.

Eloise picked up a snaffle rein. Held it just so, thumb on top, the joint slightly bent like the roof on a house. Who had taught her that? Her fist closed lightly, "Don't crush the tiny bird you hold in your fist!" She knew that bit was from Sally Swift. The snaffle exited the fist between the ring finger and the pinky, so that the horse could feel the rider "squeeze water from a sponge" on the corners of the mouth, be flexed laterally in the poll either left or right by a small movement of the wrist. She had books full of words and phrases collected over the years still rattling around in her head. All of it had been eagerly absorbed to master the intricate techniques used to communicate to the horse. Eloise dropped the rein and closed the door on the way out.

She went to her desk and turned on her laptop. And she searched for Jock. What should pop up but a photo of Whiplash. Eloise felt dizzy. She exhaled and it passed. There was her beautiful horse. In Ireland. Where she ought to be. Had expected to be. Jock had promised. Or had he? Or was it Mom? Maybe it would have happened in time if she hadn't blown it. But now? Unlikely. That bridge was burned. Yet, a tiny bit of her refused to let it go. Foolish. Looking at Whiplash, in her new life, well, understandably that was a shock. Who was that person sitting on her back, grinning at the camera?

The caption read, this person, "Suzie-whoever", had qualified for the European Junior Eventing Championships. And this person was riding Whiplash, and this person was being coached by Jock, blah, blah, blah. Well, it seemed Jock had made good use of her horse. And why shouldn't he? Jock was still in the game. Eloise was not. No horse, no farm, no coach telling her to get back up and get back on. Done.

Whiplash looked beautiful, fit, and healthy. The horse was thriving. Juniors were run at Preliminary level; Whiplash could do that easily. Jock knew the horse and he was a good coach. He had been a good coach for his daughter, once-upon-a-time. Did Whiplash like the cooler weather? And the green, green grass Eloise saw in every photo of Ireland? Eloise touched the screen and said, "Beats the high heat and humidity here. I hope that chick cares as much about you as I did. Likely worships you."

Eloise was tempted to continue her online check-up on Jock, but just thinking about it made her feel swimmy in her head. She stopped herself and went instead to "Extreme Readers." Betsy was usually online in the afternoons for about an hour or so, sharing her notes and then checking back later that night to respond to any comments that trickled in.

As it turned out, Betsy and Dabs were having an exchange.

Betsy wrote, "Really, Dabs? I haven't seen it."

The two of them continued their chat, back and forth,

Dabs going next, "I think it's new. Isn't that odd? I feel like we willed it into existence."

Betsy asked, "An entire book about the physical Jefferson?"

"Yes. I expect the treatise to be that the outside of the man reveals much about the inside. It follows your thinking, Betsy. That's why it jumped out at me. I'm always browsing new books. Bet you are too."

Betsy wrote, "I assume I'm not alone, puzzling for years at how dissimilar the paintings and sculptures of Jefferson appear."

Dabs wrote, "A Sphinx.'

"I'm enjoying studying Jefferson, Dabs, but people do feel so extremely different about him."

Dabs wrote, "I read once that by simply reading ten books on one topic, you become an expert on that topic."

Betsy was not so sure. "I don't believe that would be enough, but it's a worthy goal."

Eloise joined the conversation, "Hi."

Dabs wrote, "Hi Eloise. Did you see there is a new book out on the topic of Jefferson's person, by that I mean, bodily person."

Only Dabs would have phrased it that way. Eloise imagined him wearing a waistcoat while sitting at his computer. She asked, "Can we add it to our list?"

Dabs added, "What do you think of aiming for ten books on the subject of Jefferson?"

"Sure. Why not?"

As soon as the discussion dwindled, Eloise saw that Dabs had PM'd her.

Dabs wrote, "Did you get my present?"

"I did. It was intriguing."

"I have more pages transcribed. I rather hoped you'd let me share them with you."

He was odd. Very. Who talked like that? She didn't think she had any reason to be worried, and by that she meant worried for her "person".

She typed back, "Can you send me a photo of the dresser and the old journals? Do you think it's authentic?"

"Yes, yes, and yes. I do hope you want more pages."

Eloise wrote: "Of course I do!"

"Then madam, you shall have them!"

Eloise replied with an LOL, when she really was thinking OMG. Dabs was a real head-case. But then, who was she to judge?

Later when Eloise checked her email, Dabs had sent three photos. One was of a chest of drawers, with the toe-molding removed to show a space below the last drawer. It was hard to see this as proof-positive of a hidden shelf.

The second photo was of a clearly old, bound book. Again, what proof was that? The third photo showed the open frontispiece of what she assumed was the book in the previous photo. It had flowery writing in faded ink with flourishes. Eloise enlarged the photo enough to make out "Louisa Roberts" and "May, the Year of our Lord, 1779."

But it wasn't the writing or the flourishes that sent a chill down Eloise's spine. Below the writing was a well-executed line drawing of the head of a horse.

Eloise had, at one time, decorated every piece of paper

with sketches not unlike the one here. As a horse obsessed girl, when she had been at school, her heart was still at the barn, with her horse. In that instant, Eloise felt her confirmed notion of fraud fall away. Just like that. Eloise felt a tug between this long dead girl and herself. Dabs could still be crazy, but Louisa Roberts had been horse crazy. Louisa Roberts was her soul-sister from another century.

* * *

Eloise had the weekend off and so did Pinky. Doc had a couple of high school kids who worked kennels for him on weekends. Pinky and Buzz were headed north to the mountains, and Pinky had asked Eloise to dog and house sit. Eloise owed her. Eloise and Betsy were on for a Sunday breakfast date too. Eloise had her e-reader loaded with new Jefferson material. A good weekend was planned.

Eloise enjoyed the change of venue, and the company of the dogs. She had managed quite well to walk the three at once. "Prince" was a real Prince, who never pulled at the leash. Ying and Yang were basically exercise intolerant. They panted heavily at her heels, while Prince slowed his pace to match theirs. Once she put the "puffballs" up she took Prince around the block a second time, and she picked up the pace.

When she got back, she made a snack, got an ice-tea, and planted herself on Pinky's giant bed, propping herself with pillows. For the comfort of the dogs, Pinky insisted Eloise stay in the master bedroom where they slept. Pinky had dog-stairs for the puffballs, so they too joined her topside, along with Prince. Within minutes the little ones were snoring loudly.

This new book was well-written, easy to digest, and appeared well-researched.

The Declaration of Independence, through Jefferson's pen, had opened a Pandora's box. It addressed philosophically far more than a separation from Britain. It was more than the important earth-shaking preamble we all know. Of course, the specific sections on the slave trade were cut out at the insistence of Georgia and South Carolina delegates.

But Jefferson later, referring to the problem of ending slavery, had written that they had "the wolf by the ear and can neither hold him nor safely let him go." But the truth was that in the northern colonies, they were indeed "letting go" bit by bit, proving it could be done. Not so in the south.

In Britain, the Somerset decision of 1772 ruled that slavery was not supported by Common law or Parliament and therefore not legal in England. (Slavery was formally abolished there in 1833.) Excepted were the colonies. Why? Profitability, but also fear by the colonists of bloody retribution for the injustices slave owners dealt out daily. Abolishing slavery in America was seen as the card the British dare not play. But because of rebellion, they did dare.

Playing that "card" first was Governor Dunsmore of Virginia in 1775, who barely made his escape from rebelling Virginians. He called for slaves to run away from plantations and join him in the fight against the rebels, creating the Ethiopian Regiment.

Virginian's saw this as the ultimate call to war. Jefferson would later write, "I tremble for my country when I reflect that God is just, that his justice cannot sleep forever…" Jefferson understood that justice, if indeed dealt out by God, was on the side of the slaves, not the slaveholders.

How was that for cognitive dissonance?

Again in 1779, British General Henry Clinton welcomed slaves to fight for the British, and many did with the promise of freedom. At the end of the war, some made it to Nova Scotia, and to freedom, despite being on the losing side.

Eloise had a startling thought. Were slave holders joining the fight against Britain for the cause of political independence, or the less noble cause of retaining slavery? Taxes, though burdensome, were not existential. But maintaining slavery *was* felt to be key to survival, both economic and otherwise. They were determined to cling to the ears of their wolf. They would cling all the way to the surrender at Appomattox.

For the first time in her life, Eloise wondered if the wrong side won.

What if the American Civil War had never been fought? How many African Americans would have lived as freedmen had the British won and, in that win, delivered on the vow to free the enslaved?

The signers had pledged their lives, their fortunes, and their sacred honor, for independence and for the truth that "all men are created equal" excluding the enslaved in that pledge. No wonder the Brits considered them scoundrels.

Eloise had not noticed that Prince had left the bed.

But she felt him jump back up, and then a big hairy nose pushed something under her elbow. She ignored it initially, but his beard was wet, likely from getting a drink, and it was tickling her bare armpit.

"What?"

Ying and Yang were up too, tails wagging, all three staring at her.

There was a small velvet pillow next to her. She picked it up and turned it over. It was black velvet, trimmed in gold fringe, and embroidered with gold thread. It read, "Dog is my copilot."

"Now, where in the heck did that come from?"

Prince jumped off the bed and twirled a few goofy circles. The puff balls started yapping in excitement at Prince.

Eloise sighed and got up, thinking she might need another snack anyway. But first she walked into the tiny guest bedroom. The bed had a black paisley bedspread, perfect for a small pillow. Eloise immediately noticed the bedspread was wrinkled. "Someone" had been up on it.

Eloise had dog-escorts watching as she smoothed the spread and put the pillow in its place.

She lectured, "Now, listen, this is not a dog toy. Not your toy. Not your bed. Got it?"

Prince was intently staring at her, as if he understood every word.

They were happy to follow her into the kitchen and then examine the contents of the fridge. Eloise found the big wooden bowl she had used earlier, and this time filled it with a yogurt, cheese and ham slices, crackers, dried apricots, and chocolate covered almonds.

Eloise climbed back into bed and set things up as she liked them, then enjoyed her yogurt as she settled back into her book. At some point, Prince jumped up on the bed and curled up next to her ... with the black pillow in his mouth.

Eloise picked up the pillow, noticing the velvet was wet. "Aw, man."

"I thought you understood. This does not belong to you. Remember?"

She started to go back to the guest bedroom, but stopped herself, turning around to look at the dogs. Then she walked back into the master suite and patted the covers of the bed, saying ..."Up."

The puff balls jumped on the doggie-steps, and from the steps launched themselves back up to the bed. Prince popped up from the ground to the spot where Eloise had been sitting.

Eloise said, "Stay" and backed out of the room, pulling the bedroom door shut.

This time Eloise placed the black pillow on top of the chest of drawers. She went back to Pinky and Buzz's room, saying, "Fixed that little problem."

Prince jumped down, but was back in what seemed like seconds, with the pillow in his mouth.

"No way!" Eloise dragged herself back out of the bed.

Eloise shut them in the bedroom then walked around the small house with the pillow, looking for a great hiding place. She brushed off the pillow. Dog saliva on velvet was not a great look.

Eloise ended up in the kitchen. Pinky had open shelving, so Eloise simply put the pillow on the shelf, next to a stack of plates. It was not the most sanitary spot for a spit covered pillow, but at least the dog couldn't get it.

Eloise tucked herself back in her reading nest, she glanced over at the wooden bowl on the nightstand and sighed. No cheese or ham or crackers. At least they hadn't eaten the fruit or the chocolate since it was wrapped in plastic (and toxic for dogs). The empty yogurt cup was missing. "Someone" had hidden it. Eloise ate her apricots and chocolate and had just re-immersed herself once again when she heard a scraping noise. She froze. Prince was not on the bed.

Prince trotted in, pillow in his mouth, tail wagging furiously as he jumped back up on the bed and proudly spit out the pillow.

Eloise hopped up, e-reader in hand, and headed to the kitchen.

When she got there, she hugged the e-reader to her chest, her mouth hanging open.

A kitchen chair had been pushed away from the table up against the counter. He had used the chair as a stepstool to hop up on the counter, where he had simply reached up and retrieved the pillow from the shelving. He had done it without disturbing a single plate.

Prince barked. She looked down to find the pillow had been dropped at her feet. He backed up a few feet, held her eye and barked again.

She understood. He wanted her to hide it again. And this time, make it harder.

Eloise put the pillow in the oven.

7

Hi Eloise,

I entrust to you another entry.

I thought you would appreciate this as you admire horses and work with dogs. I look forward to hearing your reaction.

Dabs

May 7, 1779

Tonight, Father and I were, as usual, the last ones up, reading in the parlor, our candles nearly burned away. Father closed his book, and when he did so, Beast rose from my feet, yawned, and stretched, then placed his paw upon my thigh. Father said, "There is no creature I love more than a dog."

I corrected him, "Father you love your horses more and you know it."

He said, "That is not quite true, daughter, how-ever dedicated I am to our horses. The love of a horse, well, it makes us. For a horse, if we are to be his master, truly, he requires us to be without temper, calm, and brave. A horse never forgets, never, one who is unfair, or cruel. Even the accidental trauma, once experienced, is never forgotten. Because of this, a horse requires us to find those good qualities within ourselves, and bury our fears, our hurts, our disappointments. For a horse to love us, we must rise to be that person. And when we do, we experience something sublime. He grants us his power and beauty. For a horse to love his master, his master must be worthy. And for that reason, yes, I do love our horses.

"A dog is different. And for that difference, he gains his place. Let a dog see your fear, your pain. He will not draw away, but instead draw closer. He will love you most in your broken states. He will be your protector and a better medic than any man. And in return what does he ask? To share with you whatever your fortune, poverty, or riches. Dearest Louisa, that creature there gazing into your face, his eyes shine with intelligence that is hard to fathom, but look at him there, his eyes shine with love for you. I love my horses, that is true. But I hold a special place in my heart for dogs, and especially the dog that loves you."

And then I asked, "And what of men? And love?"

Father lifted his glass and smiled coyly. "If you can find a man as good as that dog there, I shall have no complaints."

He did give me a broad wink with that.

It was a beautiful and mature piece of writing. Could it possibly be from the same pen that drew the frontispiece sketch of a horse? Eloise had thought the drawing to be from the hand of a child or nearly a child.

She wrote Dabs back. She asked him the same question. But she also asked to see more. How much did he have? He had mentioned multiple journals. Were they by month, by year? Who was this person? And not only the girl, but the father too.

In her email inbox was another message. This one from Jock.

Hi Lulu,

I got that clinic booked. Below are the dates and address of the farm. It's an hour north of you. I will only be there for the weekend. Come Saturday, and I'll get you a room and treat you to a belated-birthday dinner. I need a favor. I have three prospects lined up for a client, but I need you to go ride them. One's a green-bean, one is a Prelim horse, and one is ready to go Advanced. Top quality. You know the kind of ride I like. I trust you more than anyone else to separate the wheat from the chaff. Contact info below. Give them a call and line up a convenient time for you. Thanks.

Jock

Eloise made a rude gesture at the computer screen. Jock was, as usual, calling the shots, without regard to facts. Like nothing had happened. When she calmed a moment, she wondered if this was a white flag? No. Wrong analogy. Jock never surrendered. But this had to mean something, or not.

She was stewing when an email came in from Dabs.

Hi Eloise,

Agree, the writing is mature. But her comment regarding the twenty-one-year-old soldier means she's not yet twenty-one. Now, while I am reading about Jefferson, I'm thinking about Louisa Roberts. If she lived in this house, well, she didn't live far from Monticello. I've never heard of her, but since this house was passed down to me, we might be related.

There are four journals in all. I'm transcribing between my other duties. My hay fields are cut, and it's time to tedder the cut hay. It's very time sensitive because I must watch the moisture content. Hoping for good quality hay to sell and to stack in my barn for my own use.

Are you not riding at all?

Dabs

Eloise wrote, "My Dad wants me to go try sales horses for him. But no, I haven't ridden for a few years now."

Eloise sighed. Before she hit "send" she added to her message her cell number. Was that wise?

"Ping!" Now he was texting her. Eloise grimaced. What had she been thinking?

"Your Dad rides?"

"Yeah, he lives in Ireland, but he's coming to teach a riding clinic."

"Wait. Is your Dad Jock Robertson?

"Yes."

"I'm so slow. You're Lulu Robertson?"

Eloise cringed. Once she had been proud to be Lulu Robertson, daughter of Jock. But once she had been cast off, well it felt better to reject the name herself.

"I hate that name."

The little floating dots indicated that Dabs was already typing.

"Years ago, I caught your horse. A red mare, at Rocking Horse. Mare had a wicked duck and spin, you cartwheeled through the air and landed on your feet. She left the course and ran right to me."

"That's embarrassing. It wasn't the first time, either. That's how she got her name. "Whiplash."

"She ever give it up?"

"Yeah. Best horse ever."

"I remember you. You are talented. Better than I will ever be. You ought to go ride those horses for your Dad."

"Jock."

Eloise felt anger well up in her. Lulu Robertson was just a name on the back of an old saddle in her laundry room, and Jock sure as shit had quit on her as "Dad."

Dabs did not seem to notice her correction, "Maybe one of those horses is a hot little chestnut mare. "Whiplash-redux?"

"I doubt I would land on my feet nowadays."

"I'd come with you if I weren't so far away, and if I didn't have to go tedder the hay."

Eloise felt grateful for the distance. But she did want to see more of the journal.

"Get your hay teddered, then send me more."

Dabs signed off with, "Will do."

* * *

Eloise was late. She should not have been. She had been up since dawn. Betsy was already seated at the table with a pot of coffee.

"Sorry to be late. I had to be sure that big dog had his tongue hanging out before I left."

"Oh dear, has Prince misbehaved?"

Eloise recited her adventures with "Prince and the Puffballs."

She was rewarded by Betsy's laughter.

"Prince and the Puffballs sounds like a title of a children's book. He may be trouble, but the smart one's are, aren't they?"

"Dogs or children?"

"Both. He's not content to sleep away his life. But you must stay on your toes. That's why I chose a Persian cat. Marilyn IS content to sleep away most of her life and therefore very little trouble."

"She's affectionate at least."

"Yes, and she looks good in rhinestones."

"Not exactly a role model for a modern woman."

"But entirely appropriate for a fluffy white Persian cat."

The waitress was heading their way, but Betsy added, "I like that dog very much, just not for myself."

Eloise ordered blueberry pancakes, her favorite. Betsy made sure they had plenty of crispy bacon to go with the pancakes. Once they were into their meals, Betsy brought up the dog again.

"That hide-and-seek game Prince played with you. Do you think someone taught him that, or did he think it up himself?"

"Who knows? He's not a Labrador Retriever. Those dogs will push a spit-covered ball in your lap for you to throw it until they drop."

Betsy refilled their mugs. "Do you think he got into so much trouble that someone dumped him?"

"Maybe. People get large active breeds without understanding how much exercise they need. We never had problems with any of our dogs. But they burned off excess energy and never got bored on the farm. The worst they ever did was chew stuff when they were puppies. I've had some tough horses though."

"It was news to me that you rode horses, tough or otherwise. I know so little about horses, except of course they are beautiful. Tell me about your toughest horse."

"I had a chestnut mare once."

"Describe chestnut."

"A red head. Mine was close to orange colored. There's an old saying, 'Chestnut-mare-beware!'"

"Are they really that fearsome?"

"I suppose the brighter the red they are the hotter they were thought to be. Mine had a pretty blaze face, and her nose would sunburn in the summer, just like any red-head."

Betsy added, "The same assumptions are made of red-haired people. I guess it's due to how easily they flush. The blood is visible, so if their blood is 'up' you can tell."

Eloise said, "Jefferson was a red-head."

"Indeed. But I'd like to hear more about your red-head."

Eloise smiled.

Betsy said, "I sense a story."

Eloise paused, then said, "I haven't thought of her in ages, but for some reason lately..."

"I never think these things are coincidental, do you?"

"No. I guess not."

Betsy asked, "She was trouble?"

"Yes. But that's why we got her. Jock trained and sold horses. She came to be sold."

"Jock?"

"My Dad."

"How unusual a name. But you were saying about the horse?"

"She was a hard stopper."

"I have no idea what that means."

"Sometimes horses decide not to jump. She wasn't just a stopper, but one that waited until the last possible moment, then threw her head down and spun left."

"That sounds dangerous."

"Hmmm. Jock bought her cheap and gave her to me as a project."

"Your father bought you a dangerous horse?"

"Mom wasn't thrilled. But it was the best horse I'd ever ridden."

"And you turned her around?"

"Not right away. She would duck and spin, I would fall off, and then she would run away. I don't think she liked me very much. It was humbling."

"You never got hurt?"

"Just bruises. Mostly to my ego. Jock wouldn't let me quit."

"Was he right? To do that?"

"I don't know. All I know is that she stopped spinning and running away, and I stopped falling off. By the end of our time together, I felt like she would have gone through rings of fire for me. Whiplash and I had a very good three years."

"Whiplash?"

"Jock re-named her as a joke. She's still out competing. A kid just qualified for Junior European Championships on her. She'll be representing Ireland."

"Ah, that's why you've been thinking about her?"

"Yes, that and because of Dabs."

"Dabs? My goodness, how does Dabs figure into this?"

"It's hard to believe, but Dabs says he caught her once, when I fell off. Whiplash ran right up to him."

Now Betsy put her palms flat on the tabletop. "You and Dabs have met before?"

"Dabs and Whiplash. And I guess he met whoever re-trieved my horse from him that day in Florida. It wasn't me."

"Eloise, my God, how long were you going to wait to

hand me that juicy tid-bit? Dabs knows who you are? I declare I'm suffering whiplash myself! This is astounding. Why aren't you astounded?"

Eloise shrugged, "Because eventing is a small world and because I'm not that person anymore. Dabs used to event. Jock is well known. So, Dabs put two and two together when he heard my dad was Jock Robertson. And then he remembered watching me fall off and Whiplash running right up to him to be caught."

* * *

Eloise was listening to her audio book when Pinky arrived late in the morning. Eloise had brought all three dogs in with her, putting the three of them in an empty run, since she wasn't sure when Pinky would make it back. Pinky had a new rescue dog in tow. It was a small dog this time. Eloise knew Pinky would gleefully transform it.

It pulled on the leash all the way down the stairs, gagging, and choking. When Pinky got to the bottom, she picked it up, cheerfully calling to Eloise.

"Hey Eloise, another dog got her freedom ride from a high-kill shelter. She's going to be a stunner. Let me put her on the table so you can get her "before" picture.

Eloise pulled out her ear buds and put her book on pause before dutifully taking a photo with Pinky's phone.

"That's a cutie. Poodle?"

Pinky nodded and then raised an eyebrow. "You and the pack have a good time?"

"It was nice. Betsy and I met for breakfast Sunday."

Pinky put the dog in the tub and hooked it up. Then put on her apron, starting the water, and feeling it for temperature. The little dog looked like it knew the drill.

Pinky said, "My babies here? Everyone good?"

"All three fed, walked, and snoozing on a polar fleece in a run."

"Thanks."

Eloise pulled the clean towels out of the dryer and quietly began to fold. She was tempted to put the ear buds back in but waited in case Pinky wanted to chat. The laundry was never done, but she enjoyed the opportunity it provided for chatting.

Pinky began hosing down the dog, "Other than breakfast with Betsy, what did you do all weekend?"

"I read."

Eloise added as an afterthought. "I took the dogs on long walks. The weather was perfect; but, what about you? Did you and Buzz enjoy your getaway?"

"Yeah, we heard some good bands, tried different craft brews and stayed up way too late. And the second night we sampled small plates at a friend's restaurant."

Pinky's phone rang, but she couldn't get it. She finished bathing the dog, and he was now sparkling white as she put him in a cage and turned on the dryer.

Janet called on the intercom for a dog just as Pinky looked over her list of grooming jobs, then Pinky went looking in cages for her next dog.

So, it wasn't until later when Eloise and Pinky met up again in the basement.

Pinky was soaping up a Gordon Setter when Eloise

came down and put a dog in a run. She hung up the leash on a hook on the wall as Pinky called out to her.

"That was Buzz calling earlier, by the way."

"Yeah?"

"He was going to do a little cooking for me, y'know, since he has to go in to work and stay until closing. He made me dinner for later. He's sweet that way, making sure I eat a decent meal."

"Buzz is a prince of a guy Pinky. You're so lucky."

"He started the broiler to let it heat up."

Eloise finally got it. She smacked herself on the forehead, "Oh no! I forgot…"

Pinky started laughing, barely choking out the words. "The kitchen filled with the most God-awful smoke. Set off the smoke alarm."

"Oh, Pinky I'm so sorry. I totally forgot. I'll buy you a new pillow."

Pinky, got control of herself, wiping a tear off her cheek with one of the bath towels. "Good Gawd Eloise, whatever made you put my little throw pillow in the oven?"

Eloise sighed, "Prince."

Pinky listened to the whole story, shaking her head. Finally, she said, "Eloise, why the heck didn't you just shut the door to the guest room? That's what I do."

Eloise smacked her forehead a couple more times. Damn. Then Eloise realized she still had a yogurt cup to locate in Pinky's house and a hair clip stuffed between Pinky's couch cushions. In the meantime, at least she could locate and purchase the pillow on the internet.

Doc was in his office when Eloise did her final cleanup of the litter boxes at the end of her day. She freshened up the water and set out new food, giving each cat some attention if they asked for it. Some cats relished having a few moments of petting, some preferred to sulk.

Doc called out from the office, "How's it going, Eloise?"

Eloise made her way to the office door. Doc was behind his desk, which was covered in file folders, books, magazines, newspapers surrounding an open laptop. There were cardboard boxes on the bare floors. He lacked artwork on the walls. It was stark, but he did have two faux leather rolling chairs for clients facing his desk. Eloise had sat in one of them the day she interviewed for the job. She had not sat in one since.

"Going well. All the dogs scheduled to go home are clean and walked and ready for pick up. All done up here too."

Doc asked, "If you need anything, let me know. I'm working on giving everyone here a raise. It won't be much, but I'm pleased with the business, and I want each of you to feel appreciated."

"Thanks. Doc."

Eloise hesitated then asked, "Do you miss the horses?"

"Of course, I do. I loved being close to them at the event. Incredible creatures."

"Do you miss riding?"

"Eloise, I haven't been able to ride, I mean really ride, since I started vet school. It's odd. I became a vet because it was a way, I thought, to make a living and somehow keep riding. But that wasn't realistic."

"That reality thing, it's tough."

Doc said, "Seeing all those event horses, the bug bit you, didn't it?"

Eloise detected a twinkle in Doc's eye. "You too?"

Now he was leaning back in his chair. "There's more isn't there?"

She had an opportunity. Eloise nodded.

Doc saw her wheels turning. He said, "You can come in you know, even sit in a chair. Hovering there in the door, well, it gives me the feeling you haven't decided yet if you want to tell me your plans or make a run for it."

Eloise came in but she did not sit down. "Did I mention that my Dad is a horse trainer? Eventer."

Doc looked incredulous, "No. You certainly did not. You never said a thing. Not a thing."

"It's complicated."

Doc nodded, "But now you've brought it up…"

"Only because now, he's asked me to go ride three sales horses for him. He's in Ireland and coming to teach a clinic. I mean, I haven't sat on a horse in well, years."

Doc said, "It seems to me that you are perfectly in your rights to say no."

Eloise swallowed. "That's just it."

"You don't want to say no?"

Eloise paused before speaking, "We could do two in one day, but the Advanced horse, we'd have to drive two hours just to try him."

Doc narrowed his eyes. "We?"

"We, as in you, me, and Pinky, although she knows nothing about it yet, and nothing about horses. Pinky has to promise not to say a word, not a word, while we're around the seller."

Doc looked amused, "I'm not sure what use I'll be, but if you can schedule it for a Sunday, I'll see what I can do. Could be fun. I guess taking you to that event, well, I let a genie out of a bottle."

Eloise laughed. He was right.

Eloise realized she very much did want to go try the horses. It scared her. She understood why she had asked Doc, unexpressed and unarticulated. She needed him. She could not do this alone. She had never tried horses without Jock. He would sit on them first, then put her up and coach her through the ride. She resented that Jock had the nerve to ask her to do it. True. But the longing she had been feeling, well, it had a direction for the moment. She was going to ride. At last.

8

Oddball Dabs must have gotten his hay teddered because there were more transcriptions in her inbox. Eloise hesitated, but not for long. She knew she was encouraging the guy. Whatever. History freaks seemed the wrong demographic for a murderer or rapist or scam artist. She was going along for the ride because of Louisa Roberts. At some point, she'd have to make that clear to Dabs. But not yet. Eloise eagerly began to read.

Friday May 14th, 1779

We have been blessed with a letter from Buck. Aunt Bess nearly fainted with relief. Either that or Priscilla has over-tightened her stays. Buck's rare piece of parchment did declare that he has, by the Grace of God, recovered his missing servant, Sammie. Sammie did not of course, strictly speaking, go missing. The ungrateful lad ran away. Governor Dunsmore lured many more than Sammie away from their rightful owner. We lost a few field hands and regretfully, our cook Olive and her husband Mo, who was our skilled shoemaker. I assume Buck wrote home merely to crow over this conquest. Buck also writes he is done with the State Militia. They did no more than sleep rough and go hungry. Buck writes his horses are poorly. It angers me that he would let their health degenerate so he could roam the woods to little purpose.

* * *

Saturday May 15th, 1779

Today Bud and I had a surprise. I rode Beauty and Bud rode the three-year-old filly, Fanny. We got to the creek crossing and Fanny was having none of it, tossing her head and backing up the bank while Bud flailed his arms and legs to no use. I was trying to talk Bud through it, when who would approach from the far bank, but the venerable Mr. Jefferson. He had ridden all this way to inspect the Barracks, which he does on occasion.

The sight of Mr. Jefferson, calmly riding toward us, interrupted the scene. Even Fanny stood still, though her knees wobbled. He offered his aid. I am sure the sight of the distressed child compelled him to help. Bud was one moment tearful, and the next squealing like a pig, which did not soothe the fractious filly one bit.

Mr. Jefferson greeted me by name and inquired if he could assist. He rode his young stallion Caractacus. I think it a fine horse, but not nearly as attractive as what father is producing.

Mr. Jefferson rode up to Fanny and placing his horse's tail right beneath the filly's nose, walked down the bank and through the water. Bud had eyes like saucers as the filly followed a few steps. But as she came to the edge of the creek, she bunched herself up, all four feet together. Bud squeezed his eyes tight as the filly trembled. Mr. Jefferson crossed back to try again, offering words in such low tones I have no idea what he said. This effort produced one hoof of Fanny's sliding forward into the drink, while the body of the filly recoiled backward.

Beauty had stood and watched, while the cold water washed over her legs, and the end of her tail floated on its surface. Growing impatient, she began to pound the water with a front hoof. I reprimanded her, thinking it a disturbance to the proceedings. Instead, Fanny was intrigued. Mr. Jefferson brought his horse to stand by mine and soon Caractacus joined Beauty in creating a great turbulence. Fanny had stopped trembling and made her decision. Bud shrieked as Fanny launched herself into the party. We soon had three horses flinging water while we laughed at their antics. Just to be sure Fanny had lost her fear, Mr. Jefferson and I led as Bud followed in a few practice crossings. Before parting, Mr. Jefferson invited my family for an evening of fellowship, music, and dining next week. I have never dined at Monticello, although father goes to play chess from time to time.

Bud and I finished our session. We looped back to have one last crossing for good measure.

Fanny did not hesitate. No, she forged boldly into

the depths, stopping to help herself to a drink. Thirst slaked; she performed a full baptismal. Bud does not swim, but I can attest that he does not sink either. He met the filly on the bank. It was a noticeably quiet ride back to the barn since I did not dare speak.

* * *

Sunday May 16th, 1779

We are not poor. I object to such characterizations by Aunt Bess. Indeed, the tobacco meant to ship from Norfolk is destroyed. But we are not ruined! We have plenty to eat and more to harvest. We have all manner of animals. Aunt Bess does hoard, and squirrel away much, especially precious tea and chocolate. I suppose her hoarded stores are becoming depleted and that worries her. But Father has sold many riding horses to the prisoners, at inflated prices too. Some around here have emptied the pockets of these prisoners for trifles, even the beds they slept upon. But horses are not trifles, and horses are always needed. As long as we have breeding stock, we have the "goose that lays the golden egg." We shall never be poor.

* * *

Dabs wrote, "Eureka! Can you believe it? Jefferson makes an appearance. I know he was already a famous neighbor by 1779, and I know he was instrumental with the Barracks being built, so it makes sense he would come to inspect them from time to time. But still, this is pure gold."

"Agree. Unbelievable."

Dabs added, "There is an old graveyard here, and Louisa could be buried in it. I've walked through the graveyard a thousand times but never paid much attention to the names. Until now. My folks made a point to keep the cemetery clean, the bushes trimmed. I'm afraid I've let it go wild. The stacked stone wall is still standing, but the gate is about to go. I took the weed-whacker out there today and set to clearing the mess. Then I took a dry scrub brush to a few of the head stones. I was looking for Louisa. I didn't find her though."

"She's likely buried elsewhere next to her husband."

"I suppose you're right."

"I could be wrong. We don't know if she married. She may not have lived long enough to marry. People died young then."

"Are you trying to cheer me up?"

"Hahaha."

Dabs typed, "I told you I've gotten obsessed. But this is exciting stuff."

"Agree, and I'm not related to Louisa Roberts or living in the same house where you found the journals. I don't have any connection to her, but I want you to get cracking on the transcription regardless."

"If I didn't have to go outside and work my tail off, it's all I would do."

"You get your hay baled and picked up out of the field yet?"

"I did, and it's beautiful hay. I called in back-up for baling and stacking. Exhausting."

"Sorry I couldn't help."

"I'm sorry too."

"So, Louisa writes about a creek crossing. Do you know where she was riding?"

"Sure. I see it all the time. I get up early and ride the perimeter of what's left of the farm."

"Can you still cross the creek?"

"Unless we have a freshet. Then it's too high and strong for me and Dude, but most of the time, sure."

"Freshet?"

"Jeffersonian language. Heavy run-off."

"Forever after, you'll cross that creek and think of Louisa."

Dabs typed, "And Bud."

"You're sure it's the same creek?"

"Yes. If they are riding out from this farm."

"Dude? You really named your horse Dude?"

"It was a long time ago."

"Funny. At least it sounds like you still enjoy your rides."

"It is a very tame ride. We mostly walk but Dude seems to enjoy it. You should ride again you know. You were good. I bet you miss it."

"I decided to go look at those horses for Jock."

"Wow. That's great. Could be a fun adventure."

"I'm anxious for a bunch of reasons. For one thing, Jock doesn't do something like this unless he has a reason."

"How so?"

Eloise replied, "Like a drug dealer giving out a free hit."

"You know about drug dealers?"

"It's just an analogy!"

Dabs typed back, "I hope so. But I don't see what you have to lose. Just go ride."

"It's complicated."

"But do you miss it?"

"Yes."

"Go ride the horses. Get someone to video and let me have a look. I wish I could come. It's more fun with a friend."

"Doc said he'd come, and Pinky is coming to video."

"That's great. Um, you have a friend named Pinky?"

"Yup. She doesn't know a thing about horses, but if she keeps both me and the horse in the frame, the video will be good enough."

"Well then, I'm counting on Pinky to video, and counting on you to share them."

Dabs said, "If you send me video, I'll send more transcriptions. Is it a deal?"

"You were going to send me more regardless."

"But I didn't know about the horses then, did I?"

Eloise wrote back, "How is that relevant?"

"Maybe I don't think I'd get to see the videos any other way."

"If I share the videos, you have to promise you won't show them to anyone."

"I can do that."

"I'll let you know."

"I'll just keep working on the journals until you get back to me. Deal?"

"Okay. Deal."

Eloise thought Dabs would expect to see on the video the Lulu he remembered. She wasn't up to that level. She may never have been up to that level. She did fall off a lot. But she always stood near that halo of light that surrounded Jock, and just by being his daughter a bit of it always shone on her. Jock let her believe she deserved it, that it was rightfully hers. Unlikely.

Eloise was nervous, suspicious, edgy.

Was Jock's horse shopping request an attempt to invite her back into the world he had taken from her, an attempt at an apology?

She couldn't help but want to please him as she always had wanted to please her Daddy. She was pathetic. The thought produced a feeling of self-pity, followed by self-loathing. Jock was not here. Jock should no longer have this power over her.

But here she was, saying "yes."

She briefly considered all those numbers at the bottom of Jellybean Ralph's screen. She did not need Jock but cynically she wondered if he needed her. Or her money.

But there was no turning back now.

* * *

Eloise had the appointment made for Sunday to try the most advanced horse of the three. Pinky had been excited. Eloise repeatedly told her it was not going to be exciting, not if she had anything to do with it. Doc volunteered to drive. She promised herself she would make it up to Pinky and Doc. Eloise sent Jock an email confirming the trip. It wasn't long before she got an email from Jock in return.

Lulu,

Be sure and get a feel for how the horse takes you to the jumps. I would rather have one pull my arms out than feel like it's doing the backstroke, but you know that. Have fun.

Dad

Jock expected her to jump. Of course, he did. The task ahead seemed stupider by the minute. Eloise considered calling the whole thing off. But that seemed cowardly. This was an advanced level horse. This horse wasn't an off-the-track barely trained, adrenaline-poisoned, rocket ship. But if things went south, she was done.

Eloise figured she better see if her boots still zipped. They did. She left her boots on and went looking for her helmet. Her schooling helmet was a "total" the lining was crumbling and smelled like pee. She threw it in the garbage. Had her show helmet made the move? It was also past its prime. She went into her bedroom closet upstairs and came up empty-handed. She went back downstairs and stood on the upholstered bench in her mom's huge walk-in closet, to explore the upper shelves. There were lots of boxes up there. She still couldn't reach the stuff on the top shelf. She got a hanger and worked the nearest box forward with a tiny tap-tap-tap. It fell off the shelf right into her hand.

It was her mother's old top hat. They weren't even legal anymore. It too should have gone into the trash. She examined it. Size 7, long oval. The satin band around the brim was stained. She resisted the urge to bring it to her nose. She could imagine her mom wearing it, adjusting her tailcoat while Eloise handed her a bottle of water for one more swig before going into the arena to compete. Eloise put it back in the box and managed to toss it back onto the shelf. She went for the next box. It was even harder to reach. A tap-tap-tap, another tap, and another, until the box tipped off the shelf. Eloise had caught the first box easily, even with the hanger-in-hand and stretched on her tippy-toes.

This time the box whacked her on the head, which in turn made Eloise jerk backward, which upset the bench, scooting from under her. Eloise fell backward with a thump, whacking her head hard on the wall behind her.

Eloise cursed.

Then she laughed. How was that for irony? She nearly got concussed trying to retrieve her protective headgear. She had fallen even before she had gotten near a horse. This was not a good omen.

Eloise opened the box. It was a helmet she had never seen before. She recognized the make. She remembered trying one on at a tack trailer at a horse show. It was beautiful. They retailed for what? Six hundred. Easily.

Eloise slipped the helmet out of the drawstring bag and admired its black matte finish and shiny trim. Then she put it on, a perfect fit. She noticed an envelope in the box. It read, "Merry Christmas Lulu. Can't wait to see what the new year brings for you and Whiplash."

Eloise's head throbbed as if in response to the note. Whatever Christmas this was bought as a gift, it was never given. Jock was out of their lives as soon as things got rough, and he soon had her horse too.

Who needs a helmet when you don't have a horse? But why did her Mom stash it away high up in her closet? Did her mom know this day would come? Well, at least Eloise now had a helmet to put on for Sunday. And it fit. "Yours is not to question why …" Yeah, she remembered the second half of that saying.

Eloise thought wryly that since she nearly knocked herself out without getting near a horse, perhaps she should be wearing this fancy new helmet 24/7.

Eloise sat on the closet floor wearing the helmet, her head ached, she felt dizzy, and she was giggling in a loopy kind of way that, thankfully, no one witnessed.

* * *

The two-hour car trip with Pinky and Doc did not feel like a long ride. Eloise's nerves had the effect of speeding up time. Eloise felt compelled to give Pinky a tutorial on what not to say. Also, she reviewed how to take a video of a horse and rider. There was something comforting about the fact that Pinky knew nothing about horses and would have no qualified opinion on Eloise's riding.

There was also something both comforting and astonishing about the fact that Doc and Pinky were there at all.

Eloise wore her best breeches, had her boots in a boot bag and her helmet in a drawstring bag. She brought a pair of deerskin gloves she had found in her mother's closet. They still had that soft flexibility that wears away with use and sweat. Her mother had been old-school, wearing deerskin or crochet-backed gloves with deerskin palms.

They pulled through fancy gates after punching in a code. Doc whistled softly through his teeth as they got out of the car. This was not the average eventing stable, which truth-be-told were usually more basic. This place was as high-end as the price of this horse. Eloise looked down at her phone to remind herself of the name of the trainer. Should she know this guy, Mike? She didn't, but she'd been too long out of the game.

The three of them strolled into the barn. A girl was leaning over to the side, braiding her ponytail. She straightened up, threw the braid over her shoulder.

"Hi, I'm Daphne. Mike is on his way. I need you to sign a rider release."

Daphne looked right at Eloise. Of course, Eloise had on breeches. Daphne disappeared for a moment, then returned with a clipboard and a pen. Eloise signed away her rights.

Daphne led the group to a tall bay gelding standing in the crossties. He had a wide forehead with a bushy forelock that nearly covered his eyes and a long black bushy tail to match. His mane was braided, his legs wrapped in snow-white polo bandages, and he wore fleece topped bell boots in front. He had on a jumping saddle.

He picked up his head as the group approached, and Eloise felt her heart begin to pound. The horse looked expensive standing still. Eloise felt compelled to step toward him and examine his large expressive eyes. The two creatures exchanged earnest glances.

Eloise thought to herself, "Atlantis, be kind to me, big guy."

Daphne came out of the tack room with a bridle over her shoulder. She unclipped the crossties, took the bridle off her shoulder and tossed the reins over the neck of the horse. When she pulled the halter off Atlantis, Eloise stepped forward to take it from her.

Daphne said, "Thanks" and chatted amiably about Atlantis while she finished bridling the horse. He was easy in the stables, easy in turn-out, easy to hack out. Eloise hung the halter up on a hook on the wall.

Mike walked into the barn. He walked directly to Doc, shaking his hand first, but after Doc introduced himself and Pinky, Doc motioned to Eloise and stated with an air of importance, "Eloise Robertson." The way he said it made Eloise cringe.

"Ah, yes. Jock's daughter." Mike reached for her hand, and Eloise noted the dry and calloused palm, as well as Mike's accent which was likely British.

Mike led the horse out of the barn to an outdoor arena full of jumps. Eloise carried her boot and helmet bags. There was a tall mounting block in a corner of the arena, along with two director chairs. They watched Mike mount while he gave them a run down on the horse. Atlantis had come from Canada with Mike, had a show record through Intermediate, and was ready to go Advanced. All these words floated above Eloise as Mike then walked Atlantis around on a loose rein. Eloise set her bags down next to the mounting block. Pinky held her phone in the palm of her hand, she was asking Eloise something.

"When do I start filming? Eloise?"

"What?"

Pinky frowned, "Do I record this?"

"Oh, sorry. No. I'll let you know."

Eloise sat down in one of the chairs, Pinky sat in the other, and Doc stood behind Eloise, putting one hand on her shoulder for a split second. Eloise leaned over and unzipped her boot bag. Mike picked up the reins on Atlantis and cleared his throat, giving a quick description of his basic routine. Then he proceeded to trot the horse around the arena, making serpentine lines around the many jumps.

Eloise pulled her boots from the bag. She had polished them to a high shine. Her hands were shaking as she zipped up the first boot. Then as she pulled on the zipper on the second boot, it stuck half-way up. Mike was saying something to her as he rode past, but she didn't hear it. Instead, she felt a surge of adrenaline as she tried to unzip the boot and have another go at it. The zipper would not go down. She tugged again. It would not go up. She was stuck. Mike was working the horse and Eloise was supposed to be watching. Instead, she was absorbed with her boot.

Pinky noticed, she staged whispered, "Eloise, what's going on?"

Eloise closed her eyes for a moment as if in pain. "Wardrobe malfunction."

Eloise, partly in frustration, partly as a demonstration of her predicament, gave the tab on the zipper a good yank.

It came off in her hand. With this, Eloise groaned so loudly that Mike pulled up the horse.

"Is he not your type?"

Doc answered, "Mike, he's wonderful, it's just we seem to be having a problem here with a boot zipper."

And Pinky, who had been given strict orders not to say anything said, "Looks like we'll be needing some spray lubricant and a large paper clip."

Mike laughed. Then spoke into his wristwatch, "Daphne, can you please bring the clipper lube and a large paperclip to the arena?" And then he said again, "Yes, that's right. No, I'm not kidding."

Mike gave the horse a walk break, and Daphne came at a jog to the arena, miraculously armed with the two requested items.

Pinky thanked her while Eloise sat in the director's chair red-faced. This wasn't the impression she had hoped to make.

Pinky leaned over Eloise's booted leg, shook the spray can and said, "I could get you something to bite on, like they do in the movies."

Doc cracked up. Eloise rolled her eyes.

Pinky gave the zipper a generous spraying with clipper lube while everyone looked on. Pinky then threaded the paperclip through the hole where the pull had once been attached. She looked at Eloise and said, "This is the delicate part, courage my friend." She slipped one finger down under the head of the zipper and fished around.

"Aha!"

Eloise said, "What?"

"I found the problem. You've caught some little bit of lining or something."

Pinky wriggled her finger around while staring at the sky in deep concentration, then pulled her finger out from under the zipper, and like magic, unzipped the boot.

Doc clapped his hands, "Spectacular! Good work, Pinky."

Pinky then carefully zipped the boot up and removed the paperclip.

Eloise said, "How'd you know how to do that?"

"I used to do wardrobe for theater and modeling shows. There's never been a zipper to best me yet."

Doc laughed. "Pinky, you are a wonder."

Mike and Daphne had watched the proceedings. Daphne said to Mike, "Remember that time ..."

Mike growled, "Let's not."

Eloise put her helmet on and pulled on her gloves. At least both of those items were new and unlikely to malfunction. Her hands were no longer shaking. This riding session had been "pre-disastered." Some crazy pressure she had placed on herself had been lightened.

She asked Mike to show her the canter, a few changes, and a couple jumps.

The horse looked powerful, with a ground covering canter stride. Mike showed Eloise a flying change of lead each way, then popped over a few jumps. Then he rode over to ask if Eloise wanted to see more. Eloise shook her head. It was time to get on.

Eloise felt Doc's steadying hand again on her shoulder. This time it lingered long enough to give a squeeze.

Eloise fastened her chin strap. Mike jumped down, he tightened the girth a hole, then stepped back to hand the horse to Eloise.

Eloise used her arm to measure the stirrup leathers, from her fingertips to her armpit, and raised the stirrups. She led the big horse over to the mounting block, and Mike put a hand on the left rein while she stepped up on the block, put her left foot in the stirrup and swung her right leg over, settling softly into the tack and fishing for the right iron with her toe.

Pinky waved the camera at her and yelled, "Now?"

"Yeah, Pinky. Now."

Eloise Robertson was on a horse. The neck was long, the ears a mile away. The braids were neat and tight. Atlantis had a well sprung ribcage that met her lower leg in a snug way. Eloise glanced behind her as they walked. A wide and rather flat croup swung in rhythm, hips dropping in turn as they walked. She felt both exhilarated, and "home."

Mike walked to the middle of the arena, one hand resting on the top of a jump standard. "So, Eloise, Jock said you've been taking a break from the riding, with school and all."

"It was only then that Eloise realized Jock had likely told Mike all about her.

She said, "I hope I remember how to ride."

"Jock said he put you up in the saddle at age four. It's like riding a bike. You never lose it."

Then his tone got serious, "Shorten those reins. More forward, go on, cover ground. Test the scope. Jock's going to ask."

Mike was barking orders. Pretty soon her ponytail was bouncing on her back as she sat the trot, difficult at first, but soon she found the sweet spot in the saddle. Eloise was working to follow Mike's directions. Eloise made a transition to canter and rode a couple flying changes. But she was thinking so much about her riding, she forgot her job was to judge Atlantis.

Soon, it was time to jump. Eloise shortened the stirrups a hole. Then she got up in jumping position. She started with a low vertical to vertical with six strides between. Atlantis pointed his ears forward and took her to the jumps with eagerness, she only had to stay out of his way. Mike had her repeat the line. Eloise felt her knees and ankles complain. Mike had raised the top pole on the second jump.

Mike added a third jump to the line, an oxer. Atlantis did it with no assistance from Eloise. His ears "locked and loaded" on that top rail and he fired off the ground like a shot.

Again, said Mike, and again, and on each pass, Mike raised the height of the top pole on the oxer. Eloise grabbed mane as the jump got bigger to keep herself from falling back too soon into the saddle, her calf muscles were burning. Her body remembered but her legs grew fatigued. She had to pull up. When she did, she was floored to see the size of the jumps. They were huge.

"Wow. My legs are done. But wow."

"A horse like this brings it all back, doesn't it?"

Then he pointed to Pinky, "You got it all, right?"

"I got it, alright. Man, that was something, Eloise!"

Doc grinned at Pinky. Pinky stopped talking, as if perhaps she had said the wrong thing.

The ride home was quiet as Eloise watched the video and watched it again. She was grateful to Pinky and found herself thanking her more than once. She also was happy to have Doc there too, quietly encouraging her. She was also exhausted, her legs no longer aching, but her whole body weak with fatigue.

Mike had asked if she wanted to meet him next week for a cross-country school and gallop. Tempting. At that moment though, her legs wouldn't have held her up if she had tried to hop over a mud puddle. She knew she did not have the fitness. Still, Atlantis had jumped with eagerness and power over big jumps today. Atlantis was a great horse. Jock would love him. She had done her job as requested. She couldn't help but feel eager for Jock to see the video, to get back to her and praise her riding. And she hated herself for caring.

9

Monday May 17th, 1779

*Work goes fearsomely slow at Mr. Jefferson's Monti-
cello. I pity Mrs. Jefferson, although I expect it to be
quite grand should it ever reach completion. It shall be
grander than our house, yet I prefer ours for its spacious
and most importantly, completed rooms. Their structure is currently an unfinished box. It is a two-story
red brick house of eight rooms. Mr. Jefferson has some
odd ideas, as there will never be a central staircase. I
find our staircase to be the most graceful feature of our
home. He must have stairs, but perhaps he will winch
his guests upstairs as we do our hay to the hay mow.
Mr. Jefferson and his bride avoid such a future by re-
siding on the main level. Mr. Jefferson described for us
the planned double portico. Currently the second story
portico exists only in his imagination, and the front
portico is not yet pilastered. Planks had been laid across
the entry hall floor and gaps exist between the boards
that are large enough to be alarming. However, once
over this bridge, we passed through double doors into a*

lovely parlor. That at least was complete and featured large windows that let in generous amounts of air and light, and insects too, unfortunately. Someone needs to invent a way to gain the two without the addition of the third. Perhaps it will be Mr. Jefferson, if not Dr. Franklin.

When we arrived, Mrs. Jefferson was seated at her pianoforte, with a Hessian lady, a Baroness I am told, standing before it. We had come just in time to be treated to a performance. Father had met the Baron (who is a prisoner) and Baroness previously, but Aunt Bess and I had not. Father has spent much time among the prisoners' selling horses and made quite sure that the Baroness purchased a horse to both ride and drive. She has brought along her three little girls and drives them about for air and diversion. I find it charming that the Baroness has come to war with her husband. The Baroness it seems is a bold woman of many talents. This horse father sold her is a lady's mount, safe and not easily perturbed. But the Baroness rides him with the skill of a dragoon, in tall boots and with a leg on each side. I wonder what that would be like. Truth be told, I envy her.

We took our seats, with Mr. Jefferson rising to bow to us and the small round form of the General Baron also popping up and bowing. The Baron is of puny dimensions. His lady is far more intimidating. It was only after we had taken our seats, that I noticed, and politely acknowledged the other guest who had risen and bowed, but now sat primly with a violin and bow lightly resting across his thigh. It was the young officer Bud and I had encountered at the gravesite. He nodded and I nodded back. I admit, I felt a lift of my spirits on spying him there. His addition to the party added interest.

The Baroness and Mrs. Jefferson began their performance, and all eyes were upon the Baroness as she stood before the pianoforte.

The Baroness was wearing blue watered silk with a stomacher embroidered with flowers and vines and the sheerest lace at her elbows. A large pearl drew the eye to her ample bosom where it dangled from a slender velvet ribbon around her neck. The critical effect, however, was not dependent on fashion, and I thought it was such as no gown could ever bestow upon my person.

That pearl rose and fell as she inflated and expelled air from her lungs. Yes, her tone was sweet and clear, yet it was her bosom that held great powers over the gentlemen present. I found myself amused. A sideways glance at Aunt Bess and I was soon corrected by her dainty foot pressing firmly down upon mine. This did have a steadying influence. Oh, Aunt Bess! She not only knows my thoughts, but she is sympathetic.

After the aria was completed, the Baroness received applause and curtsied. Mrs. Jefferson nodded acknowledgment. Next, Mr. and Mrs. Jefferson and the Major played together.

I did enjoy the duet of violins played by Major Schmidt and our Mr. Jefferson. Clearly Mr. Jefferson held no personal animus toward these men. I cannot but wonder how these Hessians can take to the field to do their bloody work, while having no real stake in the outcome. Certainly, they were now enjoying Mr. Jefferson's hospitality and his table without a trace of guilt.

At dinner I no longer had my good Aunt Bess to press her toes into mine to rein in my emotions. I was quite on my own. Major Schmidt had been placed directly across the table. He immediately engaged me in discussion of horses. This was deadly to my feminine decorum. There is no topic of which I am more fluent. To my shame, I flooded him with information and opinion. If Aunt Bess had been closer, my toes would surely have been bruised because once the floodgates opened, it was impossible to stem the flow. We spoke of bloodlines and handling and early training. I did brag on father who is a master of riding and driving. Perhaps I may have excited interest in more sales for father. I can only pray so.

Major Schmidt has many opinions regarding these topics and is proud of what he has achieved with the gelding we sold him. He has named him Rudy. We Roberts are invited to come watch him ride. The Baroness asked to be included as did Mr. Jefferson, so it will be a gathering.

I had to feign interest in the conversation once it turned to discussions of philosophical writings. It did give me opportunity to study the face of Major Schmidt. I believe all women are skilled at feigning interest in whatever men want to drone on about. I think I am not unlike others of my sex in this skill.

I did note that Major Schmidt has eyes and lashes quite wasted on a man. They would make his face too womanly if it were not for his strong chin, oh and his ridiculous mustache. I wondered if that wooly caterpillar was grown to add manliness to those eyes. I tried to imagine him without it. I think it would likely make an improvement.

We women soon left the table, the cloth was cleared, while the gentlemen remained for wine and nuts and further philosophical discourse.

A servant brought in the children to kiss their mothers' good night; the Baroness' "little ladies" included. I was sure to cluck and praise the little darlings. But I kept one ear tuned to the buzz from the next room, which had gained animation. More than that I could not discern.

Soon it was time for our long trek home down the steep path from Monticello to our flatter and greener fields. The days were long enough that we had still much light, and we placed our trust in our horse and servant Isaac to bring us safely home. All in our party were drowsy, despite it being obvious Mr. Jefferson watered down his wine. I knew father, once he was well ensconced in his chair in the parlor, would pour himself a cordial before bed, and that his sister would join him. Beast would greet me as if I had been gone a year, and once settled, I would pull out quill and ink. I wrote this entry by candlelight without delay as to remember the details. And now I say my prayers and keep appointment with my dreams.

* * *

Eloise read the journal entry, and paused over the description of Major Schmidt, smiling over Louisa's disdain for facial hair. It made Eloise consider that Jefferson was clean shaven. Then again, so was Washington, and Adams, and Madison, Hamilton, and Franklin. Did any of the founders sport a mustache or beard? She couldn't think of a single example. George Washington with a mustache? Unthinkable.

She loved the description of the Major's eyes. He sounded handsome. Well, Louisa had said as much earlier. But the eyes. Eloise suddenly realized where she had seen those eyes. She dug out the flier, hidden away in her zippered pocket in her backpack.

Eloise luxuriated in a long look. Oh yes. Those eyes made her stomach do a flip-flop. Joe's soulful, large, dark, and heavily lashed eyes certainly made her think of Louisa's Major Schmidt, or at least Major Schmidt sans mustache.

It was then that "Joe" of the lost and missing dog was "cast" by Eloise for the role of Major Schmidt. Once that decision was made, the "Major" went back into his zippered compartment. But his image did not. It stayed clear in her mind.

* * *

Dabs texted, "Thanks for the video clip. No one would ever know you hadn't been riding every day. And that horse! What dreams are made of."

"I was nervous. But it was all there, as if I hadn't stopped."

"Those jumps were huge."

"It took four Ibuprofen and half the day to stop gimping around the clinic Monday."

"It was worth it though. Be honest."

"Yes! Thank God my muscles remembered what to do. I'm not upset that they gave me hell for not giving them a little more preparation."

"Okay, that's funny. What did Jock say about the horse?"

"He said he could buy the two others for the price of that one. He wants me to go try the other two."

Dabs wrote, "Better keep taking the ibuprofen then. When do you try those?"

"Next weekend. They are close enough to us that we can see both in one day.

"I wish I could come."

"Makes you want to go buy a horse, right?"

"Be wasted on me. And my old guy still counts on me to take him for a spin. If I bought another horse it would feel like a betrayal."

"You're worried about cheating on your horse? That's kind of sweet. On a different topic, I was just wondering if you are correcting the spelling on Louisa's journals?"

"I take out the random capitalizations and doubling of letters. But that's about it, other than an occasional abysmal spelling. But to be fair, spelling wasn't yet standardized. Hey, doesn't she have a great sense of humor?"

"She does. Her sense of humor can be cutting, though.

She's smart as a whip, that comes shining through. And she is educated."

"She is. Since you're interested, I'll send you an uncorrected entry, double letters, weird spellings, etc."

Eloise soon received this via email.

Wednesday May 19th, 1779

Mr. Jefferson has been made Governorr and will be leaving us the First of June for Williams Burgh. Father has takin this news as urgency to sell Mr. Jefferson our Sateen and Silk. I accept credit for this suggestion. He and Isaac will deliver the team once Jefferson is settled as they are not quite ready, but Handsome and nearly perfect matched. This election of Jefferson's is received most greiviously sadd for me as I was sincerely hoping to meet again the Doe-iyed Major Schmidt at another Jefferson swarrey. But perchance If I Now see the Young Officer about the neighborhood, we have at least Made acquanitency and I Should be Able to greet him without Accusation of Wantoness (at least by Aunt Bess!)

* * *

Eloise sent Dabs a note telling him to please continue making corrections to the text.

Eloise had another message from the bank. It was Mr. Jameson's receptionist. This time she used Eloise's first name.

"Hello, Eloise. Mr. Jameson would like to speak with you at your earliest convenience. Please give him a call."

Eloise was mildly annoyed. The guy at the bank felt the need to play career counselor. Why couldn't things just stay the same? Eloise saw no reason to make any changes. Not now. Maybe not ever.

Still, here she was re-engaged with Jock and feeling vulnerable. Stupid. She had a place to call her own, a job, and evidently, assets. Grow up, suck it up, and call Jellybean Ralph.

* * *

Pinky was putting the finishing touches on a Westie with fine scissor-work on its muzzle when she spotted Eloise.

"Did you get your boot repaired?"

"Nope. I've packed clipper oil and a box of extra-large paperclips in the boot bag. You were a genius. I'm going to remember that little trick forever."

Pinky spoke without taking her eyes off the dog on her table. "Why not spring for some new boots? You could get some like those cool colored ones at the event."

"New boots cut the back of your knee and rub your ankles bloody."

Pinky turned to glance at Eloise shaking her head.

Eloise shrugged, "If they don't, they won't be tall enough after the folds around your ankles form. The boots drop. Until you get those ankle folds just right, it sucks."

"So, you break them in before you ride in them. I get it."

"My current boots feel great and only need to hang

tough for another day of riding. If I take them to the shoe-man, he wouldn't have them back in time, that or he'd tell me they were a total."

Pinky said, "The oil and paperclip trick is a temporary fix. You take them to the shoe man after this trip."

"Why does it matter?"

Pinky examined the head of the dog on the bench. Then she snipped at some invisible hair, gave the Westie a "high-five" and it picked up a paw and touched Pinky's hand.

She took it off the table and placed it in a cage, turning to Eloise.

"I don't know a thing about horses or riding. Doc does though. And he told me you were really, like really, talent-ed. What's the deal?"

"The deal? It's dogs and cats for me and for you. That's our reality."

"Reality? That horse looked real as real can be to me."

Pinky changed the subject and looked down at Prince on his dog bed on the floor. He had been quietly watching Pinky work. Pinky had been bringing him to the clinic, leaving the puffballs at home. Doc didn't mind. Pinky had started giving him extra basement privileges, like staying on the dog bed.

Pinky said, "Doc still hasn't found that chip on any reg-istry. Sad because someone invested a lot in his training. If Doc's schedule is light this week, I think he is going to do the big snip-snip. Has to happen before he can be adopted."

Eloise said, "That's big."

"That dog's been tutored, and now he's going to be neu-tered."

Then Pinky grimaced, "Did you see who my last customer is today?"

"Yeah. Turbo. I'll get him.

"I could use the back-up."

Eloise went to the small cages. The card on the front said in bold red, "Turbo - Bites."

Eloise did her high-pitched voice, shrinking and lassoing routine, and pulled the tiny Maltese out of the cage and into her arms, where he nearly clawed his way over her shoulder before Eloise delivered him to Pinky.

Pinky put Turbo in the tub. "Turbo" was a tiny thing with his engine on high rev, his nerves perpetually "shot," but more problematic was that he was sly. He had been fired by his previous boarding and grooming facility because he scrambled in the tub like a freaked-out cat, clawing at every surface the moment the water touched his back. He would climb up your arms and chest and neck, and face, scratching all the way. He also had to wear a muzzle because he was quick to swivel his neck and latch on to a finger.

Pinky practiced the patience of a Buddhist Monk. But it wasn't just surviving the bathing or brushing, or the nail trim that made the dog difficult; Turbo held a grudge.

He had a special trick of squirting urine at you through the bars of the cage door. He seemed to plan for it, pressed up against the cage front, waiting. Eloise and Pinky agreed it was retaliation. When it was time to get him out of his cage to go home, he always tried to nip. But, once he was on his trip up the stairs to freedom, he pranced happily on his leash, a soft and pretty white bundle of energy that once upstairs was willing to play with a toy or cuddle in your lap with the smallest bit of encouragement, a love bug.

Turbo was a complicated character.

Pinky put on his muzzle then turned the water on low and began by spraying away from Turbo, but he commenced scrambling and lunging. Prince, who always was good about staying in his "place," was concerned about the ruckus. He began to softly whine, as he looked at Eloise and then back at Pinky. He seemed to be asking, "Can I help?" Eloise had an idea that maybe he could.

"Prince, come over here and see if you can slip Turbo a Prozac."

Prince approached with caution then poked his hairy nose over the edge of the tub. Straining against the lead, Turbo began to wheeze loudly, but he had stopped scrambling. Pinky gave his chest a gentle push to release the tension. Turbo and Prince were busily breathing in each other's scents.

Pinky winked at Eloise. "Good boy. Keep the little bugger distracted."

Prince evidently liked the little "bugger," as his long feathery tail began a slow wag.

Eloise laughed, "Oh my God, Prince is a canine shrink."

Pinky did her job fast. She lifted Turbo out of the tub and set him on the grooming table. Turbo flailed his tail about, still leaning into his leash, releasing the tension for short moments to spit up saliva. Prince thought this was funny and barked. Pinky gave Turbo a toweling off, slipped off the muzzle, put him in a cage, and turned on the blower.

Turbo was now free to bark back at Prince and the

basement got loud as the other dogs in the kennel joined in until it was unbearable. But Turbo forgot to shoot his pee at anyone.

Eloise yelled, "Coffee break!"

Pinky put Prince in a run, and they climbed the stairs and firmly closed the door behind them.

Later that afternoon, Eloise brought a brushed-out and fluffy-white Turbo up the stairs to give to his owner. Turbo was overjoyed, doing his best impression of a jumping bean. After handing the dog over, Eloise went back to the basement and was chatting with Pinky when the intercom blared.

It was Janet yelling. "All hands-on deck y'all. We've got a bolter!"

Pinky and Eloise looked at each other and spoke simultaneously, "Turbo!"

Eloise said, "Let's get Prince. Maybe Turbo will come to him."

Pinky nodded.

Eloise grabbed Prince's leash and snapped it on. "C'mon, Prince. Let's see how well you work as a lure."

Doc was in the parking lot with the distressed owner. He nodded in approval at the sight of Prince. The owner was a heavy-set woman who was hyperventilating and pointing in the direction that Turbo had bolted.

Eloise heard Doc say, "You're in good hands, we've got a working dog here, and these women know how to handle dogs. Pinky, Eloise, Prince, ready for search and rescue?"

Doc could not be serious. But Pinky and Eloise exchanged a glance that said, "Roll with it."

The woman pointed again toward the back lane where trash cans stood in a row. "I don't know why I dropped the leash, but as soon as it left my hands, he took off that way. I've been calling his name, but he won't come, and I have a bad knee, or I'd have run right after him."

Pinky said with bravado, "Prince will find him, won't you, boy?"

Eloise played along, and commanded Prince to, "Find Turbo! Find Turbo!"

Prince played his part, nearly jerking Eloise off her feet. They were off. Eloise was jogging to keep up, Pinky right behind them saying "Find Turbo!"

Eloise heard the woman exclaim, "Wow!"

Eloise thought of Doc having to work to maintain his serious expression.

Pinky and Eloise followed Prince down the lane behind shops and restaurants and past overflowing trash cans.

Prince stopped. He ran in circles deeply inhaling, then stopped again, nose down in some nasty goop he began to lick.

Eloise said, "Ewwww, stop that. You're supposed to be looking for Turbo."

Eloise and Pinky stood slightly bent over and catching their breaths while Prince licked and snorted. Eloise weakly pulled at the leash.

Pinky began to giggle. Eloise joined in.

Pinky put her hand on Eloise's shoulder for support, "I can't believe you said, Find Turbo!"

Eloise dropped her mouth open wide, "Me? You said it too!"

Pinky added, "God that was fun!"

Pinky got a grip on herself, "You know that little rat is back here somewhere."

Eloise giggled, "And you know he's not going to let us catch him until he's ready."

Eloise pulled harder on Prince's leash, dragging him away from the goop, his nails scratching against the black top. "C'mon, Prince. We promised to find Turd-o."

Eloise tried to get Prince back on the trail, but he refused to budge. Instead, he sat down and stared up at Eloise.

Pinky said in an exasperated tone, "What?"

"Woof."

Eloise said, "No. I'm *not* going to let you lick up more of that gross stuff."

Pinky said, "What do you think he's trying to tell us?"

Behind them came the high-pitched answer. "Yip!"

Turbo, with a muzzle gummy from licking the same goop that had enamored Prince, stood behind them.

To nab him, Eloise only had to step on the end of the trailing leash.

Eloise and Pinky and Prince were the heroes of the day. They laughed themselves silly in the break room describing the scene to Doc and Janet and Suzie.

Eloise used to laugh a lot but hadn't for a long time. Until recently. It was like she had rediscovered a muscle long neglected. Like her riding muscles. It felt good.

10

Thursday May 20th, 1779

*We have no likeness of mother. I thought to make a
sketch and present it as a gift to father. But her features
are no longer clear in my mind. How can this be? I had
passed fourteen years when she departed this world. The
odd thing is that I remember more clearly her dog. He
did outlive her by several years. I will never forget the
sight of dear father graveside, her Ranger by his side.
This image I could perhaps capture in pencil. But my
beloved mother, I cannot. I do recall the shape of her
hands and feet. But her face eludes me. I tearfully con-
fessed this to father. He told me to simply stand before
the looking glass. There she be.*

* * *

Friday May 21st, 1779

*Wandering brother Buck has returned. Not to stay,
much to the disappointment of Aunt Bess. She rose*

with the sun to present him both an apple and a cherry pie for his breakfast. He has grown lean, and his skin takes on the look of leather. The pies bring both Aunty and Buck great satisfaction.

He is proud of capturing his Sammie and two other escaped men who he returns tomorrow for bounties. Sammie, I have not seen, but the two horses Buck returned to us are wasted, foot-sore, and saddle sore. He takes two of our horses and leaves his wretches. It will take six months of care to return them to health.

Buck is cool to me, which I bring upon myself by shaming him over his horses. We had hardly spent a night and a day under father's roof before we found ourselves at odds. He reminds me of my duty to wed. I reminded him that all the men are off roaming the woods looking for a fight. Perhaps I should wait and see who comes back? This did cause him to laugh, but it was false mirth.

He is much aware that our home, all of it, will in time, go to him. I shudder to think that the care he takes, which is little, should one day be applied to all at Ivy Creek.

Aunt Bess has life-estate of High Meadows, but no plan to return. If she did, she claims Carter next-of-kin, who descended upon that estate after the death of her husband, Chase Carter, would spoon poison into her morning tea. She says this only in half jest. Still, she draws her dower portion of income, knowing full well she is cheated. She has her maid, Priscilla, who she owns outright. She has been here with father, her brother, seven years; it seems all my life. We women are legally under coverture of men, with no likelihood to own anything, not even our own persons. What we do receive must come from the generosity of men, often a gift. Perhaps a servant or a silver teapot.

* * *

Tuesday May 25th, 1779

Father, Bud, and I rode out to the Barracks to watch Major Schmidt ride. The Baroness did come, an exotic creature in her split-skirt and tall boots. I admit envy. Jefferson scattered our gathering by jumping out of the woods into the open field to join the party, frightening our horses. Little Bud was mounted on Fellow, and nearly came a-cropper, but our gathering soon settled. The horse we sold Major Schmidt, Rudy, was fine of flesh and his handsome master sat proudly. It was a feast for my eyes. Such a sight contrasted painfully with the distressed appearance of Buck's mounts. I sometime think horses too generous. Buck deserved to be unseated by his mounts and left in the dirt to walk home. But then what did Sammie gain by his rebellion?

Jefferson departs to take his seat as Governor, and we shall have no more social engagements. I pray that dear father will live forever because it will not be only horses that suffer by Buck's management. But I look about me and see very few old men.

I expect I will be foisted upon some Albemarle gent.

Aunt Bess will have life retainer at Ivy Creek by her nephew to bake pies. Perhaps my consolation, when I am cast off, will be to take my dog and horse. And yes, the silver tea service.

* * *

Dabs sent a text. He said, "Louisa's humor has turned dark. And you and I know that the war has yet to reach Virginia."

"We know, roughly speaking, how the war turns out, but we don't know what happened to these people. Do we?"

"No. I have never heard of Louisa Roberts. The Carters, though, were prodigious breeders. Famously King Carter had nineteen children. I'm sure I'm related to one of them."

Eloise wrote, "'That would be the same family as the 'The spoonful of poison in the tea', Carters?"

"I expect so."

Eloise typed, "No drama quite like family drama. Don't you feel sorry for Louisa, having lost her mother so young."

"The same age Thomas Jefferson lost his father."

"So young. And Aunt Bess has lost her husband, and Mr. Roberts his wife."

Dabs wrote, "And where is 'little Bud's' mother?"

"No mention of a mother for Bud. Sad."

Dabs wrote, "What is going to happen has already happened. And yet I find myself caring about them. Very much in fact."

"Your parents?"

"Dad died years ago, Mom three years ago. She is the

143

reason the house is in bad shape. She was a hoarder. She stopped doing maintenance and repairs. The place was slowly being reclaimed by nature, rotting so to speak. I had to jack the foundation, re-level floors, do mold abatement, new wiring. The chimneys are unusable. Mom just wanted to be left in peace with her dogs and horses. After her death, I was left with one dog and the three old horses. The dog died in his sleep."

"That had to be hard."

"Sometimes I feel like she is right around the corner in her favorite chair, reading. My mother and I shared a love of reading. I was lucky to have had my mother for a lot longer than Louisa. But at least Louisa has her father. Losing a parent at so young an age, well, it must have profound effects on a person. At fourteen, you are no adult. Louisa Roberts as much as Thomas Jefferson."

Dabs continued, "What bothers me is that historians have assumed Jefferson had a troubled relationship with his mother. But Jefferson guarded his intimate relationships. The man who invented a copying machine to copy his letters for posterity, left no trace of letters to or from his mother or his wife. If there were tender or heated words on paper, he made sure no one would ever read them."

Eloise wrote, "But we do have Louisa Roberts. So much has changed since her time. But experiencing loss of a parent, I'm not sure that changes. You could be walking where she walked. Looking at views she would recognize. How does that feel?"

"It's my childhood home, and it is my home now. I have

wireless internet, central heat and air, and modern lighting."

"I should hope so."

"Flush toilets too."

"Louisa would be amazed. So, did you live somewhere else?"

"Yes. DC. I came home when Mom became ill. I thought it was temporary. But I'm still here. My divorce settled matters."

Eloise paused. Dabs was divorced. She was unsure how to respond.

"I'm sorry."

"It's okay. I am enjoying being a country squire and tending to the place and my animals. I'm fascinated by the history here, both Jefferson and the family that possibly tread these old floorboards."

Eloise almost asked Dabs how old he was. But then scolded herself, "Do not give him the wrong signal." So, he was a divorced guy, living someplace interesting, with an alluring historical journal. The allure was the history, not the lonely old guy.

She tried to wrap things up, typing, "Keep transcribing and keep reading. I am absorbed in the new reading assignment from Betsy on the Hemings family. Aren't you?"

"I'm interested in everyone's story. Everyone."

Eloise thought to herself, "Ick. For God's sakes!" But she didn't write anything in response. Eloise turned off her computer without a farewell. She went back to her book, reading over again a paragraph that kept eluding her. She acknowledged to herself that she cared about Louisa Roberts, whoever she was. If Dabs was part of the package right now, she could deal with that. But it was Louisa's story that had captured her interest. Not Dabs.

Eloise had added a basic timeline of the American revolution to her reading list, so she knew what was coming for Louisa. If this were a novel, she could skim or skip ahead. But who was she kidding? Eloise never skipped ahead when she read. Reading about hard things was a lot easier than living through them.

Whatever hardships and heartbreaks lay ahead, no one could prevent them, they must be endured. Or not. Such was the flow of life. Hard, cruel, with no promise of more than happy moments, mostly blindly under-valued at the time they were experienced.

Eloise put down her e-reader and started her shower. She went into the closet, sitting down on the upholstered bench. She took off her shoes and socks, then stood to finish the job of undressing. By this time, the shower had steamed up the mirrors in the bathroom.

Eloise had her shower and stepped out of the shower to a fog that seemed a gentle embrace. She missed her mother. Louisa too had no mother. By the time she had dried off, the mirrors had cleared. It was with some surprise she heard the words, "there she be" come back to her from Louisa's journal. Her eyes felt hot, but dry.

She was not Louisa Roberts. She was not her mother. Her mother had been much fairer than Eloise. But Eloise could still recognize traces of her mother in herself. She should count herself lucky to have had her mother for as long as she had. But she did not feel lucky. Maybe it did not matter how long you had your mother, if your mother was a good and loving person, her death would always feel too soon.

Dabs had lost his mother three years ago. Eloise had lost her own mother right about the same time. Dabs had revealed a bit about himself, hadn't he? And she had, in a way, left the room. Dabs evidently was close to his mother. He credited her with his love of reading. Dabs did mention he was divorced. Divorce. What an ugly thing that was. Eloise felt a pang of compassion for Dabs.

Eloise went to the long cabinet in the bathroom to look through the multiple jars of her mom's "lotions and potions." Eloise still hadn't used them all up. The body lotion was the same scent as her mom's cologne. It smelled of spices and she realized it had a faint scent of cinnamon.

She decided to use it. She rubbed it in well, then instead of reaching for her own hairbrush, she picked up her mother's.

She did not brush her tangled mop of damp brown hair. Instead, she turned the brush over and looked at the hair tangled around the bristles. Eloise pulled one single hair from the brush and wound it around her pinky finger. It was blonde, likely not her mother's natural shade. It had once been part of her though. Eloise put the brush up to her nose. The shock of recognition flooded her entire body. A vivid memory. Her mother and she were lying side-by-side, heads upon the same pillow. Eloise sat down on the floor of her bathroom. She found herself leaning over the bristles of her mother's hairbrush, the presence of her mother summoned like a spirit. A hair of her head, the scent of her scalp had summoned her like a magic incantation. But that scalp and all the rest of her mother's body resided inside of a satin lined, highly polished wood and brass box. Eloise had seen her there, had placed her handful of "dust" in the grave along with the other mourners. But that was not her mother, that was the empty shell. Her mother was here. She felt her here. Just as Dab's felt his mother was in the other room, reading a book.

Eloise left the strand of hair around her pinky finger. People tied a string on their fingers to remember. She would never forget.

* * *

Pinky, Doc, and Eloise sat in the corner of another arena. She wasn't sure why they agreed to take another precious day off to be her security blanket. She was glad they had. Although she was less anxious this week, she wasn't ready to fly solo. Not yet.

When Eloise pulled her boots from the bag, Pinky stepped forward like her show groom.

"Eloise, don't you dare yank on that zipper. I'll zip up your boots."

"Why do I feel like I have a Ladies Maid?"

Pinky lifted an eyebrow, mumbled something about watching too much "Masterpiece Theater" but then she squatted down and ever so gently with the large paperclip, zipped up the damaged boot, and then gently zipped up the other boot.

148

"All good."

"Thanks Pinky."

Doc was standing outside the arena, and said, "Beautiful mover. Holsteiner, I think he said?"

Pinky frowned, "Aren't those cows?"

Eloise chuckled, "Holstein cows, Holsteiner horses. It is a Holsteiner, Those gaits could clean up in dressage."

Pinky said, "Whatever it is I love the color. And that tail!"

Eloise nodded in agreement. "Sadly, grey horses don't stay that color. They get whiter as they age. But he'll keep that gorgeous tail."

Eloise watched the horse and admired it too. But once she got on, she knew this wasn't Jock's ride. It was not a horse that offered a gallop, it was a horse you had to make gallop. The trot stride that looked so powerful from the ground, felt like it spent too much time hovering in the air.

She pulled up before jumping, even while the trainer was setting rails. Eloise wondered how her mother would have phrased this.

"He's just lovely. Beautiful mover and all..."

The trainer could have played poker.

Eloise continued, "I know Jock's type though, and he's the one it has to suit, not me."

The trainer looked resigned. "Why don't you consider him for yourself then?"

"I wish," she grinned. "He'll get snapped up quick. He is a beauty."

And not terribly graciously the trainer called for a groom to come fetch the horse, and Eloise and her "team" were soon shaking hands and making their way to the parking lot.

It seemed a long ride to see the final horse. Doc and Pinky had questions regarding the fancy moving Holsteiner, dappled and full of tail, that Eloise had rejected. Doc "got it" but Pinky took a bit of convincing.

Doc pulled up to a gate quite different from the previous two. There was no code and no electric opener. There was a rock on the ground for propping it open. Eloise got out and opened it and then closed it after Doc pulled through.

The facilities were large but mostly empty. The three of them walked into a barn that was old, but with a high ceiling and wide aisle. They walked past empty stall after empty stall. The floor was packed dirt but swept clean. The air was humming with large industrial style fans. At least the few horses there were, were nibbling at full hay nets, looking content and in good flesh. The horsewoman who greeted them was old and had clearly been overexposed to the elements for years.

Her first words as she stuck out her bony hand to Eloise were, "Jock's girl?"

Before Eloise could finish introductions, her attention was drawn to the loud rhythmic clanging of a pawing horse.

The woman, whose name was Bev, growled, "Quit, mare!"

Eloise softly laughed, "That the one?"

"Yup, 'Red-Devil'."

The mare was leaning into the cross-ties, front feet in the barn-aisle instead of in the concrete bay of the wash stall. Her ears were alert as she studied the party before her.

She was new-copper-penny chestnut, with a wide blaze and two little white socks in front. She was slight of build but a good height. Of course, she would bulk up with age, being only five years old, she had lots of maturing left to do.

Bev had not braided "Red-Devil." The mare wore old neoprene boots that had once been white but were now Georgia-clay-red. They were scuffed on the strike pads. The knee rolls on the jump saddle had cracks in the leather. And there wasn't a groom anywhere to be seen.

Eloise asked, "You do all the riding?"

"I got a girl; she rides real early. Red here went once this morning on the longe, just so's you know. They go out all night if the weather don't kick up, that keeps 'em settled too."

Bev pushed the mare back into the wash stall, scolding her, "Red, get back in there. These folks are going to think you're a pushy thing." Then Bev winked and stage whispered, "She IS a pushy thing."

As Bev slipped on the bridle, old as the rest of the equipment, she made eye contact with Eloise. She said, "Jock tell you 'bout this one?"

"Just that it was a young prospect."

"Top quality mare. Top. But not for everyone. Wouldn't be fair though to hold back on you."

Doc asked, "She's not dangerous, is she?"

"Depends who's riding, I guess."

Now Pinky chimed in, "I don't like the sound of that."

"Jock swore you were up to it. She's fast as greased lightening, and 'bout the scopiest jumper I ever saw."

Eloise tipped her head. "So, what is it then?"

151

"She's hot as a two-dollar pistol. That, and she can spin. Always going to be to the left, but she'll have you sitting in the dirt quick as you can say, 'Jack-Rabbit.' So, don't go to sleep on this one."

Bev snapped a longe line on the left ring of the snaffle. Eloise grabbed her boot bag and the three of them followed her out to a large sand arena full of jumps. Bev untied the reins and tied one to each side on the girth. Then she sent the mare out to the end of the line with a few clucks of her tongue.

Eloise leaned over and asked Doc, "You ever see anyone tie their reins to the girth instead of using proper side-reins?"

"My Dad."

"Oh," Doc's comment reminded her that he, like her, had been raised by a horseman. Eloise felt lucky to have Doc ringside. He was looking after her.

The mare did not put one foot wrong. In fact, she longed beautifully and obediently, following Bev's simple voice commands instantly.

Doc leaned over and spoke quietly, "When a five-year-old horse longes that well, it means they've spent a lot of time on the longe line."

"But that's good, right? Too many people don't spend enough time on groundwork. It'll serve the horse well all her life."

"True. But sometimes it means that no one wants to actually sit on the horse."

Even Pinky understood that line. "Maybe you shouldn't want to sit on this one either."

Bev longed the mare both ways and then untied the reins, tightened the girth, and nodded at Eloise.

Eloise said, "You're not riding her first?"

"Would have been my cup of tea, back in the day. I'd never let her go if I wasn't old and my bones gone brittle. Climb on up, Lulu. Just don't take it personal if you get your britches dirty."

Eloise's inner voice said, "Run, run away now!"

But this horse was for Jock. He liked them hot with drive and speed and scope. It was her job today to evaluate the prospect. She couldn't put her tail between her legs and run away now.

Eloise stepped forward and measured the stirrups against her forearm. She thought to herself that the key to following a quick reactive horse, was to stay centered. Sit deep, heels down, shoulders over hips, hips over heels, and your spine over the spine of the horse.

The other key was emotional stability. Calm and confident and in control. Eloise knew on that score she was likely not up to the task. She needed to channel Jock. Jock never showed any negative emotion, or any insecurity. Never. At least never in front of Eloise.

The mare stood like a rock while Eloise mounted. As she gathered the reins, she realized Bev had never asked her to sign a rider release. At least she had health insurance through the vet clinic.

Eloise put her focus into the ride. The mare swished her tail noisily when Eloise put her leg on. "Red" was a touch-me-not. Well, that would have to change because those types needed to learn to take confidence from a touch instead of over-reacting. Eloise got a feeling of Red in all three gaits. Bev directed Eloise over a few small jumps. The mare felt eager, her ears alert and searching for the next jump. Once, Red threw in one small buck on landing, but it was rideable.

When Eloise walked, Bev nodded. Then pointed toward the gate to a large pasture, "I got a track around that pasture. Start in trot, and when you make that turn up the grade, you let her out. She'll come back at the top of the rise. Push your pedals up one notch first."

It seemed not an offer, but a command. Eloise obediently shortened her stirrups. Doc, Pinky, and Bev stood by the gate while Eloise left them.

Eloise felt shaky. She just wanted to survive this. She bridged her reins, leaning down on her hands, pushed down her heels and stood up in her stirrups in anticipation of being run off with. Instead, the "Red-devil" found a steady trot. Eloise tried to relax into it. But she couldn't. Her heart was beating too fast, and she was, as usual, light-headed. On the one-hand she was scared, but on the other-hand she was about to take a thrill-ride, and in no way wanted off. She felt the mare's anticipation build as they skimmed the bottom edge of the field and followed the fence line as it made the turn up the hill. Her knees went weak, and she internally scolded her muscles to fire up, God-damn-it, and do their job.

The mare leaned into the reins. Eloise didn't ask the mare to canter, but she allowed it to happen. And it happened in a way that felt like a jolt. Eloise didn't fight it. She bent forward and stayed centered, just as she had planned, leaning harder on her bridged reins in front of the mare's withers. She felt Red's hind legs punch the earth. This mare felt incredibly sure-footed. This was her hill, she knew it, and she ate it up with the feeling of an athlete that knows the job-at-hand and finds it easy. And it was easy. Eloise was not being "run off with." She realized she wasn't in danger. Instead, a thrill washed over her and made her face burn and tingle as tears were blown from her cheeks. It was a feeling she thought dead to her forever. She was Lulu. This was her ride. Her only thought as she sat down at the top of the hill and let the mare jog down into a walk, was "Damn you, Jock."

11

Dabs asked, "So, what was dangerous about the mare?"

"Not sure. Never put a foot wrong."

"What did Doc think?"

"He was crazy about the horse, and so am I."

"Jock?"

"Vetting both the mare and the advanced gelding."

"Without sitting on either one himself?"

"It's not his money, so why not?"

"Wow, so you got to be the one to test for him whether the horse was really dangerous. You did a lot for him, you know. When does he come teach his clinic?"

"Two more weeks. I'm kind of dreading it."

"Sorry to hear that."

"Did I mention I'm thinking of getting a dog?"

"No."

"He's a stray that showed up at the clinic. He's big and hairy, solid black, high drive and full of mischief. He's off-the-charts smart and trained, too. Pinky has been fostering him for the rescue organization where she and Doc volunteer. Dog's not up for adoption yet. Has to be neutered first."

"Sounds like a lot of dog. I get the impression that you like your animals with a lot of…"

"What?"

"Not sure how to tactfully frame this."

"What?"

"Issues."

"Oh please! That is such a squishy word. I hate that word. I think you of all people can do better."

"I don't know whether to be flattered or insulted. I agree that using the word "issues" is a dodge. I *can* do better. You didn't like the fancy moving horse because it wasn't "high drive." You instead have fallen for the horse that was referred to as dangerous."

Eloise stared at the screen a moment, typed something too defensive, then deleted it. Finally, she replied with, "But it wasn't, was it?"

"Clearly you rode her well. Some horses and dogs require a higher degree of skill. There it is. Be flattered. You have the skill. That mare needs you or someone like you. Probably same goes for the dog. I'm thinking you should get both."

"Well, the horse is for Jock, and as far as the dog, well, I haven't made a final decision yet."

"Don't you think you have? You would not have mentioned it otherwise."

Eloise had grown uncomfortable, "Maybe. Maybe not. But, on another topic, why haven't you sent me another journal entry?"

"Why don't you say, 'Please' first?"

* * *

July 2, 1779

Mr. Jefferson has now left the neighborhood to take up his new post, and Mrs. Jefferson has gone to her sister. The Baron and Baroness have gone to Berkeley Springs to take the waters. It is wartime and no one comes to visit. We are an island, and a dull one.

Buck has not yet returned, and Sammie has taken a turn for the worse. He may have brought him home only to die. There I say it. Aunt Bess has expertise and confirms my fear. If he is to suffer with outcome certain, I wish the end would come fast rather than slow. Is that wrong to wish?

This suffering harkens back to Maisie's slow and painful death. Little Bud was placed in my arms while all dissolved around me in grief. No one came to take the child from my care. And he is still more than servant to me though he goes to the quarter at night. If nothing else, I will make him a horseman like his brother Sammie and his brother Isaac. Skills mastered early are retained for life. Sammie was lost to us once before. We likely must mourn a final time.

* * *

Dabs sent the entry without comment. Though it was short, it revealed much. It was an entry heavy with tragedy that explained much to Louisa's readers, so distant from her time. Bud was a slave child. Sammie and Isaac and Bud were brothers and slaves. The children of a slave by the name of Maisie, who had tragically died, leaving Bud motherless. Sammie had been lost to them once, a runaway, and now was likely dying. Eloise understood why Dabs did not comment. She wasn't ready to comment on it herself. In fact, she felt a need to take a break. She was going to get one too. Eloise and Betsy were joining Pinky and Buzz, (and dogs) for a concert in the park.

* * *

There were times when Eloise envied Pinky. This was one of those times. Pinky was looking spectacular, with pale blue feathers braided into her hair and a multicolored dress, belted at the waist with a swirling skirt. She had beaded pale blue moccasins on her feet that had tiny little bells that jingled as she walked. Pinky looked loose jointed, and light footed, as if she could at any moment begin to dance.

Buzz, Pinky, Eloise, and Betsy had carried coolers and baskets, blankets, and candles, and brought all three dogs to the free concert in the park

She felt like a plain brown sparrow next to a peacock. Eloise could never pull off "peacock" without feeling absurd. Eloise had worn jeans and a button-down blouse and brought along a black cotton sweater just in case. At least Eloise had Betsy along, who also was dressed conservatively.

Pinky had even adorned the dogs. While Ying and Yang sported blue feathers in their top knots with aplomb,

159

Prince, like Eloise, could not pull off "peacock." He greet-ed Eloise with lowered head, dreadlocks, and blue feathers drooping behind his left ear.

Eloise said, "Prince, I love you, but that is NOT your look."

Pinky chided Eloise. "Give the guy a break. He was beg-ging for attention when the puffballs were getting decked out, so I obliged." Then she lowered her voice, "Buzz al-ready laughed at him. He's taking it hard. Just lie and tell him he looks sexy."

Eloise had to suppress a guffaw because she was pretty sure Pinky was serious. She looked to Betsy for back up. Betsy said, "Sexy? I'd rather tell him he looks joyful, be-cause that dog is a joyful spirit, and that's no lie."

Buzz had changed the subject by handing them white wine in plastic glasses and passing around bruschetta with various toppings. The smells made Prince forget his hairdo, his nose seemed to expand and grow wet as he inhaled the scents.

They had set up their blankets on the edge of the park, since they didn't want the dogs near the speakers, and not everyone would appreciate the size of Prince, although the blue feathers did diminish the intimidation factor. Pinky had packed squeaky toys for each of the dogs, tiny ones for the puffballs, and a big dinosaur for Prince. So, as they passed around the food and wine, the air was filled with not only the sound of the recorded music that preceded the show, but loud and irregular "squeak-squeak-squeaks."

People continued to gather, the grass to be covered by blankets, food, and people. The sun was setting, and someone came out on the stage to tell jokes and settle the crowd. Pinky was leaning against Buzz with her eyes half-closed. Pinky had consumed a lot of wine already, and the evening was still young. The puffballs, miraculously, were already snoring.

But everyone came back alive once the first band got going, shocking them out of their food and wine stupor. Before long Pinky and Buzz were on their feet, dancing. Eloise was enjoying the music, but she just couldn't get to her feet. Instead, she gathered the leashes on Ying and Yang, who were pushing their faces into the folds of the blankets rooting for crumbs. Prince had already earnestly licked clean the platters. Buzz had saved what was left of the cheeses by wrapping them up and putting them back into the baskets. They had decided to wait to pour the coffee he had packed in a thermos and open the tin of homemade Biscotti. The party was in full swing, with the crowd having grown dense. It seemed like everyone was on their feet, as they were asked to clap along with the song and sing the refrain.

Eloise and Betsy finally got on their feet. Prince stood on his hind legs excitedly and Eloise took his front paws and danced him about. Then he ran, got his dragon, and presented it to Pinky. She tossed it into the air for him to catch.

He then took the dragon to Buzz who repeated the toss. And so, it went, the green dragon next presented to Betsy, and then Prince took it to the people who were dancing next to their blankets, and they too obliged.

Soon Prince and his dragon were making the rounds to adjoining parties. Everyone appeared to enjoy his antics.

The upbeat song ended. It was time for ballads. Pinky and Buzz swayed together while Eloise and Betsy sat back down with the dogs. Ying and Yang were soon snoring again. Eloise was feeling sleepy and closed her eyes to listen to the music, Prince stretched out between Eloise and Betsy, which felt protective, and sweet. Eloise thought to herself that she too had consumed too much wine. Her last thought before she drifted away was that she smelled pot. Yes, the scent was unmistakable; she had smelled it many times during college, though she never partook herself.

She was startled awake by Pinky. "Shiiiiit."

Eloise sat up. Pinky was sitting cross-legged next to her, holding a baggie.

Eloise opened her eyes wide, "Is that what I think it is?

Buzz was standing over them, "What the hell?"

Pinky said, "Prince just dropped this in my lap."

Betsy said, "Oh my."

Prince was wagging his tail excitedly, and then he did a "play-bow" inviting Pinky to do … something.

"Oh, my God, what do I do?" Pinky jumped to her feet, bells jingling as she held the baggie away from her body. Buzz put his hands out to stop her, or at least quiet her down. The second band had finished their set, and people were standing on their feet clapping and holding up their cell phone with the flashlight apps, yelling, "encore."

Buzz said, "Pinky, I think it's from our neighbors over there. Let me take it back over."

Pinky was having none of it. "If you got caught. You already have shit like this on your record, Buzz."

Buzz made a grim look, staring directly at Pinky. She said, "No."

And she marched away. Eloise jumped up to follow her, turning to say, "I need to go to the ladies anyway. You all mind waiting?"

She had to jog to catch up to Pinky. She said, "I need to use the restroom. Let's go, Pinky."

Pinky looked agitated. She stood and fidgeted in place. Then she said, "I'm tempted."

Eloise opened her eyes wide in disbelief. "No way."

"Aw, Eloise, you're a peach. Okay. Let's not then, although it would be great to get stoned with you, y'know, watch you relax. But yeah. Let's find a trash can. The bathroom is over that way."

Pinky linked her arm through Eloise's, and the two soon saw a trash can, overflowing with refuse.

They walked up to it. Pinky said, "Maybe we should go find another one."

"Pinky just get rid of it, okay?"

"Ick. I'm going to have to like, shove it down into that nasty pile."

Eloise hissed, "C'mon! We handle dog shit."

Pinky rolled her eyes and fished the baggie out from her bra where she had shoved it. She was poking it into the trash can, right at the edge, under a paper tray of half-eaten French fries with ketchup, when right behind them a deep voice boomed.

"Lovely evening isn't it, ladies?"

A male arm reached around from behind Pinky and daintily flicked the ketchup-soaked paper off the heap, letting it land on the ground. Then he pinched the exposed edge of the baggie and pulled it out of the garbage.

Pinky and Eloise sighed in concert. It was a cop, of course it was. What were the odds?

Eloise said, "I know it sounds crazy, but our dog found it."

Pinky said, "Cross my heart and hope to die" as she made the motion with her finger across her chest.

"That's a great story." He held up the bag and shone his flashlight on it.

"Lucky for you there's not much here. Why would you want to go and throw it away? Mad at your boyfriend, are you?"

Eloise realized she really, really, really, DID need to go to the restroom now. She said, "I realize you don't believe us, but we have this big ole dog that steals stuff and brings it to us."

The cop said, "Like a cat burglar, except he's a dog."

"Totally. He's a thief. I smelled pot, y'know, but we didn't have any, really." She saw the cop raise an eyebrow.

She was getting excited now. "I'm telling you the truth. The dog brought it over and dropped it in Pinky's lap."

Pinky added, "And then he did his play-bow, y'know how dog's do, and wanted me to like throw it or something."

The cop started to chuckle.

Eloise said, "Um, I really need to go use the ladies' room. I don't mean to be rude, but it's starting to feel urgent."

The cop was laughing now. "The dog...did what?"

Pinky spread her arms wide and lowered her shoulders;

she wiggled her hips and looked up at the cop. She could tell he was enjoying it, so she said, "Woof-woof!"

Well, the cop just lost it. Then Pinky and Eloise lost it too. All three of them were now laughing.

Eloise said between gasps, "Oh my God, I'm going to wet my pants."

The cop said, "Go, both of you! Go on! And next time you try that excuse, at least bring the dog along."

They ran the rest of the way to the bathroom, only to find a line. It was brutal. But they made it.

Eloise and Pinky returned to Buzz and Betsy and play-acted the scene with the cop for them. They had laughed until they were crying. Prince had jumped up and down and barked, and Ying and Yang yapped happy yaps right along with their laughter. Then they had gathered their things and joined the flow of people strolling down the sidewalks to wherever they had parked their cars.

Eloise was exhausted, her newfound laughing muscles in her belly fatigued, but loosened and relaxed, released. And though it was late, her head was clear. No dizziness.

Betsy offered to drive Buzz' car, which was smart as Buzz and Pinky had together consumed a lot of alcohol. Eloise sat next to Betsy in the front seat, while Buzz and Pinky and the dogs filled up the back seat.

Instantly it seemed, a chorus of snores serenaded them. It was Ying and Yang, as usual, but Buzz and Pinky were adding to the music. Prince popped his head over the back of the front seat between them and panted.

Eloise said, "I think he's feeling crowded back there."

Betsy said, "Prince buddy, you want to come up here and sit with us?"

Eloise was about say, "No, better not," but it was too late, Prince was climbing inelegantly over the seat.

Prince scrabbled halfway over the seat, knocking into Betsy who said, "Hey!" tightening her grip on the steering wheel.

"Stay in your lane, Betsy! I can't be telling a cop it was the dog's fault for the second time tonight."

Eloise grabbed Prince's collar and pulled him the rest of the way over, his tail smacking Betsy in the head. Eloise got him settled and Prince sat up tall and proud between them, still taking more than his fair share of the seat.

Betsy murmured, "Perhaps that wasn't my best idea."

They pulled into the driveway of Pinky and Buzz' bungalow.

Eloise said, "Why don't I unlock the door and get the dogs put up while you gently wake up our hosts?"

It took Betsy a few tries to wake up Pinky and Buzz, but once they were up, they managed to take themselves into the house, and still being the gracious hosts, with half closed eyes, Buzz invited them in for a night cap.

Betsy answered, "Thank you, Buzz, but no. We all had a wonderful time though."

Betsy and Eloise had each driven themselves to Pinky and Buzz's, so they had separate cars for the trip home. They stood by their cars before leaving.

Eloise said, "Pinky and Buzz are the nicest people I think I've ever known."

Betsy said, "I'm not a likely member of their crowd. It's so kind of them to include me."

"The same can be said of me. I'm not sure why Pinky befriended me like she has."

Betsy said, "That dog is the life of the party, isn't he?"

Eloise nodded.

Betsy said, "Take him, Eloise. You'll never be bored."

"Why don't you take him?"

"Ha! I'm too old to keep up with that one. But you are not. You told me about the red mare, and how she was a pistol, but was your kind of ride."

"I said it was Jock's kind of ride."

"Hmmm. Maybe you and Jock like the same kind of ride? This dog, he is a wild ride if I ever saw one. As dogs go that is."

Eloise grinned, "Controlled chaos?"

Betsy opened her car door to leave, "Oxymorons are wonderful, aren't they? But only a few can get away with using them effectively."

Betsy and Eloise got into their cars. Eloise was full and tired. She had danced with a handsome "Prince" and laughed until she was weak. She had friends.

Eloise thought of Mr. Jameson. Why she wasn't sure. But Mr. Jameson had asked her what she wanted, and Eloise had not been able to tell him. But she knew.

As she drove home, tired, and slightly drunk, she knew what she wanted she could not say out loud or to anyone, really. She wanted her mother. She wanted not "Jock" but her God-like "Daddy," and the Daddy who had loved her mother. The three of them had been one

"unit" with a dog and horses. Those things were so tightly entwined that even the idea of recovering one thread
from the ruin and clinging to it, felt pathetic. And Eloise
knew one thing for certain, she did not want to be pitied
or pitiful.

It had been a great night. It was a night to remember
and memorialize through retelling. But, even so, Eloise was
surprised to find herself wiping tears from her cheeks as
she drove home.

* * *

Eloise had been absent from the discussion on Extreme
Readers and had not been texting Dabs. But then this
came, and it felt like being thrown a lifeline to pull her
from herself and take her far away. This was something to
grab onto. And she did.

* * *

July 3, 1779

Sammie hangs on, but now we are quarantined.
Indeed, Buck and Isaac best remain in Williamsburg.
Aunt Bess was the one to diagnose, and our Doctor has
confirmed Sammie has pox. The white members of this
family are safe due to the influence of Mr. Jefferson,
who had convinced father to take us to Philadelphia for
the treatment years past. But none of our servants had
the treatment. Indeed, it was illegal for a time in my

*country to inoculate. Now, even if we could, no one in
this country inoculates servants.*

*No servant can safely care for poxy Sammie. The
burthen falls to Aunt Bess and myself with father also
engaged. It is a messy business, but I take reading to the
quarters to occupy the hours. I still ride out daily with
Bud and this keeps me from tearing out my hair. I shall
document here the progression. Perhaps as an old woman (God grant that I may one day be one) I will wish
to refresh my mind and share with the young what we
endured through these trials.*

* * *

July 10, 1779

*Wondrous news. Father has taken on Major Schmidt as
a laborer. The availability of prisoner labor is well uti-
lized around here, and benefits both sides. The Major
is immune to pox, so we put him in no danger. He will
move into the empty quarters behind the kitchens. His
labors are not gratis, but father has agreed to exchange
for labor one of the three-year old's we were planning
to bring up from the field last month but postponed.
The Major offers to do the work of training himself, but
first he must take his turn administering to Sammie.*

*Major Schmidt's cabin is run rotten with rats,
and birds have nested in the chimney which smokes
terribly. I handed him Cleopatra, who smelled the rats
and commenced hunting as soon as her feet touched the*

*floor. The Major is tempting her to reside in his quar-
ters by putting cream in her saucer. He has also sought
permission to borrow from father's library, and father
generously grants it. The Major speaks English more
than tolerably well, and I suppose I am impressed that
he also reads in English. No one hereabouts thinks anyone need know another language, especially a woman.
Many hardly care if a woman read or write, if she can
keep charge of the house servants and produce living
children.*

* * *

July 12, 1779

*I'm afraid I shock Major Schmidt. I simply asked if
the quarantine would be lifted in the event of Sammie
succumbing. It seemed a reasonable question but elicited
grim silence before I was graced with an answer. The
answer was no. A month must pass without anyone
falling ill.*

*Sammie has a mouthful of painful bumps, a terrible
fever, and bowels that have turned to water. The bumps
make eating and drinking difficult. I suggested trying
mush like we feed the field-hand's babies. That was
summarily rejected by Sammie who snarled his answer.
His temper is mercurial, being sullen and resigned to
death one moment, and full of rage the next. When he
deems it necessary to speak to me, he is beyond impertinent. I try to exercise patience but am not entirely*

successful. His predicament is not my fault. Aunt Bess is an angel and I wish I could be more like her but then Sammie treats her with respect.

Major Schmidt relieved my shift with Sammie by bringing a pot of chocolate. He was able to get Sammie to sit up and take a cup. I was amazed Aunt Bess allowed her secret stores to be raided for such a purpose. Major Schmidt neglected to offer me a cup. Sammie looked over the rim of his cup at me with something I can only describe as glee. I bore it without comment.

* * *

July 15th, 1779

The Major and I had a tortured literary discussion. Must everything be political? I suppose these days the answer is yes. I have long enjoyed Mr. Swift's tales. Being a horsewoman, I recognize the irony of the "Land of the Houyhnhnms" because I know and appreciate the nature of horses better than I know the nature of man. The Major sees the story only in terms of our current practice of African slavery. I asked him if we "Yahoos" should then give up riding horses due to Swift's story. He answered that we should merely release all those living under a lifetime bond of service as they are not horses, nor cows, but men. I told the Major that he may as well write stories himself, for such a thing will not happen in my country, unless it happens by force. To which he replied that such an undertaking was currently underway. I tried to correct him over the purpose of this conflict, but he countered with a lecture. Taxation, according to the Major was a debt we owe the King for fighting the last war on our behalf. To claim enslavement by the King whilst engaged in enslaving Africans was, according to the Major, outrageous hypocrisy. The Major claims that if we had paid our debt by paying our taxes, the King would have allowed the practice of African enslavement to be gradually eradicated, but now it must be completely ended as punishment. The Major stated that all the land we sit upon, was gifted to our progenitors by those who ruled before King George. The British made us our power and wealth, and true, the African slave trade was begun by those prior rulers. Slavery's evils are now understood far and wide, and even acknowledged by the very men in British America who live and enrich themselves from it. But It must end with this war.

For the Major, this is justification enough for him to fight, beyond his duty to his own Prince. He says with a smile that despite all this, we must be friends. He claims that he and Jefferson agree upon this point.

I marvel at this. Jefferson has never manumitted any of his slaves. In fact, he has sought to have returned to him any who have absconded. As was done by my brother Buck.

12

Betsy commented on Extreme Readers, "Eloise, I haven't heard your reactions to our current book."

Betsy thankfully, had kept private their wild evening!

"Finished it."

"And?"

"I'm obsessed with the Hemmings story. The new DNA evidence confirms Betsy's son, Eston, passed on Jefferson's DNA."

Betsy wrote, "DNA from Eston's descendants could have come from twenty Jefferson men in the area. Jefferson had uncles and cousins galore and one brother."

Dabs chimed in, "Ah, but Thomas Jefferson was at Monticello nine months prior to every one of Sally's children's births."

Eloise wrote, "Plus, the practice for widowers to take a slave 'concubine' was not uncommon. Martha Washington, like Martha Jefferson, kept her own half-sister as a slave. Ann Dandridge. Not only that, but Martha's son Jacky Custis allegedly impregnated Ann. The system, as Jefferson points out in 'Notes on Virginia' perverted both slave and master."

Betsy wrote, "I'm not sure about that story."

Eloise was on a roll. She realized she was angry. What was it about Founding Fathers, or fathers in general? So adored, so worshipped, and yet duplicitous? Why did they get to walk away like heroes from their own messes?

Eloise wrote, "Maybe George Washington was a pillar of virtue, but if he had engaged in sexual relations with his slaves, there would be no offspring, no descendants to test for paternity ala' Jefferson. He was sterile from smallpox."

Dabs wrote, "I can understand that it's natural to want our founding fathers to have risen above base sexual impulses, especially when it came to abuse of power. These men were supposed to build a country based on the highest principles of the enlightenment. We expect them to be exemplar models of virtue, and in large part they were. But they were human."

Eloise wrote, "Sex between master and slave was commonplace. Martha Jefferson's father sired six children with his slave. Betty Hemmings was the product of a slave and a white man. Sally's sister Mary was rented by Jefferson to a Charlottesville merchant who sired children with her. Later, one of Mary's daughters from an earlier liaison, Betsy, would become the concubine of Jefferson's son-in-law. How can that context be ignored?"

Betsy typed, "You have a valid point. But we must be careful not to swing the pendulum too far in the other direction and knock heroes off pedestals simply as sport."

Eloise wrote, "Truth matters. The historical record matters. This 'scandal' over Jefferson and Sally was not the 'moral impossibility' his grandchildren insisted. Jefferson never denied the relationship. He left it to his daughters and grandchildren to deny it for him."

Dabs wrote, "And pin it on their Carr Cousins."

Eloise added, "Who were cleared by the DNA evidence."

Dabs added, "Must have had it in for their cousins."

Eloise added, "Jefferson's grandsons also tried to paint Sally as everyone's good time. Vile."

Dabs typed, "Why? Long-standing resentments? Jealousy? Shame? Remember that the Jeffersons were left with nothing *but* their pride. Jefferson was a spendthrift. Even before his death. His grandson and namesake couldn't afford to go to college. Yet Jefferson continued importing wine and buying books. After his death, all were evicted from Monticello, homeless. That they fiercely defended their grandfather's reputation. I get it. It was all he left them."

Betsy added, "I feel compassion for the heirs."

Eloise wrote, "I feel angry at Jefferson."

Betsy wrote, "Perhaps Jefferson understood the depravity of the system because he knew himself to have been 'depraved' by it. But in the end, he was still a slave owner and a plantation owner, a member of an elite social class and he could not rise above it."

Eloise wrote, "I've been thinking about Martha's extracting a death bed promise from Jefferson never to remarry. So, I don't let her off the hook either. Sure, she didn't want her daughters to suffer stepmothers as she had, but my thoughts are also less generous. Maybe she thought a slave liaison would suffice for Jefferson's needs, as it had for her own father. After all, no slave concubine would ever gain her status. No progeny from a slave would ever be equal to or challenge the status of her daughters. A concubine could never give Jefferson what she had given him. She was protecting her daughters, and in a way, securing her place for eternity, as Jefferson's only wife. She knew he would hook-up with a slave."

Betsy appeared shocked. "Eloise, how cynical."

Eloise added, "Maybe I am, but come on, a mother who is dying looks after her children before anyone else. And Martha's own history would have guided her. And that history included far more than wicked stepmothers."

Betsy concluded the discussion, "I admit you seem to have unusual insight here that makes sense. Yes. Protection of self, protection of our loved ones, is instinctual. I think that's what Jefferson's family, and many of his biographers were doing, protecting a loved one. But historians have a duty to search for the full story. It's only fair to weigh the good against the bad. Judge Jefferson, and his wife and Washington too, both by our standards, and the standards of the time. We ought to seek understanding so we can show mercy in our judgement."

Although Betsy could not have known fully why, Eloise felt chastised by Betsy's final comment.

* * *

Thursday July 18th, 1779

I relieved the Major of his duties with Sammie this

morn, but not without engaging him once more. Truth be told, I had disturbed my rest with formulating my thoughts. My feathers were not but a little ruffled from our earlier discourse. I asked him, if he were so enchanted by the assertions of innate equality by Mr. Jefferson, then how could he serve his Prince, or for that matter, King George. If all men were born equal, what right has a man to be born into the lofty throne of Prince or a King? An accident of birth should not give one-man powers over another. How can one who castigates the practice of African slavery bow to King or Prince, who has neither earned by merit the power they wield, or the riches they possess. The Major claims I make the argument for Mr. Jefferson. But he posited the question of how to effect change that aligns with that philosophy. Because those who hold the reins of power rarely yield them without the shedding of blood in the struggle. An army cannot fight on too many fronts at once, so the greater wrongs should take precedence. The Major sees the fight against British America as rational and noble if it eradicates our practice of enslaved labor. After that, he sees no reason to resist reforms in all states across the globe, including his own. I fear Major Schmidt is a radical. And in this I see that if not for the question of our African bondsmen, he would be fighting for our side.

* * *

It was a quiet afternoon at the clinic and Pinky had Prince

in the tub, giving him a vigorous shampooing. Eloise was folding towels by the dryer.

"Don't scrub his hide off, Pinky."

"He's getting neutered tomorrow. I want him surgery-ready."

"Oh."

"Then he'll go up on the "Adoptables" board."

Eloise only made the noise, "Hmm." She felt herself being backed into a corner.

Pinky lifted an eyebrow. "Time to commit, Eloise. It's only $200.00. I can spot you if you don't have it."

Eloise looked down at her towels, "It's a life-changing commitment."

Pinky said, "That's kinda' the point."

"I have the money. But thanks."

Pinky was squeezing the excess water out of Prince's coat. "I can put together the paperwork as soon as my hands are dry."

Eloise said, "You, Ralph, Doc, Betsy, and even Dabs have all told me to adopt the dog. I was resolved to say no."

"It's a once-in-a-lifetime dog, Eloise. I don't know who Ralph or Dabs are, but they are right, and we've all been patient. And he chose you, didn't he? I mean sitting on the steps like he was sent to you by your guardian angel?"

"That was weird, I'll give you that."

"Who turns down their guardian angel? It's way bad juju."

"You believe in that stuff, don't you?"

Pinky said, "I believe in love."

"That sounds so corny."

"You take that dog and let him heal you."

With exasperation Eloise replied, "I don't need *healing*!"

To this Pinky rolled her eyes, and put Prince carefully down from the table, gave him a quick toweling off, then put him into the large cage, turning on the blower.

"You think I need healing?"

Eloise thought Pinky was just being her woo-woo self, or maybe she was probing. Whatever the reason, it was making her light-headed.

Pinky shrugged, "I think you want him badly. I think you did the day he showed up at the front door. Something is holding you back. You don't have to tell me if you don't want to. But at least be honest with yourself."

And with that Pinky dried her hands. She looked over her shoulder as she stopped on the bottom step. "I'm taking a coffee break. I'll make a folder of the contract on Prince from 'Good Stewards,' but the final decision is yours."

Eloise had to lean against the washer, her head, again.

She knew that if she took the dog, she was never going to move to Ireland. Even should an invitation come. And it likely never was going to come. And even if an invitation came, Eloise would have turned Jock down to make him plead with her. That was foolish to the extreme. Jock had not asked. Jock would certainly not plead. He had not forgiven her. She had not forgiven him. No one had budged.

Eloise would not adopt Prince to leave him or give him away. If he were her dog, it would be "til death do you part." Because, if you really loved someone, you did not move away to a foreign country and leave them behind.

Eloise folded towels: she started another load of laundry. She wondered if Pinky was up there talking about her to Doc.

Finally, Pinky brought down a folder with Prince's name on it.

This was it.

Pinky put the folder on top of the washing machine. "Well, what's it going to be?"

Eloise experienced a strange rush. And when the feeling had passed, she felt strangely warm and tingly all over. Eloise thought maybe she had just experienced a hormonal surge.

She nodded "yes" at Pinky, and Pinky slapped her on the back, stared at the ceiling and said, "Thank you, Jesus!"

Eloise smiled at her friend, "You weren't wrong. I do want him."

Pinky pointed at her, "It's time to take off that hair shirt, Eloise. What you want, what you need, go get it."

Eloise said, "You never cease to amaze."

"Moi?"

"Hair shirt?"

"Did I use it wrong?"

"Nope. You did not."

Eloise was smiling, but Pinky had touched a nerve. How the hell did Pinky know what she did not? Again. Adopting Prince was the easy part. All it would take would be filling out the form, paying the fee, and Prince would be hers. This time around he would get a micro-chip, and this time it would get properly registered. Registered to her. Eloise was making a commitment to Prince and to her life in Atlanta. Tomorrow he would go "home." He would be her Prince.

But the hair-shirt comment? An uncomfortable moment of clarity. Bullseye. She had cast herself out as much as she had been cast out. She assumed Jock had meant this separation to be a punishment, and she had accepted that, had blamed herself as much as Jock because, well, she deserved it. But part of her believed she would be reunited with her horse and her dad and regain some part of what had once been, sentence fulfilled, all forgiven.

If Jock had wanted "Lulu" with him in Ireland, he would have made it happen. He would have fought for her instead of with her. Because he had not, it followed that it was not what he wanted.

But Jock had kept her horse. It was clear what Jock valued.

Well, maybe now she was staying, that she was never going to go, ever, now she wanted her horse back. Pinky told her to take off the hair shirt and go get what she wanted, what she needed. Well, she wanted her horse back.

She knew what to tell Ralph.

Eloise filled out the paperwork, one copy went to Good Stewards, and one copy was for Eloise's files. She then went to the website and paid the $200.00 adoption fee.

Eloise found Pinky brushing out a Sheltie. "It's official. I just paid the fee."

"Let me put Daisy up. I've got something for you."

Pinky took a slicker brush to the hair on her smock, then washed and dried her hands. She reached into her tote and pulled out a bag with a bow on it.

"I've been carrying this around for a week, waiting for you to get off the pot."

She handed the bag to Eloise, who gave Pinky a hug, and then Eloise untied the bow.

Eloise pulled out a heavy leather collar with blue contrast stitching. Already dangling on the collar was Prince's rabies tag, and a large blue tag in the shape of a dog bone. One side of the tag read "Prince" and on the other side was printed, "Eloise Robertson" followed by Eloise's phone number.

Pinky said, "There's something else in the bag."

Eloise opened the bag wider and pulled out what appeared to be a "onesie."

"What the heck? I'm not having a baby."

"It's a post-surgery suit to keep him from licking his sutures. Beats the 'cone of shame.'"

"Now I've seen it all."

"See, easy Velcro on and off, for when he needs to, um, go outside. Then, one-two, the essential area is covered. Believe me, you do not want him bumping into your furniture with one of the cones we sell here. He'll be breaking some priceless family heirloom."

"Pinky, how did you know I would adopt him?"

"Everyone knew, has known, not just me. You knew too."

"But I didn't. It's just today, honestly just minutes ago, that things became clear to me. It's like a curtain has lifted."

Pinky said, "Isn't it weird how we keep secrets from ourselves?"

Eloise's thoughts were interrupted by the intercom. Janet needed a dog brought up. Eloise grabbed a leash and crossed paths with Pinky who had grabbed another brush-out from the cages.

"If we get a slow day, I'll give Prince a free clip for you."

Eloise had another strange sensation, this time an unpleasant one, that ran all the way down her spine. "I like him au naturel, but thanks."

* * *

The next day was "the day" it became real. Eloise was taking Prince home. Putting on his "onesie" he shoved his wet muzzle under each of her armpits, making her look like a heavy sweater. Prince looked ridiculous. It was a look that a toy poodle or a chihuahua could have pulled off. Not so much a giant hairy dog like Prince. But, as usual, he was cheerful about it. It felt odd to walk him to her car, put him in the back seat, and drive him to the townhome. Her usually silent and short drive now featured the soundtrack of heavy panting and hot breath on the back of her neck. Prince's perpetually damp chin hair tickled the back of her neck and made her shiver.

"Silly boy. There's no need to be nervous. You're going home."

Eloise patted the space behind her right shoulder, fingertips finding some bit of silky ear as Prince managed to rest his muzzle on her shoulder. Eloise firmly said, "Stay!" as she recalled how he had scrambled over the seat the night of the concert.

Prince's nails made tapping sounds as he trotted briskly from the garage into the kitchen, his nose testing the air, his tail wagging wildly. Eloise let him explore the house while she unpacked his bag. Dog food, bowls, treats. It went into the laundry room on a shelf above her tack.

They had an early dinner. Then Eloise went to the bedroom, saying, "Good digs, right?"

Prince hopped up on the bed, and Eloise sat down at her computer. She wanted to tell someone about Prince.

Eloise picked up her phone. She knew it was irrational but went to her call log and hit the symbol next to the word "Mom."

"The number you have dialed has been changed or disconnected."

"I got a dog." It was all she could get out before she felt her throat close.

"Shit."

Pinky had said something about healing. And it had touched a nerve. She wanted to tell Betsy and she wanted to tell Dabs. At least on the internet they could not see her, couldn't see how the simple act of getting a dog had made her wobbly emotionally. But things felt too raw. Acknowledging that rawness was all she could do today.

Instead, she took her latest read, the family letters of Thomas Jefferson to bed and read. Thomas Jefferson wrote to his daughter's, he wrote to his grandchildren, he wrote to his sons-in-law. Letters. People used to write letters. They saved letters to be read again. And again. They saved them to exist after they no longer existed.

Prince stretched out on his side, head on a pillow, and was softly snoring by the time Eloise turned off the light. The onesie had done its job. Prince had left his incision alone. She would have the new task of getting him out to relieve himself each morning. She had a small fenced-in patio area with a tiny grass patch and a few bushes. That would serve. Eloise scrunched herself down in the bed.

She rolled over on her side and pulled Prince up against her body. He was dead weight, warm and soft. He smelled slightly from the surgery. A mix of alcohol and betadine, but when she buried her nose in his coat, he smelled of lavender, thanks to Pinky.

Eloise woke up early to find Prince in the same spot but rolled over to face her. He was gazing at her. He propped himself up on his elbows when he saw she was awake, his tongue lolling, one paw placed on her forearm. Eloise picked up her hand and stroked his head, his ears, then touched his new ID tag, the one with her name on it.

She whispered to him, "You left someone, didn't you? Did you mean to? Or did they leave you?"

Speaking to Prince, even in a whisper got his tail thumping.

"Seems you're an early riser too. I'm glad. This is our space, our time to think. This is where we gird our loins for the day. I used to have this time surrounded by my animals. But stuff happened to me, just like stuff happened to you."

Eloise reached over and ran her hand over his silky head and ears. So different from the first time she had touched him.

"No more hair shirts. From here on, it's you and me."

13

July 20, 1779

*Only minutes into Buck's shift caring for Sammie,
he stormed into the house. He was speaking in such
tones as called us all to the front of the house, alarmed.
Priscilla lifted her apron over her face and crumpled
to her knees. She thought Sammie had passed. Instead,
Buck was saying to Father that he would not suffer to
be in the same room with Sammie and that the Devil
take him for all he cared. He declared Sammie must be
sold to Georgia as soon as he was fit. Priscilla began
to sob. Father asked Aunt Bess to attend to Priscilla then admonished Buck to not speak so in front of
the ladies. Father pulled Buck by the sleeve into his
study and shut the door. We began to climb the stairs
when Priscilla dropped upon a step and clung to the
pilasters. She had stopped her bellowing, and instead
was straining to listen, staring at Father's closed door.
Truth be told, Aunty and I did the same. We could hear
Buck's raised voice but make out no words. When the
door swung open, Buck passed through in a rush, not*

seeing us in his haste. *Father though raised his eyes and said in comforting tones, "Sammie will not be sold. He may still be in danger from this illness, but he is in no danger from me, nor will I allow Buck to harm a hair upon his head."*

Priscilla whispered, "Yes, sir."

Father said, "We'll hear no more upon the subject."

Though Aunt Bess and I nodded, I felt sure we would be discussing this incident. Aunt Bess did however take a moment to question her maid servant. She said, "You and Sammie are sweet on one another?"

Priscilla looked terrified but nodded.

"He'll likely run again."

Priscilla once again nodded.

Then Aunt Bess said, "Men are forever fighting for dominion. It is the fatal flaw of the sex. And we are too often simply another bit of territory over which to struggle."

She told Priscilla to strip the cherries from the tree in the back, and once rinsed clean, they would find a cool spot and pit them for making Cherry Bounce.

I gleaned from this scene that Buck and Sammie's relationship as master and servant was permanently asundered. How they could both occupy Ivy Creek Plantation seemed to me unworkable. Father would need to task Sammie to the ground, never more to work in the home quarter with the horses. Sammie being the excellent horseman, would chafe at the demotion. I expect, unless put in iron hobbles, Sammie would run again, and Father had already stated he would let him go. Like a feral cat, Sammie would take to the woods, never to be tamed. How such had come to pass, I had not an idea.

* * *

Pinky was shampooing a large German Shepherd, but stopped to point a wet soapy finger, covered in dog hair, at Eloise. "You're going. That's all there is to it."

"I don't even understand why there's a dinner."

Pinky put her back into her task while explaining, "Doc takes his payment in-kind for the Miller menagerie. Their restaurant is high-end. Doc blows the whole account on us. Last time we still had a balance left to burn after dessert, so Doc ordered Dom Perignon. It was crazy!"

"How did I miss this?"

Pinky started to rinse off the big dog, pulling hair from the drain and throwing it on the floor. "Doc waits until the bill gets big enough before he books a table. Last time was before you started working here."

"How dressed up do I have to get?"

"Just wear a dress. Buzz wears a sport coat and tie."

"I hate wearing a dress."

"Um, okay, wear some nice pants and accessorize. Add sharp shoes, maybe a cute jacket."

Pinky was wringing the excess water from the coat of her large client who realized his bath was over and wanted out of the tub.

Pinky yelled, "Whoa, Bubba!"

Then she scooped her arms around the wet dog's chest

and under his belly, lowering him to the floor where he gave a mighty shake that slung water everywhere.

"Eloise, I saw a closet full of beautiful clothes. Surely you can find something in there."

Eloise wiped water from her face. "Ugh. I'm as wet as if *I'd* given him the bath."

"Not even close. Hand me a towel, please."

Eloise opened the dryer door and pulled out a large towel.

She used it first on her face and arms. "Still warm. Here."

Eloise said, "That was Mom's closet. It's all her clothes."

Pinky put the Shepherd in the largest cage and turned on the dryer.

"Don't you think she'd want you to use and enjoy her things?"

Eloise's voice got soft, "Yes."

Up went Pinky's eyebrow, "After work today I'll help you put something together."

Eloise nodded, looking serious.

Pinky said, "Think of her watching over us and getting a kick out of you looking sharp in her outfits."

"Okay. Okay."

Eloise had relented. Mom *would* want her to find something from her closet and think of her when she put it on. She would do it. For Mom. But it would hurt.

* * *

When Pinky came by later that day, she inspected the

clothes on the racks as if she were shopping. Eloise plopped down on the upholstered bench. Backed into Eloise was Prince, his butt firmly planted on her feet.

"Your Mom must have been petite."

"Curvier. I'm taller."

"Isn't it cool how she organized her clothes by color?"

"She loved to organize things, people."

Pinky pulled out a short black and bronze silk dress. "With your brown hair and hazel eyes, perfect."

"No dresses. And besides, my eyes are brown."

Pinky stared at Eloise, squinting, "Nope. The irises are rimmed in gold. Hazel. One of your best features."

Then Pinky added, "Black and brown. Like a Doberman Pincher. Classic."

"Dress like a dog."

Pinky shook a wooden hanger at her, "You laugh. Nature doesn't make mistakes."

Eloise said nothing. Nature did make mistakes. Her mother should have had many more years.

They settled on black slacks, a black sleeveless knit top, with a tan micro-suede duster and leopard print high heeled pumps. Her toes were squished. Eloise was nervous about the heels, but Pinky said, "You only have to walk from the car to the table and back again. Those shoes make the outfit."

The closet had a tri-fold mirror. It gave Eloise a good look at herself, even from the back. The pants were a little short, but at least she wouldn't trip on the hem.

"You have anything for your neck? Ears?"

Pinky and Eloise looked through a selection and picked

out a necklace of amber glass beads, and simple hoop ear-rings.

"You are *not* carrying that backpack."

"I guess not."

"Why not use that beautiful bag up there."

"Which one?"

"That leather satchel. I noticed it last time I was here. On the top shelf. That color will go great with the duster."

Pinky grabbed an umbrella that was hanging on a hook on the wall. "Got something for me to stand on? Lawsy, these ceilings are high."

"Be careful, I took a tumble trying to do that the other day."

"Spot me, okay?"

Pinky cleverly hooked the handles on the satchel with the crook of the umbrella handle. Then pulled. She hollered, "Incoming!"

The satchel slid down the shaft of the umbrella, and Pinky jumped off the bench, dropping the umbrella and the bag, which landed with a heavy thunk.

Pinky hefted the bag excitedly, chirping like a bird. "Oh, it is just as soft as I imagined it. I would carry this every day if I were you. You are not a student anymore. Time to look like a grown-up, and a stylish one at that. Ooof it's heavy. Let's empty it."

Eloise went to the kitchen and found a paper bag. When she got back, Pinky had emptied the contents on the bed, and she was still chirping, "Two zippered pockets and three compartments. You are going to love this bag."

191

Pinky held the handbag up against Eloise. "I knew it. It looks great against that Duster."

Eloise looked at the pile on her bed. Letters. She picked up one set, saw Jock's familiar printing in the corner with an unfamiliar address.

Pinky glanced over, "Important?"

Eloise shrugged.

"Look at those later."

Eloise picked up another, and saw it was from her grandmother, someone she never knew. A few other sheets of paper were paper clipped together.

Pinky said, "At least take off your outfit."

Eloise silently put the letters into the paper bag. Her inner voice was not so silent. Were these kept for her to find? She thought of Washington and Jefferson burning letters. Well, not all of them. They only burned what they did not wish to be read. Her Mom was a planner, an organizer. But damn, it would have been nice if she had left more specific directions about, well, about everything.

Pinky admired Eloise's outfit again. "You look elegant as hell. Wouldn't your mom be so proud."

Eloise was surprised that she could answer in the affirmative, this time without a lump in her throat because whatever else, she knew her mother would want her dressed in her good clothes and going to this dinner. She would do it for Mom.

* * *

Even though Eloise did not look at the trove of letters,

knowing about them sat heavy in her gut, like an undigested meal. She thought about her parent's divorce. And the excuses she was given. And it made her think, oddly enough, about the preamble to the Declaration of Independence. The part about "dissolving bands" and "declaring causes that impel separation." But who is ever truthful about that sort of thing? It's all about making the other side look bad, isn't it?

She wrote on Extreme Readers, "I wonder if the wrong side won the American Revolution."

Betsy answered, "Why would you say such a thing?"

"Did you know that the British promised freedom to any slave that fled slavery and served in the British forces. Of course, those who stayed were promised nothing but a lifetime of slavery for themselves and their children. Abigail Adams wrote, "... *It always appeared a most iniquitous scheme to me—to fight ourselves for what we are daily robbing and plundering from those who have as good a right to freedom as we have.*" Abigail was honest enough to "own" the hypocrisy. Of course, they owned no slaves. Patrick Henry cried, "Give me liberty or give me death!" All the while keeping slaves. Samuel Johnson wrote, *"How is it that we hear the loudest yelps for liberty among the drivers of negroes?"* How must slaves have felt hearing the words, "... *all men are created equal*" or that "... *they are endowed with unalienable rights, that among these are life, liberty, and the pursuit of happiness.*"

Of course, Eloise could not say anything about how Major Schmidt, through Louisa's journal, had been the first to make the argument clear to her.

Dabs typed, "Really, Eloise? Jefferson's words reset the arc of history. I mean that. They have the moral authority of truth. They were ahead of his time. He just could not rise above his world as it existed."

Eloise wrote, "Or was unwilling to make the personal sacrifices required to do so."

Dabs again defended Jefferson. "If Tarleton had captured him, and he nearly did, Jefferson would have been hung for treason, if not here, then in Britain. Every one of the signers put it all on the line."

Eloise wrote, "But Jefferson was up to his neck in the business of tyranny. He owned thousands of acres, multiple farms, all being worked by slave labor. His home was filled with Martha's slave family, six of them Martha's half siblings."

Betsy joined Dabs in Jefferson's defense, "He believed in the natural rights of man. And he was bending history on a righteous arc. But consider, Eloise, that understanding an entrenched evil in society is theoretical. Self-examination, condemnation of one's own wrong actions, and being willing to make huge sacrifices that affect not just oneself, but one's family? How many of us can do that?"

Eloise wrote, "I think he gave up because he was too entangled in it all. He gave up, understanding that other's blood was to be spilled in the future and other fortunes were to be lost to settle the question. But personally? He was burning through his fortune and living well. He punted."

Dabs wrote, "Perhaps. But his bright and shining moments illuminated the world and guided the future. Freedom of religion. Separation of state and religion. Equality of mankind. Public education. The University of Virginia (my alma mater, ahem). We wouldn't be America without him."

Eloise said, "Why would any of that matter to any person held in bondage, or even their descendants?"

Dabs asked, "Betsy, do we have a Tory in our midst?

* * *

July 30, 1779

No one has fallen ill since Sammie's confinement. Still, Aunt Bess says we must not fail in our vigilance. Sammie is still able to spread pox until the last scab falls from his ravaged skin. We must remain an island for two weeks more, the rule being 30 days without new cases. I have spoken too freely of his disfigurement in front of Priscilla. She mopes about the house with visage most tragic. Sammie's face has not a smooth inch left upon it. The hard centers have become pustulent and many scabbed over. It is an ugly thing, pox. If it does not rob the life of its victim, it robs their beauty. Not all cases are as destructive as Sammie's. Sammie is finely formed with regular features and large dark eyes. His dusky complexion formerly was unmarked, but is now ruined.

Sammie continues sullen though the fevers have subsided, and his appetite improved. I have never treated him badly. I am not my brother. I feel his scorn is undeserved.

When I relieved Major Schmidt of his shift today, I

*walked into the quarters to find the two sharing a joke.
One they had no intention of sharing. I expect it was
lewd.*

*Major Schmidt continues to extoll the virtues of
Cleopatra, who daily presents him with a rat. She has
a bellyful of kittens, which is an annual event. Schmidt
has asked if her kittens are as fearsome as she. And
yes, indeed, she has supplied many of our friends with
skilled hunters. He asked if he may provide kittens
to the barracks. Father agreed. It seems the barracks
are infested with both insects and rodents. The Major
boasts that rats know better than to now invade his
cabin, as crossing the threshold is death certain, and
fewer and fewer attempt such foolishness.*

*I am happy to report that the Major no longer
appeals. Even with his eyelashes and doe-eyes. He still
sports that wooly caterpillar upon his upper lip, but I
expect that it is his proximity that has dulled my fasci-
nation. He is no longer an exotic. Aunt Bess however
has fallen under his spell. When he plays his violin in
the evenings, she puts her knitting in her lap, her nee-
dles gone still, until he finishes.*

* * *

Dabs texted Eloise, "Hi. Hadn't heard back from you
since I sent those last journal entries. I hope you are still
interested."

"Of course, I'm interested. Louisa is a trip, although I'm
not sympathetic to her right now. She doesn't even register
the injustice of Sammie's situation."

"Don't forget she is young and not worldly, though well-read."

"Really? I'm young, not worldly, and I am well read."

"Ah, but you are existing 240 years later."

"There were plenty of writers in her time that understood."

"None more so than Jefferson."

"Words without action make it worse."

"Harsh."

"Sorry. I'm feeling out of sorts tonight."

"Worried about seeing Jock?"

"Maybe. But no. I've got a dress up dinner on Saturday night with the Doc and the whole staff of the clinic."

"You get anxious in social situations?"

"Not that. I'm wearing my mother's clothes, jewelry, and carrying her handbag."

"Bittersweet."

"You are a nice guy, Dabs. Yes."

"I don't think any guy likes being told they are a nice guy. But I'll try and take it with my chin up."

Eloise texted a laughing emoji then wrote, "There is something else."

"Yes?"

"The handbag. I emptied it out and it was full of letters. Some from Jock. Some from my grandmother. Do I read them? It's a breach of privacy. Ideals. Living up to them. I mean if I'm going to come down hard on Jefferson and Louisa…"

"Do you think your mother kept them so that one day you would read them?"

"I can't ask her."

"They could have been kept for sentimental reasons."

"They divorced."

"Letters are kept or destroyed by intent. Don't assume otherwise."

"There you go again, being a nice guy."

Dabs changed the subject. "By the way, I am beginning to have a sense of urgency about getting the journals finished. Some of the pages and binding feel like they could disintegrate into dust."

Eloise said, "There could be nasty mold spores in that dust. Be careful."

"That's the second nice thing you've said to me today."

"I must try not to do that too often. You'll get spoiled."

"I could get used to being spoiled."

Ugh. Dabs was flirting.

Damn.

And she was being far too cute in return.

Double-damn.

14

It had been an uneventful day at the clinic. A day where Eloise's mind kept trying to replay all her terrible decisions and regrets. Yes, and resentments. And she found again that she was angry at Jock, but oddly also Thomas Jefferson. God, she was weird and knew it.

Eloise was handing a freshly bathed Marilyn to Betsy.

Betsy said, "Dabs is impressive. I think he's the only one I've heard opine who is your equal."

"He's single, Betsy."

"How do you know that?"

Betsy's blue eyes had gone wide, her stare intense.

"Communicating privately, are you?"

Betsy winked in an exaggerated way.

"It's nothing like that. He's sharing original revolutionary writing with me, and by-the-way that's confidential."

"Why? Is it significant?"

"Could be. But you're right that Dabs is smart. And he seems like a nice person, sort of fatherly."

"Fatherly? What's the fun in that?"

"Stop. Yes, he's fatherly. He's retired from his law practice. I think he's lonely."

"Retired? Well, maybe you're right. But let's not "pool our ignorance, shall we? I'll ask."

"Oh no, please don't Betsy. What does it matter anyway? We're in Georgia and he's in Virginia."

"I guess you're right, but still, we've read Jane Austen. If he's a single man who may be possessed of a good fortune...we should know his age."

* * *

Eloise transferred everything from her backpack into her mother's satchel. She had not forgotten about the flier in the zippered pocket. Eloise placed the flier into a zippered pocket in her "new" bag, but not before opening the flier and kissing her finger then placing it on his lips. Joe was just as bewitching as ever. There was nothing complicated about her feelings toward Joe.

Eloise looked at the paper sack of old letters sitting on the floor of the closet and felt that lead weight creep back into her belly. This was stupid. She could at least sort through a few. She dumped them again on the bed and sorted the letters by sender and by postmark. It seemed less intrusive to read the letters from her grandmother than from her father. After all, she never really knew her Robertson grandmother.

Eloise settled herself in her usual reading spot in bed. They must have been important to her mother to have saved them all this time. Prince tucked himself next to her contentedly. She was soon totally absorbed in the letters.

Dear Elly,

While I certainly am surprised by your news, I have nothing but the best wishes for you and Jock. His father is still unaffected I'm afraid. Robertson's are stubborn and proud and as unmovable as the sun, with a history of holding grudges to the grave. He will not relent. I, however, am not my husband's obedient slave. I want to hold my grandchild and be a part of his or her life. Once the baby arrives, and you are ready to receive me, I intend to come.

I understand the nuptials will be quiet with only a few in attendance. That is proper under the circumstances. However, I am still sending a gift. Hope it will be well received by my prodigal son.

Please call me by my given name. Let's not stand on formalities now my dear.

With love,
Anne

Eloise, it seems, had been an "oopsie." Stupidly, this was news to her. If any letter deserved burning, surely it was this one. On reflection, it seemed it was her mom who had bravely written his mother with the news, not Jock. And clearly, Jock was already on the outs with his folks, being the reckless black sheep. This disappointment to his parents included Mom. And Eloise.

Eloise read the other letters, but they were polite and careful in the extreme. Why save any of them? She couldn't shake her anger. She wasn't dizzy though, and the heavy feeling, dread perhaps, had left her stomach.

It was very late when she sent Dabs a text. It was a foolish impulse, but it felt good to vent. She didn't expect a reply. It was one of those times when she should have just written it all out and then hit delete. But she didn't.

Dabs wrote back right away.

"I'm sorry. Life is messy. It doesn't mean you weren't loved. I've been thinking about the one strange overlap of my life with your life. And that I handed off your horse "Whiplash" to an attractive woman wearing a Burberry raincoat. She was blonde, and elegant, stylish for being at an event. Could it have been your mom?"

"That was Mom. Burberry all the way. Weird, isn't it?"

"Yes."

"Thanks for writing back. It's late. I'm sorry."

"You going to be able to sleep tonight?"

"Not likely."

"I'll send you this then. Maybe it will take your mind off those letters and give you a laugh."

* * *

August 7, 1779

Major Schmidt came to the house to announce that Cleopatra was queening. Aunt Bess, Priscilla, and I, accompanied by Beast, followed the Major to his quarters. I gave Beast strict instructions to wait outside.

We entered the dark and damp interior. Aunt Bess

held her tongue, but I could see her disapproval at seeing our homespun blanket in the box the Major had constructed for Cleopatra.

Cleopatra had a dreamy look upon her face and was purring contentedly and kneading the blanket as three little charcoal-colored lumps nuzzled into her teats. A fourth kit, solid grey like a turtledove, shook and cried, blind and lost. The Major gently picked up the kitten and pushed it up against Cleopatra's belly, where it began to root about.

Bess, noting the color of our white cat's litter remarked, "Cleopatra, where have you been? I've not seen any sable-shaded Tom's about."

Major Schmidt spoke without turning his head saying, "Nature is nature, ladies. It is as blind as these little kittens."

That remark drew a frown from Bess.

Cleopatra began to pant and stood, her kittens dropping away and making pitiful squeaks as they did. The Major put a finger to his lips and winked at us. Cleopatra threw herself on her side, then sat up to try and lick beneath her tail. Major Schmidt began to stroke her along her back and she visibly relaxed and once again lay flat. He continued to stroke her along her side, speaking to her sweetly in his native tongue. I could see her eyes halfway close. She must have been in pain as I could tell her focus had drawn inward. Yet the Major slowly ran his hand over her coat and murmured something. Cleo stayed there for a minute or so, all of us quietly in attendance. And then she quickly *stood, and there deposited in the folds of the blanket, another sooty little form. It did not move, nor did it squeak as it should. Cleopatra roughly stroked it with her tongue.*

Aunty Bess asked, "Is it dead?"

The Major answered, "I do not like the looks of it. But give Cleopatra a moment to rouse it with her tongue."

Cleopatra was doing her earnest best to stimulate the little form. The Major pulled up a corner of the blanket and added his efforts to Cleopatra's. When that seemed to do no better, he picked up the kitten between his palms, cupping it firmly, stood and swung his arms downward a couple times. Cleopatra looked on with interest. Then he did the strangest of things. The Major put his two thumbs about the muzzle of the tiny form, placed his mouth over the mouth of the kitten and blew gently. The Major drew his mouth away, and miraculously the kitten opened its mouth wide and squeaked. We all gasped, along with the kitten. The Major then chafed the kitten between his palms briefly and handed it gently back to Cleopatra, who took it in her mouth, made a circle, and then lay back down, dropping the kit into the blanket. The Major lined up the kits to Cleopatra's teats and stepped back to join us.

Priscilla said, loudly enough, "Never seen that trick. Don't think I'd like to kiss a kit that just been where that one had been, though."

Priscilla, not one known for her comedic abilities,

had us laughing so hard we had to excuse ourselves from the maternity ward.

* * *

It was Saturday night. Doc's big treat, and Pinky had forced the issue. She was going, dressed in her mother's clothes.

Eloise looked at herself in the three-way mirror, ready to go, and thought, "So, I'm an oopsie. I know I was loved. I do. I thought we loved each other, like forever-together-love. But Jock and I are cowards. He bolted. I wanted to. I'm so sorry, Mom. I'm so sorry."

Eloise pulled herself together. It was just a dinner. A treat from her nice boss, and with people she saw every day. Her mom would love to see her dressed up in her clothes. If it had not been for her cramped toes and her mascara-stiffened eyelashes, she could almost say she was comfortable.

She could still bag it, stay home, and read in bed with Prince tucked warmly against her. Just make up a story as an excuse. Pinky would never let her get away with that. Nope. Just be the last there, first to leave. That was her plan.

Eloise was pleased when the host led her back to a banquet room to see the first part of her plan had been successful. Doc came around the table and pulled out her chair.

Doc said, "Now the festivities can really begin! What would you like to drink, we have three wines on the table, or maybe you'd like a cocktail?"

Doc went to his seat at the head of the table. Eloise sat at the end, with Pinky and Buzz to her left and Susie and Janet and Janet's husband on her right. There were small plates of this and that being passed around and multiple wine glasses at each plate.

Pinky said, "I was just about to call you. Get cold feet?"

Eloise lied, "Just fashionably late."

Buzz said, "You look wonderful, Eloise."

Pinky said, "It's true. And did I mention I adore that bag?"

"I believe you did."

Then she took a good look at Pinky. "Pinky, you look stunning."

Pinky's dress was the color of a hot pink azalea. Across the shoulders she wore a fuzzy white shrug. But it was the neckline that drew Eloise's gaze. Eloise had never seen Pinky's décolletage on display. It was, impressive. In fact, they seemed amazingly round and gravity-defying. Hanging above the cleavage was a large cut crystal pendant that refracted the pink from her dress and twinkled like a star.

The chatter was happy as Buzz waxed poetical on each new bottle of wine. He also gave a flowery disquisition about the menu (Buzz knew the Chef).

After dinner, more bottles of wines and cordials arrived along with desserts. After that came snifters of expensive brandy to blow out the last bit of credit on Doc's account.

Finally, Doc stood to make a toast.

"We all of us here have much to be grateful for…"

Buzz loudly said, "Like Pinky's dress!"

The room exploded in laughter. Pinky did not blush, but she did poke a grinning Buzz with a pink fingernail.

Doc continued, "My little clinic could never be possible

without all of you making it work for the human and animal clientele. Each contact they make with us, with any of us, can provide confidence or create concern. That each of you does the former, is all-important to them, and to me. I feel blessed and grateful."

Doc raised his glass, said, "Thank you" to a chorus of, "here, here!"

Susie made a toast to Doc, for his mentorship, and for his encouragement in her applying to vet school.

Janet and her husband toasted Doc for being a great boss who had created a business with a healthy work culture.

Buzz made a toast about how saving mutts from the streets was one thing that Pinky and Doc had in common. They shared a passion of "no dog left behind." And he liked to think he was Pinky's finest rescue.

Pinky rose to say she and Doc had become friends after she had brought in rescues from Good Stewards for vaccines. Doc had invited her to join the staff as groomer. It had been a great decision and she had been there six years. Pinky was grateful to Doc for sticking with the rescue all this time.

Buzz said, "Eloise, your turn."

Eloise realized she was slightly intoxicated, enough to feel relaxed. Or maybe that was because she had slipped off the pinching shoes and left them under the table. Eloise had no idea what she was going to say. Public speaking was not her forte'. This was an area where Jock shone brightly. Jock would make 'em laugh, Jock would make 'em cry. Channel Jock.

Buzz banged his glass with a knife and said, "Speech, speech!"

Eloise raised her eyebrows and tipped her chin downwards to get a good look at Buzz. He was certainly drunk. Suddenly she knew what she was going to say.

"You all know I read a lot?"

The room murmured assents.

"Tonight, when I saw Pinky in that dress, I was transported 240 years back in time, to a particular scene with a particular woman. The woman was referred to as the "Baroness," In my reading, the Baroness sang an aria. As she sang, the room was transfixed by the rise and fall of the bellows that provided the Baroness her ample lung capacity. Bellows, you know, her um, chest."

Eloise paused to check her inebriated listeners were with her, they were looking amused and expectant. So, this is what it was like to hold an audience like Jock.

"Pinky, let's just say, that your 'bellows were impressive tonight, even though you did not sing."

Eloise was gratified to hear the room erupt into laughter. "I'm grateful to all of you, but tonight I want to thank Pinky, the 'Baroness,' who is much more than a set of bellows. Brilliant with clippers and scissors, patron Saint of lost and unwanted pets, and my friend. So, to our Baroness, our Pinky!"

"To Pinky!"

Pinky was looking straight at Eloise, brow lifted, head tilted, and for the briefest moment, the two of them marveled at each other.

Eloise sat down, amazed at herself, especially for giving

a semi-lewd toast, without anxiety, and that she was able to offer her toast to the person who worked "below stairs," elevating her with an aristocratic title to boot.

Eloise had only to draw from Jock and her reading and the toast had come easily. Jock who she was so angry with, Jock who had bolted and cast her off and then replaced her. Jock who she was so much like in so many ways.

With a scraping of chairs, hugs all around, and thank-yous to Doc, it was time to go home. Buzz was about to order an Uber ride home, but Eloise decided she was sober enough. Eloise would drive them. Pinky sat up front with Eloise, and Buzz sat in the back seat. Buzz was snoring within a minute.

Pinky looked over the seat. "Can you believe him?"

"It's the booze."

"Buzz can sleep anywhere anytime. It's like he can do it at will."

"Nifty trick."

Eloise pulled up in front of their bungalow, and said, "I'll help you get him into the house."

"That is so sweet."

Pinky opened the back door and put one knee on the seat, "Buzz, let's go in."

He said, "That was great, babe."

"C'mon, upsy-daisy."

Buzz rubbed at his eyes and scooted toward the door.

"Watch your head, sleepy boy."

Buzz said to Pinky, "You looked amazing. You tipped good?"

Eloise watched them slowly make their way to the door.

Pinky's bag was still on the front seat. Eloise grabbed their bags, locked the car, and hurried to help.

Buzz said, "Hi, Eloise."

The puffballs were by this time screeching behind the door.

Pinky unlocked the door, saying, "They'll really need to pee."

"You help Buzz to bed, I'll walk Ying and Yang."

When Eloise returned with Ying and Yang, Pinky was sitting on the sofa.

"I made you a mug of Sleepy-Time tea. It prevents hang-overs."

"I've never heard that before."

"I just made it up. But it's true."

"That makes zero sense."

Pinky, doing a Zen-master voice said, "Things that are true often make no sense."

Then, "Drink your tea and I'll massage your feet. To-morrow morning, you'll see that I was right."

Eloise gave in, thinking a foot massage sounded nice. She pulled off the pointy-toed leopard print shoes.

"Now that is an offer I can't refuse. Wearing these shoes reminded me of foot-binding. Have you ever seen photos of what they did to those poor women? I mean, Pearl Buck *The Good Earth* kind of stuff?"

"Do you have a literary reference for everything?"

"Maybe, Baroness Pinky, maybe."

"Baroness Pinky? You would make the better Baroness. But wow, nice of you. You've loosened up, you know."

"I felt good in my mom's clothes." When she said it, she

realized it was not only Jock standing up there giving the toast. Mom. Mom was there too.

Pinky said, "And that bag. That gorgeous bag. I hope you never use that backpack again. Use it if you go hiking or something."

"About that bag."

"Yeah?"

"All those old letters we dumped out. It's history. Not the important kind of history. Just my history. Why is it that we dive right into the lives of strangers, but hesitate to investigate our own?"

"I'm not really listening but keep talking."

Pinky started to massage Eloise's feet by pulling on each of her toes, then putting her fingers between the toes and slowly moving them.

Eloise said, "I didn't read the letters that were from Jock. That would be wrong. I decided to give them to him next weekend when I see him."

Pinky now was working on Eloise's arches, but she did nod. Eloise took that as encouragement.

"I glanced at some pages of scribbled gibberish, un-signed. I'll read those later."

Pinky nodded again.

"The other bundle of letters were from my grandmother. I thought those would be okay to read. Both women are gone, and Mom saved them for a reason. Maybe I was that reason."

"True."

"And I read them."

"And?"

"And I found out that I was an oopsie. Y'know, an accident."

"You are no accident. Just because your mom and Dad didn't plan you."

The foot rubbing stopped. Bummer.

Eloise nodded, "Yeah, since here I am, clearly Mom and Jock's oopsie was a keeper. I know I was loved. I get that."

Then Eloise glumly added, "It's just, the marriage didn't last, did it? They married because of me. And in the end, their love for me wasn't enough. I wasn't enough."

Pinky went for the other foot. "Life takes sharp turns, not everyone can hang on. Hey, you're the one who had the horse named Whiplash, right?"

"Ha-ha. A metaphor for life."

Pinky shrugged.

Eloise continued, "I don't get it. It's not like they fought, at least not in front of me. We had a perfect life. I had a perfect life. We had a barn full of horses. I had my very own horse, a good dog who slept at the end of my bed. Well, mostly at the end."

Pinky shrugged, "Every story ends the same damn way. Someday you and I will have to dance right off the stage too. Sucks. I saw my mom say good-bye over and over again to her friends. Mostly they were reckless and addicts and stuff like that. Suddenly it was her turn. One heck of a sharp turn for me."

Eloise studied Pinky as she rubbed Eloise's heels and ankles. Pinky, bright flower that she was, had her very own story. Of course, she did. Clearly, it was a story with plenty of sad parts.

"I'm sorry, Pinky."

"Mom never caught a break. But she didn't make the best choices either. Smoked like a chimney, drank like a fish. Never finished school. Went to work at sixteen, got preggo and never stopped working 'til the day she dropped."

"And your Dad?"

"Never knew him. That's probably why I had trouble figuring out what a good man was. First dude I hooked up with was abusive. But, when he kicked my dog, I was out of there." Then she looked over at Eloise's mug. "Drink up, Eloise."

Eloise drained her mug, then sat up, pulling her feet from Pinky's lap. "Thanks for taking such good care of me, Pinky."

"I just might sleep right here on the couch tonight, Buzz snores like a freight train when he's drunk."

"Can I get you a blanket?"

"I'll get it, I'll have to lock the door behind you."

Eloise picked up her shoes. No need to undo Pinky's great massage.

At the door she turned. "Your Mom didn't name you Pinky, did she?"

Pinky shook her head and smiled, one eyebrow lifting, "Sadly, no."

"Who gave you that name?"

"I did." Then she shrugged. "I decided pink would be my signature color. So, I dyed my hair platinum, dyed the tips pink, and named myself Pinky."

"Did you change it? Legally, I mean?"

Pinky shook her head. "Damn thing is on my license."

"So, what WAS it?"

"You don't tell a soul?"

"Lots of people surely know. Doc has to fill out your withholdings."

"And has the good grace and sense not to mention it."

"As will I."

Eloise sealed her promise by crossing her heart, then running her fingers across her lips.

Pinky nodded then stage-whispered, "Darlene."

After a moment of shock, Eloise said, "I've never known any Darlene's."

"There was one in the Mickey Mouse Club. That's where Mom got the inspiration." Pinky winked, then stepped back in and closed the door.

15

Eloise wore the same clothes to have dinner with Jock. Well, she found some suede ankle boots to wear instead of the toe-crushing leopard print stilettos. She brought Jock's old letters, determined to find a quiet moment to return them.

When Eloise entered the restaurant, her heart began to pound, hearing Jock's voice before she saw him. A hot wave of dizziness washed over her. How many times had she fantasized a reunion that had not happened? Too many. She remembered she was wearing her mom's clothes. She wondered if Jock would notice. Her legs, feeling slightly wooden, moved her forward.

Eloise made her way to a back section of the restaurant that had a long table, Jock was at the head, presiding, the sole male, a King among his courtiers.

He stood up and strode across the space to her, like he was gliding on ice, and gave her a bear hug. Then he stood back but with an arm across her shoulder and presented her to the group.

Jock's voice boomed, "May I present my daughter, Lulu Robertson."

Jock walked her to his end of the table, and she noticed a chair next to "himself" had been saved for her. Eloise had forgotten the way he took up space, although still fighting trim. She knew every one of the women at that table, who would be seeking his approval tomorrow in her riding lesson, would have paid a hefty fee for his undivided attention.

Jock said, "You look wonderful, darling." And patted her on a knee.

Eloise's mouth had gone dry as dust, but she did manage to say, "You look great too. Clearly, life is agreeing with you."

His eyes twinkled, "As long as I have a good horse in the barn, and good company, life is good."

A waiter came in with a bottle of wine and poured a bit in Jock's glass for his approval. He took a sip and nodded, and added, "My daughter has just turned twenty-one, and for the first time ever, her old man is going to buy her a drink." With that, the waiter turned over Eloise's wine glass and gave her a modest pour before proceeding around the table to fill everyone's glass.

One of the ladies politely asked, "Lulu, do you ride?"

Eloise said, "Not so much these days."

Jock smiled, "I just had her test ride a few sales horses for me."

Eloise asked, "And, what's the latest?"

"Going to buy both, that's how much I trust your judgment, kiddo."

Eloise had a sip of wine, unstuck the inside of her lips

from her teeth and used her best business voice, "The gelding is top class, and that red mare is dynamite."

"Bev said that mare took a cotton to you."

"Bev is a hoot. You two go back a bit?"

"Bev's old as dirt. Everyone knows Bev."

Jock changed the subject, talking to the table, "My daughter always has her nose in a book. She ate up those Harry Potter books. You know how thick those books are?"

Another woman said, "I was the same way. Weren't they wonderful?"

It seemed it was a table full of Potter-heads. Jock had never read a single Harry Potter book, so he went elsewhere.

Jock asked Eloise, "What's the latest reading obsession?"

Eloise began to speak about Jefferson and Virginia, and although most of the table tuned out, as they discussed Dementors and Voldemort, Jock seemed genuinely interested.

He said with authority, "We're related to Jefferson."

Eloise rolled her eyes at her dad. "Oh please, you once told me we were related to George Washington. But then I learned he never had children!"

"You weren't listening. We are related to Martha Washington. It was her son Jacky who married a Calvert. We are related to the Calverts."

Eloise smiled and shook her head, "I know who Jacky Custis is, and what you're saying means that not only are we *not* related to George Washington, but we also have no blood ties to Martha Washington."

"I'm just trying to pass on what I was told. I'm sure my mother would debate you on our being related to Jefferson. She knew this stuff."

"Okay, I'll bite. How are we also *not* related to Thomas Jefferson?"

"Listen and learn, since for some reason I remember this stuff. Thomas Jefferson had an uncle named Field."

Eloise lifted one corner of her mouth. Already the connection to Thomas Jefferson was getting remote, and the name "Field" was so weird that she momentarily wondered if Jock was making it up as he went.

Jock continued. "Uncle Field married one of the Robertson girls. I can't remember her name. But it's no joke that Robertsons were FFV."

"Aha! Just as I suspected. No blood ties to Jefferson either."

Someone at the table chimed in, "FFV?"

Eloise knew this one. "First Families of Virginia. Second and third sons of the British Aristocracy who came to Virginia to grab land and get rich by the labors of slaves."

Jock looked hurt. "They came to make a new world in the image of the old world, since that's all they knew."

Eloise added, "Instead of peasants, they had African slaves. Those raised in old Virginia were 'educated in tyranny.'"

"And you are quoting?"

"Thomas Jefferson."

"Looks like you know a lot about our famous ancestor."

"I don't think we're related, but if we are, maybe you should know that he died broke. All his assets were liquidated to pay his debts, including his human assets. His only living daughter spent her remaining years drifting from one child's home to another. Apologists would like us to believe the slaves grieved his passing because they loved him. But their grief was likely because his passing meant catastrophe for them."

Jock shook his head sadly. "Look, I'm really impressed at how much you know about Jefferson ..."

Eloise continued, "Do you know he wrote down every single penny he spent? But he seems to have never added up those numbers or made a budget. Did you know he patented a plow? Yet, he failed as a farmer, even with slave labor."

Jock raised his eyebrows, "I expect my mother just turned over in her grave. But no matter. My question to you is, what are you going to do with all this new-found information?'

"What does anyone do with new-found information? You begin to see the world around you differently."

Jock looked serious, "I see that. You seem passionate about the topic. It occurs to me you might stay in school, go for an advanced degree. You have a tremendous amount of freedom to chart your own course, you know. Unlike Jefferson, you are not broke. You have more options than most people your age."

Eloise was dumbstruck. But only for a moment, then she blurted out, "I got a dog!" She realized she sounded like a ten-year-old child. She wasn't sure where that had come from, but she had said it with great feeling.

Jock laughed so loudly that the table went quiet and turned their faces to Jock.

He announced, "Lulu got a dog. Tell us all about the dog, now everyone wants to hear."

Eloise was sure her face was red, but she shifted into story-telling mode. She could do this, take the floor, own it like Jock always did. She recognized it as the same state as when she made her toast to Pinky. Except this time, she understood she was practicing the skill as a protective device.

Eloise related, with dramatic flourish, the appearance of the shaggy dog. And then how his chip wasn't registered. And his antics. Jock had taught her how to spin a yarn as well as ride down to a solid fence at speed. Whether it was embellished or not was not what counted. People would do all sorts of things for you in exchange for a good story well told. But the most important person in that room was Jock. And she could tell, in every sideways glance, that she was pleasing him. The twinkle was back in his eye. And pleasing Jock felt good, filled her with warmth and hope and pride. Maybe he would stop being angry at her. And she could stop being angry at him. She softened toward him, and looked forward to giving him the letters, later, in a quiet moment.

When it came time to pick up the tab, it was all paid for by the clinic organizer. Eloise followed Jock back to the hotel, where he got her a room. But before she headed upstairs, he asked her to sit down for a chat.

Eloise made herself a cup of tea, and noticed they had "Sleepy time." It made her smile and think of Pinky. She had not had a hangover last time, just as Pinky had promised.

Eloise sat down and stirred her tea, letting it cool.

Jock sighed. "When you walked into the room you took my breath away."

"I'm wearing Mom's clothes. And carrying her hand-bag."

"You're so grown up. She would be so proud of you. That college degree, man, she was adamant that you do that. She wanted you to have a normal life."

"Whatever that means."

"It meant, not my life."

Jock abruptly changed the subject. "Do you have a fel-la?"

"My dog's name is Prince. He's my only fella'. But I'm ready to get back in the saddle. Do not smirk, I mean hors-es, not "fellas." Trying those horses for you reminded me how much I love riding."

"You need to ride, Lulu. It's who you are. You have tal-ent. I mean that."

Eloise drew a deep breath; she wasn't sure why she was suddenly nervous, but she was. "So, this new horse, the ad-vanced one. He's for your young rider?"

Jock said, "Totally. It's all about the kid. She's ambi-tious. And she can ride."

"I guess they're really happy with your coaching?"

Jock nodded again.

Eloise finally said, "Kid's learned a lot from Whiplash."

The time was now, so Eloise spit it out, "You know this isn't what I wanted. I know you were angry at me. I de-served it. I have a right to be angry too, you know. I can't say I'm sorry another time. But you've benefitted, this kid has benefitted from my horse. I'm ready to take my horse back. I want to have Whiplash back."

Jock looked thoughtful, then simply nodded his head.

Eloise felt a surge of relief, she had done it. She might not be going to Ireland to be part of her dad's life, but she would have her horse. Her exile, some self-imposed, could come to an end. She spoke quickly, "I'll pay for everything. I know shipping and all, and quarantine for a mare is what?"

Jock said, "She's good where she is, Eloise. You should think about Whiplash."

But then he paused a beat and totally changed his tone. "I have no doubt you can afford it. I do know a great quarantine farm in Kentucky. Mares stay two weeks."

Eloise felt she was about to clinch the deal. She brightened, "I'll pay for it. I can get Ralph to give me the funds."

Jock froze. "Ralph?"

Eloise felt confused. "Mom's money manager."

"I know who Ralph is. He thinks he's a damn dragon guarding a treasure. He was a pain during the divorce settlement. Surely you can do better than fussy little Ralph."

Eloise had apparently touched a sore spot regarding the divorce settlement. That treasure? That had been left to her. Did Jock resent that? Had she just blown it? She felt another hot wave wash over her. Jock had plenty of reasons to be angry with her, but she never had thought for a moment that he was jealous of the money left to her after her mom had died.

Eloise deflected. "Seems like a nice group you're teaching here. Cultivating a new base for business?"

She entertained for a nanosecond that maybe Jock was

returning to Atlanta to train and coach. If Jock worked here, she could be his assistant trainer. She could compete Whiplash, once again under Jock's coaching. The notion got shot down before it could be fully formed.

"No. I have too good a gig in Ireland. Besides ..."

"Besides what?"

"Lulu, I've decided to remarry. I expect that is hard for you to hear."

Poof went the fantasy, replaced by a hollow feeling in her chest, followed by anger then cynicism. Jock was closing the big deal. This trip had nothing to do with her. Nothing to do with trying to reconnect or express any sort of love or regret toward her or her mother. Instead, Eloise felt hurt on behalf of her mother.

She said matter-of-factly, "Must be the sponsor who just bought those two horses."

Jock shrugged, as if to say, 'You got me, there.'

"Is she connected to that young rider? The one who has my horse?" And when she said, it, she felt a flush of jealousy. "It's her *mother*?"

Eloise was suddenly very dizzy. She was glad to be sitting down. But she knew she needed to put her head down and slow down her breathing, so she did.

Jock stood up; he placed a hand on her back. "You still get those dizzy spells?"

Eloise was able to lift her head and say, "It always passes."

"I'm sorry, Lulu. I've upset you. Please, have breakfast with me tomorrow. You and I will be the only ones up so early. Let's say six am. Really, Lulu, this changes nothing."

Jock was right. This changed nothing. No matter what stories she concocted, what words she spoke, she had never been able to change a thing.

Eloise made her way to her room and got ready for bed. The sleepy-time tea wasn't working. She went through the motions, got into her pajamas, and tried to read. She decided to text Dabs, half hoping he wouldn't answer. He did. He must have been up late too.

"I just had dinner with Jock. He told me that I'm related to Thomas Jefferson (through marriage). He said a Robertson married Jefferson's Uncle Field."

It was several minutes before Dabs texted back, "I did a search and Field Jefferson was TJ's uncle. The older brother of his father Peter. Field Jefferson (Field was their mother's maiden name) married Mary Frances Robertson, and they had nine children. Jock knows his stuff."

"He's such a blowhard, I assumed he was spinning."

"Seems you come from old Virginia stock. But how was it otherwise to see your dad?"

"He told me he's decided to remarry. It's stupid, but it hit me hard."

"I'm sorry."

"I brought what I believe are Jock's old love letters to Mom. I imagined the way he took them from me would be a sign that he still loved her. I didn't even mention them. I'm not going to either. I can't believe I just told you all that, because until this moment I would never have admitted such a romantic bullshit notion."

"Don't be embarrassed."

"Why would I think such utter crap? He wasn't here

for me, or Mom when she got sick, but he took my horse. My horse. And now, what? He's got a new wife and a new daughter to coach, riding MY horse. He's replaced us. I did ask for my horse back. At least I'll get Whiplash back.

"I wish I were there with you."

"I think I'll burn the letters."

"That seems rash."

"But that's what happens in the movies, right?"

"I don't watch those kinds of films."

"OMG! How old ARE you? When you say stuff like that, I wonder."

"Some days I feel ancient. And some days you seem very young, although I know you are twenty-one. I'm thirty."

"How can you be only thirty? Honestly, I assumed you were retired like Betsy."

"I married young, went to law school, and got a job. Then my mother needed my care and attention, so I took a leave-of-absence. And then my marriage ended. The farm had become mine along with a trust fund when I turned twenty-one. Because of that, well, I was able to quit my job and stay here and try to figure things out."

"And have you figured things out?"

"No. Sorry to say. Regardless, don't let Jock tear you up, because he can't be what you want him to be. You can make your own family now. You have that power. Go ahead and use it."

"Thanks, Dabs."

"You're welcome. You really can't sleep?"

"No. And why are you still awake?"

"I'm transcribing the journal."

"That must be it."

"What?"

Eloise wrote, "Why you sound so old. In your head you're in the eighteenth century."

"True. Well, you are too, right?"

"Not as much as I'd like to be right now. Do you have something to send me?"

"I just finished up one. If you're sure you can't sleep."

"I'm counting on it."

"To the 18th century we go then. Good night, Louisa."

Eloise frowned. He had called her Louisa. She hesitated, then decided to humor him, as he had been a good sport, and had in fact calmed her down.

She typed, "Good night, Major."

* * *

August 1, 1779

We are free from quarantine at last. Buck jumped over the traces and ran to town the moment he could. He imbibed to excess and found a fight, returning home with ruddy cheeks and a scrape on his chin. Aunty Bess scolded him, not that it made an impression.

Myself, I visited Mary for an afternoon of diversion. Honesty prevents me from extolling the gaiety of the visit. Mary has a new babe and can talk of nothing else. It made for tiresome conversation.

Buck's foray to town has not made him less cantan-

kerous. Father had the boys bring up the remaining four-year-old horses to be started. Major Schmidt took the red gelding he had been promised as compensation, we call him Fox. Buck chose the large bay mare, we call Fashion. Isaac took the mule faced brown gelding called Friend. Father took the leggy red filly we call Flame. Father directs the process. Major Schmidt has a calm and steady hand, and Fox has made speedy progress.

Father believes that once the horses are accepting a rider, they learn from each other, so they ride as a group. Friend is placid by nature, so it was that Isaac led the group around the paddock, and the others followed.

I know why Buck chose Fashion. She is large, proud, and alert, without a trace of femininity. To look at her is to see a horse as they are depicted in military art and statuary. He works her without regard to her tender age or innocence. She looks like what she has not yet become. She will not suffer Buck's strong hand. I said so privately to both father and Major Schmidt.

Things came to a pass yesterday. Fashion had been bullied and reprimanded one time too many for not obeying commands she does not yet understand. She stood straight up upon her haunches, so straight that Buck slid down her spine and landed standing on his feet behind her. Fashion landed her front feet, then meant to kick the troublesome Buck with both hinds. He stood so close that she merely bumped him with her hips, knocking him to the ground.

Buck's pale complexion had turned florid. I feared

for Fashion. But instead, he pointed to Major Schmidt and said, "Step down, Major." He said it with such venom it stoppered all our mouths, even Father's. The Major stepped down quickly.

Buck then lightened his tone, but there was no sincerity in his voice. He said, "That gelding will likely run through cannon fire for me. I'll take a stalwart common soldier any day over a frightened female no matter how comely. You take the mare."

The Major quickly made the trade. Father made light of the moment, saying, "Major, ride Fashion next to Isaac. Ladies do enjoy believing they are in the lead."

The session recommenced with no further disturbances. Buck was sullen for the remainder of the day, but it appears only his pride was injured in the fracas. Later when I asked Bud, he said the Major was satisfied with the trade, as the mare is the better horse, and quite possibly the beginning of his own breeding program. Father, though, has lost his best young mare to the Major.

Major Schmidt has been performing for us after supper on his violin. It does cut into our reading time, but Father did remind me that one day when this war is over, Major Schmidt will be gone to his home across the ocean, and we will fondly remember these evenings of music.

Bud is quite taken. Bud has been so bold as to ask our guest to teach him. I told the Major he need not bother. But he claims to enjoy the boy. Bud does now babble on about it as we ride. He tells me he is mighty bad, that the instrument cries like a cat when he draws the bow across the strings. Bud is undeterred. He wants to learn to read music too. But how that can be when the child is untutored in even writing his own name? His die is cast I am afraid. As is my own. Kicking at traces or rearing upon one's hind legs, seems to me a pointless struggle.

16

Janet's voice was loud over the intercom, "Grooming appointment for Pinky, but I have a special request for Eloise to fetch this one."

Pinky looked up from the tub. "Expecting someone?"

Eloise shook her head.

Eloise jogged up the stairs, and into the waiting room to find the jellybean aficionado, purse-strings guy she had just been thinking about: Ralph.

Ralph had at heel a stocky Scottish Terrier, very much in need of grooming.

Ralph grinned, "Murtagh is well past needing a bath and grooming, and was overdue for vaccines, and so here I am, the new client."

"Murtagh, you named him Murtagh?"

"Yes. A character from Outlander. Murtagh was reserved but loyal and brave. This little fellow's love is of the reserved and dignified kind."

"You're an Outlander freak?"

"Oh yes. Books and show."

"Me too! Outlander is the best!"

Eloise knelt to meet Murtagh, His tail wagged in a slow

mechanical way, his nose began to vacuum her knees and moved up the front of her smock while she stroked him. Although he was stout, he was well formed, with muscular thighs and straight legs, and a short thick tail.

He stopped his inhalations to make eye contact. Lovely round eyes met hers in a probing examination. Here was a dog unafraid of making judgments. She felt, when he broke eye contact, that she had, in fact, passed muster.

Eloise said, "He's perfect! I expect Murtagh will keep your yard free of squirrels and chipmunks."

Eloise slipped her lead over Murtagh's head and un-buckled his collar. "Funny thing, I was going to call you."

Ralph bowed slightly, "At your service, Madam."

She giggled, feeling Ralph was role-playing from Out-lander. Then she got to the point, "I had dinner with Jock."

"Oh my. Jock is here?"

Ralph leaned in a little closer, as if Jock might hear him.

Eloise reassured Ralph, "No. He's on his way back to Ireland. But he's got my horse over there and I've decided I want her returned. I'll have to come up with the money to ship her back and find a place to board her. Then there's the money I'll need for the farrier and vet, tack, and supplies. Keeping a horse isn't cheap. I thought I'd never have a horse of my own again, but now, now I want to try."

Ralph looked serious and conspiratorial; his voice low. "You send me a budget and we can talk. Make sure it's realistic. No need to go where the prices are exclusionary by design. I am familiar with these things you know, because of your mother."

Eloise returned the serious expression; meant to show

Ralph she would not be frivolous. But inside she was glee-
ful. She met Ralph's eyes and he smiled, the corners of his
eyes creasing, his lips pursed as if to keep himself from
laughing.

"I think I just made someone happy."

Then he looked down at Murtagh, "Murtagh warms up
to people slowly, but he's a grand little man. I can't wait to
see him freshly barbered."

"Pinky is the best groomer anywhere. We'll make him
feel proud of himself."

Ralph left and Eloise realized she *was* happy. She felt
safe and although full of a sort of buzzy energy, relaxed.

Janet asked, "Who was that guy?"

"My financial advisor."

"You have a financial advisor?"

Eloise nodded.

Janet squinted her eyes and folded her arms across her
chest. "And you have a horse in Ireland?"

"It's a long story, but yeah."

Janet shook her head, "How do you get a horse here
from Ireland? Like do you use Fed-Ex or what?"

Janet looked both confused and slightly annoyed. Eloise felt her defenses soften. Soon everyone would know she
had a horse. Her horse.

She answered, "Sort of. Lots of companies fly horses.
They have special crates for the horses that look like the
horse trailers you see on the road, except no wheels. The
crates lock into the floor of the plane. Horses fly all the
time."

Janet uncrossed her arms, her brow wrinkled, "I've always known you were different, Eloise. But you're a different kind of different from what I thought."

"Um, I guess that beats being just the same old kind of different."

Eloise couldn't wait to see Pinky, her friend, who was not the same kind of different as Eloise, but a different kind of different just the same. She couldn't wait to share her happiness. Being happy made her want others to be happy too.

The morning flew by as Eloise brought Pinky up to speed. Soon it was lunchtime and Eloise had a new journal entry from Dabs to read.

* * *

August 30, 1779

On our second set of horses, Bud said, "Miss Louisa, I never ask for much, ain't that true?"

My ears pricked sensing danger. I said, "Well, now, you're no better than you must be. I gather you are about to tell me what this is about."

Bud, his demeanor serious, said, "I ask only for the grey kitten."

I nearly granted him his request then and there, as Father would not mind Bud taking a kit to his cabin once they were weaned. Cleopatra's kits were all skillful at containing vermin and had always been of use to us.

Instead, I reminded him, "Nothing can be yours, by law."

The lad began to cry, which shocked me. I had injured his feelings. I do not think of myself as cruel, and yet poor Bud was injured. I tried my best to mend the injury I had inflicted, I said, "It is the same for me, Bud. Father owns everything, and it is only by his good graces that I call this horse or dog my own. The law does not see it thus."

"So, it is Master Roberts I got to ask?"

I nodded thoughtfully, then asked, "You have set your heart on the grey one, then?"

Bud brightened, "Oh yes, Miss Louisa."

"What makes you want that grey kit so?"

"He's not white like Cleopatra, and he's not black like the Tom. He's half and half like me."

I suppose I should not have been, but I was struck dumb while the child prattled on about never having had his own pet, no cat nor dog nor horse, and did I think Father would allow it?

Bud was noting the obvious. Maisie's boys were all of a light tone. Around these parts, the slaves came in all shades, some nearly as fair as I. It was not a topic of polite conversation, but always noted for the purpose of identifying runaways.

Bud continued about "his" kitten. He was a child like any child. He loved the horses; he loved my dog. I even think he loved me, and I him. Yet, he could never hope to have even my freedoms, limited as I saw them to be.

Bud must have felt emboldened, for next he said, "Major Schmidt, he says I'm doing better on his fiddle, that if I study and practice that one day I may best him with my playing. Ain't that something?"

Since I had already made Bud cry once that day, I refrained from pointing out that Major Schmidt would leave us one day, and most certainly take his "fiddle" with him. Then Bud said the most outrageous thing, He said, "Major Schmidt, I think he sweet on you."

I said, "Don't be impertinent."

"I thought you would like that, Miss Louisa. I heard gals like it when a fella was sweet on them."

I was becoming increasingly irritated, I said, "I could never love a man with a caterpillar slouching across his upper lip."

Bud began to giggle. And I couldn't help but join in. By the time we returned to the barn, we were barely containing ourselves. The Major, Buck, and Isaac were putting away their young string, and the Major noticed. He asked what had caused such merriment.

I answered seriously, "As it is soon to be fall, Bud and I were discussing wooly caterpillars. They are harbingers of winter you know."

The Major looked interested. "And you and Bud, you saw such a sight on your ride?"

Bud, the imp, said, "Yes, Sir, Major. We see 'em every day, and Miss Louisa, she takes a special aversion to them."

And then Bud and I made eye contact, which sent

us into a new fit of the giggles, puzzling the poor Major.

* * *

Eloise texted Dabs as soon as she finished reading the entry. "Thanks for the latest entry. Louisa is such a good storyteller. She includes pathos and ethos but cleverly ends her entry with humor."

Then she couldn't help herself, she had news to share. "Guess what? I saw Ralph, my financial advisor, about the expense of bringing Whiplash back to Atlanta. He said to draw up a budget. First, I got Prince, and now I'm getting Whiplash, the stars are beginning to align."

"You're going to be very busy. I hope you'll stay interested in our little project.'

Eloise thought it a strange reply. "Of course. I just thought you'd be interested in hearing my news."

"I just wanted you to know that if you get too busy, I'll understand."

Eloise frowned at the text, she was supposed to be sharing her happiness, but Dabs wasn't reacting the way she expected. "I won't get too busy. Don't worry."

"Do you know where you're going to keep her?"

"Not yet."

"You'll want more than basic board. Around here winter requires an indoor arena. That comes at a premium."

"We had a small indoor at our place. We needed it in winter, and in the summer when the rains came too. Yes, I'll want either an indoor or a covered arena."

"Why not board at your old farm?"

"Can't. It's private."

"Too bad. I'll bet you know everyone in the area. Call your old riding friends."

Dabs couldn't know why that wasn't an option. She couldn't face any of them. She couldn't revisit any of it, even to herself. She'd let everyone think she was moving to Ireland. That she'd been with Jock training horses since, since the funeral.

She deflected. "Did I tell you that Jock scored a big money sponsor and possibly the next Mrs. Robertson by using my horse. Ugh."

"You told me, but perhaps you shouldn't dwell on it. Focus on the future. You have friends. I hope you'll consider me one of them."

Dabs was sounding old and weird again, and pitiful, like he needed bucking up. And he was dragging down her happiness.

She said, "Of course. And yeah, that's good advice. Thank you for sharing Louisa's journals with me. They are not just history, but likely your history, and I feel privileged to read them."

"They are special. Louisa is special."

Was Dabs depressed?

Eloise piled it on. "Because of you sharing, I've been given a rare opportunity. Insight. This makes the world of Thomas Jefferson, distant and foreign, feel close and personal."

Dabs replied, "We *are* reading firsthand of this strange land where slavery existed, and it's nearly unthinkable that it all was right here. I think of Louisa holding Bud as a baby. They grew up together. She enjoyed recounting their joke on the Major. But there is a boundary that exists because of slavery, that cannot be crossed. I find the situation heartbreaking. This all happened right here in my home."

"Dabs, are you okay?"

"Yeah. Sorry. I'm just feeling the weight of it all today. That's all. I'll go take a break with Dude and get some fresh air and be right as rain."

* * *

Eloise quickly forgot about Dab's weirdness. Instead, she began her search for a boarding barn by calling Bev.

Bev picked up before the second ring and shouted, "Whatever you're selling, I ain't buyin'!"

"Is this Bev? It's Eloise Robertson."

"Jock's girl?"

Eloise cringed. Because of course, she was "Jock's girl."

"Yeah. I came and rode the red mare for Jock."

"Mare's still here. You want her?"

"Jock told me he bought her."

"Rather sell her to you. You two got on good."

"Jock's not going to buy her?"

"Maybe. If you're not going to, then why'd ya' call?"

"I'm looking for a place to board my horse. I just thought you'd give me a good recommendation. Plus, I need to make up a budget, and I'm not sure how much I should expect to pay."

Bev bellowed, "Cool your jets, Jethro. I'll get you when I get this one put up."

Eloise realized Bev was yelling at a horse, not her.

"What time you plan on riding each day?"

"I get off work in Buckhead at three pm, but some days I run a little late."

"Traffic's a bitch from Buckhead to anywhere. Tell you what, you come on up tomorrow after work and see how long it takes. Dress to ride. Red needs a gallop."

"Uh, sure. Can I bring my dog?"

"Long as he don't chase horses."

As Eloise put down her phone, she had a vision. She was cantering Whiplash around that field of Bev's, and up ahead of her ran Prince. The vision evaporated but left her with a hopeful feeling. She didn't mean to invite herself to board at Bev's. It was probably too far a drive. Eloise hadn't seen a covered or indoor arena and winter was coming. However, at Bev's she wouldn't have to see "people." If nothing else, she would enjoy another gallop and give Prince some exercise.

* * *

It was mid-afternoon when Janet buzzed through. "Eloise, Doc's ready for Murtagh Jameson."

Murtagh was leaning against the front of the cage, his eyes closed, his mouth open. Eloise opened the door and he nearly fell out. "Hey, buddy, naptime is over." She slipped the lead over his head, and he dutifully trotted behind her up the stairs.

Doc was chatting with Susie when they came in. Doc said, "You can stay, Eloise. I'll be done in a jiffy. I'll try to meet Mr. Jameson too when he comes to pick up..."

Doc looked at the chart, "...Murtagh?"

Eloise met Doc's eyes, "It's a character from Outlander. You know, the books and tv series."

Eloise hoisted the little dog up onto the exam table with a grunt, "Murtagh, my friend, you are a lot heavier than you look."

Doc performed his usual exam. Susie briefly held the dog while Doc drew blood. Murtagh was stoic, standing like a rock, devoid of emotion.

Doc said, "He is solid. Powerful hind legs."

Eloise added, "Front paws made for digging out Badgers."

Doc continued, "Long muzzle for poking down holes."

Eloise said, "Thick of neck, stout of chest, sharp of tooth."

Susie rolled her eyes, "You two! He'll spend his time sleeping on the furniture. And in the winter, he'll be trotted out on a leash wearing a plaid coat. And those teeth, the only guts they'll be tearing out will be the guts of squeaky toys."

Doc laughed, "Well, we are in Buckhead."

Eloise said, "He's owned by my um," and she glanced at Susie, "my banker. He's helping me learn about budgets and stuff."

Doc gave Eloise a sly smile. "Budgets? Let me guess what costly thing you are trying to afford. Could it be...horses?"

Susie rolled her eyes again, shaking her head.

But Eloise couldn't hide her excitement, "Yes! I'm ready to take Whiplash back. Jock didn't offer to pay the transport costs. Ralph, I mean Mr. Jameson, and I are going to figure it out though. I've got to come up with the money to import her. It won't be cheap."

Doc warned, "With a mare, you have a longer quarantine. That adds to the expense. Don't forget the shipping from JFK to the quarantine in Kentucky and then to Atlanta."

"Ralph didn't say no."

Eloise pulled out her phone and pulled up the photo of Whiplash that she had found online. It was too bad that the photo had the kid on her instead of Eloise. Eloise passed the phone to each of them to have a look because suddenly it did not matter that Doc and Susie knew about Whiplash. She was happy and anticipating more happiness.

Susie scowled, "That's your horse?"

Doc pulled his glasses up to look closer, "She's a beauty."

Doc added, "Where will you keep her?"

"I'm going to Bev's this afternoon. It's a possibility."

Doc nodded, "I approve. That old gal was tough as shoe leather, but she reminded me of my old man."

Doc gave the Scotty the vaccines he had lined up on the counter, and then a few rubs, and the dog's tail did a slow tick-tock wag before Doc set him back on the floor.

Doc said, "I can't wait to see this little guy after Pinky clips him."

Susie added, "Betcha' Pinky puts a plaid scarf on him."

Eloise smiled, "I think I saw one in her collection."

Before Eloise left the room, Doc said, "Eloise, I'm feeling a bit jealous."

Susie looked from one to the other and said, "Noooo! Doc, no way. You told me you quit large animal because you were getting beat-to-hell. You can't be serious about going back to all that. Please don't catch the horse bug from Eloise."

Eloise said, "Doc and I already had the bug, it's just been dormant. But it's not dormant any longer, is it, Doc?"

Doc just went, "Hmmm."

Eloise smiled; she wanted Doc to feel as happy as she felt right this moment.

"I wonder if Bev has anything you could ride?"

17

Bev greeted Eloise as she got out of her car, Prince on a leash. "Might as well turn him loose. I got other plans for your two hands."

Eloise did as she was told. "Stay close, okay?" She realized, as she turned Prince loose, that she trusted him. And she was right. Prince stayed by her side as Eloise followed Bev into the barn and straight down the aisle and out the back. To Eloise's surprise there was another long building directly behind the barn.

Bev walked into the building through a dented metal door. "Damn if I didn't run the drag right into a rotten spot in the kickboard. It ain't going nowheres like that."

Eloise followed Bev through the dented door with the open-mouthed reverence of someone entering a cathedral. "You have an indoor arena!"

"Built thirty years ago. Took me twenty to pay the damn thing off. Comes in handy though."

Eloise refocused on the tine of the arena drag that was stuck in the rotten base board.

Bev asked, "You want to drive or pull?"

The tractor looked like it was held together by rust.

243

"Pull."

"That's best. I got no grip strength. Sure am in a pickle. Can't go forward, can't back up with the drag down. So, I'm gonna' use the lifter to pick up the drag a skosh, see if you can pop the tine out at the same time. Grab that old longe line off the wall."

Eloise got the longe line, and Bev ran it around the frame of the drag. Then she handed it to Eloise.

"An inch just might be enough."

Prince stood by Eloise's side; head tipped as if he was studying the problem, a member of the team. Bev got into the seat of the tractor and started it up. Diesel fumes coughed out of the tailpipe before the engine purred loudly. Bev started to fiddle with the lifter. It looked hopeless, but Bev was undeterred. She yelled over the engine, "On the count of three. Dig in your heels and put your back into it."

Eloise could see the frame of the drag make little spasms as the tractor tried to lift the drag.

"One, two, three, PULL!"

The tine popped out with a satisfying "Ping!" Bev popped the clutch and the tractor reared up and the drag bounced. Eloise, who had put all her weight into the line, found herself sitting in the arena sand. Prince bounced around barking. Mission accomplished!

Eloise stood and dusted off her butt.

Bev put the tractor in gear and drove away from the rotten kickboard.

"Good you came. Couldn't have done that myself."

Eloise hoped Bev's comment was a sign she might let her board there.

She shut off the tractor and got off stiffly. Eloise pulled the longe line off the drag, then wrapped it into a figure eight and tied it off, just as her parents had taught her. She handed the line to Bev.

Bev said, "Go on and get Red. I'll finish up here. I set her stuff by the wash stall."

"Will she mind Prince do you think?"

"Guess we'll find out."

When Bev finished dragging the arena, she joined Eloise in the barn. Eloise had tacked up a very wiggly "Red." Prince was in a "down-stay"…mouth open, tail thumping.

"Dog's got some training. You do that?"

"No. Someone else. He's a rescue, but what a good boy. That's why he's called Prince."

"I like him. He's welcome here."

Then she lifted her chin toward Red. "Best give her a twirl before you climb on."

"Is it necessary for every ride?"

"Maybe you like to gamble? Jock sure did. Jock always thought the odds were in his favor. Mostly he was right."

Eloise felt her jaw tighten. "I'm not Jock."

"Day will come that you'll skip the longing because the mare is stronger and more trained, like that dog there."

"My odds will be better?"

"It ain't gambling if you're certain of the outcome."

Eloise had not yet asked Bev about boarding. But she intuitively knew not to. Bev was watching her, judging her.

The red mare was perfect on the longe. The ride in the arena was uneventful again. Prince too was well-behaved ringside.

After about fifteen minutes of riding, Bev sent her to the field. Eloise called Prince to follow, and he bounced up from his down-stay and ran to her in a crazy zoomie zigzag. Red spooked and twirled a complete 360 degrees. Eloise managed to stay in the middle of Red's back, giving her a kick and a cluck to encourage her to go forward after the dog who was already through the gate as if he knew the plan.

She heard Bev cackle, "You're Jock's girl alright."

Eloise had accomplished Jock's number one rule for riding. She had kept the horse between herself and the ground. She couldn't help but feel proud of herself. Her body had remembered.

The three of them made their way around the field. Red was watching Prince out of one eye, head tipped, wary but growing braver.

Eloise picked up the trot, and Prince managed to keep with the horse as they completed a lap. But then Red took the hill at a gallop, leaving Prince far behind.

Eloise pulled up at the top of the hill and waited for Prince, Red blowing. There he came, loping up the hill, tongue hanging out. The three of them stood in silence, gazing out at a grassy hillside that was going to seed. A large Cooper Hawk drifted overhead, and Eloise stroked the neck of the mare and tugged gently at her mane. There in the field, atop a red mare, a good dog by their side, re-emerged from some hidden place the wounded Lulu, ready to try again.

Some wheel had turned, some inexplicable something clicked into place, not in her head, but in her heart. It was an internal click and catch that lifted Eloise, just for that moment, and gave her a sense of expectation, of hope. What she had said was never to be again, was finding its way back to her, unbidden, but welcome just the same.

* * *

September 3, 1779

I have been remiss in my writing. But today was eventful and I am compelled to take up my pen.

Major Schmidt has taken to joining Bud and me with his new mare Fashion on our ride each morn. Fashion has taken a shine to the Major. I do believe she would move into his cabin with him, Cleopatra, and her kits. Bud too, but he spends every moment there as it stands. What odd companions. But war, it seems, makes for strange bedfellows. Fashion is a talkative mare. She will call to the Major, she will call to Beauty, and she will call to Fanny. The three mares enjoy each other's company. If the younger fillies get nervous, they look to Beauty, and they emulate her behavior.

This morning the Major was first to the barn, and had prepared his mare, and surprised me by having Beauty prepared too. But the true surprise was to find the Major sans mustache! I am appalled to admit that my first impulse was to kiss him. And then without having uttered a single word or moved an inch from my spot, I was mortified to realize he had read my thought. A grin had spread across his lips.

247

He said, "The verdict? I confess to some measure of vanity, Miss Roberts. Please tread gently."

I said, "I never would have thought you a vain man, Major."

He said, "No less than most men I expect. But you do not yet say if it is an improvement."

Beast sat down on my feet. Something he often does when I stay in place for a spell. It allowed me to look down and stroke his head. I did not look up as I answered. I said, "I will not be coy. Yes."

The Major must have taken my assent as referring to much more than his loss of facial hair. With Beast wedged between us, he placed a warm hand behind my neck and gave me a tender kiss that was finished before it was started. My arm reached naturally around his back. But, too soon, he was back at the side of Fashion, tightening her girth, as Bud joined us, prattling on about his kitten.

Even now as I write this, I recall the warmth of his kiss, the smoothness of his lips. I felt dizzy and quite honestly, disappointed at the brevity. But I do feel grateful for the large bulk of my dog, grounding me. I thought about how easy Beast was, including himself in our embrace. I also admit to not possessing any instinct for restraint.

I have been kissed before. I will not lie in my own journal. But such puppy fumbling as I have experienced do not compare. I shall stop before I appear cruel, even in my own writings, it is too much.

Bud and the Major have named the kittens, al-

*though how they tell the blacks apart I have not a clue.
Bud's grey kitten they have named Lady Jane. Bud had
to be told who Lady Jane Grey was. I didn't have the
heart to tell him of her unfortunate end. I had no idea
how they determined it was female. Bud did attempt
to explain. He said the Major told him it was a matter
of grammar. He said this in all seriousness. I asked for
clarification. Bud explained, female kits sport an up-
side-down exclamation point while male kits punctu-
ate with a colon. When I asked where the punctuation
marks could be seen, he looked surprised at my ignorance. Bud said you only must lift the tail. Bud cannot
read or write, and now his first lesson of grammar has
been pure sophistry. I did not laugh but thanked him
for educating me. This may be the only grammar the
boy ever need know.*

*The war news is scarce. Buck and Father follow the
papers, but the news is always old. Savannah is still
held by the British, though under siege. Buck is itching
to return to the fight. Jefferson is calling for our militia
to go to South Carolina. But no Virginian would leave
his country unprotected knowing the enemy will surely
turn toward us soon. And so, Jefferson is frustrated.
Father is not willing to see Buck leave yet and Aunt
Bess is adamant he stays. We go about our business.
But we are always waiting for something to change,
knowing it could, one way or another.*

*And our Major Schmidt has woven himself into the
fabric of our lives. Father has discovered that the Major is a fair opponent at Chess. They have quiet games*

that oft run into multiple days of play. Buck used to play. But for this too, he now has no patience. He is an unsettled man. When Buck enters the room, all grow wary. Priscilla nearly hugs the walls to pass him by.

Sammie is well enough to work on jobs that are not taxing. He is a fair hand at strap-work. And now he is to clean all our tack at the end of each training day. Much of this can be done while sitting. Father still expects Sammie to run from us once he is stronger. But where? And if he runs, he leaves behind Priscilla who did declare her feelings. But I have not seen Priscilla and Sammie together, not even to nod at each other. Just the opposite. The two seem like opposing magnetic fields, they repel instead of attract, backing away from any path where they may collide.

* * *

The next morning Doc brought in a flat of donuts, set it on the counter and poured himself a cup of coffee. He held up the pot in a salute to Eloise, "Top off?"

He picked up Eloise's mug, topped it off, handing it to Eloise. Next, he handed her a donut. "They're still warm."

Eloise took the donut and bit into it. "Thank you."

Doc leaned against the counter. "So, how was it at Bev's?"

"I stayed two hours."

"Two hours?"

"I rode the Red Devil again. I took Prince too."

"Bev didn't mind the dog?"

"Bev liked him. And when I went to the field, he kept up with us. It was great."

"Bev's an interesting gal."

"She asked me to come ride Red after work weekdays and help her do evening chores."

"Isn't the mare leaving soon?"

"She said she hadn't cashed the check. She didn't say why."

Doc, took a donut, took a bite, then looked thoughtful. "Strange."

"I get the feeling I'm on trial. She never told me how much for boarding and I was too chicken to ask outright. But at least she asked me to come back."

"That's not going to satisfy your friend Ralph. Better call around. At least give him a range." Doc turned to leave.

"I forgot to tell you the most important part. Bev has a small indoor. It looks rough, but at least the footing has been maintained."

Doc turned halfway. "Wow. Somehow, we missed that. You may have stumbled into a good arrangement, as long as you make yourself useful to Bev, that is."

"Bev's an odd duck, but I don't mind. Plus, she liked Prince."

* * *

Dabs texted Eloise, "So, it looks like we may have a budding romance."

Eloise felt her face flush as she texted back, "???"

"Louisa and the Major. Oh, God, Sorry."

Now it was Eloise's turn to feel embarrassed, "No, I'm sorry. I have been so absorbed and excited about the prospect of getting Whiplash back. I'm slow to switch gears, but I DID love getting the latest entry. In a way I'm a tiny bit disappointed in Louisa, though."

"Why?"

"It seems so, I don't know, a normal teenager type entry for a journal. And yet, she is certainly not a normal teenager."

"But why wouldn't she and Major Schmidt become an item? She has clearly been attracted to him from the first. Even Aunt Bess saw it. Then there is proximity."

"Or lack thereof when he returns to his homeland. It's bound to have a sad ending."

"That's cynical. Plenty of Hessian's chose to stay."

"You think they have a future? Buck's going to inherit the place, and he doesn't like Major Schmidt. Major Schmidt is opposed to slavery. Slavery will not end for what, um hold on, eighty-five years. So, it is not going to be one happy household, not after Mr. Roberts is out of the picture."

"Well, clearly you are not a romantic."

Eloise typed, "Reality bites. But there it is. And besides, the only thing we know survives that war is that house you are living in."

Dabs wrote, "Better to have loved and lost..."

"OMG. You ARE a romantic."

"The man shaved off his mustache for the girl!!!"

For the first time ever, Eloise thought Dabs didn't come across like some 18th century prude.

She smiled to herself, "Okay. He deserved that kiss. But Louisa better watch herself. Aunt Bess will not be best pleased."

Now who was sounding like an 18th century prude!

Dabs said, "Watch your inbox for the next installment."

* * *

Eloise opened her email hoping for a new journal entry from Dabs. Instead, she found a note from Jock.

Hey Lulu,

I need a favor. Bev is not returning my calls or texts. Can I get you to check on her and the mare? The gelding shipped last week. We have him here and he looks terrific. I've just ridden him lightly, but so far, I'm impressed. Good work!

Whiplash sustained a mild ligament injury. We have put her on stall rest and shock wave treatments. She should be fine in about six weeks. Please don't worry, we have first class care here. We even have an aqua tread down the road we can use for reconditioning work once she is given the green light to rehab.

It was great to see you and I'm glad you are making a life for yourself there. I sure am glad to hear you are ready to get back in the tack. You need to be riding.

Let me know what is up with Bev.

Jock

Jock's email hit Eloise hard. Horses did sustain injuries, but why now? Whiplash had made it into her teens without ever hurting herself. Whiplash was a tough mare with exceptional balance. If she stayed sound, she would have years and years of competing ahead of her. Jock had used her horse to get what he wanted. And now, now that she wanted the ride back, the mare was out of commission. This was a pin in her balloon. "Man plans and God laughs."

And the Red Devil? Jock was anxious about closing that deal and taking delivery. That ride would go to Jock. Where did that leave her? With nothing, that's what.

It felt like Jock was punishing her. Again.

Her one consolation was Prince. When they climbed into bed, instead of stretching out, he propped himself up on his elbows, placed a paw across her forearm and stared at her. Eloise stroked the top of his head with her free hand and began to calm. Prince had been amazing today, staying with her, staying with Red. After a few minutes, Prince removed his paw, got up and turned a circle, and settled, job done. She did feel better.

The next day, Eloise was walking dogs. She had a padded strap around the hindquarters of an old Keeshond with neurological problems, helping "Elsa" to squat on the grass, and wobble her way back to the cage where she was resting on a thick cushion. Eloise had the job of making sure Elsa was taken out extra times a day for gentle supported movement, because of concerns of pressure sores and circulation.

Eloise found herself wiping tears from her face. When Eloise returned from the walk with Elsa, she found Pinky counting the number of grooming jobs for the day, coffee cup in hand.

Pinky narrowed her eyes studying Eloise. "You've been crying. I've never seen you cry before."

"Seeing Elsa wobble around did me in this morning."

"She's a really old dog, Eloise. But she is also a happy dog. Eating, peeing, and pooping. If she is comfortable, safe, and getting and returning affection, well, life is not so bad for Elsa, is it?"

Eloise nodded, put Elsa in the big cage at floor level, squatting down and getting her settled, the canned special dog food placed right at her chin, a bowl of fresh water next to it. Elsa wolfed down the food, then lapped at the fresh bowl of water. Eloise waited for her to finish before removing the bowls. She arranged her hind legs in a way that looked comfortable, then leaned in and kissed the dog on the top of her head.

Kissing the dog on the head started the tears flowing again. Eloise thought to herself that no one likes to be pitied, no matter how pitiful.

Pinky crossed her arms and leaned back against her grooming table.

"You going to tell me what's going on?"

"Okay. Yeah. Jock is back in my life and it's killing me."

Then she showed Pinky the email on her phone.

Still looking at the email, Pinky nodded at it, "I agree with one line for sure. You need to be riding." She handed Eloise back her phone and looked her in the eye. "You can ride with or without Jock in your life. I don't know why you give him so much power."

18

September 15, 1779

Beast and I found Buck into his cups sitting with no light but the glowing fire. I meant only to take my book from the table, but he put out a hand and stopped me from leaving. He asked me to sit, and I obliged, but with trepidation, one hand upon my dog.

Buck said, "This prisoner is no proper match for you, sister."

I could not see the hackles rise upon the back of my dog but did feel his body stiffen. As long as father lived, Buck had no power over me.

I asked, "What eats at you so?"

This disarmed my brother. He frowned and looked thoughtful.

He then said, "If we lose this war, we will be brought to heel. Those who led the rebellion will be hanged. Nearly the first of those hanged will be our illustrious neighbor."

I opened my mouth but then shut it. Buck's eyes were glassy, his body slumped to the back of his chair.

He seemed to be speaking to himself. My dog was beginning to let down his guard, reading the body language of my drunk brother as no threat.

He continued, "If we fail, they will confiscate the land and property of all who took up arms against the King, and all of that will be given as spoils of war to the loyalists."

Buck refocused on me. "I must go back to the fight. But here all is uneasy for me. You fawn over a man who would fight to take all from us. He is the enemy, Louisa, no matter the music he can make, how grandly he sits a horse, or how much father enjoys his game of chess. If I meet him on the field of battle, I will be obliged to kill him."

Beast lifted his head to watch my reply, stiffening his body once again. I tried to speak in level tones, though my innards quaked.

"Major Schmidt is a good man who has left the fight. He is a prisoner of war. You will not meet him on the field of battle. He is a friend to me, to father, and especially to little Bud."

"Bud?" He snorted in disgust. "Major Schmidt is subversive. Bud is what he will always be. Our property. There is an order to this world we live in, and once turned upside down, all is lost. Sammie must be sold off because his mind is ruined, and Major Schmidt must return to barracks, because both seek to subvert the rightful order. We must assert our rights, because once we yield them, we invite our own slaughter."

"Buck you are over-reacting."

257

Now he slammed his fist into the table, causing both myself and Beast to startle.

"Louisa, look about you! There are far more servants in our country than masters. Do you not read of uprisings?"

At this I rose from my seat. I said, "The tyranny of our race over the darker complected one far exceeds the tyranny of England over us. Yet, you are willing to kill good Major Schmidt to be freed of British tyranny? All whilst fearing reprisals for your tyranny over the likes of Sammie. Your inability to see the hypocrisy of your position, well it appalls me."

Buck appeared shocked. I had surprised myself, realizing where my words had been borrowed. Major Schmidt had indeed affected both my opinion and my boldness.

Buck growled his retort, "And your naivete' sickens me. You have been reading the flights of fancy of our neighbor. I intend to keep what is mine or die trying."

Buck was not finished.

Buck sneered again most threateningly. "You must have a husband and babes. And not with our enemy."

I nearly lost composure, gripping the scruff of my dog, lest he try to do my fighting for me. I answered with steely reserve. "You have made your feelings plain. You must do as you see fit. And I will do the same."

I left the room quick as I could, book pressed to my chest, my other hand pulling Beast's scruff to stay at heel.

* * *

Betsy and Eloise brought Prince along to dine and people-watch at a sidewalk Bistro. Buckhead was buzzing with shoppers. Betsy ordered salmon salad, and Eloise the Asian salad. Eloise pulled a chew-bone out of her satchel and handed it to Prince when their food arrived, and he stretched out with it by her feet.

Eloise had revealed to Betsy tidbits of Louisa's revolutionary story, breaking her confidence with Dabs. Betsy pressed her for details, and pressed on, until Eloise had folded and revealed far too much.

Betsy said, "I really wish Dabs would let me see it too."

"I'm a rat to have said what I've said. These are his ancestors. The journal is his treasured find. If he found out I told you, I might never see another word. I feel like I've betrayed Dabs."

"I promise. You need not say more."

"Thanks, Betsy."

"How about we discuss it in light of Jefferson, that takes some of the heat off you. The journal doesn't have to be explicitly mentioned."

Betsy was crafty.

Eloise said, "Well...You know how in fiction people get zapped back two hundred plus years ala' 'Outlander?' They experience the past not as those of the time did, but as a person from their own time. That feels like me. I can't help but judge them by my modern standards. But still, mind-blown by what they have to say. Stuff that has stuck with me."

Betsy agreed, "You get to know, or even love, people long dead, and though you can't change them, they can change you. Isn't that remarkable?"

Eloise leaned in and lowered her voice, "I kind of have fallen in love with Major Schmidt. Louisa, not so much."

"Ah, but don't forget it is Louisa who made you fall in love with him. Have you considered that?"

That thought made Eloise pause, then sit up straighter and frown.

"Oh my God. Wow. That thought changes everything. Louisa is a sharp and witty observer but not often kind. But, when she describes the Major, it is always in ways that makes him admirable. Her father too. And her Aunt. Not her brother. She describes him well, but not ever in a flattering light."

"Point of view is always something to consider…"

Prince jumped up like he'd been bitten by something.

A woman screamed.

Chairs scraped against the pavement as all the diners rose from their seats. Women reflexively grabbed their bags.

The shoppers on the sidewalk parted like the Red Sea. People were shouting and pointing.

The words "STOP THIEF!" was the loudest.

A man came hurtling through the crowd, loaded down with … pocketbooks?

Prince was off like a bullet. Someone screamed in terror. Prince somehow understood which body was the target. The thief, loaded with pocketbooks in his arms, saw the dog too. He came to a skidding stop, head swiveling to look for another path. Prince plowed into his chest at full force, the dog's jaws clamping down on the arm he had flung across his throat.

The man landed hard upon his back on the sidewalk, yelling "Help!" Eloise ran to her dog, who was now wagging his tail and rolling his eyes up at her under his bushy eyebrows. Prince gave the man's arm a couple of good tugs and shakes.

He was crying out, "He's biting me, he's biting me!"

Eloise told Prince to "LEAVE IT!" and he let go and backed away, barking with excitement.

Some man had put his foot on the thief's chest, telling him to freeze. A blubbering salesgirl was crying and thanking everyone.

Eloise took Prince's trailing leash and backed away from the crowd. Sirens soon followed and, in an instant, police were swarming around the perpetrator. All for a shoplifter? Well, it had been dramatic.

Eloise made her way to Betsy.

Betsy took charge. "You hold onto him; I'm going inside and settle up."

Eloise saw someone point her out to a police officer. They made their way to her, and she answered their questions and gave them her contact information. Then she noticed that a local TV station van had pulled over and double-parked.

Betsy came out of the restaurant and took Eloise by the elbow, "You don't look so hot."

"I get dizzy when I get too excited. It passes. But let's get out of here."

"Police through with you?"

Eloise nodded back, but before she and Betsy could step away, a reporter walked straight up to Eloise smiling, his camera man at his back.

"Here is our hero of the day. I understand this dog knocked down the shoplifter. That's extraordinary. Your name?"

"Eloise Robertson."

And your dog's name?

"Prince."

"Well, everyone here says your dog is the reason the shoplifter was stopped. Tell me Eloise, is he a trained protection dog?"

Eloise's voice was nearly a whisper, "I don't think so. I got him from a rescue. He's a great dog though."

Prince, who had retrieved his bone, was sitting, tail thumping as the cameraman zoomed in for a closeup. He looked proud of himself.

The reporter enthused, "I'd say so. How about that? A rescue dog was the hero of the day. I have to say, he doesn't look like an attack dog. What breed is he?"

Eloise shrugged.

The reporter reached over and gave him a pat on the head, but Prince was not looking at the reporter, he was studying Eloise. And she was studying him. She loved him. And he loved her, she felt that to be true. But he did not really belong to her. She needed him, she deserved him, he had looked for her and found her. He was her Prince. And they lived happily ever after, too. But then why did this amazing incident, further proof of his canine genius, make her feel sick?

The reporter looked into the camera, "There you have it folks, today a rescue dog stopped the theft of high-end designer handbags, worth thousands of dollars."

Eloise was relieved to get Prince into her car and sit down because the light-headedness had gotten bad, but still, she started the engine and drove away.

* * *

At work Eloise had been required to repeat the story of the Prince takedown. For once, Eloise put no effort into story-telling, and the day and the topic, driven by more pressing tasks.

But Pinky, once they were in the basement, kept probing for details, lifting an eyebrow in that way she did.

Then, oddly, Pinky asked if she could tag along to watch her ride Red. Eloise couldn't think of a reason to say no, and why should she? She'd enjoy Pinky's company.

So, after Pinky had finished her last dog, Eloise followed her home, and then Pinky climbed into Eloise's car.

Prince thought having Pinky in the front seat was exciting. And honestly, Eloise felt better for her company. Eloise's mood had been lightened.

When they arrived, Eloise introduced Pinky again to Bev.

"Bev, you remember Pinky. She came with me the first day we tried Red."

Pinky raised her hand, "Hiya. I'm the friend who is totally ignorant about horses."

263

Bev squinted at Pinky, taking in her blue high tops and pink hair.

"Don't get yourself bitten, kicked, or stepped on. Horses are damn dangerous."

Pinky did not seem to notice the twinkle in Bev's eye.

"Yes, ma'am. If you see me about to do something stupid, please save me."

"It'll likely take both me and Eloise to keep you unscathed. No promises, but we'll do our best, won't we, Eloise?"

"Bev, she's the only human company I have in the basement where I work at the clinic. Can't let anything happen to her."

The three of them, (well, the four of them if you count Prince) headed into the dark and cool barn, as Eloise spoke to Bev. "Jock is irritated with you."

Bev nodded.

"He wants to know what's up with the mare."

"Course he does. Whiplash?"

"Not good news I'm afraid."

"He ain't gonna' turn her loose, is he?"

That stopped Eloise in her tracks.

"What? How did you . . . ? That's my horse. Jock has reasons to be mad at me. But it doesn't give him the right to keep what's mine."

Bev nodded.

Pinky was silent, but grim-faced, not making any sense of it, but reading Eloise loud and clear.

Eloise deflated, "But when I saw him, he agreed to send her back."

Bev turned to Pinky. "See that hose there on the reel. Turn it on and start at this end and top off all the buckets. Down one side and back up the other. Don't let any of the fresh ones take a finger off."

Pinky saluted and headed for the hose reel, looking only a tiny bit nervous.

Bev turned to Eloise. "Now the way I see it, we've got something Jock wants. And Jock, he got something you want."

"Jock said Whiplash has a ligament tear. Six weeks of rest and then rehab."

"Could be true. Could be Jock come up with that to put you off, buy him some time."

"You think he made it up?"

"Maybe you know a different Jock than I do?"

Eloise was appalled, as much by Bev as by Jock. She didn't mean to sound angry. "You have something against Jock?"

"Don't be gettin' your dukes up. I got a warm place in my heart for Jock. But that don't mean I'm blind to imperfections. Still, I once felt real sorry for him. Jock walked away with nothin' but the good looks and charm God gave him. Elly and Jock were a right good match, one wasn't cleverer than the other. It's just that Elly won that round."

Eloise heard what Bev had just said, but she wasn't really listening.

"Whiplash belongs to me."

"Hmm. Jock never was one to let facts get in his way. Didn't you say his Junior went to Europeans on the mare?"

Eloise nodded.

"Went well, did it?"

"But he just bought that fancy advanced horse for her."

They had stopped in front of Red's stall, and Red picked up her head and came to the front of the stall.

Bev said, "Red Devil in the right hands, now there's a top-notch prospect. I thought Jock could use her, put a feather in his cap after the hard knocks he's suffered. But I ain't so sure now."

Eloise's head was spinning.

Bev continued, "Don't seem right that one kid gets three good ones, while the other kid gets bump-kiss."

"Jock's planning on marrying her mother. Did I mention that?"

"Well, well. That just raised the stakes, don't it?"

Eloise raised her voice in disbelief, "He can't give away something that isn't his.

"Oh, Jock don't give nothin' away. But old Bev don't either."

Bev squinted at Eloise, raising a boney finger, "Now listen here, Missy, pull yourself together before you get on Red. You can't be churning inside if you mean to ride. That filly is light on her toes and can catch you out."

* * *

It was an easy fall as falls go, almost like a familiar dance move. She found herself making a balletic dismount she knew finished the performance.

Red had longed well, and she had done a few minutes of warm up trot in the arena, but Eloise wanted Pinky to hike the field with her, just walking and enjoying the sunshine with Prince before she did her laps at trot and canter. She wanted to impress Pinky with the charms of horses and nature. She wanted to show off how Red could take the hill. She had been showing off.

When they walked, Prince ran ahead, disappearing in the tall grass, circling back from behind, then scooting past them with glee before once again disappearing. Red didn't mind. Pinky and Eloise chatted as they walked, Pinky getting winded and stopping from time to time.

Pinky was leaned over and resting her hands on her thighs on one of her breaks. "So, your dad is going to marry the mother? This girl who rides your horse, she'll be your stepsister?"

"Who has had MY horse and gets two brand new horses too."

Pinky straightened up and she and Eloise and Red began to walk along the fence line at an easy pace. Pinky was quiet for a moment then said, "What else?"

"What, that's not enough?"

Pinky took her open palm and moved it in circles, "This stuff with Jock, you yourself said it's killing you. I get that. Crazy stuff with the dog, and that shoplifter. That was wild. I'd be bursting my buttons I'd be so proud of my dog. Except you looked spooked. I'd like to think I was someone you could talk to."

"I'm trying, Pinky. Maybe if I can just get Whiplash back…"

They followed the fence line as it turned. The ground rose in front of them. Eloise turned to look down at Pinky. "I'm going to do one easy warmup lap before I gallop." Pinky nodded and Eloise trotted away, Prince following.

As Eloise finished her warmup lap, she pulled Red up to walk next to Pinky. Behind her trailed Prince.

Pinky was sweating and out of breath. "I'm dying on this hill. Riding has to be easier than walking, the horse is doing all the work, right?

Prince flopped onto the grass in front of Pinky and by kicking his feet, proceeded to slide down the grassy hill, grinning all the way.

Prince came to a stop at the bottom of the hill and hopped back up.

Eloise said, "You guys hang out. Red and I have two more laps to do. I'll trot one more then finish with a gallop. Watch how she takes this hill. It's something!" Eloise picked Red back up, trotted off.

It wasn't long before Eloise had lapped them, as she passed, she kicked Red into a gallop. Eloise bent low over Red's neck while Pinky hugged the fence line.

Eloise hollered, "Yippee!"

Eloise felt the mare lower her haunches and kick into gear. Her heart pounded; the wind whipped at her eyes. But, man-oh-man, this mare, her mighty stride, her solid feel, and her confidence in her own power, was something extraordinary. Red blew up the hillside, boom-boom-boom-boom.

And then from her left out of the woods and sailing over the four-foot board fence as if it was nothing, a magnificent deer. It was stout and fat and shiny, with huge ears and antlers too. She took in all the details instead of focusing of Jock's number one rule, "Keep yourself between the horse and the ground."

She had lost focus. Her balletic cartwheel was unstoppable. And she had nothing under her but air and a left foot that was still in the stirrup. Bad. She managed somehow to lose the stirrup, but also the horse.

She watched Red's glorious copper-colored ass, rippling with gloss and muscle, head down the hill at full tilt, without her.

Eloise was running after her knowing she could never catch a galloping horse.

Over the crest and down the hill she ran after Red. She saw Pinky down the hillside standing stock still, with the added chaos of Prince running toward Red barking furiously. A disaster in the making. Prince, however, ran right past Red toward Eloise.

Pinky, her arm now outstretched was yelling sternly, "Red, come! Red, come!"

Red, broke to trot, and bounced down the hill, straight toward Pinky, tail lifted, neck arched, expelling air through her nostrils in tremendously loud bursts that seemed to emanate from deep in her chest.

Eloise was whispering, "Please don't run her over, please don't run her over."

Eloise stopped, stitch in her side, breathing hard, and as Prince came close enough for her to place a hand on his head, she watched Red trot right up to Pinky, stopping at the last moment, inches from her face.

Pinky reached for a rein and tugged it hard. Eloise noticed that she remembered to walk on the mare's left side.

Pinky led Red back up the hill toward Eloise, her right arm fully extended, carefully minding her feet and her fingers.

Pinky called out, "Oh thank God you're okay! God, horses *are* dangerous."

"I'm fine. A deer jumped in front of us. Just caught us by surprise."

Pinky was yelling, "Did you see me catch her? She came to me. Red came right to me!"

"Boy, am I glad she did. They usually go all the way back to the barn. Horses are prey animals and when they get scared, they seek safety. The barn feels safe to them. But Red saw you as safety."

"Really? Wow that is so cool."

Eloise looked thoughtful. "Just like Whiplash running up to Dabs. Isn't that weird?"

"Dabs? Who's Dabs?"

Eloise then told Pinky about Dabs, about Extreme Readers, and without telling her about the journals, told her about all she and Dabs had in common and how they had forged a long-distance friendship.

Pinky then addressed the horse. "Red, I believe you are what is commonly referred to as a facilitator. Eloise finally opened up to me. So much to process here. So, how do you take your fees? Carrots or sugar cubes?"

Eloise laughed and asked Pinky if she could give her a "leg up" onto Red.

Eloise gave instructions. "See I just bend my left knee like so, while I put my hands-on top of the saddle. Put both hands around my shin. Yeah, like that. I'm going to hop three times on my right leg, and when I say 'three' you give me an assist at the top of my hop. Just push. I'll swing my leg over the back of the horse. Got it?"

Pinky looked serious, gripping Eloise's shin and ankle, tongue stuck out slightly between her lips.

On the count of three, Pinky pushed so hard she nearly tossed Eloise over the horse to the green grass on the other side. Eloise dug her left heel into the saddle, grabbed mane, and wriggled herself back into the tack.

"Sorry, sorry. Are you okay?"

Eloise was giggling. Pinky joined in, and they giggled until they were wheezing. Prince joined the jollity by barking.

Red, bless her, stood patiently.

Eloise said "Red, you're a really good girl. Isn't she grand, Pinky?"

The two girls composed themselves before heading back.

Pinky looked at Eloise and shook her head.

"Dabs, huh? Whiplash ran right to him. Just like Red just ran to me?"

"Then he returned her to my mother."

"Oh, I like him, Eloise. I really like him."

"That's silly. You've never met him. And why he gets props for handing Whiplash back to Mom, I do not get either."

"You just taught me that. What do prey animals seek? Safety. Whiplash saw Dabs as safety. Red saw me as safety. The horses have given our characters the green-light. Like passing a security clearance. Animals don't bullshit. And you know what else, if you think about it, Whiplash introduced Dabs to your Mom. Oh my God, there is so much going on here."

"I'm not sure I followed all that."

Pinky added, "Don't you wonder what she thought of Dabs? What do you suppose she said to him?"

"Thank you. She was polite."

"And Dabs?"

"Probably, 'You're welcome.'"

"And now you and Dabs are being drawn back together, by ... ?"

Eloise sighed, "We're in the same online study group."

"With Betsy as leader!"

Now Pinky was moving her hands again, this time in a gesture that looked like she was playing an accordion. "So many connections, Eloise. Like this beautiful circle of trust built upon animal instinct."

Eloise grimaced, "Coincidences."

"And what is the common denominator in this weird and amazing herd?"

"I don't know."

Pinky opened her hands now, the accordion vanished, "You, you my friend, you!"

Eloise saw absolutely no logic whatsoever in Pinky's euphoric ramblings. But they were back at the barn.

Bev knew. Eloise could tell by the look on her face.

"Got your britches dirty, did you?"

"Yes ma'am."

Bev gave a brisk nod. "Strange to say, y'all look like it done everyone a heap of good."

19

Riding Red had filled Eloise with a vague feeling of anticipation, expectation. Maybe it was hope. Although Emily Dickinson wrote that "Hope is a thing with feathers..." for Eloise, "hope" had a chestnut mane and tail.

Even watching the bubbles multiply in her laundry room sink had her feeling uplifted. She had dumped in her old brushes and filled the sink with hot water and antiseptic soap. She let them soak while she and Prince trotted back into the garage to pull everything else out of her trunk. Prince was taking interest in each item. Eloise made two piles, keep and toss. When she held up a sticky bottle of Koppertox, he wrinkled his nose and turned his head away.

"Yeah, I agree. This we toss."

Her galloping boots were stiff and moldy, and her saddle pads had a funky odor. But a wash with a spot of bleach and they should be salvageable.

Eloise pulled out an extra-large zip lock bag, stuffed full of old bridle numbers. These she had collected from every horse show she had ever entered. These paper tags each had an aluminum tab on the back that slipped through the side of the browband. They were required by show rules to be on the horse, either the bridle or the halter, every time the horse was brought out of the stall. Eloise had saved them from shows big and small, successes and disasters. Most people threw them away. When she began competing, they were often the only "prize" she had to take home. Once Eloise had started the practice, she never stopped. Saving her competition bridle number had become one of those rituals that had turned into superstition.

When Eloise opened the bag, it was as if a genie had been released from a bottle. Both Eloise and Prince drew back. Was it the smell? Musty metallic and paper? She laughed at Prince who had flattened his ears, and now hunched forward, smelling them carefully as if they might jump out and bite him.

Eloise dumped the pile in front of her. She turned one over and read the back.

"Got through water complex, lost both stirrups."

She turned over another. It said, "Won dressage."

The next one said, "Got run off with, made time."

And then, scrawled in tiny letters to fit the small space. "Won. Best weekend of my life."

Some were clearly written by a child. Most did not have a date. But each proved she had been there.

In every memory, behind each cardboard disk, were her father and her mother. Her Mom to help her dress and memorize her tests and her courses and hold her horse while she ran to the porta-potty, again. Her Mom, who made sure she ate and stayed hydrated.

And always there was Jock. He never missed a ride, had coached her through every warm-up.

They cheered for even her mediocre performances and consoled her after her many failures. Eloise felt a familiar flush of sadness and with it an equal measure of guilt.

She never imagined they would not be there, would not be here.

Eloise reached over and stroked Prince on the top of his head. He melted, rolling partially over, head on her knee, eyes upturned, mouth slightly open in that happy grin he often made. She rubbed his tummy and his long-fringed tail beat time on the concrete floor.

Eloise stuffed the numbers back into the bag, took one more inhalation of the musty smells, then zipped the bag closed.

Eloise was getting stiff sitting on concrete. It was time to get up anyway, start that load of moldy stuff in the washer and rinse out her brushes.

She had just started the wash when her cell phone rang. It was Jock. Bizarre. She had every intention of telling him about finding her bag of show numbers, about the happy memories they elicited.

"Hey Jock. I was just thinking of you."

"Hey Lulu. I've been thinking of you too. I just had the strangest conversation with Bev."

"I'm glad she returned your calls."

"I'm so glad I've got my girl on the ground there, since I may need you to help me get this deal done."

"What do you mean?"

"Bev's suddenly decided the mare isn't for sale."

"What?"

Eloise felt a rush of guilt. Bev was exercising her "leverage" on her behalf. She hadn't asked her to, but she knew it to be true. Red was being held hostage until Whiplash was for sure on her way to Atlanta.

"You know anything about this?"

"Um…"

"We tried the mare, we vetted the mare, we agreed to a price. She's up to something."

Eloise had no intention of being mined for more information. After a long beat she said, "You still there?"

Jock said, "Hey, yeah, sorry, I think our connection is coming and going."

She deflected by asking, "How's Whiplash?"

"Great. She's great. Getting fat."

"Don't let her get too fat, please. I want to be able to bring her back into fitness without having extra pounds to shed."

Jock's next words were careful and intentionally light, "Hey, are you by chance riding that mare at Bev's?"

Eloise felt herself flush, get dizzy and angry. She tried not to let it show in her voice. "Yeah. Isn't that what you wanted? For me to get back in the tack?"

"Sure, honey. Sure. Just know that Bev isn't like me or your mother."

Jock continued, "Bev's got a temper and a tongue that can blister paint. Years ago, we had a falling out. Thought that was ancient history. But I'm not sure now. Just don't go losing your heart over that mare, because she may be using you to get back at me."

Eloise said nothing. Jock said nothing.

The line seemed dead. It was dead for so long that Eloise simply hit "end." Jock could think they lost the connection. It wouldn't be wrong.

* * *

October 20, 1779

I suspect father is unhappy that Fashion was traded without his consultation. Fashion may be the grandest horse father has ever bred. She could have brought us much needed income. And perhaps the greater loss, she now cannot contribute to our breeding program.

Buck has not one word to say in her favor since he traded her to Major Schmidt. Buck, always unsatisfied, has traded horses again, this time for Isaac's ride. The mule faced gelding is a sturdy soul who will best serve his purpose, in that regard Buck judges correctly.

The Major has set obstacles for us to traverse on our rides; fallen tree logs, snake-fences, drops, and banks, and we include the creek. The Major also leads us in merry chases, but if Fashion falters in her courage, Beauty and I take the lead. Bud brings up the rear, squealing with excitement when the pace quickens. We see fox and deer and groundhogs aplenty. No one hunts these days, so the foxes breed unchecked. I like to see them slink along the grass. Come winter, their coats will grow full and show brightly against the

277

white ground. Even now, when they blend among the browning grasses, the white tips of their tails give them away. The bird life is also on the move. Red-winged blackbirds scavenge the harvested fields in large and noisy flocks.

Winter will soon come upon us, and so it is no time for Buck to head to the woods to sleep rough and make war. His horses too would suffer and lose flesh with sparse forage. Buck endures. Barely. When the spring grass is up, he will be gone. Until then, we must bear his restless spirit.

Major Schmidt and I have had but few opportunities of privacy. Buck when he does cross our paths makes narrowed eyes, and Bud confesses he is under direction from Aunt Bess not to leave us alone.

Dear Aunt Bess. I am not all together disappointed in her strictures. I cannot describe the way the Major looks at me nor its effect. It makes me feel ashamed even though I have done nothing wrong.

I repeated to Major Schmidt what Buck had said whilst in his cups. This led to the Major returning confidences, describing his trials as a soldier and prisoner.

After the British defeat at Saratoga, he held hopes that terms, or the conventions as they are called, would be affirmed by both parties, and all captured would be returned home. England had only to agree that none would be allowed to return to the fight. This they would not do. This led to trials and despondencies with no hope of freedom until hostilities cease. The

Major did describe deprivations and hardships. His winter quarters in Canada were not survived by all. Then his march to us in bitter winter ended in bitter disappointment. Misery, illness, and death followed them here. He has seen much death, some gruesome and bloody in the heat of battle, but most from disease and hardship. No glory there. No glory anywhere. It is a hard business, war, whence the business of it commences. It is just as hard a business between battles. Major Schmidt vows he will leave this life of soldiering when he can. But unlike others, he will only leave it honorably.

Father reports all but one of our mares is settled in foal. Joyous news. We shall have new life next year. For now, our herd expands.

Our stallion is elderly. He must have his hay and grain soaked for lack of teeth, but age has not yet dimmed his ardor. When he is gone, we have no replacement of his quality. This worries father.

Yet amidst our troubles and the unanswered question of our freedom from King George, the cycle of life continues. We will have new foals. With that happy thought, I lay down my pen and wipe the ink from my fingers. My candle is nearly gutted, and Beast snores in my corner chaise-lounge, the fabric soiled from his muddy paws. He has ruined it. I do not care.

* * *

Betsy wrote online, "Jefferson may have lived by a complicated code of ethics we hardly comprehend today, but although he was no deity, he was no monster."

Dabs wrote, "Of course not. His Declaration of Independence and his Statute for Religious Freedoms are what makes us Americans. But his mighty ambition for himself and his young country drove him to do things he would never accept in others, like the executive over-reach of the Louisiana Purchase. It turned out to be a brilliant move."

Eloise wrote, "Rules for thee but not for me?' It's not just his four decades with Sally. Jefferson's idea of the noble farmer struck me as ludicrous. He never plowed or planted or weeded a day in his life. That labor was done by slaves. And Jefferson looked down his nose at merchants and bankers. Instead, he should have sought their advice. He was a terrible manager of his finances. He inherited debt and added to it all his life. He even foolishly secured someone else's debts and that man defaulted. Who does that?"

Dabs wrote, "Who does that? Aristocrats who rely on an old notion of honor among their class. He made a lot of bad decisions and privately he was not the public persona he cultivated for the ages. As much as he disparaged the merchant class, and glorified the rural life, he tried using his slave's children to start a manufacturing concern. His only profitable operation; nail making. They started slave children in his factory as young as ten."

Betsy wrote, "I am sure he saw nothing wrong with that."

Eloise added, "We've come so far."

Dabs typed, "And yet, the tensions that existed then, well, they haven't disappeared. Rural and urban. Federal laws and restraints, versus unregulated or left to the States. Each side loves to claim and quote Jefferson, just as they did before, during, and after the Civil War. They usually forget to say which Jefferson they claim, or even recognize that there truly was more than one Jefferson."

As soon as they signed off, Eloise had a message from Dabs.

* * *

Hi Eloise,

I'm sending this poor-quality photo of a painting that hangs in my bedroom. I always admired it growing up because it has a horse and a dog in it. My mother called it an amateur effort. She told me the frame was worth more than the art. I never gave it another thought, until recently. The painting has collected a lot of grime over the years and that makes it dark even in the best of light. I got a flashlight and examined it closer. I'm grinning as I write you this. In the corner I found initials. "L.R."

Dabs

* * *

Dabs,

OMG! Louisa Roberts!!! Jealous!

Eloise

* * *

Eloise,

Come see it in person. Consider it bait. Maybe in the Spring? It's getting colder by the day with gusty winds that make my rides less than comfortable. But Spring in Virginia is glorious.

I'm still interested in those old headstones. I read that if I take charcoal and thin paper, I can do a rubbing. I'm going to try it. Wish you were here. More transcriptions to come. I promise.

* * *

When Eloise got to the barn, she was excited to pull the cover off her dressage saddle to show Bev. "This was custom made for Whiplash."

Eloise had decided to enjoy Red until she had Whiplash back.

Bev nodded, "Let's see if it'll work on this young'un."

Eloise lifted the saddle up and placed it on Red's back,

first without a saddle pad, to better judge the fit. She placed it a little too far forward, placed her palm on the pommel, and gently pushed until it did not want to go back any further. This was a trick her mother had taught her to find the natural "saddle-platz."

The "static" fit didn't look bad. The seat was level, not tipped forward and not tipped back.

Bev said, "That girth ain't gonna' fit. Too long. Let's see if one of mine'll do."

Bev returned with a dusty dressage girth. It fit.

Once girthed, the two women took turns on a step stool, checking the clearance over the spine and the withers, then looking from the rear. Bev walked back to the front of the horse and ran her hand under the flap where the shoulder blade would need to slide under the tree points as the front leg moved forward.

"Tetch roomier than need be. Let's find you a half-pad to make up the difference."

Bev returned with a fluffy sheepskin half-pad, saying, "It's like puttin' on an extra pair of socks when your shoes are too loose."

As soon as Red was tacked up, Bev warned, "A dressage saddle don't make a dressage horse."

Eloise nodded, "And I'm no dressage trainer. Mom was the real dressage rider in the family. Wish she were here."

"Just pretend Elly's in the corner watching. You'll do fine."

Sitting in her old saddle was like putting on a favorite pair of jeans. Familiar. Comfortable. A weird sort of homecoming.

283

Red was no dressage horse. Bev was right. She remind-ed Eloise of a kid who could do a cartwheel, but whose knees are bent, ankles flexed. There was no technique there yet, just enthusiasm and raw talent.

Red must find simple balance, equilibrium, at all three gaits, on curved lines and straight lines, and in leg-yields. Building muscles takes time, finding balance takes time.

Her mother's voice was faint in her mind. Eloise had to block her own voice and focus to hear it.

But it came. "Repetition is the mother of all learning."

"Patience."

"Reward approximations."

"Preserve the horse's desire to try."

"Make her feel proud."

Bev was filling up water buckets when Eloise led Red back into the barn, stirrups run up, girth loosened. They had finished the ride with a walk around the field. No gallop today, no leaping deer, but the walk gave Prince a chance to run. Red and Eloise enjoyed watching. Red stood quietly in the crossties as she was untacked. Even the look in her eye was different; softer.

Bev said, "Looks like you dun good."

"I imagined Mom there, even heard her voice in my head."

"Ain't that fine? You never do ride alone. None of us do."

""I never thought of it like that before."

"When your soul needs soothing, get on a good horse and listen."

Bev's comment disturbed her good feelings.

Pinky talked of healing. Bev talked of souls to be soothed. Their pity was oppressive, a burden. She had intentionally cut herself off from all that oppressive pity to make a fresh start.

Eloise was rebuilding. She was slowly losing that hollowed out feeling. She had this great dog that was performing miraculous feats. Because of Bev, she would get her horse back; she would make it happen. She had a job she loved, and amazing friends from different walks of life. As Jock had pointed out, she owned a house, debt free. She even had a monthly flow of cash she had not earned, did not deserve, but was given to her anyway. She was unbelievably privileged.

But Bev's comment reminded her that she was evidently, still, after all that, someone whose soul needed soothing, who needed healing, and she wanted to scream out loud that she was working on it. She was. She was doing better. She was back in the saddle.

But still, she felt some trepidation, knowing that a hard spin could put her right back on the ground. And she wasn't sure she would have the strength to get back up again.

20

It was about a week later when Janet buzzed the basement with an odd sound to her voice. The day was done. Pinky had sent her last dog home and was cleaning her clippers while Eloise described her latest ride on Red.

Janet said, "Eloise, Doc wants to see you in his office. Don't take Prince up there, okay?"

Eloise looked at Pinky. Pinky shrugged. "I'll put Prince in a run. You go on up."

Eloise instantly had dry mouth. She knew the tone of bad news. By the time she climbed the stairs, her heart was pounding. She wanted to turn and run, felt the pull on her back trying to take her the opposite direction than her feet.

When she got to Doc's office, the door was closed. She'd never seen the door closed before. She felt light-headed and strangely heavy-footed. It was like she had two blocks of wood instead of feet. She knocked lightly. Doc said, "Come in."

When Eloise stepped into the room, a man rose from the corner where he had been sitting. Everything came into hyper focus. Doc's diploma on the otherwise bare white walls, the tile floor bare of rugs. Doc's desk looked cheap. There was a coffee ring on the top. But what came into the sharpest focus of all was the face of the man who had just stood up.

Doc said, "Eloise, why don't you sit down?"

Her only thought was to run away, but there was nowhere to run. She was caught, trapped, and consumed with guilt as Joe moved toward her.

In her mind, Eloise stepped forward to take a seat. That's not what happened. What Eloise *had* done was make a sudden grab for and then lean on the back of the nearest chair. And as the chair had casters, it rolled. Well, it more than rolled, it scooted. Eloise's body lurched forward, but those wooden feet of hers had grown roots and stayed in place and the chair she had tried to use as support seemed to fly away.

The tree that was Eloise was felled, and somehow Eloise's branches did not find the floor before her trunk. Timber. The last bit that hit the floor was her head. She did manage to turn her body, so that at least she did not break her nose. In that twist, the spot to take the blow was the same spot that had gotten a good knock in her mom's closet when she fell off the upholstered bench.

A low voice was murmuring in her ear. Sweet. This was a dream. Eloise had always had vivid dreams. She opened her eyes to look into large heavily lashed brown eyes, brows drawn together in concern. Oh, she knew who he was. She could enjoy this. He placed a hand gently behind her neck. Eloise reciprocated by placing a hand behind his neck too. Wow, this felt so real. He leaned in closer, and Eloise kissed him as it seemed the obvious thing to do. As their lips parted, she sighed, "Major Schmidt" but then feeling confused said a bit louder, "Joe?"

It was time to roll over and go back to sleep because she was tired. Which she did, tucking both her hands under her chin and turning toward the wall onto her right side.

"Eloise, wake up!"

Wha? What was Doc doing in her bedroom?

A jolt went through her.

Eloise managed to sit up, her hand finding a sore spot on her head, and Joe, (Oh my God, yes, it was Joe) supported her back and shoulders as she did so.

Doc said, "Eloise, you fell. I'm not sure how it happened, but you've hit your head and I'm taking you to the ER."

Doc hit the intercom. "Janet, get Pinky up here, and tell her to bring Eloise's purse, oh, and leave the dog. Eloise has injured herself."

"Is she okay?"

"Likely fine, but a knock to the head has to be examined. If you and Suzie can close up that would be great."

Joe helped Eloise into a chair and was being solicitous. He was asking her what day this was. He asked her if it was before lunch or after lunch. He even asked her where she was. Eloise knew the EMT drill. And she was not *that* confused, just embarrassed. She wasn't totally clear on what she had said or done. Well, what anyone heard or saw.

Doc turned to Joe and asked, "Joe, may I assume that you two have met before."

Joe pursed his lips and Eloise beat him to a reply, "No. Hi, I'm Eloise Robertson. I'm so embarrassed to have tripped like that. So stupid. But really I'm fine."

Joe extended his hand and introduced himself.

Doc looked confused, "You two haven't met before?"

Joe looked him straight in the eye. "I don't believe we have."

Pinky burst into the room, her own bag over her shoulder and Eloise's in her hands.

"What in the world?"

Then Pinky looked at Joe and lifted an eyebrow. "Hiya. You look familiar."

Doc said, "Joe, can we postpone this? I think I need to go to the ER with Eloise."

"Of course. I'll come back later then."

Then Joe turned to Eloise. "I hope that bump on your head is nothing serious."

Pinky had Eloise by the elbow and was leading her out the door. Once they got halfway down the stairs, Eloise was babbling to Pinky, "Oh my God, that was so embarrassing. One moment I was walking and the next moment, wham!"

Pinky asked, "Why was that guy here?"

Eloise did not answer. But her internal voice was shrieking all sorts of expletives.

* * *

Doc had borrowed Eloise's wallet to get her checked into the ER. He had insisted Eloise and Pinky sit while he took

289

care of the preliminaries. He came back and sat down with them.

Eloise said, "We could be here for hours. When you aren't having a heart attack and you're not bleeding out and you're not an overdose, you get put to the end of the line. They do nothing for a little bump on the head. I'm serious, I'm fine. We should go or we could be here all night."

Doc said, "You seem to know too much about the ER, Eloise."

"My Mom."

Pinky touched Eloise's arm and said, "Sorry."

Doc said, "It would be negligent to let you go home until someone examines you."

Pinky said, "Sometimes a long wait is a blessing, in the right company that is."

Doc lifted his chin and he and Pinky exchanged a long look. It was a look that ratcheted up Eloise's anxiety level. Bad news was going to find her. Fainting had just postponed its delivery. Her heart began to pound again.

Doc calmly stated, "Eloise, you said you had never met Joe before."

Eloise didn't like where this was going.

"But you called him by name."

"I did?"

Doc nodded. "Right after you kissed him on the floor of my office."

Eloise stood up, looking like she was about to bolt. "That's absurd!"

Pinky stood up too and took Eloise by the arm. "If Doc said it happened, it happened."

Eloise put a hand over her mouth and slumped back down into the chair. "Oh, my God. Doc, I'm sorry. I'm so embarrassed. What must Joe think of me? He must think I'm insane. Maybe I am insane."

Doc looked at Eloise. "How did you know his name?"

Eloise slowly opened her purse and fished out her little travel-pack of tissue. She pulled it open and grabbed a tissue, blew her nose, and then wiped at her eyes. Then she unzipped the pocket where "Joe" had been in residence, and handed the flier wordlessly to Doc.

Doc handed it to Pinky who carefully began to unfold it, took a long look, and then exhaled, "Oh Eloise."

It was the disappointed sound a mother would make who had just discovered their child had driven the getaway car in a bank heist. Pinky handed the flier over to Doc.

Doc said, "So, that's how you knew his name was Joe."

Pinky tapped the photo of the dog, "That's Prince."

Doc nodded, "That's why Joe was at the clinic. A friend had seen the clip on the local news about the shoplifter. Joe tracked Eloise down once he had found the right rescue site."

Pinky pointed to the dog. "That explains why you didn't take up my offer to clip Prince. He'd look too much like this photo."

Eloise felt like she might throw up. Despite her prediction of being at the ER for hours, a nurse opened a door, and miracle of miracles, Eloise's name was called.

Eloise grabbed her purse and fled.

When Eloise came out again, hours later, Doc was gone. Pinky, however, was waiting. Pinky stood up and reached out to grab the discharge papers Eloise had clutched in her hands.

She read, "No driving. No aspirin or ibuprofen. Seven days' rest. Acetaminophen and ice for pain."

Pinky put her arm through Eloise's arm, pulling her to the door. "Doc left us his car and took an Uber."

Eloise resisted Pinky's forward pull, and managed to whisper, "I want my dog."

"Yeah. Okay. I can take you home and get you settled and then get Prince."

"No. Prince first."

"Okay. Stay calm. Prince first."

Eloise was still barely moving. "I can't leave my car at work. I mean I live so close by."

Eloise came to a full stop. "Oh my God, I never called Bev! I'm such a flake for not calling or showing up for Red today."

Pinky pulled her forward. "I called her. I mean I had all that time sitting on my butt. I simply asked to hold your purse while you were getting your scan, and I found her number in your phone contacts."

"Oh."

"Now I have her number in my phone, so I can tell her she won't see you for a week. No riding."

Eloise followed Pinky and got into the car like an obedient child.

Pinky did all the talking.

"You knew it was his dog and you didn't say anything. Okay, I can understand. You were having a war with yourself. Do the right thing, and you lose the dog, and you really, really want and need the dog. Or say nothing and see if Doc and Suzy find the owner anyway since he was chipped, and if they don't, bingo, the dog is yours. Totally explains how you hemmed and hawed over committing. But then why save the flier? Should have burned the flier. That flier proves you knew all along."

Eloise protested weakly, "I kept the flier because I had a sicko crush on his photo. When you threw it away, I found it in the trash and kept it."

Pinky looked over at Eloise incredulous. "You folded it up so that the dog was hidden."

"I didn't know it was Prince in the photo."

Pinky was shaking her head, "You hid the dog. You hid the dog. Give me a break. You knew it was Prince and you hid the evidence from yourself."

Pinky was not done. "Was it to keep, oh, what do they call it, plausible deniability? Like, 'Oh I never noticed that was Prince in the flier.'"

"No. But I get your point. I put the flier in my backpack the very same day that I found Prince waiting on the front stoop."

"Are you trying to say you never put two and two together?"

"I didn't."

Eloise had to wonder for a moment why hadn't she put two and two together? She had found Prince at the front door and moments later was digging that flier out of the trash. But she hadn't. Or had she?

Pinky's voice was steely, "By hiding Prince's photo you made sure that you never would, either."

Eloise felt judgement in the tone of Pinky's voice. It stung. She whispered. "What? Are you saying I was trying to deceive myself?"

Pinky parked the car right next to Eloise's and turned in her seat. "I don't blame you for wanting that dog. He's the best thing that's happened to you in a long time. I'm in your camp there. But, as handsome as that guy Joe is, I still don't get why you kept the flier or why you kissed the guy."

Eloise felt her cheeks grow hot. She had tried to bend the universe to her will, again. Again, it had not worked, and again she had not only humiliated herself, but wrecked the only friendships she had. Just as she had wrecked relationships in the past.

Eloise moaned, "He's probably at some bar telling his friends about the psycho who stole his dog and sexually assaulted him."

Pinky shook her head. "It seems to me that what you *really* need right now, even more than a dog, is a real flesh and blood boyfriend. I mean, you're twenty-one. The way you kissed Joe, Doc made a not so huge assumption that there was some history there."

"There isn't. Argh! I never meant to ever meet Joe. I don't care about Joe! The man I'm in love with has been dead for around 200 years. I hope I never see Joe again. Never, ever. But I love Prince and Prince is my dog now, and he's not getting him back."

Eloise was out of the car and headed into the clinic to collect her dog and go home.

* * *

When they got to the townhouse Pinky asked Eloise for her car keys. Pinky said, "I know, I know, you think I don't trust you *not* to drive. But, if I have the keys, you won't be tempted."

"I might need to go to the grocery store or to the pharmacy or something like that."

"Nope. You have me and Betsy."

Eloise then recalled that she had a magnetic box under the wheel well with a spare key in it. She handed the keys over to Pinky. "Wait, my house keys are on that ring too."

Pinky closed her hand around the keys. "You won't need those either since you're staying put."

"What if Joe turns up and tries to take Prince?"

"He wouldn't dare."

"But what if he does?"

"Don't answer the door."

Eloise nodded seriously.

Pinky tried to reassure her. "I'm sure Doc will be in your corner. Hey, spend your week reading books and sleeping. I know you'll miss cleaning up dog poo but there will still be plenty to pick up when you come back."

Eloise remembered she had a spare house key hidden in a fake rock outside.

Once Pinky left, Eloise grew restless. Prince followed her as she paced around the house. Joe wanted his dog back. Why else would he have bothered to track her down? He knew where she worked now and might even know where she lived. He also likely thought she was a lunatic. A lunatic had his dog.

What about Doc? What about Pinky? She hated to think what they thought of her. That she was dishonest. That she had been having some erotic fantasy over a guy in a lost dog flier. Eloise could feel the agitation building, she started to get light-headed. Eloise stopped and sat down on her sofa. Prince sat too. Then he crawled up next to her. She wanted to take her dog and go where Joe couldn't find her, or Prince.

Eloise got up and walked into the bedroom. She grabbed her backpack off the closet floor and threw it onto her bed. She tossed in her toothbrush, e-reader and charger, pajamas, slippers and clean underwear and socks and a few clean shirts. She could wear the same pair of jeans.

She zipped it up and set it by the front door. Then went to get a tote for Prince. Two bowls, a large zip lock baggie of dog kibble, a plush squeaky toy and a handful of dental chews, a short leash, and a long leash. Eloise set the bag down next to her backpack.

The doorbell rang. Eloise froze. Prince erupted in a flow of deep barks. What if it was Joe? Prince had stopped barking, had begun to whine and to wag his tail. Eloise's heart began to pound. He knew the person at the door! Should she hide?

Whoever it was had opened the door a crack. For God's sake, why wasn't the door locked? The door opened wider.

"Aren't you a good guard dog! It's just me, you silly old dog." Betsy saw the bags at the door. As soon as she did though, she went right to the issue.

"Just where do you think you're going?"

And even though she had not formulated a plan, she answered as if she had.

"To visit Dabs."

"Pinky said you suffered a mild concussion, and you're not allowed to drive."

"Oh, I'd rest once I was there. I thought I could help Dabs transcribe some of the journal entries. Maybe go for walks. I really feel fine. If I get a headache, they told me to take Acetaminophen."

"Pinky said she took your keys."

Eloise couldn't think of a thing to say in her own defense.

Betsy shrugged. She turned on the stoop, pointed her key fob at her car and with a little "beep-beep" the hatchback lifted.

"Put your stuff in the back. Prince must stay in the back seat, okay? No climbing over the seat."

Then looking at the floor Betsy added, "At least you pack light."

"You can't go. Who'll take care of Marilyn?"

Betsy rolled her eyes, "Pinky will look in on her, although Marilyn will snub me for days after I get back as punishment."

Eloise found the fake rock near the front door that held the spare house key and locked the door behind them. Prince bounced up and down all the way to the car, leaping into the back seat when Betsy opened the door.

Once Betsy started the car she turned and assessed Eloise. She said, "Really, how are you?"

"Fine."

"You look like you're on speed. I know we're driving to Virginia, although I'm not sure where in Virginia, but for sure we've got a long drive ahead, so I figure you're going to get around to telling me what the hell's going on."

"We're going to Charlottesville."

"How wonderful. We can tour Monticello! If you're up to it that is. I can post about it, Monticello I mean, on Extreme Reader. It makes a perfect cover story."

"As long as we have a safe place for Prince while we tour."

"I'm sure Dabs can make a plan for Prince." Then, she added, "Eloise, please call and tell Dabs the change of plans. That I'm tagging along. I hate to come uninvited and unannounced."

"Don't you need to swing by your house to pack a bag?"

"I packed myself a bag to stay at the house with you. Pinky had a feeling you were up to something."

"She didn't trust me."

"Should she have?"

From the back seat came a series of muffled barks. Eloise looked over the seat back to see legs twitching. Prince was already asleep and dreaming.

Eloise was still agitated. She said, "Prince still trusts me. I can't let Joe take him away. I had to make a new plan."

Betsy raised her eyebrows, "Dabs doesn't know we're on our way to see him, does he?"

"No."

"Don't you think you'd better call?"

"We've actually never spoken."

"Oh my. How have you two been communicating?"

"By text."

"I think it's past time to call. And I want to be able to talk to him too."

"About me?"

"No. About Thomas Jefferson! Really Eloise, we're about to descend upon him, uninvited, a concussed pen-pal and retired schoolteacher he's never met, bringing a large hairy dog. The least I can do is explain why we must impose on his Virginia hospitality."

"Right. To explain that Eloise has gone loopy."

Betsy chuckled, not unkindly though, and said, "Well, certainly that's part of it."

21

The GPS led them closer and closer to Dabs Carter and Ivy Creek Farm. Betsy would not let Eloise take a turn at the wheel, and so they spent a restless night at a motel along the highway. Prince appeared to be the only one who slept, but Betsy said she had at least "rested her eyes."

The closer they got, the more rural the vistas and the colder the temps. There would be "frost on the pumpkins" up in old "Virginny."

Eloise had time to search online and find two historical markers she wanted to visit: The Albemarle Barracks, of which nothing remained, and the burial grounds for the POW's who perished there. Dots on a map but close together.

Finally, they pulled up to a mailbox with the correct address. Betsy hesitated. Nothing could be seen from the gates but a gravel drive, unkempt, scrub pines and overgrowth obscuring any view of what lay beyond. The white gates stood open and sagging with peeling paint.

Betsy said, "Are you sure the address is correct?"

Eloise nodded.

"It's not very welcoming, is it?"

"Are you worried?"

"I've been worried non-stop since Pinky called."

"I don't think Dabs is a mass murderer. But my judgment hasn't been stellar these days."

"Keep cell phones charged and on our persons at all times. I've got three bars, how about you?"

Eloise gave a thumbs up. "We're rural, but not that rural."

The driveway was a rough ride in a car that was never meant to go off-road. But it was soon forgotten as they rounded a curve.

Betsy said, "Oh."

Eloise echoed Betsy. "Oh."

It was a big box of a house, beautiful, but spooky as heck. Virginia red brick. The glass in the tall casement windows was rippled. The front steps were wide and flanked by white columns that supported a portico.

Prince was panting anxiously and whining as soon as the house was in view. Eloise rolled a window halfway down so he could take in the crisp air and smell of damp grass and leaves. Once they stopped, his tail began crazily thrashing the seat back. When Betsy put the car into park, his whines turned into deafening barks.

"Eloise, please get him out. What's gotten into him?"

Eloise opened the door and Prince leaped from the car and took off behind the house.

Eloise jogged after him. As she rounded the house she was stopped in her tracks. There was the barn, just as she had imagined it. To the right a fenced off field. She noted a depression in the ground from the gate to the barn, where horses had trekked back and forth for over two hundred years.

Betsy had come to stand beside her. Prince and Dabs were framed for a moment between the sliding doors of an enormous barn. Dabs rested a large hand across the top of Prince's head. Prince was looking up at Dabs, mouth open in his usual grin, tongue hanging out the side. It struck Eloise as dreamlike. The moment passed as Prince broke away and tucked his butt and zoomed around in crazy trajectories, causing all three of them to laugh.

Betsy said, "Prince seems to think he found a prize!"

Dabs walked over, first to Betsy and gave her a brief hug. "Betsy! Finally, we meet."

Eloise put her hand out and Dabs took it and held it for a moment. "You look exactly as I remember."

Eloise was surprised that he had remembered her.

She examined his face and noted his square chin, heavy brows, and a thick unruly mop of reddish-brown hair. At first, no recognition at all. Then Eloise suddenly realized she had seen that face before, when it was much younger, a boy, versus this man, but she said nothing.

Dabs noticed, "I clearly didn't make as much of an impression as you did."

Eloise felt a bit shy as she said, "You weren't being flung from your horse on a regular basis."

Betsy was about to say something but was stopped by the sight of Prince coming toward them at an alarming speed.

Prince flew up to Dabs, twirled around and plopped his butt down on his feet, then leaned against Dab's legs, and lifted his chin to look up at him.

Betsy's laugh was one of relief, "Prince seems quite enamored with you, Dabs."

"As soon as Prince found me, I knew who he was, and who was here. But I'm being a terrible host. Let me get your things."

Dabs looked disappointed when all he was directed to carry to the house was a backpack, Betsy's overnight bag, and Prince's tote.

"Looks like you two made a quick getaway."

Betsy said, "We're not wanted by the police, just so you know. But, yes, it was a hasty departure, and Eloise does have a mild concussion."

Dabs raised a questioning eyebrow.

"I did NOT fall off a horse, but that's all I want to say about it now."

Dabs said, "I wouldn't dream of pressing for more information than you're ready to share."

Betsy said, "Dabs, you really are a Virginia gentleman."

Eloise frowned, "Dabs, I told Betsy all about the journals. Don't be angry. I just want Betsy to be part of it too."

Betsy added, "I hope you don't mind. We had such a long drive, and Eloise decided all current affairs were off the table. So, we went to the 18th Century."

"Ah, well, I see; happy to have you join us. I'll need to get you up to speed on our revolutionary journalist, Miss Louisa Roberts. I think you will be as charmed as we are."

As Dabs opened the front door, Eloise was struck by the sight of the grand staircase in the wide hall. She became aware of the unevenness of the wide plank flooring beneath her feet.

Eloise said, "Charmed is too mild a word. Bewitched? Louisa can write, and it all happened right here."

Eloise added with reverence, "I can see them there, can't you? On the stairs. Aunt Bess, Louisa, Priscilla." Then she turned to her left, pointed at a front room, not too large.

"There's Mr. Roberts' study."

Dabs nodded and gestured back to the wide hall, saying, "My mother used to refer to the house as 'Mostly Hall.' The dimensions make it not only the longest, but the widest room in the house. Long ago, dances would have been held in the hall. It was a practical design before the days of air conditioning. Open both doors at either end and the casement windows too, and the house had cross-ventilation. Also, likely flies. The barn is too close to the house. Dining room is behind the study originally, then came the butler's pantry with a covered walk to the outdoor kitchen before it was demolished to build a modern kitchen. Over here is the formal parlor. That's where they would have spent the evenings reading, playing Chess, playing music. Behind that, Mr. Roberts bedroom; my room now.

Dabs continued, "Of course, indoor plumbing changed things. Not sure when the first kitchen was built or how many times it's been renovated. The space under the stairs became the powder room and the back bedroom had a closet and bathroom added. I have you ladies upstairs. One of the bedrooms was converted into a bathroom."

Dabs led them up the stairs.

Dabs showed Eloise her room, "I can't know which room was Louisa's, it could have been the current bathroom for all I know. But my gut says this one was hers."

"Hope it's okay for Prince to sleep in here."

"Of course. It will be nice to have a dog in the house again."

Betsy said, "It's so kind of you to take us in like this."

Eloise remembered her manners, "I don't know how to thank you. I feel lucky to be here, to see Louisa's home, to get to sleep in what may be her bedroom. I imagine Louisa would be most excited by Prince."

"Isn't it odd that all the years I grew up here, I thought of this house as my house. And now, I think of this house as the Roberts' house."

Betsy said, "Aren't you a Roberts descendent?"

"Don't know. The one person who could have answered all my questions is my mother, and I'm afraid it's too late now to ask her."

* * *

Dabs made a strong cup of Earl Grey. He offered ginger-snaps, and they were just the ticket with the tea. Eloise marveled at the sight of the enormous barn, as she looked through the kitchen windows. This glass was not wavy, but part of some long-ago renovations.

Dabs was saying, "Betsy, I'll make you a copy of the completed transcriptions. I think you'll find them fascinating."

Eloise broke in, "When can I see the chest with the hidden panel? And the original manuscripts? Oh, and the family cemetery. And the art. I can't forget the artwork."

"And there's more transcribing waiting to be done."

305

"Everything. I want to see everything."

Betsy added, "And Monticello. Don't forget that we only have five days, including drive time, Eloise."

"Five days. Oh, I can't think about that right now. I can't."

Dabs sighed, "That's not enough time."

Betsy said, "Eloise, you are supposed to be resting, remember?"

"I don't feel like resting."

Betsy raised her eyebrows, "I do. Dabs, if you print off those documents, I'd like to take a lie-down. Neither of us slept last night."

Dabs refilled teacups then excused himself to print off the transcribed pages of the journal for Betsy. They could hear the mechanical hum of the printer. When he returned, Betsy and Eloise had cleared the table and washed the teacups.

Betsy took the proffered pages and excused herself.

Dabs turned to Eloise, "It's about a mile to the family cemetery if you care for a walk."

"I'd love to. I've been cooped up in a car and Prince could use the exercise."

Eloise and Dabs headed out the back door with Prince trotting ahead like he knew where he was going. They turned to the right, away from the barn down a well-worn path.

Eloise walked alongside Dabs, Prince running ahead then circling back. They were mostly silent, except for brief moments when Dabs would point something out, a bird, a plant, an old fence-line long gone. They seemed to be walking an old road, although it had not been maintained, it was still evident that wheeled vehicles, likely tractors, had used it not too long ago.

The landscape was mostly gently rolling terrain with fallow fields on either side of the path, but then led into woods, then to a hill that rose sharply before them. Dabs indicated a narrow path that left the road and disappeared into tangles of growth. Prince led the way; the path became steep. Evidence of weed whacking littered each side and kept the brambles from attaching themselves to Eloise's jeans, but she noted there were plenty of thorny canes.

On the crest of the hill, framed by blue sky, stood Prince. He made a familiar profile and it recalled to Eloise, with shame that prickled the back of her neck, his photo in the flyer.

They joined the dog, and walked toward a low stone wall, its iron gate open and tipped crazily on one hinge. A cemetery. A place of old bones. Perhaps bones of people she had come to know.

Dabs stepped through the gate. "My mother and I used to ride up here all the time."

"To visit family?"

"For the view. Look."

Someone with an artist's eye had carved a large "picture-frame" in the heavy foliage that ringed the track around the wall enclosure. Below was the house and barns and fields of what was once Ivy Creek Plantation. Eloise spotted three horses with their heads down grazing.

Dabs looked at Eloise and smiled, "Dejavu. Odd feeling, standing right here, showing you this view. I'm not quite sure that I won't turn around and find myself alone."

Eloise had to look away. "You will find me gone soon enough. I'll have to go back, even though I've ruined everything."

Dabs gently cradled Eloise's elbow, pointing again at the view. "Enjoy the view. Mom couldn't keep the place up anymore. But she always kept that view open, even when she couldn't enjoy it herself."

The three horses had lifted their heads and ambled a few feet before resuming grazing. The air was crisp and carried the musk of dead leaves and wet clay. She was here with Prince. They were safe. For now. She could rest.

Eloise refocused on Dab's face. It was a kind and open face. A face without a trace of self-consciousness. She asked, "Why do you think it was so important to her, to your mom?"

"The connection to the past feels strong up here, as if the buried are the watchmen and women, the observers of all that came after them. As Mom got older, she got more and more interested in her forbears. I totally get it now. I'm not sure who is buried here. Mom never spoke of anyone specific. There are no recent graves. And by recent, I mean since reconstruction. She felt a duty to them, I suppose. And now it's my duty."

Eloise turned her eyes to the graves around her. "No sign of Louisa?"

"Think of the years of wind and rain wearing away these inscriptions."

"Did you try to do rubbings?"

"No. Thought I would, but I read it could be damaging. I've read that the safest and most effective way is to use an extra flash not connected to the camera. You put an umbrella over the marker to make the face of the stones dark, then set up the extra flash at an angle to the stone. It will cast shadows in depressions, highlighting what is otherwise unobservable."

Eloise and Dabs began to stroll. There were headstones but also stones set at the foot of some of the graves, helping to demarcate the length of the grave. The rows weren't straight, the stones were not grand. Here and there a larger stone was placed. Some were readable. Taylor's, Epps's, and Randolph's and a few Carters, who were surely kin, but not a single Roberts'.

Eloise asked, "Isaac and Sammie and Bud and Priscilla? Where?"

"Hidden, for good reason. The University used to dig up recently deceased slaves to use them in the Medical school."

"Oh, my God."

"Gruesome business. Finding cadavers for the fledgling medical college was a challenge. It doesn't surprise me that the graves of slaves were held less sacred. The bodies of slaves were never their own in life. It makes perfect sense that the sons of the gentry continued to use their bodies after death."

"Brutal."

When they got to the middle of the walled circle, the inscriptions were completely gone on the markers. The ground was depressed, the headstones and the footstones pitted and blackened. A few that had once evidently been upright were now flat against the ground. One headstone was shaped like an obelisk pointed not upward toward the sky but listed to the side like a drunk.

Eloise asked, "What do you suppose happened here?"

"I think we can assume this is the oldest portion of the cemetery. Virginia is hot and wet in the summer, and cold in the winter. The ground settles and shifts. We've had earthquakes and tornadoes. At least the residents are safely 'below deck.'. When I get to the project with the flash and camera, I'll start here; see if anything turns up."

Eloise squatted next to a headstone that was near the tipsy one. She rose and moved to the one next to it. "These two go together, don't you think?"

Dabs nodded solemnly.

Eloise rose, and Dabs briefly took her hand.

Prince was standing just outside the gate. He had been studying them. When they headed toward home, Prince turned and trotted down the path.

Prince led them all the way back to the house. He knew exactly where they were going.

* * *

Eloise always thought of a garret as a small dismal sort of room. But this one was not. At least it was not small. Prince had cautiously made it up the narrow stairs, and then sat just inside the door, looking wary.

"It's all right, Prince."

Dabs said, "I don't blame him. It's kind of a fire trap up here. Lots of old paper and wooden crates, dust, a tiny window set up high in the peak, only one exit and a narrow one at that. Smart dog."

Betsy had joined them and the three of them began wandering from pile to pile.

Betsy said, "Is there any sort of order to it?"

"If there was, I've long since lost it. Much of this stuff was stacked all over the house. After mom died, I brought in a dumpster and started to heave-ho. But I almost threw away a lock of hair that had been tied up with string and stuck between the pages of a book. It said, 'Freddy.' Hit me hard. My mother's name was Freddy. I had almost thrown it away. So, instead I hauled nearly everything up these awful narrow stairs and added to the heaps of stuff already up here. Once I had the boxes and stacks of papers out of the way, I found I needed a bedside table. And there were loads up here to choose from."

Eloise added, "And that's how you found the journals."

"Yes. And now I'll never throw any of this mess away. I've become my mother, trapped in a Sisyphean task of moving it around for the rest of my life, while I study Jefferson and transcribe those journals and live with one foot in the 18th century. It's a lonely task. That's why I joined Extreme Readers. But I don't see how anyone can be as Extreme as I am."

Eloise asked, "Can we see the chest?"

Dabs did a full turn, "I've been moving things around, it's, yes, behind that trunk, we just need to move that forward, oh, don't use the handles. They're dry-rotted."

Eloise had almost done the unthinkable, damage one of these either priceless, or worthless old things. Either

311

way, she suddenly felt like joining Prince by the stairs. She stepped back and let Dab's carefully pull the old steamer trunk out of the way.

Betsy said, "Look at that old trunk. Did someone take the 'grand tour' do you think?"

"My mother and Grandmother. Studying the art and architecture of the old world. Marvelous when you think about it. Here. Isn't it a lovely little chest?"

Betsy said, "How in the world would you get that down those narrow stairs by yourself?"

"With Henry's grandson. Henry can't get around anymore, although he used to do everything around here for Mom."

Dabs leaned over the chest, "See, you pull out this little piece on the side, and there, the panel was false, see, a secret shelf."

Betsy said, "Very clever."

Dabs stood up and pointed to a dressing table with a discolored mirror. Sitting on top was a leather box, rather plain, with a hinged lid. "Here, I dug this out of a pile recently. Heavy. Stuffed full."

Dabs lifted the hinged lid and picked out a very blackened metal disk.

Eloise made a funny squeaking noise. "That's a harness brass."

Dabs nodded, "All identical. I meant to clean one up, but then, you know, amateurs who try to clean up antiques often ruin them."

Betsy said, "I think harness brasses are rather common. That one looks awfully far-gone."

Eloise said, "May I take a look?"

Dabs handed it over.

"Can we take it downstairs where the light is better?"

"Of course."

It was with great relief to Prince when they left the attic, turned off the single glaring bulb that cast more shadows than light, and carefully descended the narrow staircase.

Eloise saw something that made her come to a full stop. "Dabs, this has an 'R' on it."

"Really?"

"Don't you see it? The letter 'R' with vines and leaves around it."

Dab's squinted at the disk in her hand. "It's so corroded. How can you be so sure?"

"Because I have one just like it."

22

"Would you two like to keep me company while I bring in the geriatric herd and feed them?"

Betsy demurred. But Eloise and Prince were eager. The three of them walked to the pasture to find horses ambling toward them in a sort of line dance.

Dude was in the lead, the other two following. Dude got to the gate and hung his head over with ears pricked, looking straight at Eloise.

Dabs spoke to the horse. "Yes. We have visitors."

The gate was barely secured by a chain that was hooked over the head of a nail. Dabs unhooked the chain, opening the gate by lifting it off its sagging hinges. The horses waited politely, then Dabs gestured, and the old gentlemen continued single file along the beaten path.

Dabs turned to follow, but not until he gave a small bow to Eloise.

Eloise asked, "You never put a halter on them?"

"They aren't going to stray."

The barn was chilly and dark. Dabs flicked on the lights, and they hummed. The horses had put themselves into the correct stalls and were munching hay. Eloise followed Dabs into a feed room. Three buckets were covered with towels.

"I soak the feed for the old guys."

Dabs handed Eloise a bucket and took the other two and they stepped back into the aisle.

No hanging plastic corner feeders here. Each stall had wooden feeders built into the walls. Once the horses were fed, she and Dabs stood for a moment.

Dabs said, "Makes me feel good to see them eat."

Eloise then wandered down the aisle. It was a huge barn with a high ceiling, despite the loft. There was an open space over the back of each stall where hay could be pushed into the stall directly from the loft. It must have been quite the chore to load and stack hay up there in the days before electric hay conveyors. Even with the convey-ers, Eloise knew it was a big job.

At the end of the row of box stalls, Eloise came upon something she had never seen before.

She asked, "Standing stalls?"

Dabs nodded. "Never used in my lifetime."

Eloise walked into the stall to get a closer look. The floor was pitted, but hard as stone. The partitions were wood with curved iron bars to separate the heads of the horses. There was a sort of wooden shelf, with a rack for hay above it. The flat part of where she thought feed would go had a hole on the left side.

Eloise turned to Dabs. "Why the hole?"

"For the tie-rope. It had a wooden ball on the end. I have a box of the balls here somewhere. They're called 'tie-bob-bins.' The 'tie' rope was long enough that it allowed the horse to lie down, but when the horse stood, the extra length would be pulled down the hole again by the weight of the 'bobbin.' No extra rope to get tangled in the horse's legs."

"Clever."

Dabs pointed at the hay rack. "Mom always called it a hay 'rick.' But she also called the hayloft a 'hay-mow.' Spelled like 'mow', but rhymes with 'cow'. Strange old-timey words."

Eloise examined the rack that ran along the back wall, then looked up to see the opening above to the loft where the hay would be stored.

She said, "'Mow?' I've never heard that term before, although 'rick' sounds familiar. How did they get the hay up there before the days of gas or electric conveyors?"

"Winched it up with a hook and ropes and a swing arm into the big loft door. Same door we still use."

Eloise smiled because it made her think of Louisa's description of Monticello's lack of a staircase. She counted the standing stalls. There were ten of them, each slot about five feet wide.

She said, "Can you imagine walking down your barn aisle and looking at ten equine behinds in a row? Must have been quite a sight."

"I have to imagine it because we only used the box stalls. The box stalls were already here when Mom grew up. It can't be healthy for the horses to be so limited in their movements."

Eloise nodded, "Especially in the winter when the weather was too harsh to be outside. Moving is how horses stay warm. They must have gotten awfully stiff."

Dabs nodded. "And if the horses couldn't get turned out and go to the water tank or the creek to drink, water had to be hauled by hand."

"Remember reading about the terrible winter here in 1779? We have it so much easier today. We have freeze proof hydrants, although we have to take the hoses off and leave them in the wheelbarrow in the heated tack room at night." Then she corrected herself. "Well, when we had a farm."

Dabs pointed again to the wooden feed box in a standing stall. "Look at the smooth depression in the wood. Feel it. It's like a turned bowl, only made of marble. Recently I've wondered if we have met the horses in the journals who made those depressions."

Eloise laid her palm flat against the wood and imagined Beauty, Fashion, Rudy, and Fanny. Any of those long-ago horses, could have slowly shaped this wood with their tongues as they ate. She had her hand touching what they had touched. Eloise closed her eyes and felt herself reach back through time. A chill passed over her, but her hand, the palm of her hand, pressed against the bowl created by the horses, well her palm felt so warm it began to sweat. Eloise pulled it back suddenly.

Dabs said, "As soon as the first depression was made, the grain would roll into it, and the next horse would make the depression deeper. It happened over time. Time way before anyone can remember keeping horses in these stalls. You felt it?"

"I'm not sure what I felt Dabs. But feel the palm of my hand."

Dabs took Eloise's hand in his and gave it a gentle squeeze.

"Your hands are like ice."

Eloise *was* cold, but she wanted the sudden heat of her palm to be true, to believe she had made a connection to the creatures of the past. Wanting things to be true was not the same thing as true, though. Wanting by itself was complicated and painful but also exquisite. Like memories. Shadows of what was but is no longer. Her hand had been cold. Not hot.

Dabs added, "Let's get inside. I've got fixings for spaghetti. I hope you like spaghetti. You eat meat? I can leave the meat out if you prefer."

"I love spaghetti, and I eat meat. Betsy eats bacon, that I've witnessed, so it's all good."

Dabs looked relieved. "That's good. It's my mother's recipe. Well, then."

* * *

Eloise could not sleep. Dinner had been delicious. Her tummy was nicely full. That wasn't it. A low-level of anxiety continued to buzz through her. She was expecting, what? That the trip to Ivy Creek held an answer to all her problems?

Prince had hopped up into the high four-poster and tucked himself against her. The room was cold, and he was warm and heavy against her stomach. She had thrown an arm around his curled-up form and pulled him into her for extra warmth. A dead weight of relaxed and sleepy dog, he offered no resistance. He was the best thing in her life. She had dared to want what was not hers as some sort of cosmic compensation for losing what had been hers. But loss was, it seemed, to be a constant in her life. She would in time, lose him too.

They were safe for the moment. She was seeking, what? Magical intervention on her behalf?

But the thing was, she felt there was magic here. She felt it like a weightiness in the air. It wasn't enough to have made it here to Dabs. She wanted to flee to Louisa.

Eloise decided she would use her insomnia to begin an imaginary discussion thread on Extreme Readers. Of course, it had to be about Jefferson and the founders from Virginia and not Louisa Roberts, and especially not about Eloise Robertson and her giant fail.

These Virginian's were the undisputed elites of their age. Did they believe their own ornate rationalizations for their injustices? Or did their failings eat at them? Did they feel deep and private shame in the dark of night?

Failings. Shame. Maybe she had lofty company. These were her thoughts as she finally drifted off to sleep.

Eloise was awakened by the rapid thumping of Prince's tail and muffled barking. Thumpa-thumpa-thumpa-thumpa. She lifted herself onto one elbow to look at her dog. His lips made little popping sounds as they puffed away from his gums. Eloise wondered who it was that made him so happy. Eloise glanced toward the window, to check the light. Had the sun begun to break over the horizon yet? It was still dark.

Eloise stiffened. A densely dark shape backlit by a

lighter darkness filled the corner. She felt that she should not breathe too loudly. That she should not move. But if there had been someone there, Prince would have barked, surely. Eloise reached slowly for her dog. She felt the warm arc of his ribs, the knob on his sternum. She pulled him into her. He stretched and rolled unto his back, as if asking for a belly rub. Silly. No one was there. She took a breath and stroked the soft underbelly of her dog, settled back into her pillows, and closed her eyes, no longer scared, but instead feeling that she had summoned Louisa. And that was something.

Then she heard words. Or imagined them. It was the way you "hear" words when you are reading a book

It was Louisa, and she said, "I never thought him my enemy. But then I had not yet felt the war. To see him there with Bloody Ban, well, to take my most precious possession, it was the breaking of me. Or so I thought at the time."

Eloise tried to pick up the thread, to hear more of Louisa's story, there was no more "there" there. She had put the "book" down. Eloise felt very tired.

The next time Eloise looked at the bedroom window it was tinged in pink. The sun had broken the horizon to peek into her room. The room was freezing, and Prince seemed disinterested in getting up. Eloise let him be while she pulled on jeans and layered all her tops, including her jacket. Louisa's words clung to her. Louisa had lost something too, had something taken from her. Or Eloise had spun out her story like a piece of fanfiction. Or that.

She and Prince tip-toed downstairs. Eloise let Prince

out the back door while she found the coffee and filters. She got the back door open before Prince could bark to come in. Then she fed him his kibble.

Eloise had her first cup gazing out the back of the house at the barn thinking of the night, and her creative delusions.

The only noise was the occasional hiss and burp as the coffee finished brewing. Prince curled up under the kitchen table, pushing a chair out of place. The sun hitting the cold ground made a low fog. Eloise rested her chin in her cupped palm, her head fuzzy. She wondered if Priscilla would already be up, checking the fireplaces, getting the stove ready for breakfast? Would Isaac and Sammie have fed the horses? And little Bud? Would he be helping them? Eloise almost expected to conjure their forms as she had conjured Louisa's voice.

A low voice spoke gently behind her. "You're up early."

She did not startle, although the tone of his voice indicated he thought that she would.

"Old habits die hard."

He saw the coffee was made. "I'm not used to such treatment."

He filled a mug. "Did you sleep well?"

"Prince and I had visitors. Or at least that's how it seemed."

"I'm so sorry. The squirrels in the attic used to keep me up, but I had this expensive system installed with a one-way exit door so they can leave but they can't return. I'd thought by now they'd all be gone."

"Not squirrels. I woke up from a deep sleep and thought

I saw a shape by the window. A dream, yeah, I know. But it was Louisa, and she spoke too."

Eloise repeated the words as best as she could. Dabs surprisingly brought her a pen and she committed them to paper.

"So, clearly I'm making up a good story."

"Bloody Ban is Banastre Tarleton. His Charlottesville raid was in 1781. But of course, you know all that. We read about how Jefferson was accused of cowardice by fleeing."

"Yes. I know who Bloody Ban was and all the political machinations later to smear Jefferson."

"Still, that's some impressive dreaming."

"How can you live here and not have those sorts of dreams all the time?"

"Maybe not dreams, but I have plenty of daydreams. When I was young, I spent a lot of time rambling around this countryside. I imagined running across Indians, and later, Jefferson. And now that I have the journals, I dream of meeting Louisa. It's kind of wonderful."

"It *is* wonderful."

Dabs leaned back against the counter, "So much has transpired here, on this very ground. Some days I feel like the space I am taking up, although it looks empty, is crowded. Every room is occupied. Every stall is filled."

"I don't feel that way in Atlanta."

"No? Think of the Civil War. But it's not just famous people or battles that give a place a feel. It's all the lives that tread the ground we walk over. Even the lives of our own parents."

Eloise frowned, "Mom sold our horse farm. Where I

grew up. Where they ran their business. It was the only home I ever knew. Mom bought a townhome and that's where I live now. It's not home. It never will be."

"Isn't it still full of your things, your mom's things?"

"Yes."

"Don't you feel her presence through those things?"

"Not really."

The lie slipped easily from her lips but filled her with shame. She remembered how she had come undone over her mother's hairbrush.

Dabs changed subjects, "Hey, come have a look at the newest journal entry."

"I'd love that!"

"And if you're really nice to me, afterward, I'll let you help me muck stalls."

"Bet you use that line on all the girls."

"No. But, in hindsight, I should have used it to screen out unsuitable matches."

Eloise deflected, "Three stalls isn't hard, it's more like a session of meditation."

"Agree. The sifting of manure from shavings, well, it's not unlike tending a Zen Garden."

Eloise nodded, "A Zen Garden of poop."

Eloise followed Dabs into his study, and he put on cotton gloves. He had wrapped each journal in acid-free paper. He unwrapped the one he was currently working on and set it on a table. Then Dabs used a flat stainless-steel instrument that almost looked like something from the autoclave at the vet clinic. Dabs called it a spade.

"I'm going to go to the page I'm working on."

Louisa's writing had faded to a faint brown, the letters long and elegant, with loops and flourishes, and densely packed. Even the margins were filled with the last line of each page making a circuit around the edge.

Eloise found her hand had lifted. Touching the page would be like touching Louisa, or close to it. But she caught herself, her hand dropping to her side.

Dabs added, "Every now and then she adds a little sketch, horses, dogs, and ivy. Not so many in this section though."

Dabs drew his brows together, "Toward the end of this journal, there are spots and crumbling edges."

"I suppose the less you handle it the better."

"I try not to touch the page. The faded letters are hard to see, but I have this." He pointed to a flexible stand with a lighted magnifying glass."

"Where in the world did you find that?"

"Can you believe it, my mother had it. With this light and magnifier, she could read any book, even as her eyesight deteriorated. The lamp is actually designed for doing fine needlework."

"'Needlework?"

Betsy answered from the doorway, surprising them. "Oh Eloise, needlework was once a required skill of every proper lady. Now, let me look at the journal too."

Betsy had to grab Prince by the collar and pull him back so she could look.

She lectured the dog, "Prince, you don't even know how to read."

After Betsy had a moment to examine the journal she exclaimed, "Oh my!"

Betsy leaned closer, squinting at the faded ink. "May I?" She turned on the light and swung the magnifier over the page.

"Extraordinary."

Dabs said, "I've transcribed and typed up a new entry and made us each a copy. Now that I've shown you the journal, I can put this up for now and we can read the printed transcription over breakfast."

Eloise nodded and added, "Once the horses are done."

"Okay. We finish our cup of coffee, then we muck, I'll fry up omelets and we can read and talk about the latest entry."

Betsy lifted her eyebrows.

Eloise laughed, "Betsy, you don't have to muck."

"I am of the opinion that I'm unqualified."

Dabs said, "Perhaps you would prefer a walk with the dog."

Betsy added, "Or better yet, ruminate over my cup of coffee."

Eloise smiled. "Or that."

* * *

December 26, 1779

Aunt Bess and father have handed out winter garments and extra rations to those who labor in the ground. The numbers have dwindled through these war years as those who left us to seek freedom with the enemy have not returned, except Sammie. Winter has settled upon us, but the labor is never done. The fields are not yet too frozen to chop in manure that is hauled by wagonloads. It is hard work. But I wonder if those who have left us and avoided the job have not chosen a worse fate. Or in fact, have perished.

Major Schmidt has introduced us to a new Christmas tradition. He used the washpot to boil water, then added wheat bran and molasses to make Christmas soup for the horses. We ladled it into their troughs and watched as they drank the soup and smacked their lips, some suckled like foals to savor the bits stuck to their tongues. Bud found this amusing, and truth be told, I did as well. However, it has made a mess of the wash pot. And it is far too cold to clean up the mess at present.

Christmas morn we exchanged gifts. I made drawings for each of my family. For father I drew a portrait of our stallion, for I know he cannot last many more winters and is much beloved. I captured him most nobly I think, without the signs of age he now wears.

Dear Aunt Bess. She is the most selfless of souls. I drew her portrait, with a kind eye, in the act of knitting.

Buck, I drew holding a brace of duck, thinking that scene would please him most. I did well enough to escape my brother's opprobrium.

Father outdid us all. My gift, of which I believe Aunty most heartedly did disapprove, was a fine new saddle for Beauty. Although it was well padded and quilted, it was most scandalously not a side-saddle. The Baroness, it seems had convinced father that riding astride was not only sufficiently healthy and modest for a lady, but in fact, far safer than aside. Aunt Bess tut-tutted but agreed to design an appropriate over-skirt to protect and cover my legs.

Buck was delighted with his present from father, a long gun of the type used on the frontier. It is much touted for its accuracy. We pray the enemy is not thus armed.

The Major joined us for our Christmas board, which was so filled that there was no place left to place the mince pies. Priscilla had to clear the platters as they emptied to make space.

I made a point to take a platter out to the cabins later. It was only right that Isaac, Sammie, Bud, and Priscilla enjoy the bounty in privacy without being called away into service. And when I found Bud, I was able to give him the drawing I had made of his precious Lady Jane.

A happier child I have never seen. But, not due to my gift. The child begged me to sit while he took a violin from a case. I knew it was not Major Schmidt's because this case was lined in blue satin. I was aghast.

Sammie cut me off before I could speak. "Bud worked real hard at his lessons. That prisoner going to be gone one day, and so will his violin. Bud had to have his own."

Bud then performed a simple tune to prove his

brother's words true. And I applauded heartily at the completion of the ditty.

I left the servants to their leisure, feeling unsettled. And in the yard, I met Major Schmidt who appeared to be going to visit the cabin, his own violin case in hand.

"Do you have a duet in mind with your student?"

He answered, "No duets of yet. But the student learns by watching as well as practice. Bud is in that golden time when learning comes easily, but it passes. We must make the most of it while I am still here."

I said, "It is far too grand a gift. It will only cause jealousy, envy, and frustration."

He said, "I had little part in it."

I was not believing his words. "The gift was not yours?"

He said, "I helped locate it. A student's instrument, but it will serve the boy for years to come."

I foolishly raised my voice, "Who would give a servant child such a lavish gift?"

The Major leaned closer and spoke slowly, voice low, brows knit, eyes narrowed, he said, "His own father."

I am ashamed to admit at that moment, I was confused. Major Schmidt saw it, knew it immediately.

Before I could make my way past him, he did utter, "Louisa, surely you know this to be true."

This "truth" the Major delivered had breached all fortifications of my heart and mind. It arrived now like a flaming arrow, and I felt the heat of it. And yes, indeed, once uttered by the Major, I did indeed think it true. But still, I was enraged.

I said nothing in return but walked on.

23

Dabs and Eloise returned from feeding the horses to a warm and fragrant kitchen. Betsy greeted them. "Dabs, I've invaded your kitchen. I've a frittata in the oven."

Eloise exclaimed, "Frittata? Whatever it is, it smells wonderful."

Betsy laughed, "It's a fancy name for a baked omelet. Dabs, I threw in what I could find, cheese, onions, bacon. I baked some potato wedges too."

"You can invade my kitchen any time."

Eloise experienced Deja' vu. Growing up, Jock and Eloise always got up early to feed. Animals came first. Always. That was true at the clinic, too.

Eloise realized, for the first time, that by taking the job there, she had tried to recreate her childhood routine.

Dabs brought them the newly transcribed pages, and all activity stopped while they read.

Once it was clear they had all finished, Betsy put down her mug, "So. Mr. Roberts is Bud's father. I confess, it had occurred to me."

Dabs added, "I had wondered, after all we've read about Sally Hemings. And Eloise, your additional research

330

showed that such a relationship might have been common practice."

"You both had guessed it? That Bud was her half-brother?"

Betsy looked surprised. "I would expect you to have guessed it first."

"But Mr. Roberts?" Eloise's voice trailed off.

Dabs quoted Jefferson's granddaughter. "A moral impossibility?"

"No, I guess not. Here, like at Monticello, a shadow family could have existed. Louisa did get something correct though."

Betsy asked, "What?"

"Louisa said the gift would create jealousy, envy, and frustration."

Dabs asked, "Ah, but whose jealousy, envy, or frustration?"

Betsy said, "Louisa's willful ignorance is not an uncommon protective response."

Eloise sighed, "Okay, but like Eve's bite of the apple, once you know, you can't 'unknow. Oh, wow, now I see and get Buck's resentments. Sammie is their half-brother too."

Dabs said, "Bet all three boys are his father's children, Sammie, Isaac, and Bud. Buck knows."

"Oh."

Betsy added, "Jefferson and Sally, Mr. Roberts and Maisie, there is always the possibility of love, isn't there?"

Eloise looked thoughtful, "When someone holds complete power over you, and has every legal right to play the tyrant, can you truly love them, even if they are kind?"

Betsy said, "Well, what you just described, Eloise, has been legally true for women until very recent history."

"Oh."

Dabs said, "We can't know if Mr. Roberts loved Bud's mother, or if Jefferson loved Sally, and if those feelings, if they existed, were reciprocated. It would be foolish to make assumptions. But I think it fair to say that no one likes to have to compete for affection or feel that their children must compete for affection or material well-being or anything else. A good argument against bigamy."

Betsy said, "Times change, but jealousy, envy, and festering resentments, those are eternal."

* * *

After they had cleaned up the kitchen, Dabs announced, "I'm making a run to the electronics store to buy an auxiliary flash so we can try that experiment with the headstones, then I'm heading to the grocery store. Any requests?"

Betsy said, "Please let me buy groceries. I love to cook, or I could treat us to dinner out. Either way, I'd like to contribute."

"Oh no, I want to play host. You're here such a short time. Go see Monticello."

Eloise looked surprised. "Really?"

"You two should play tourist while I shop. While you're touring, I'll work on the next transcription."

Eloise frowned, "But what about Prince?"

"We'll have a guy's day while you two historians do your research."

Betsy said, "We accept!" before Eloise could lodge a protest.

Eloise did want to see Monticello. But there were a couple of other stops she wanted to make first.

* * *

The GPS said they were there as soon as they turned out of Dab's driveway. Betsy pulled the car over and cut off the engine and the two women got out; a bit confused because they saw nothing.

Betsy said, "It should be here."

Eloise zipped up her jacket against the cold. They walked along the road, eyes scanning the landscape. Betsy spotted it first, a low stone base with a brass historical marker sitting in the shadows.

Betsy read the inscription in a soft voice. "In 1779, 4,000 prisoners, British and their German auxiliaries, captured at the Battle of Saratoga in 1777, marched over 600 miles to quarters, called 'The Barracks', situated a half mile north of this site. Traditionally, some of these prisoners who died were buried near this memorial marker, which was placed here by the Albemarle County Historical Society in 1983 to mark the presence of the British and 'Hessian' prisoners during our American War of Independence."

Eloise said, "So, no headstones. No real way to say where the men are buried, just 'tradition' to go on. There are bodies here, near here, at least."

"Yes. A marker and some shrubs."

Eloise said, "So far from home, in unmarked graves, their names un-noted, forgotten."

"The fate of many a soldier."

Eloise looked down the road, "Louisa would have been over there, somewhere." Eloise pointed. "Her first meeting with Major Schmidt, sitting on Beauty, Bud at her side, her dog attending the funeral, uninvited yet tolerated."

Betsy said, "That was over 240 years ago. Still. It was on this ground, or very nearby. The creatures that walk upon it change, but the ground endures."

Eloise added, "Louisa wrote it down. Or we could never know what she experienced that day. I wish I could let her know that we are so glad she did. That because she did, we can pay our respects."

Betsy said, "Brr. Let's get back in the car and turn on the heat."

Eloise said, "I feel like we should give a benediction or something."

Betsy did the honors. "Dear Lord, bless these brave men, let them know we are no longer enemies, but friends. All is forgiven. May they rest in peace. Amen."

"Amen."

Betsy turned the heat on high to thaw out as they drove the short distance to the marker for the Albemarle Barracks. The marker sat near the entrance to a horse farm, looking out over vast pastures. The wind was gusting as they walked up to the sign.

Betsy said, "That wind makes me think of those poor men, having marched 600 miles in winter weather, just to find themselves here in a deep snow with no real shelter."

"Let me take a photo and then we can get back in the car."

Once in the car, Eloise enlarged the photo and read it to Betsy. In addition to the basic facts, it read:

"Most prisoners lived in primitive huts spread out over several hundred acres of the barracks camp, where they endured great hardships. Supplying and guarding the Convention Army taxed the resources of the community and militia. By Feb. 1781, the last of the prisoners had been relocated."

Eloise frowned, "That can't be right. Jefferson wrote that the camp brought in something like thirty thousand dollars a week into the local economy."

"Are you sure that's correct?"

"That's the number Jefferson claimed as a minimum went into the local economy. He wrote it in a letter to Patrick Henry."

"So, you think the local community was not as "taxed" as the marker claims?"

"Well, for sure, Jefferson did not want them moved away from Charlottesville. He thought the camp a boon to the local economy. But Patrick Henry was upset over the expense and logistical nightmare it was for the state. Maybe the truth lies somewhere between the two. Here we go again with jealousy and resentments. Those two were always at odds. It was war time, and Washington couldn't get his troops provisioned or paid, and yet the state was forced to house and feed the enemy while our own soldiers froze and starved."

Betsy added, "The treatment of POW's is always

fraught with emotion. They are the enemy, killing your countrymen."

Eloise said, "Yet good Major Schmidt with the other prisoners finished the work Virginia had promised to provide but had not. They built their barracks, planted gardens, raised livestock. The officers rented houses, even remodeled the homes they rented, and built additional living spaces. The prisoners even built a theater. They got on with it, trying to better the conditions. And Jefferson obviously did not resent them. He entertained the officers in his home."

Betsy countered, "Ah, but Jefferson in 1779 had the luxury of being far from the fighting."

Eloise said, "He was no soldier. True."

Betsy added, "The war comes right to his doorstep later. That doorstep is not far from here. Shall we go visit the "Master of the Mountain?""

* * *

Prince had his wet beard resting on Dab's knee, while Dabs rubbed behind his ear. "Well Prince, it's you and me buddy. I know your Momma rarely puts the leash on you, but I'm taking no chances."

Dabs fetched the leash and clipped it on the dog's collar. Prince pranced by his side as they headed out the back door. Dabs couldn't remember when he last had company. Or if he ever had any since his mother's passing.

Dabs once again climbed the hill to the old cemetery.

He let Prince lead the way up the steep part of the path, trying to flatten with his feet the downed vines and canes to create a wider path.

Dabs cleared the tree line and stopped to admire the view of Ivy Creek. Then he thought of the residents of this hill who were likely no more than mulch, or less than mulch at this stage. But they had once been as alive as he was. Did they too once enjoy this view?

Prince had put his snout down and was snuffling about, so Dabs dropped the leash. "Go on, enjoy the smells." The dog wandered past the hanging iron gate into the interior of the walled cemetery. Dabs followed, looking at the forlorn and unkempt space. He had spent an afternoon trying to tidy up, but the neglect was obvious.

Dabs started by walking the circumference of the walled space, then spiraled in, and by doing so, came at last to stop right in the middle. He stood by the side-by-side depressions, the pitted headstones. The ground was depressed, the stone at each end aslant, the foot stones not much more than chips. Dabs stood on the grave site, hoping to decipher something, anything, on the stones, when it came to him that the ground felt spongy, and he stepped aside. The hairs prickled on the back of his neck. Prince had stiffened too, the hackles standing up on his back.

Dabs spoke to the dog. "Oops. Must have walked over your grave, well not your grave, but someone's, and they weren't too happy about it."

Dabs picked up the leash and gave it a tug. "Maybe I was standing on someone's head." He chuckled. His laughter broke the spell. Regardless, they started back down the hill at a brisk pace.

* * *

Dabs let Prince sit next to him on the bench seat of his truck. It reminded him of days long past when he had an oversized black Lab who went everywhere with him. It felt good to see Prince cram his nose into the small space Dabs had made by rolling down the window, his permanently wet beard leaving streaks on the glass. Dabs stopped first at the electronics shop to get the auxiliary flash, then the grocery store. He was making roast beef for dinner with mashed potatoes and green beans. For dessert he went the easy route and bought ice cream. Ice cream had been a Jefferson favorite. Dabs also bought a bag of dog chews to augment Prince's supply.

Once he returned to the farm, he found himself talking to the dog. "It's rib roast. Sadly, not for you, although I'll bet, we can put gravy from it over your kibble. Doesn't seem fair though, does it?"

Prince was waving his long-fringed tail in reply, bright eyes intensely focused on the grocery bags.

Dabs opened the bag of dental chews and handed one to Prince, who took it eagerly and pranced out of the room, his head held high.

Dabs hoped for Eloise's sake that all could be worked out back in Atlanta with the prior owner. It would be a shame to have to give the dog up. But that would wait. Right now, he was ready to get back to the transcription.

He knew Eloise and Betsy would expect a new one when they returned. Monticello offered more than could be absorbed in one visit. They would likely be chilled to the bone, footsore, and overwhelmed by the experience.

Like most historic houses, like the very one he stood in, Monticello was so much more than bricks and stone and lumber. How could inanimate things come to mean so much to so many? Well, here he was. He had left his career, his marriage, his friends, to devote himself to this house and this land. Well, initially, it was to devote himself to the care of his mother. But that had been over three years ago, and here he had remained. And even though every inch was familiar to him, with the discovery of the journals, he realized he knew almost nothing of it.

Dabs got settled at his task in the study, putting on his glove liners to handle the journal, carefully placing it on a stand that was designed for holding open a dictionary. He used the "spade" to open the journal and turn to a new page. Louisa's dense and loopy lettering in faded brown ink thickly covered nearly every inch of the page. He turned on his mother's embroidery lamp, swinging the arm over the page and leaned forward to look through the illuminated magnifying glass. Dabs then pulled up his rolling chair to the desk, got his pen and paper, placed it next to the stand, sat down, and began to transcribe.

Louisa's words always absorbed him fully. And so, he was startled to find a very wet muzzle across his thigh.

"Hey, not so close to the desk." Dabs pushed gently on the stand that held the journal, placing it a safer distance from the edge. Prince did not budge but looked up through his shaggy black mop.

"What? You ate the chew too fast?" The long tail waved slowly back and forth, the eyes still asking for something.

"Potty break? Okay, but it's going to be short."

As soon as Dabs stood up, Prince was bouncing around and barking.

"Sorry, to be so dense."

Dabs fetched the leash and marched the dog down the driveway and back to the house, satisfied all was accomplished. Dabs gave the dog a second dental chew before settling back down with the journal.

Dabs got well into his transcription. Each line he transcribed he rechecked against the original to be sure he had not made unnecessary changes. He became aware at one point that Prince had joined him, sitting like a sentinel in the doorway. Dabs turned momentarily in his seat and noted that Prince was holding one of his shoes in his mouth. He ignored the dog and then heard the dog's nails clicking against the wood floors. Better to lose a shoe than to lose his place in the transcription.

Dabs realized the dog had returned. This time Prince had what looked like a rag doll draped gently in his mouth. Dabs was sure he had never seen the doll before. Dabs rose and walked over to the dog, who spit the doll out at his feet.

"I'm sorry but you'll have to entertain yourself until the ladies return."

Prince drooped and walked away, head lowered, shoulders hunched, tail listless.

Dabs went back to his task in earnest. Once finished, he pushed his chair back from the desk, swung the arm on the magnifier back and turned off the light, put on his glove liners, and carefully wrapped the journal and placed it back in his drawer. Safe. Now, he needed to move to his other desk where the laptop was waiting for him to type up his transcription, creating a document.

Dabs checked his watch. He needed to get the roast in the oven. He got up, but not before printing out "How to cook the perfect roast every time." The directions were simple. Dabs had a moment of pride, envisioning his perfect roast being presented to his guests. Then he shook himself. It wasn't a perfect roast yet.

Dabs got the roast going and set the timer. He left the potatoes and green beans on the counter, filled the pot with water for boiling potatoes later. He felt organized.

He returned to his laptop and opened a blank page, named it, dated it, rubbed his hands together in anticipation, and began to type from his notes. It did not take long to become fully immersed.

Prince was so stealthy that Dabs didn't hear him before the dog wedged his big head under his right arm, dampening his right thigh. This time his bushy eyebrows were full of "dust-bunnies."

"Well, hello. Clearly I need a housekeeper."

At that the dog spit something out of his mouth onto Dabs' lap, and backed away, ears pricked, tail waving slowly, expectantly.

Dabs looked down, horrified at the dark object that appeared to have a tail.

"Ick, disgusting."

Dabs pulled gingerly at the long dark and twisted thing, breathing a sigh of relief that it was not in fact a desiccated rat corpse. It was a strip of leather, hardened and twisted, and at the end of the "tail" hung an ornate but blackened key. Dabs held it up and away from himself to get a better look, and Prince did a backward-hopping dance, as if he thought Dabs would toss it for him.

"Where are you getting this stuff? Okay, the shoe came from my closet. But the doll and the key?"

Prince turned and left the room. Dabs followed. Once out in the hall, Dabs noted that Prince had not gone far, had in fact stopped just outside the room and was waiting at the foot of the stairs.

"Damn. Sucked me into your game. Okay then, where are we going?"

Dabs soon found himself in one of the upstairs bedrooms. He scanned the room, felt awkward, and began to back out the door, fiddling with the leather fob and key as he did. What was he doing?

"Come on. Let's check that roast. Surely you'll find that more stimulating."

Prince was happy to watch Dabs slide out the roast for a look. It was going to be beautiful. He went back to his computer, typing away, only stopping once to finger the rag doll and the key and fob.

Dabs thought of his mother. How she had slowly, very slowly withdrawn into the past, hoarding everything, assigning great import to stuff that looked like junk, squirreling things away, demanding that nothing be tossed or moved. He had dutifully waited to do anything until after she had died. And even now, he had mostly shifted the piles up to the attic space to add to the many piles already there.

She was clearly not the first packrat in the family, as the attic space had proven. Dabs looked at the doll again. The doll no longer had a face, although it did have a cap and faded dress, likely created from some ladies' sewing scraps for a daughter. Children then, like children now, needed a soft toy. But who was this sad little bit of faded cloth made for? Who took the time to put it together? He re-examined the doll, wishing he could find a face, but age and light had faded away what surely once was there, likely drawn in ink.

Dabs put down the doll and lifted the key by its fob. And where did this go? Where did the dog find it? Then he thought of his mother's steamer trunk in the attic.

24

Dabs walked away from his laptop. Prince again led him up the stairs but hesitated once Dabs had passed Eloise's room. Dabs opened the door to the garret stairs. He left the door open for additional light, climbing the narrow steps and flicking on the light. He carried the doll in one hand and the ancient key in the other.

He went straight for the steamer trunk. It was clear, once he got to the trunk, that the key he held in his hand did not belong. Still, he held the key up against the lock. He turned to go back to find Prince standing in the doorway, staring at him.

"Found your courage, did you?"

Prince advanced, performing the stiff-legged walk he had done earlier at the cemetery. The dog was afraid, but being a brave and loyal companion, and all that sort of thing, felt compelled to join him.

"C'mon, nothing up here but a lot of old stuff covered in dust."

Prince put his nose down and began to move in a jagged line, intent.

"We got rid of the rats, or squirrels, or whatever."

Dabs sighed, "Still, I don't even want to think about how much rat poop is still up here. Some of it, likely vintage."

That thought made him smile. Gross. But probably true.

Prince had now wedged himself between piles of stuff, far to the back. Then the dog went off like a fire alarm with furious barking. The noise echoed off the rafters.

Dabs began pushing stuff out of the way, trying to get to the dog. He was yelling at the dog to stop, but his shouts merely added to the cacophony, as if the two creatures were barking in unison.

Whatever Dabs was expecting to find, it wasn't this.

Prince was barking viciously at a gigantic wardrobe. How someone toted that thing up those narrow stairs was a mystery, but it sure wasn't going to go back down those stairs, not in his lifetime.

Dabs grabbed the dog's collar and pulled him back. The hand he used had a rag doll in it. In the other hand he still held the key by the twisted piece of leather. And then he noticed. The wardrobe had a lock. And it looked about right for the old key.

Dabs spoke to the dog in soothing tones. Prince stopped barking, backing away from the wardrobe as Dabs stepped closer. Though the dog was quiet, he clearly wasn't mollified. Prince had his hackles up and his ears flattened back against his skull with his entire body rocked slightly back.

Dabs examined the flaking varnish, loose hinges, and the hardware, filigreed and fine. It must have been a valuable piece of furniture in its day. He wasn't surprised when the key slid easily into the lock and with a bit of jiggling back and forth, turned. Dabs gave a tug, but the door remained stuck. A firmer tug and the hardware of the latch seemed to loosen in his hands.

Dabs gave as hard a pull as he could muster, determined to get the thing open, but instead of the door opening as it should, it seemed to fling itself off the furniture, the door edge whacking Dabs on his head, causing him to yell out, from both surprise and pain.

Dabs too, had managed to punch himself in the forehead with the old key. He had nearly tipped the whole damn thing over on top of himself. Instead, it was only the contents that burst forth, having at one point obviously been over-stuffed into the wardrobe. The lead item appeared to jump at Dabs from above him, teeth and claws bared. Or at least that's how it appeared to both man and dog, although really the tippy-top shelf was simply disgorging its contents.

Dabs used the door as a shield to frantically swat the half-seen thing away, then he threw the door like a weapon, still yelling while observing, irrationally, that the attacker was what was traditionally referred to as a Catamount. Its mouth was open, its large canine teeth bared, even though it was quite dead.

Prince jumped into battle while Dabs stumbled backward, leaping over Dabs and attacking the (quite dead) beast. The dog and the great cat of the mountains appeared to be engaged in a life and death struggle in the tight and dusty space between mounds of junk. It was noisy, it was fierce, and the dust and fur flew. Dabs, holding the rag doll to the cut on his forehead, had extricated himself as far back as an old ladderback chair with a missing spindle. He sat down heavily, the chair collapsed with the sound of splintering wood, and Dabs found himself wedged between the chair legs, half sitting on the floor. Somehow, through the chaos, way behind him, he heard Eloise's voice.

"Dabs? Prince?"

Dabs waved a rag doll over his head like a flag. "Here." He did not even try to get himself untangled from the chair.

Eloise began making her way around stuff.

Prince, having heard Eloise's voice, stopped his attack.

"When we walked in the timer was going off. Betsy rescued dinner. And then we heard thumps and barking."

Dabs called back to her, "Oh my God, the roast."

"Wow, you look stuck. Why are you holding that doll to your head?"

"I got attacked by a Mountain Lion. I think Prince finished him off."

"Um, you're talking crazy-talk, but let's have a look at your head."

Dabs pulled the doll away and Eloise squinted at his forehead. "Just a scratch and a bump. Did you say it was from a cat? Prince likes cats, he wouldn't kill a cat. Well, anyway, let's put some ice on that."

Prince joined them in the tight space, looking self-satisfied and relaxed.

Dabs said, "There's the man of the hour. Let's go look at the kill, shall we?"

"If you can extricate yourself from that chair."

Dabs put out his hand and Eloise grabbed ahold and

on the count of three gave a tug. It was awkward, but Dabs got to his feet.

"As one who has recently experienced a head injury, let me say that if you saw a Mountain Lion after hitting your head, your secret's safe with me."

Dabs rolled his eyes and led her back toward the busted wardrobe and the heap of furs on the floor. The Mountain Lion pelt was worse for wear, but the head intact.

Dabs picked it up, poking it at Eloise and mock roaring. "RAAAHHHHR!

Prince barked once, but now with enthusiasm if not pride. Prince had fluff from the pelt around his mouth and hanging from his chin hairs.

"You aren't delusional after all. Wow, look at that!"

Eloise took it from him and examined it. It wasn't just a pelt. It had beading and fringe on it. It was a headdress.

Eloise placed it on top of her head, the front legs of the cat dangling over her shoulders. Prince backed away a couple steps, confused.

Eloise exclaimed, "It's a Native American headdress! Isn't it cool! What else was in there?"

Dabs bent down and picked up the next fur. A full-length heavy coat. He handed it to Eloise who put it on in addition to her headdress. The next item was a mink stole, with a desiccated head still on.

Dabs scowled, "Why in the world was this ever a thing?"

Eloise, weighted down with furs and a headdress, looked at the wardrobe, the broken hinges, cracked wood, and the door on the floor.

"What a shame."

Betsy appeared behind them. "Eloise, that's an interesting if not macabre outfit."

Eloise added, "And surprisingly heavy."

Dabs picked another jacket off the floor. "Beaver?"

Prince leaned forward and sniffed, his hackles once again rising.

Betsy looked at the doll still held by Dabs. "Oh my. Look at that doll."

"Prince found it, I've never seen it before."

Betsy took the doll from Dabs and examined it closely. "Look at the fine needlework. This is very old. Look at the cloth. This seems hand loomed. It makes me feel a bit sad. The child mortality rate was so high. Maternal death rates too. How tenuous and fragile each babe's chance of survival. A woman sewed this doll for a precious baby of the house. I can nearly feel the love just holding it."

Betsy looked distracted as she handed the doll back to Dabs.

Dabs broke the spell by asking, "Did I ruin dinner?"

"No. Nipped it from the oven just in time. Roast is resting on the counter; potatoes are on the boil and the beans we can zap in the microwave. I don't like my beef rare anyway."

"Bless you."

"Eloise, that headdress looks mangy. It's likely infested. Head-lice are more common than you'd think."

Eloise snatched the headdress off her head and handed it to Dabs, then removed the heavy coat.

Betsy added over her shoulder as she left, "Scrub those hands before we eat."

Once Betsy left, Dabs and Eloise began to giggle. Prince too seemed to get the joke, his tail wagging and his mouth hanging open, his eyes brightly watching the two of them.

Dabs pulled off the fluff that was still hanging from the dog's beard.

Eloise had to stifle her giggles to speak, "We leave you two guys alone for one day…"

"That dog could get a Saint into trouble."

"He keeps things interesting, for sure."

"I get why you want to keep him, though. He's wonderful."

Eloise nodded. But then found that she could not speak.

The two stood silently next to each other, and Dabs became uncertain, but finally found his courage to break the silence.

"Betsy told me a bit about what happened."

"I can't talk about it."

"That's fine. I just wanted you to know that I know. Well, mostly. I know too that you lost your Mom. Both my parents are gone. It doesn't matter that I'm thirty, I still feel like an orphan. No one chooses to be an orphan. A dog, a horse, well, they don't make things feel right, but they are all those things that Mr. Roberts spoke of in Louisa's journal. They help. I get it."

Dabs switched topics, "Hey, let's eat that roast and you can tell me about your day. And I'll tell you about mine. I'm almost done with the latest transcription. I'll be able to print out the document for you and Betsy to read before bedtime."

Eloise looked at the mess around her. "Shouldn't we clean up?"

Dabs reached down and turned the pelt of the mountain lion, so its eyes faced the floor. Prince looked at Dabs and wagged his tail.

Dabs smiled down at the dog, then at Eloise, and said, "Not tonight."

* * *

Betsy handed Dabs a plateful from the sideboard and said, "Monticello has a republican feel even as it's grand too. Don't you agree, Eloise?"

It felt natural, letting Betsy take charge. Eloise made a mental note to offer to do the cleanup.

Eloise agreed. "It wasn't a bit ostentatious. No gilt, no heavy ornamentation. Many of the rooms were modest. And as promised, no grand staircase. I mean, the entry hall was an intriguing museum that advertised intellect and travel and scope of knowledge, but after that, it was simply a lovely home with lots of light and air."

Betsy added, "I agree with Louisa. The lack of a central staircase was odd."

Eloise said, "When you walk outside you realize that Jefferson's home was a village. With slave cabins and workshops, and little factories. Then the livestock. And the underground rooms and passages, nearly invisible to the casual onlooker. It wasn't a bit modest in scope. Not really. Like Jefferson's crafted public persona, it was designed to hide how grand it really was."

"Did you go upstairs?"

Betsy answered, "Oh yes. We climbed that narrow staircase and visited the dome room on the third floor. We exhausted ourselves trying to see everything. We did have to give up finally our explorations on the outside because we were frozen solid. But we visited the Sally Hemings exhibit. We wouldn't have missed that for the world. It was touching."

Eloise picked up the narrative. "Those alcove beds. Except for Jefferson's, they looked claustrophobic. Imagine eleven grandchildren living there, all having to sleep in those alcove beds or pallets on the floor."

Betsy smiled, "Except for Aunt Marks, she had a real bed. No alcove bed for her!"

Eloise said, "I was rooting for Aunt Marks and her little four-poster. Good for her."

The three of them polished off loaded plates. Prince was not forgotten, getting drippings and scraps. Everyone sat slightly stupefied, halfheartedly spooning ice cream from custard cups.

Eloise remembered. "I'm cleaning up. You two vamoose."

Betsy didn't argue. "I'm going to go on Extreme Readers and share my impressions of Monticello. Jefferson must be smiling down from heaven on the impeccable condition of the estate. Once he had completed it, he no longer had the funds to maintain it."

"Post one of the photos I took of you by the Sally Hemings exhibit."

"Of course!"

Betsy thanked Dabs for the dinner, and he once again thanked her for saving the meal.

Dabs said to Eloise, "Let me help, that roasting pan looks awful."

"Nope. I saw scouring pads under the sink. I'm on it."

Eloise nearly pushed Dabs from the room.

Soon the only one left in the kitchen with Eloise was Prince.

Eloise let the roasting pan soak in hot sudsy water while she loaded the dishwasher and wiped down the counters. She started the dishwasher then got to the earnest business of scrubbing the roaster with steel wool. The effort felt good.

The results were not as satisfying, but then the roasting pan had been well used. Eloise smiled as she thought that many a happy meal had been made in that pan. She really was, at heart, an historian. Who else would feel fondness toward an old stained roasting pan?

Once the kitchen had been put to bed, Eloise opened the back door and watched Prince bound out, disappearing in the moonlight. She stepped outside and watched her breath condense in the chill air. The stars were incredibly bright, the darkness dense, the barn, so near, a denser black. Black on black made her think of the previous night, a shadow of a shade, perhaps. Or her bruised brain working overtime. Eloise felt her skin go gooseflesh and crossed her arms, wishing Prince would reappear.

Instead, Dabs was at her side. "Prince enjoys his freedom."

"I wish I could see him or hear him."

"He'll come in when he's ready. You shouldn't worry."

"You don't worry?"

"Oh, I do. Not as much since Mom passed. Before then, I worried all the time. But, bit by bit I've lost reasons to worry. Hey, there's your dog."

A streak of black was barreling toward them, passing, then circling back to land on the doorstep, hitting the door with a twirl and a dull thump from the side of his body, tail wagging.

Dabs bowed, in a charming, old-fashioned way. "Shall we?"

Prince led them into the house, nails clicking on the hardwood floors, heading straight for the staircase to lead Eloise to bed.

Dabs stopped at the bottom of the stairs; Eloise then noticed Dabs was holding something. She pointed at his hand, "Our bedtime reading?"

"Yes, of course. I nearly forgot. Please give Betsy her copy."

Dabs held her eye just a moment too long as if he had something to say, but then cut his eyes away as if embarrassed to be caught looking.

"Sweet dreams, Dabs."

She started up the stairs, noticing that Prince was sitting above her on the landing, watching, mouth open, looking oh so amused.

Truth be told, Eloise was wearing a similar expression.

* * *

March 30, 1780

The British have turned south, having been stymied from success in the north, but in their exodus by sea, God near drowned them all. Sadly, their horses per-ished. This alone I regret. The target is Charleston, pro-tected by Benjamin Lincoln. Buck is itching to go now, but Aunt Bess and Father are begging him to remain to protect Virginia. Should the Carolinas not repel the British, who would then be left here to protect us? Lin-coln failed to liberate Savannah, and that even with the help of our French allies. This is cause for concern.

Buck mounts his horse and flies away from his du-ties to gather gossip at every opportunity. He is fright-fully contrary with everyone. I stopped myself in the nick of time from stumbling into Buck and Aunt Bess hissing at each other and was able to back away before they could discover my presence. Auntie was remon-strating Buck, though it was unclear why. It had to do with Auntie being the rightful owner of Priscilla, and Father being the rightful owner of Sammie.

While I wish Buck no ill, secretly I wish him gone, as he cannot for a moment forget the war and devote himself to his labors. We depend on Major Schmidt, Isaac, Sammie, and Priscilla at the home quarter for labor. Father oft sends Sammie to work at the breeding barn to get him out of Buck's path. Father mostly works alongside Isaac and then late at night at his ledgers.

Father's health suffers. The mares are large in foal. New life comes regardless of the fates of men. We have what we need aplenty, even with scarcity of coin or specie; a good poultry yard, full smoke house and dairy with additional stores sent to us from High Meadows.

Mr. Jefferson has decided to relocate our Capital permanently to Richmond. Father sees opportunity for commerce. I expect the society of Williamsburg mourns. The assembly will be safer with the greater distance should the British sail up the James. I pray the patriot forces in the Carolina's will do what our men did at Saratoga and Trenton and Princeton, and no such event will occur. If only General Washington would come back to his home country and defend us!

The kits have become cats. While Lady Jane is spoiled by Bud, and Cleopatra reigns supreme in the Major's abode, the others have been gifted to Major Schmidt's compatriots in the Hessian barracks. He reports they are doing splendidly as there is no shortage of pests to be hunted.

Bud is likely never to become a master horseman. He listens not to a word I say but sings or hums loudly through our rides. He would play his fiddle while he rode if he could. Father indulges him greatly, as do his brothers. He should be grateful to work about the horses and not toil on our bottom lands with a hoe. Major Schmidt claims the boy is making great strides as a musician. Father says Henry, for that is what he is now calling the boy, will one day be in demand for dances and such. I have heard him play and find such optimism hallucinatory.

Priscilla is moping about and Aunt Bess refuses to discuss her melancholia. I expect Sammie has bruised her heart. He and she do not seem to so much as cross paths. Major Schmidt and I also have little time when we are just we two. I assume this has been mandated by Aunt Bess. The Major and I enjoy our daily banter, and I confess I do look forward each day to our ride.

Bud, I suppose I should now say Henry, is always present when we ride out and filling the air with chatter or song. The Major seems to feel for the lad as much as he feels for Fashion or Cleopatra, which is no small thing. I do not let his fondness stir jealousy in my breast, but instead see it as demonstrative of a fine temperament and a patience for children. And while I continue riding out, I am yet finding time to practice drawing and visit this journal. Someday I hope to look back at these pages as a documentation of these difficult war years.

Post Addendum: Buck has come flying up the drive with news that Charleston is under siege. None of us can judge yet whether Lincoln has prepared the city to sustain itself. Nor do we know if support will be forth-coming from the French or the Continentals. Other than creating a sense of dread, we have no idea if this affects us.

357

* * *

Dabs found Eloise in the kitchen the next morning, not long after daybreak. The coffee was made, Prince was licking his emptied bowl. Eloise was sitting at the kitchen table, chin in hand, looking relaxed and thoughtful.

Dabs said, "How is your head feeling?"

"Better. Much better."

"I'll expect you'll be ready to get Red back into training once you're home."

Eloise dropped her eyes, her voice was low, "I've let Bev down. I didn't even speak to her. I didn't speak to anyone."

Dabs answered softly, "You bolted. Like a panicked horse."

"Hmmmm."

Dabs deflected, "I've got everything I need to try our experiment with the headstones."

Eloise felt the pressure ease. "I hope it works. I hope we find Louisa. Or at least Mr. Roberts or Aunt Bess. Do you suppose Aunt Bess' given name is Elizabeth?"

Dabs nodded. "Sounds likely. Prince and I walked back up there yesterday. I figured out where I want to start, in the middle, those two side-by-side plots. We can sketch the space and block it off into quadrants."

"A map. Makes sense."

Dabs had started with an oblique approach, not dissimilar to how one would try to catch a wary horse in the field, but now he went straight at the topic. "I hope you get to keep Prince. But even if you don't get to keep him…"

Eloise stiffened, but Dab's held up a finger, "Even if you

don't get to keep him, you kept him safe. He could have been hit by a car, or starved, or injured, or attacked by another animal, or whatever. He landed in a safe space and was loved and cared for. And that was a gift, to him, and to you too."

"He's my dog."

"Yet his prior owner never gave up hope. We always seem to assume, myself included, that no one can love like we love. But I think you shouldn't assume that he doesn't love that dog just as much as you do."

"Are you saying that I'm selfish to want to keep him?"

"No. But you need to be prepared to give the dog back. I just want to say that it happens all the time that we lose what we love. Not necessarily like this, this is unusual, I get that. But it seems to me that loss is what we accumulate as we live. I'm sympathetic, really, I am. But consider that from Prince's viewpoint, it may not be a loss at all."

Eloise's first impulse was to yell at Dabs. He was lecturing her like he was her dad, and she was a child whose goldfish had died. Loss had been her reality for years. Eloise somehow bit the inside of her cheek. It stung. But it helped her pull herself together. She did not yell at Dabs. Instead, she noted how distressed he looked. Dabs knew loss too. And not just the loss of his mother. Death of a parent was not a choice, but Dabs was divorced too. Divorce was a different kind of loss, but a loss, nonetheless. It occurred to her then that Dabs had not chosen that either.

Eloise did not mean to sound harsh when she asked, "She wanted the divorce?"

Dabs looked surprised. "Yeah. She did. But 'c'mon, I've

lost my dad, my mother, my marriage, my dog, my career. My great old friend Dude is on his last legs, along with Mom's herd. Maybe that's why I'm hanging on to this house and every bit of detritus stuffed up in that attic. Maybe that's why Mom became a hoarder. Maybe that's why I've fallen in love with people who are dead. They are safe, aren't they? From harm, from loss, from whatever. I am loving them, with no chance of losing any of them."

Eloise was momentarily stunned by his candor. Then nearly whispered, "I am in love with them too."

"Eloise, we have a lot in common, you and I."

"We do."

"You know what lasts? The written word. It transcends time and space. But it does have its limitations."

Eloise was silent.

Dabs raised his eyebrows, "No beating heart."

Dabs continued. "Books led me to you, the journal brought you to me. When you needed to bolt to somewhere safe, you bolted to Ivy Creek."

It was all true enough.

Then Dabs said something totally sappy. "Unlike the written word, I, however, have the advantage of a beating heart."

Dabs was making a play. It broke the spell. Inside her head, Eloise was thinking, "Dabs, Dabs, Dabs, not yet. Not now. Not yet. Not now."

Eloise was feeling too anxious about what lay ahead of her, too mortified by what she had done, to think too much about Dabs. As wonderful as he was, she couldn't take on his losses, his beating heart, and his melodramatic speech.

But he was right about one thing. When she bolted, there was no question where she was headed. It had little to do with Dabs or his beating heart. She was bolting to Ivy Creek, that was true. But where she meant to go with Prince was the Ivy Creek of 18th century. Eloise had, once again, badly screwed up her present, so much so, that only some vague intercession or insight could set things straight.

25

April 2, 1780

*Major Schmidt and I have had a heated discussion
regarding the siege on Charleston. I can only hope they
do not suffer the fate of Philadelphia, or the calamity of
Savannah. When the British held Philadelphia, they
feasted on the backs of the citizens and catered only to
themselves in ways obscene, and when they departed,
slipping away in the dead of night, they left a city
stripped bare and in ruins. Stolen goods were smuggled
to New York, and hardship ensued for all. Poor Savannah now suffers. No good can come from being invaded
and held as a prize by the enemy. None.*

*Major Schmidt assuredly sees it differently. Savan-
nah and Charleston are to be cut off to bring "the rebels" to heel. He says this with no malice, but as a military strategist. I ask him how well this plan worked in
Boston? He calls me saucy. He does listen when I say
that the length of this conflict sharpens commitment
to independency, not lessens it. Once we called ourselves British Americans. In hindsight, absurd! I have*

never seen Britain, nor shall I. I have never seen King George, nor any King. I shall not have a King. Instead, I shall live by my neighbor Jefferson's decree, that all men are created equal. While strangers and fools fight here for a distant King and Country, we defend this, our country, and these, our homes. American's who remain loyal to a faraway land and Regent will find that land and that Regent will do naught for them once this conflict settles. Those they once called neighbors and friends will take no pains to help them who supported tyranny. They will find themselves adrift with no country nor home once fighting closes.

The Major tirelessly returns to the inequity of holding persons in bondage. The Major has made his point fluently. I cannot deny its validity. How this tangle should be unknotted? I think Buck wrong to claim this the natural order of things. As I think Buck wrong on claiming dominion over my freedom to steer my own destiny, due to my sex. If such were true, that we should accept such lots as life has given us, then logic demands, as the Major points out, we as a people would have no basis to change the order of King and subject.

When the Major says this, I know that he could be brought to our side, to cast off King George, because we do demand as our human right, to sever this relationship. Injustices should not be blindly accepted as immutable. In return, I accept his point regarding human bondage.

I have grown fond of him and our frank discus-

*sions. He is the only person I can speak to thusly. For-
tunately, the Major is out of the battle. On this point I
take solace.*

*I see that Henry (for so I shall call him henceforth
to form the habit) and Sammie and Isaac and Priscilla too, love the Major (more than they love us). Since
the Major has no more responsibility to them than his
naturally amiable company provides, they see him only
in a favorable light. Father takes the burden of seeing them fed and clothed and trained in a productive
occupation.*

*Father cannot see the outcome of this conflict any
better than Buck or myself, but he toils alongside
those he holds in bondage and come end of day, no
longer idles with us in the parlor by the fire with
book and libation but burns his candle down over
farm books.*

*Aunt Bess too seems overly attentive over her Pris-
cilla. I do wonder who is servant and who is master.
There is a heavy burthen upon both stations, and it
appears to grow heavier by the day. Such dangerous
times in which we are placed by God.*

*Buck strategizes where to join the fight, and under
whose command. He is writing letters and is anxious
awaiting replies but speaks not of it to women. He
confers with Father behind closed door. I only fret over
which horses he will take. Any he chooses I will mourn,
as they cannot but have hard usage.*

*I see from my window that the Major and Henry
are sitting outside on upended buckets performing a*

duet of a simple tune, apparently for an audience of two cats and a couple chickens scratching in the dirt. Cleopatra and Lady Jane Grey seem most attentive. Henry's skill is improving. As I watch I see that Father has come out to add to the audience, the players stop and Father waves them on and they take back up the bows. When the tune is done, Father applauds, and speaks to the lad with a pat upon his head. I do not hear what Father says, but I am discovered at my window by Henry, who waves excitedly, and the Major now waves, and so I applaud heartedly. Henry gives me the broadest grin and I nod approvingly at him. He is proud of his progress. I feel a pang in my chest that nearly takes my breath. I do not know why I am affected thusly.

* * *

Even though the wind was chilly, the sky was blue and the three of them, well, four if you counted Prince, hiked up the hillside as if they were heading out for a picnic. Eloise was carrying a large umbrella as if she were expecting it to be a picnic disrupted by rain. It was one of the types carried in a golf bag, orange and blue stripes and the word "Cavaliers" printed in large cursive on one of the stripes. Dabs was a graduate from Mr. Jefferson's University, and proud to be a Virginia Cavalier. He entertained them with the school cheer, "Wahoo-Wah," which made exactly zero sense.

Betsy carried a sketch pad and, in a tote-bag slung over

365

her shoulder, a collection of colored pencils, eraser, ruler, and a folded plastic tarp, so if she wanted to sit down, it wouldn't be on damp ground.

Dabs carried a tripod like a walking stick and a shoulder bag full of sundry camera equipment, as well as a thermos of coffee and paper coffee cups.

Prince led the way, tail high, nose down.

When they got to the turn, Dabs pointed the way.

Betsy asked, "Surely there was a better path at some point, Dabs. How would they drive the corpse to the cemetery? What about guests coming for the service?"

Dabs answered, "I'm sure we could figure out where a cart path used to open onto that loop around the cemetery if we looked hard enough. I expect this path was always here as a short-cut for a rider or a person on foot. But it's the only way I've ever known."

Betsy asked, "When do you suppose the last person was buried here?"

"Mom said it was long before her time, or her parent's or grandparent's time."

Prince had long since reached their destination and ran back down the trail to check on them, as if bewildered at their slow progress.

Betsy said, "I wish I had as much energy as that dog."

Prince charged back up the hill.

The group broke out of the heavily shadowed path into the bright blue of the sky that made them stop their chatter in appreciation of the view.

Betsy noted, "Someone crafted that view of your farm, Dabs."

"Someone did. Mom always kept things tidier up here than I have, but then she had more help."

Eloise strode to the walled enclosure, stepped through the broken gate, to find Prince circumnavigating the space.

Eloise said, "Prince has the right idea. Betsy, do you want to start work on our map? I'll step off the distance so you can draw it on a rough scale, then add your grid."

"Sure. It looks like a circle, maybe not a perfect one."

Betsy set down her tote bag and opened the sketch pad and fished out the measuring stick and a pencil.

Eloise began a rough measure of the space. She started with her back against the wall too, sighted a line, and then began taking big strides, counting as she went.

Meanwhile, Dabs was examining what he assumed were the two oldest graves.

Eloise called out the number of paces when she reached the wall on the other side, then tried to determine the next line to pace, centered and perpendicular to the one she had just paced. She wished she had brought string. Well, another day perhaps.

But it occurred to her, there might not be another day. Tomorrow she and Betsy would have to begin the long trip back. Eloise shook the idea from her head.

Eloise got on with it, sighted her new line and began her march. It was her "show jumping march" a practiced three-foot stride she used to find her distance and take-off spots for her show jumping round. It felt good to stride boldly toward her focal point across the cemetery, arm pointed at the spot, and hopefully striding toward true center, the convergence of the two lines.

Unfortunately, it was her toe that found that convergence spot. It sent her flying. Eloise heard the wind being forcefully expelled from her lungs as she contacted the ground, hard with almost no chance to break her fall with her hands. She did not land upon flat ground either.

She heard Betsy shriek her name, "Eloise!"

Eloise would have liked to reassure Betsy she was fine, because she figured she *was* fine, but she was too preoccupied with being able to draw a full breath. She was able to roll over and sit up, putting her elbows on her knees and her head down while she tried to suck in fresh air.

Prince was there first, licking her face. Dabs and Betsy were there soon after, with Dabs saying, "Are you okay?"

"Yes. I guess I wasn't paying attention to the ground. Bad mistake for an eventer."

Dabs took the toe of his boot and probed around in overgrown weeds and grass. "It's my fault for letting this place get so overgrown. I'm sorry, Eloise. Let me get my gloves from my bag. You tripped over something."

"Maybe. Maybe not. No matter where I go, or what I do, I seem to have a talent for falling."

Betsy offered Eloise her hand and Eloise took it and rose to her feet. "Don't be so hard on yourself. I'm just glad you're okay."

Eloise nodded back; the holiday mood having dissipated. "I did trip on something. Let me try again, and this time, not fall down."

Eloise backed up against the wall where she had started pacing off the second line and used her arm again to find her sight line. Betsy understood immediately, walked back to the wall to where Eloise had started her first line, pointed across the cemetery, and began to step, *carefully*, and when the two women met in the middle, they stopped. Eloise kicked at the ground.

"Here."

Dabs had been "off" by at least ten feet, and sure enough, there was something there. Dabs squatted down and began to pull at the weeds and then dig with his fingers and wipe with his hands, delineating the edges first, then the flat surface of the top. It was not the right shape for a tombstone. It was square and as he exposed the block of granite he discovered it had an ornamented edge.

Dabs next went and brought the thermos of coffee. Betsy and Eloise exchanged curious glances. Dabs opened the thermos, and instead of pouring them coffee, poured coffee onto the block, wiping the surface with his now very wet and muddy gloves.

There was nothing to see. It was an unmarked but roughened square of rock, the only ornamentation appeared on the edges.

Dabs said, "A plinth. Right here in the middle."

Eloise said, "I pride myself on my vocabulary, but what's a plinth?"

Betsy and Dabs answered in concert, "A pedestal."

Betsy brightened, "Well, then, I expect there's an angel around here somewhere."

Dabs said, "It must have flown away ages ago. I'd remember an angel. There's never been any statuary here. Not in my lifetime."

Betsy said, "Well, we've already made one big discovery. Shall we see if we can make another?"

Betsy spread her plastic tarp on the ground and sat down to begin her mapping project. She had used her ruler to make her scale "one inch per one Eloise stride" which she marked on the page as her legend. Then Betsy had drawn the gate, which she admired as quite a good artistic rendering for a "bird's eye view." Then she drew the plinth that marked the center of the cemetery.

Betsy's next step was to create a grid, and then place located graves within that grid. A good start, even though she hadn't yet placed a single grave on her map. She would have found the activity more enjoyable if it hadn't been so chilly and if the wind weren't blowing. She would have loved a hot cup of coffee.

Dabs and Eloise were preparing to photograph the first two headstones. Eloise held the huge umbrella as steady as she could in the wind, to provide a shadow over the headstone. Dabs took the photo with the auxiliary flash. The umbrella should, in theory, keep the inscription in shadow, providing contrast as the flash bathed the stone in light.

Betsy stood up and stretched, deciding to make her own "Eloise strides" to place the two graves being photographed onto her map. But when she did, her plastic tarp folded itself, and rose like a magic carpet and began to float, and then roll as the breeze gusted it away from its spot. It settled on the ground again, but as soon as Betsy got closer, another gust carried it away, and on the third attempt, the wind picked it up even higher before setting it down further away.

Betsy yelled, "That's not funny! Stop with the games!"

Eloise and Dabs watched as Betsy played "catch me if you can" with the plastic tarp. The wind seemed to be gusting harder than ever.

Betsy protested, "Dabs, the residents up here are playing games with me!"

The plastic took flight again, but this time blew smack into the stone wall directly across from where it had started.

Eloise said, "Looks like they can't leave the walled enclosure."

Betsy stiffened, "My goodness, now you've spooked me."

"Sorry. At least you got your tarp back."

Betsy began to fold the thing up, but the wind was making the job challenging. The tarp seemed to fight her. Eloise started to go and help, but then Betsy seemed to have won the battle.

Eloise and Dabs went back to their project, setting up then taking the photo of the second grave.

Betsy called over, "Dabs, do you recognize the name Buchanan?"

"Sure. President James Buchanan."

Eloise snorted, "That Buchanan isn't buried here, Dabs."

Dabs face slowly changed expression, as a thought took hold. "Did you know that James Buchanan's nickname was Old Buck."

Eloise's eyes widened. "Oh my God!"

Betsy added a voice of caution, "I suppose it could be Buck."

Soon Dabs was there with his muddy gloves again, because this headstone was not standing, but flattened and mostly covered in decaying leaves and red clay. At some point it had toppled over onto its back. The face of the stone was badly pitted and mostly worn away, but the word "Buchanan" was faintly discernible, but nothing else could be deciphered.

Dabs poured what little coffee he had left in the thermos on the stone and tried again to wipe it clean. Then Dabs brought over his equipment and Eloise held the umbrella and they set off the flash and got the shot.

Betsy went back to her map-making, and Eloise and Dabs photographed more headstones before they were too cold to continue.

They packed up, but as they walked through the gates, Eloise realized Prince was not with them. She called his name. Prince came crashing out of the woods and performed a "fly-by" at great speed. But, instead of heading down the path, he veered off along the wood line and ducked back into the woods.

Betsy said, "Now there's a dog on a mission."

Dabs added, "Just what that mission might be, only he knows for sure."

For a moment, all three of them stood on the cleared area that circled the walled enclosure of the cemetery and gazed after the dog. Eloise fidgeted with the big umbrella, tapping the tip against the hard surface of the old roadbed. The wind buffeted them as they stood there, but still no one moved.

Eloise pulled a strand of her loose hair from her face

before she said, "Along here somewhere lies the mouth of the old carriage road."

Betsy hugged her sketch pad against her chest. "If you two would like to search, that's fine by me. I recall you purchased the makings for beef stew. I make a fine stew. And I saw a mix for cornbread in the pantry."

Dabs said, "We do have stew and cornbread on the menu tonight."

Betsy nodded, "I'm happy to head back and get it started while you two explore."

Betsy turned around and scanned the edge of the woods, clearly unsure where the goat-path began.

Dabs stepped forward and offered her his arm. "Eloise, let's walk Betsy back first."

Betsy protested, "Really, Dabs, I'd make it back fine on my own."

"Well, you did see that skin we found of the Catamount. Who knows if there are any more of those about?"

This time when Dab's put his arm out, Betsy took it.

Eloise shook her head at Dabs who winked. Eloise knew that if she went in, she would be too tempted to stay in the warm house.

"Prince and I are going to stay a bit and look for that old road-head."

"I'll be right back. Don't go too far afield."

"I've got my cell phone. You'll be able to find me."

Eloise watched the two of them head down the path, then set the big golf umbrella down as a marker and walked the outer perimeter of the cemetery. She called Prince to her a couple of times; he came crashing through the brambles to appear at her side. Once she gave him a greeting and a rub, he was off again, disappearing into the gloom of trees and underbrush.

She had almost made it back to the umbrella without noticing anything that indicated the cut of an old road-head, when Prince began barking excitedly from the woods. She grabbed the umbrella and used it to push aside brambles as she walked into the gloom.

She soon stepped into a clearing. There was nothing exceptional about the space, just that there were no trees. The ground was covered with a musky carpet of brambles, vines, and moldy leaves, but here and there the ground rose in small clumps. Prince was digging into one of them with glee. She walked over to a clump and took the umbrella tip and gave it a stab. It was rock. She gave it another stab and the pile shifted. That gave her a start. Eloise gingerly began to pull the vines away. And with a small amount of effort, she saw what looked like natural field stones. A stack of them. She straightened up and scanned the area. Then she wandered over to her dog, who backed away from his digging project in a few acrobatic scoots that made her laugh out loud. The sound of her voice quieted her instantly. It was as if she had laughed in church. She squatted down while talking quietly to the dog, hairs rising on the back of her neck.

"Please don't have dug up someone's remains."

Eloise had only the tip of the umbrella to use as an instrument. With a little work with her hands, she was relieved to see that Prince had not dug up bones. But what he had dug up was some sort of box.

Dabs called from up the hillside, "Prince? Eloise?"

Prince bounded off to greet him.

Eloise waited a few beats, then yelled, "Prince, come!"

Prince returned, excited to get back to his digging project, Dabs followed, cursing as he approached.

She squinted into the shadows and called out, "You okay?"

"Ouch, damn it! Even with my coat and gloves, I'm getting caught in the brambles."

"You need me to come free you with the mighty 'Wahoo' umbrella that doubles as a machete'?"

Various other curse words were now being uttered, but closer. He was making progress.

He made his way to her, and found her pawing at the ground, not unlike her dog. He said, "Clearly you did not locate the old carriage road."

"No, but Prince found a buried treasure. I'm hoping it's gold."

"It's trash. Could be very old trash though. Mom said this area was the farm's landfill. Folks used ravines and such to throw their trash in them. Saved everyone the work of digging. This was a ravine once made by storm runoff rolling down this hill."

Eloise felt a wave of disappointment. What had she expected? Still, she wanted to excavate the box. Dabs saw her look.

She said, "So all those little humps in the ground are trash?"

"Yes. But go on. Dig it up. Whatever it is, it's yours. It will be a keepsake of your visit."

"Really? Even without knowing what it is?"

"I promise. Now let's see what we have here."

The poor umbrella, sturdy as it was, was never meant to be a spade. Dabs used it to continue the dig, then freeing one corner, used it as a lever. Things began to budge. Prince barked. And finally, the metal box was freed.

Dabs picked it up. "I suggest we open your treasure box tonight, so Betsy is in on the reveal."

"You're going to make me wait? The agony!"

Dabs sang "Anticipation" loudly as they made their way back up the hillside and then as they turned down the goat path and then toward the house.

At some point, Eloise changed the tune to, "Yo-Ho, Yo-Ho, a pirate's life for me!"

26

Walking to the house, the cold wind pushed at their backs. Eloise had a flashback of grade school, walking down the hall with a boy. Mike? Except they called him Mikey then. Mike was friendly at a time when boys thought girls had cooties. A boy taunted them from behind as they walked, giving them little shoves on their backs. He said, "Kiss her, Mikey, kiss her if you like her so much." At a certain point, "Mikey" *had* had enough. He spun around and head-rammed the boy in the gut. Soon the other kids were yelling, "fight, fight, fight" as the two boys grunted and scuffled and then tumbled onto the floor. A male teacher pulled them apart and marched the two boys into the principal's office.

Mikey never walked with her again. She had cooties. Big time. The obnoxious kid that had taunted them? Incredibly, he and Mikey became best friends.

The house came into view just as another cold gust gave Eloise a hard shove.

Eloise said, "That's a cruel wind."

Dabs said, "Or a kind one, urging us to seek shelter and warmth. Come on, take my arm."

Eloise looked up at Dabs, surprised. She did not have cooties it seemed. And the wind was not going to start a fight. She tentatively took his arm. He noticed she was smiling and smiled back. Her inner voice taunted, "Kiss him, kiss him if you like him so much" but she ignored it, although she did not reject it entirely, or fight it.

Dabs and Eloise got to the house, arm in arm, and it did feel welcoming. She had found both shelter and warmth. Dabs was her friend. Maybe that was worth savoring.

Betsy said, "There you are. I was starting to worry. That wind is blowing in a storm. I checked the radar on my phone."

Eloise went to the sink and washed her hands, while Prince looked up at her. "Yes, it's your dinner time. I haven't forgotten."

Dabs said, "I'm taking these items to the laundry room."

Betsy was searing cubes of floured beef. Mounds of vegetables were piled next to the sink, waiting to be washed and cut.

Eloise said, "As soon as I feed Prince, I'm at your disposal."

Betsy pointed her chin to the veggies. "I'll need the onions and celery next."

Dabs came back in with the box. "Should we wait to open this?"

Betsy squinted, "What in the world?"

"Eloise and Prince found a buried treasure."

"I see. Well, this needs to cook for 90 minutes. And you two need showers. So, let's put the big reveal off a bit longer, shall we? I would think you'd like to get cleaned up and warmed up."

Eloise said, "Well, sure, but ..."

Dabs said, "Betsy, the voice of reason."

Betsy pointed a wooden spoon at Dabs. "However, you can make cornbread. I noticed you have one of those cast iron skillets with the dividers in it."

"Mom was a devoted fan of cornbread. That skillet was essential. She taught me to heat butter in the skillet before you pour in the batter."

Betsy nodded approvingly. "Your mother knew what she was doing."

Eloise delivered her chopped onions and sliced celery, and then was put to mincing garlic, cubing potatoes, and slicing carrots.

Dabs got the cornbread mixed and into the oven and set out butter to soften.

Betsy continued at her station by the stew pot, adding tomato paste and Worcestershire sauce, salt, and pepper, then flour. She added a bottle of beer along with thyme and bay leaf and one of those boxes of chicken stock (not beef stock, she explained with a wink) and a small box of frozen peas.

Once the stew was simmering, Betsy ordered them to take showers. Dabs was given a dire warning not to over-cook the cornbread. And he made a solemn pledge, but also made a show of setting the timer on his watch.

When Eloise turned off the shower and stepped out onto the cold tile floor of the bathroom, she could hear rain. She walked over to the window. Rain was blowing in sheets across the barnyard. She hoped Dabs had done the barn chores and that the horses were snug and dry.

When she got to her room, Prince was on the bed, chin resting on crossed paws.

"What a day we had."

When Eloise and Prince came down, Betsy and Dabs were sitting in the parlor, each with a glass of red wine, the bottle and another glass sitting on an end table.

Betsy was saying, "I'm not usually that enamored with a red, but this is delightful."

Dabs rose and poured a glass for Eloise, "I hope after all this enforced waiting, the reveal isn't too disappointing."

Eloise felt her stomach flip. The wind, and now the rain had created an overture for the scene. For a moment she stepped outside of herself, into the audience, watching the play.

Betsy chimed in, "Dabs said whatever the contents, the prize is yours to keep. Even if it *was* only a landfill, hardcore archeologists are thrilled to excavate trash pits."

The house was shaken by a burst of thunder. Prince, ever the brave protection dog, sat on Eloise's feet, leaned against her, and began panting.

Dabs had pulled the cornbread out of the oven long since but offered to check on the stew as he went to fetch the box.

Betsy called after him, "Use the wooden spoon to scrape at the bottom, and if it sticks, turn down the heat!"

Eloise thought to herself, "For God's sake, what other errand can Betsy send him on?"

Dabs returned, gave a good report on the stew, and then produced the box, wrapped in a towel. He had done his best to clean it off, but it was a rough surface that held on to the grime, with a fragile looking hinged lid that Eloise feared would be hinged no longer once they opened it.

Dabs reading Eloise's mind said, "I oiled the hinges."

Then, "I hope you aren't expecting gold. It's not heavy. Shall you do the honors?"

Eloise felt her face flush, she knew her hands would shake. "No. No. No. You do it, Dabs. I can't."

Eloise and Betsy leaned forward in their seats. Eloise felt her fingers curl into her fists. A strange buzz ran through her fingertips. She wanted something. What, a letter addressed to her from Louisa? Silly, but not far off from her heart's desire.

Dabs took out a pocketknife and worked the edges a bit before lifting the lid. The hinges miraculously held.

He said, "Well, look at this. Intact."

He gingerly lifted out a clay pipe. "I used to find stem fragments around the place growing up. Never the bowl, and certainly never unbroken."

Eloise had a hard time hiding her disappointment, "Why bury a box with a pipe in it?"

Betsy said, "Unlikely buried. You know what a 'Tel' is? It's a hill that is made from one civilization building upon another. That box may have been buried by time."

Dabs was examining the contents. "My God, there's even a leather pouch of tobacco, or at least remnants of tobacco. Look, a little metal stick."

Betsy said, "Well, a smoker needs tobacco, and a pipe smoker needs a stem cleaner."

Eloise hid her disappointment. A pipe. No story came

to mind to connect such a thing to Louisa Roberts or to herself. Still...

"May I?" Instead of reaching for the pipe. Eloise lifted out the small leather pouch. And when she turned it over in her hand, she gasped.

Dabs leaned closer and the two examined it closely then stared at each other, Eloise giving a small nod. This was not a letter to Eloise. But it held a letter, nonetheless.

Betsy grew impatient. "Well, what?"

Dabs answered. "A little brand, burned into the leather pouch. The letter "R" surrounded by a wreath of ivy."

Betsy asked, "Like the harness brass?"

Eloise answered, "Very like it, yes. The design is like the one I have at home. The one that was passed down to me through Jock's family."

Eloise placed the bag in the palm of Betsy's hand. And after a good look, Betsy handed it back to Dabs.

Dabs carefully replaced the pipe and the bag into the box and gently closed the lid.

"For you."

"You're really going to let me take this?"

"A gentleman keeps his word. Without you and Prince, it would still be buried on that hillside."

Eloise had felt, irrationally, that she had a stake in this place, in Louisa, in that cemetery on top of the hill, and in that vine covered clearing where this little treasure box had been found. She had felt it in her gut, and even dreamed of Louisa. But here was a tangible scrap that maybe her feelings were anchored in fact. She found herself cradling the box against her body. She understood that she had made up stories. But this was real. That "R" was the same as Jock's "R."

Betsy asked, "Dabs, are you certain that hillside was a refuse site?"

"Why would my mother have misled me?"

"Oh dear, I don't mean to imply anyone misled anyone. At least not intentionally. It's just that attitudes have changed."

Another booming thunder shook the old house. Prince shuddered against Eloise's knees.

Dabs muttered as if explaining to himself. "Those ravines had been filled slowly over the years with refuse, used as a landfill, to slow down the water. Watershed ravines are unusable for planting, and the trash has to go somewhere. Stuff is naturally going to work its way up as soil compacts and shifts. Stuff just like this."

The stovetop timer went off in the kitchen. Betsy was on her feet in an instant, "Let me see if the meat is tender."

That left Eloise and Dabs alone with a nervously panting Prince planted on Eloise's feet.

Dabs broke the silence with a low voice. "I'm not ready to see you go. Betsy promised you wouldn't leave until after lunch tomorrow. She said she preferred breaking the trip into two days of driving. That leaves time for another look at the cemetery."

"I'm not ready to leave either, but at least this way we can take one more walk to the cemetery."

Dabs slapped his forehead, "In the excitement of finding the box, we neglected to look at the photos we took!"

Betsy yelled from the kitchen. "Come and get it."

* * *

Getting chilled, warming up, wine and the best beef stew ever, had everyone stupefied. Oh, and the cornbread was perfect, crispy on the outside, soft in the middle, and they slathered it with butter.

Dabs brought his laptop to the kitchen table and the three of them pulled up chairs.

They started by looking at the two side by side stones that were set in the center of the cemetery and presumed to be the oldest. Those were the first ones they had photographed.

Eloise had her pen and paper ready to record whatever they could decipher. She sketched the shape of the headstones and labeled them, "#1 and #2.

When Dabs put the first photo up on the screen, Eloise felt her shoulders sag. No one spoke. There were some incomplete shadows cast into the shallow depressions, the face of the stone was illuminated brightly to add contrast. The technique seemed okay. But the damage of time was almost complete. No names or dates appeared. Only a few broken lines remained, but nothing connected or formed a letter or number.

Betsy said softly, "Perhaps some of the others?"

Eloise proclaimed, "It's Louisa's mother and father. It must be. We know from the journals that Louisa's mother had died, and they are all still living here in this house at the time she was writing. They would have buried her mother here in the home cemetery. And surely Mr. Roberts was buried beside her."

Betsy said, "Perhaps. But do we really know that? Dabs found the journals here in an old chest. But we don't know the provenance of the chest, do we?"

Dabs took the tip of his pen and gently pointed at the screen. "You'd think we could find the letter 'R' right about here, if it is the letter 'R' that is."

Betsy said, "You need to examine the one we found that said Buchanan. That's your best shot."

Dabs right clicked through the photos until he got to the right photo.

Betsy pointed, "Eloise, there you go."

Eloise squinted at the screen, her heart thumping in her chest.

She leaned forward, squinting, and speaking slowly. "Buchanan. Elijah. Roberts. Oh."

Dabs whispered. "It's Buck. It's definitely Buck."

Betsy said, "There is your provenance for the journals. Buck is a Roberts. These Roberts of Louisa's journals were here when Buck was buried. Dabs, we still don't know for sure that they are your relations. Houses do change hands. But they buried their son in that graveyard. My goodness, this is an important find!"

Eloise felt her eyes sting. "I'm not sure why, but I feel, I feel, well, I'm not sure what I feel. Sad. I feel sad."

Betsy said, "We all knew he was dead, for goodness' sake. They're all dead."

Dabs said, "Read the rest. Buck died on October 23, 1781."

Betsy shook her head as if to clear cobwebs, "When did the British surrender at Yorktown?"

Dabs tapped at his forehead, "I know that. Why can't I say it?"

Eloise said, "October 19, 1781."

Eloise sat back in her chair. "Wow. I hope someone was able to tell Buck they had won. Because prior to Yorktown, things had been looking grim. Aw, man, he was a young man."

Dabs sighed, "Twenty-five."

Eloise exhaled loudly, "Buck didn't get the chance to grow into a good man, husband, or father. Maybe he would have, in time."

Betsy had also sat back in her chair, "Must have been heartbreaking for Mr. Roberts, for Aunt Bess, and for Louisa."

Eloise's eyes opened wide, "This would have changed everything for Louisa. Wouldn't it?"

Betsy asked, "Dabs, would the property pass to a relative? Or would Louisa inherit?"

Dabs nodded, "I only know this because of your study group, Betsy. It was because of Jefferson the laws changed. Jefferson's only living children were daughters, so he had good reason to see the laws changed."

Dabs pulled up something on his phone and read to them, "The law of primogeniture was abolished in 1785."

He looked up from his phone, "If Mr. Roberts were still alive then, he could leave it all to Louisa."

Eloise sighed, "I feel relieved."

Dabs said, "I do too."

Betsy added, "Silly of course, since she is well beyond those worries."

Eloise whispered, "But not to us. Louisa, the family, well they haven't sent Buck off to war yet. When she does write about that day, and we read about it, we will know what she doesn't know. He won't survive it."

That was a sobering thought. They were silent witnesses, but now omniscient ones, to Louisa's story.

Prince put his head on Eloise's knee, rolled his eyes up at her, and thumped his tail, breaking the solemnity of the moment.

Dabs turned off the computer. "I'm going out to check on the horses. I really had wanted to work on the next journal entry, but honestly, I've got nothing left in me tonight."

Eloise said, "It's still raining, isn't it?"

Dabs offered, "I'll take Prince, clearly he needs to go out. You two go on up."

Prince seemed to understand and bounced over to the back door, barking.

Eloise let them go, climbing the stairs with Betsy, her legs leaden with fatigue. She did not want the day to end. There was so much more to look at, to read, to explore, to think about. But her body was done. The contest between mind and body was already decided.

* * *

Eloise made it to the bathroom, bedroom, and into her pajamas. Then she fell face down onto the bed. Someone opened her bedroom door to let in the dog. She felt Prince jump onto the bed.

Eloise was dreaming a vivid dream, 'though she knew

it was a dream. She looked through chestnut ears, large and loose in the sockets, falling slightly to the sides, then swiveling back to check on her, before swiveling forward to point the way. An unseen dog kept pace in the shadows as they rode along a rutted road. The road was winding its way up a hillside. It was narrow, with an occasional turn out for pulling over should one meet another coming the opposite direction. Eloise met no one.

As she broke through the tree line, atop a hill, she knew where she was. The cemetery. Eloise had just traversed the old road. The color of the sky was robin's-egg blue, but the air was frigid. Her feet were cold in the stirrup irons, her fingers icy as she held the reins. Where were her boots and gloves? What horse was she riding? She felt the dream begin to recede, as if chastising her for allowing her rational mind to intercede.

She begged for another chance. She would ask no more questions. She wanted something from this dream. She could not go home tomorrow without something more. An old pipe and a leather bag with the "R" and the ivy was simply a clue to a bigger puzzle.

The scene returned. She was still astride the horse, though much was indistinct, the way dreams often were. But certain bits were vivid. She was staring straight through the landscaped picture frame at Ivy Creek Plantation below.

Eloise gave a cluck to her horse, passed by the gate, now intact, and made her way around the road that looped the stone wall. She heard music. Her horse froze, ears alert, worried, but the dog dashed off.

Eloise was listening to a mournful tune on a violin. Violin. Her heart began to pound thinking of Henry, dear Henry. Eloise found two piles of fieldstones that marked a steep path downhill. She dismounted and led her horse to the fieldstones, peering into the gloomy clearing below. She saw a knot of people, their backs to her. A tall lean figure played the sorrowful tune on his violin, back also turned, but now with her dog sitting next to his legs, leaning against him. Prince? The figures were indistinct, but the music was not. It was clear and sweet, and she heard it perfectly. This was unlike any dream she had ever experienced.

Eloise thought she could commit the tune to memory. It was beautiful but so sad that Eloise felt her eyes sting. The man was wearing heavy boots and a long coat, but no hat. His hair was grey and tied back. She understood this dream. This was no trash pit. This was the slave's graveyard, no matter what Dabs had said. She stood with the reins of her horse gripped tightly in her hands, fingering the leather between thumb and forefinger. Henry, she thought, must finish soon, must turn, and see her. It was her heart's desire to see him too.

And then her mind, her rational mind, scolded her. This was a dream. A vivid and most wonderful dream. But all this was what she already believed to be true, had imagined, in her mind. Except the tune.

And the tune, which had gone on for some time, the chorus repeating, ended, finished, on a long and lingering note. A mourner turned, seemed to see her, disgust on their face. She was not welcome.

Eloise backed away, throwing the reins back over the

head of the chestnut horse, a horse she knew, but did not know. She climbed back into the saddle, feeling chilled to the bone. The dog, came to her, a black blur. And then, finally, the shadowy figure, the violinist, turned as if to walk back up the path. And briefly, ever so briefly, he seemed to see her too, to catch her eye and hold it, before looking back down at his feet.

It was not Henry. Could not be.

It was a white man. An old man. Tears had streaked his face. Eloise felt ashamed. She felt a pressing need to turn the horse and urge it away. The horse was quick to respond, as anxious as she to flee. Eloise held on as the horse ducked down a narrow trail, a tidier version of the path Eloise had traveled that very day.

Eloise woke up. The edge of her pillowcase was twisted and gripped in her left hand; the sheets and blankets pushed onto the floor. She was so cold. Prince was curled up on the floor amidst the pile.

Eloise tried to commit her dream to memory on a bit of scratch paper before it did as most dreams did and burrowed itself away into some irretrievable wrinkle in the brain. She was intent on capturing the tune. She hummed the first five notes, but the sixth note had been wiped away. And then even the first five notes evaporated. The tune was not hers to keep. Still, she was sure she would know it if she ever heard it again.

Eloise got herself and Prince back under covers, and finally warmed up enough to fall into a dreamless sleep. But still, she got up before the sun. This would be a day of parting. She had not handled partings well in the past.

Who decided they should be called "goodbyes?" They never felt good to her. She had to leave this sanctuary, and head back to take whatever was coming. But first…

This was a day that she could not let sneak up on her, blindside her. She needed space, margin, a time to gird her loins for the battle to come. She needed divine intervention is what she needed.

She tip-toed down the stairs with Prince. He led her down "Mostly Hall," site of country dances in days of yore. The floorboards creaked beneath her feet. The furnace kicked on and blew warm air through the register, making the house sigh and moan.

Eloise let Prince out the back door. The sky was lighter, but the sun hadn't broken the horizon. It was a dark and sodden world. Eloise could see her breath. She zipped up her hoodie and crossed her arms. The barnyard was full of puddles and leaf litter and branches from the storm.

Eloise called Prince and he appeared from nowhere, eager for his breakfast. Prince did a happy dance while she poured his kibble into his bowl. The crunching of the kibble as he chewed seemed extra loud.

Eloise got the coffee going, and sat while it brewed, hissing, and burping and finally pouring into the carafe. The sun broke the horizon, and suddenly the yard was filled with the sounds of birds, the chatter of squirrels. The world was coming awake in a show that felt like it was being performed just for her. The sky was going to be clear, swept clean by the storm, but presently was painted in hues of orange and pink.

Eloise sipped coffee and watched the sun come up, feeling herself in that special state of consciousness somewhere between sleep and awake. It was a space in the margin. White space. Waiting to be filled. An invitation from her.

And in walked the image of Jock. It seemed intrusive. Not at all who she wanted to think about. Jock, who made a claim on both George Washington and Thomas Jefferson. Jock the Virginian, the horseman, the FFV, or so he claimed. Jock whose Horse-Brasses with the "R" monogram were entwined in ivy. Jock who had used the old brasses as paperweights on his desk. The ones that looked just like the corroded versions Dabs had in the attic. Jock who she loved desperately. It was pathetic, but true.

Jock had created a magical world, with the aid of horses and dogs and long gallops and stories. Eloise had been steeped in them. Stories of future glory, and the romance of the past. Jock who had coached her over so many hurdles, inspired her, filled her with ambition and drive, and made her laugh, would tell her whatever story he thought she wanted to hear. There was a time she never doubted him. But now she understood that his stories were crafted to always benefit himself with no room for someone else. Not even her.

The apple had not fallen far from the tree. Her dreams? Her visions? Her romantic notions of the wind, of the long-dead horses speaking to her through the polished wood of the bottom of an old feed trough? That the "R" meant Robertson as much as Roberts?

Oh Jock. She was delusional at best. Manipulative and dishonest were harsher words for her behavior. But she had earned the harsher words. She had proven to herself that she was just like Jock. She had done it all in a way that left her an out. "Plausible deniability." She had not admitted, even to herself, that she had recognized the dog. And she had not allowed Pinky to clip Prince, so he would look like the dog in the flyer. And this fiasco was even worse because it was not her first attempt to bend the truth to get what she wanted.

These manipulations she did without a conscious thought, to benefit herself. Why Jock always pulled it off and she never could, seemed unfair. But life was not fair.

Loathing Jock for his moves, for his success, was easy, loathing herself, not so much.

Eloise tipped up her mug and drained it. The night was gone. It was full on morning. Her last day at Ivy Creek had begun. Dabs and Betsy would soon join her. They could not know how awful she really was. Jock knew, and he no longer loved her. If he ever had.

A bright red cardinal landed outside the window. She had forgotten how orange the beak was, how the top of his head was tufted, how dark and bright and round was his eye. His coat was fluffed to trap his body heat. She recalled that many birds' mate for life. Was the cardinal one of them? Just then, as if summoned by her thoughts, his mate landed next to him. And although she had a coat of browns streaked with red, the bright orange of her beak stood out better by the stark contrast.

Behind her, Dabs said, "Aren't they beautiful? Cardinals."

The pair flew off.

Eloise asked, "Do they mate for life?"

"I think so. They're said to be angelic, Cardinals."

"Really?"

"Spiritual messengers."

Eloise who had just lectured herself for such romantic foolishness, still could not reject such a lovely idea. She realized her eyes were glassy with tears. She pulled herself together.

Dabs walked over to the coffee maker. "Refill?"

Eloise lifted her cup, feeling relieved to focus on something mundane. "I'll take coffee, but I won't eat until after I help you get the barn done."

Dabs took her cup and refilled it, "Stay put. I'll go drop grain. Then we can sit for a minute. I won't turn down the offer to help clean stalls, though."

He turned to Prince, "Coming?"

Prince ran to the door. Eloise watched them walk to the barn, the dog bouncing around Dabs in circles. Dabs sliding the heavy barn door open enough for the two of them to squeeze in. Such a big old barn. With only the three old-timers in it. What that barn needed was more horses. Unbidden came the fuzzy vision of a chestnut horse, ears pricked. Eloise squeezed her eyes shut and thought to herself, "Stop it, just stop."

27

Betsy cleared the breakfast dishes, saying "Eloise, We can't tarry too long. I don't want to drive in the dark and the sun sets early this time of year."

Dabs piped up, "Betsy, leave the dishes by the sink. I'll have lots of time after you're gone to load the dishwasher."

"I hate to leave your kitchen in this state."

"Please, humor me."

Eloise asked, "Should we take more photos of head-stones?"

Dabs said, "That's going to eat up too much time. Let's just stretch your legs and enjoy the vistas. First, let me find you two some warm layers. Now that the wind has pushed the rain out, it's gotten colder."

Dabs left and reappeared shortly with caps and scarves and gloves. Betsy was delighted with her scarf, "Cash-mere!"

"My mother's. Here, the cap is not quite as elegant, but very warm."

Dabs handed Betsy a bright red lumberjack's hat. It was lined with shearling lamb and had ear flaps that could be tied under the chin. Eloise was handed her own fashion statement, a red plaid scarf and a knit beanie that was a size too big. Dabs handed mittens to Betsy and lined deerskin riding gloves to Eloise.

They were jolly as they followed Prince up the road and onto the path to the cemetery, startled momentarily by deer crashing through the brambles. Prince followed in hot pursuit, but soon gave up, reappearing, panting hard but happy.

The path was more open having been beaten down from their recent trips. As they walked, Eloise, who had been debating keeping her dream to herself, decided to tell Dabs and Betsy. There was no way to convey the emotional weight of it because each time she tried to describe a detail; it eluded her. But she could tell them there was music.

"I wish I could hum the tune. It was achingly beautiful."

Betsy said, "Violin?"

"Yes. I so wanted to see Henry because of Louisa's journal entries. Louisa never describes his face or build, but I have created in my mind *my* Henry. I do that. Cast people and faces for roles."

Eloise and Betsy glanced at each other knowingly.

Eloise continued, "I was sure it would be Henry. But it wasn't Henry. He turned and seemed to see me for a moment, and he was an old man, with white hair. I could see the tears on his face."

Dabs said, "You do have the most incredible dreams."

"It *was* vivid. I felt ashamed for spying. Well, more like ashamed for being caught. I was riding a chestnut mare. She was nervous about the gathering in the woods."

Betsy smiled, "How would you know it was a mare?"

Eloise shrugged, "Casting decision?"

Dabs frowned, "You were in the woods?"

Eloise exhaled and saw her breath hang in the air. "The funeral of my dream wasn't in the cemetery. It was in the woods, where we found the box."

Dabs said, "I guess you went to sleep thinking about that box, and where you found it."

The path opened onto the roadbed that once circled the cemetery, and they paused to enjoy the view. In the cold morning air, there was nothing dream-like about it. They inhaled deep lungsful of frigid air, slightly winded from the climb.

Prince bounded through the broken gate into the cemetery.

Betsy said, "Our activity director is urging us to move along. Let's go pay our respects to poor Buck, shall we? Let's tell him we won the war and thank him for his service."

They did. Eloise squatted down and placed her hand on the dirty and pitted surface of the headstone, still lying on the ground.

Dabs spoke to the headstone, "Your death must have broken your father's heart."

Betsy added, "And his aunt's and his sister's too."

Eloise held her hand on the stone and thought of Buck.

"Louisa and Buck may have had a contentious relationship, but he was her only brother."

Betsy tipped her head, "Not exactly true." Then she added, "Dabs, can you say a few words?"

Dabs took a solemn tone, "Buck, we won the battle of Yorktown, and we won the war. You helped create a new country. Well done, Buck."

They were silent for a long moment and then Eloise stood back up brushing her hand against her jeans.

Betsy looked thoughtful, "Why do you suppose Buck was buried so far away from his parents? I mean assuming those center plots are his parents. He's all by himself over here. You couldn't get any further away before you'd have to bury him outside the wall."

No one had an answer.

Then Betsy turned and Dabs followed. They were heading back.

Eloise was not ready to head back to the house. Not yet.

She said "I know my dream last night was just a dream. But it doesn't mean my brain wasn't trying to make sense of things while I was sleeping. Do you mind if we have one last visit to the hillside?"

Dabs turned and gallantly waved Eloise past him.

"Not at all. Lead the way."

Prince bounded ahead, stopping on the old roadbed to check they were following.

Eloise said, "Clearly I'm not the one to lead the way here."

Eloise did stop to enjoy the view, then pointed at the woods. "In the dream, the carriage road to the cemetery came out near the trail we've been using. I rode the chestnut horse on the carriage road on my way up, and I rode the shortcut trail on the way back."

Betsy reminded Eloise, "In a dream."

"Yeah, in my dream the carriage road was cut so that those coming up would be immediately struck by that magnificent view, the same one we see when we come off the trail. It was built to impress."

Betsy said, "Well, I do see how that makes sense."

Eloise continued, "I remember how it was narrow, one-lane, with turn outs for meeting someone coming the other way. It wouldn't take much for nature to reclaim such a narrow road."

Eloise was now walking where she had ridden the chestnut mare in her dream, Prince leading the way.

Eloise walked slowly along the edge of the wood line, thick and full of brambles. She said, "There should be remnants of the two drystone gateposts that marked the path to the slave graveyard."

Eloise saw Dabs glance at Betsy. Betsy shrugged. They were indulging her.

Eloise saw. "I do know, it was a dream. But wouldn't a slave graveyard, set in the woods, wouldn't it have a path for the pall bearers and guests? Why wouldn't that path be marked by gate posts? Why wouldn't the graveyard be set near the family plot. They needed a practical place where the wagon could carry the coffin. It was a dream, but so many elements of it make sense."

Betsy said, "If indeed there is a slave graveyard in those woods, what you say is perfectly logical."

Dabs spoke slowly, "Before you get carried away do remember, wherever that slave graveyard exists, and it likely does exist somewhere on this place, at some point, slaves and their kin didn't want those graves to be found."

Betsy said, "You mean that if there had been a well-marked path, if there had been stone gateposts to mark it, they may have been destroyed deliberately."

Dabs merely made a sound.

Betsy asked, "Did your mother know about any burial ground for the slaves of Ivy Creek?"

Dabs said, "If she had known the location of the graveyard, she would have told me."

Then he added, "I assume, she did not know because its location was hidden long before her time."

Prince broke out of the woods, then bounded back in. He was leading her. She followed. And behind her, with a bit of reluctance, came Dabs and Betsy.

Eloise could hear Dabs escorting Betsy, "Let me get that out of your way." And "Watch that bramble cane, wicked things."

Eloise and Prince emerged into the clearing. Eloise tried to summon the scene, to position the mourners, the gravesite, the old man playing his violin. Reality did not match her dreamscape. There was no carpet of brambles and vines in her dream. Distance and perspectives were off. Eloise wandered, feeling frustrated, disoriented.

Eloise was walking along the vine covered ground when she stumbled over a mound of fieldstones. She cursed loudly more from frustration than pain.

Dabs called out, "Are you okay?"

Eloise called back that she was fine and waited for the two to catch up.

Betsy was scanning the area. "Dabs, I thought you said the area was a natural watershed?"

"Yes. The runoff made the ravines. Then the ravines were filled as trash pits."

Betsy said, "You'd think an area that once was a watershed would still draw storm water. It's quite the opposite, isn't it? We had a lot of rain last night. Your barnyard was full of puddles. But, in here, not a sign of rainwater, no puddles, no run-off."

Betsy was saying, "If nature has reclaimed the old carriage road, why didn't nature totally reclaim the old landfill?"

Dabs said, "I think nature has done a pretty good job on this area myself."

Eloise said, "Someone might have tended it. At least while there were still relations in the area. The state it's in now could be recent. And by recent, I mean, after the great migration, when so many fled north, looking for something better than share-cropping."

Dabs cut a disbelieving look at Eloise. He looked irritated.

Betsy noticed, She said, "We are just musing, Dabs. Thank you for indulging us."

Dabs seemed to relax. He said, "Please enjoy your musing. I don't claim to know all the secrets of Ivy Creek Plantation. No one person could. Be my guest. Enjoy."

Betsy narrowed her eyes, scanning the area. She stepped carefully up to Eloise, leaned over, and pulled at the growth covering the pile of fieldstones. "I think…"

Dabs asked, "Betsy, what *do* you think?"

Betsy straightened up and wandered off without replying, absorbed in thought. Eloise did too, but in a different tack. Each woman found fieldstones, pulling at the vines that grew around and over them, until they had further exposed the stones.

Dabs watched as the two women worked silently exposing just a few stones so that they could be clearly seen among the vegetation, before moving on. Somehow, they had, together, without forming a complete sentence, made a plan.

Standing back, he scanned the partially exposed fieldstones. A pattern was emerging. Not exactly rows, but groupings. He exhaled a long breath. Then he began to walk from pile to pile.

Dabs grabbed at a vine and pulled, watching as it came loose in a line, the damp earth giving way easily. Dabs had joined their effort.

Even with heavy gloves, the three occasionally had a thorn drive its way through a glove. In that case, the silence was broken by curse words carried clearly through the chill air.

They worked diligently, working up a sweat despite the temperature. Dabs was silently toiling with them, yet apart, saying nothing.

After a good half hour of work, Eloise straightened up to scan the area. The misty memory of the dream flooded back. Sadness washed over her. These slaves had not had gravestones. All they had were the stones they could pull from the fields. And by the looks of the growing number of piles the three of them had uncovered, there were plenty of residents here, not far from the final resting places of those who had owned them.

There was indeed a story here. It was not about her, this story.

She cast a sideways look at Dabs. Then looked back at the small piles of fieldstones.

Eloise recalled that Mr. Roberts and Louisa had referred to the "servants" as family. And in some cases that was literally true. But that "family" was not entitled to be buried inside the stone enclosure above, or have their names carved into stone.

Eloise said, "This is a stark reminder, isn't it? Of the injustice of it all. No names or dates, just the stones that could be gathered like ancient cairns. Separate was never meant to be equal."

Dabs didn't answer. He was busy.

Betsy and Eloise stopped what they were doing, their sodden and filthy gloved hands hanging by their sides as their attention was turned to Dabs. Prince went to his side, absorbed too in watching his efforts.

Dabs was pulling weeds from a tall mound of fieldstones, flinging clumps in a manner that seemed angry. They watched as he sank to his knees, flinging vines and litter and red clay. He was saying something, muttering to himself, cursing under his breath.

Betsy and Eloise exchanged worried glances, then walked over to Dabs.

Dabs was saying, "All buried on this hill. Right here. All this time? Oh, God!"

Dabs rocked back on his heels and stopped digging; his face contorted.

Betsy squatted down too and brushed away the loose

mounds of dirt Dabs had been creating, then, Eloise saw what Dabs and now Betsy had seen.

Betsy was right about this hillside being a "tel." It would take a lot more digging to free what had been well buried under years of decaying matter. But still, but still, it was clearly no stack of field stones. A carved stone hand, missing the tip of an index finger was pointing toward heaven.

Betsy exhaled, "Well, I think you've found the angel that once stood on that plinth above."

Dabs murmured, "Someone put her here. Stole her from her original site and brought her here. And they must have done it a very long time ago."

Eloise said without thinking, "I've an idea who it was."

Dabs turned and looked at Eloise. Eloise felt her blood rush to her cheeks and her stomach clench. He was not happy with her. And yet she had been right. But right wasn't always kind. But she knew who had moved the Angel and why. She knew it as a certainty. And she knew why he had done it. She now knew who was playing the violin in her dream. Major Schmidt. She knew it, not just because of her dream, vivid as it was. But because Louisa had told her story in such a compelling way. She understood that Major Schmidt loved Henry as he would a child of his own. Major Schmidt had moved that angel, for his beloved Henry who was not allowed burial inside the walled enclosure above them. It was his beloved Henry whose funeral she had attended in her dreams. But she would not say any of that now.

All she said was, "I'm so sorry."

He rose and stood so close that Eloise could feel the cloud of his breath touch her face.

Dabs looked away and down at the hand of the angel, freed once again to point toward heaven.

"I don't know how you could know more about this hillside than I do."

Betsy put a hand gently on Dab's arm. "You wear the place like a second skin. You see it from the inside looking out. That's all. Eloise and I are fascinated by the history here, and place it in historical context, but this is your history."

Eloise could see that Dabs was listening, calming.

Dabs nodded, "Yes, I do see that. You don't see my mother or father, or grandparents, or great grandparents. You only see what you know from reading and from the journals of Louisa Roberts."

Betsy shifted gears artfully, "Didn't you say your mother had local help with the labor and maintenance on the farm?"

Dabs nodded again. "Henry."

Betsy echoed Dabs, "Henry? Really? Well, that alone is interesting. Might Henry be a descendent of those buried here? He might offer some insight."

"Maybe. Henry is ailing these days and feeble. His granddaughter says he's been diagnosed with dementia."

Betsy said sweetly, "The oldest memories are the last to go. He could still be an important resource."

Dabs nodded, "Yes. I feel guilty. I'm overdue for a visit anyway."

Betsy placed her hand in the crook of Dabs' elbow.

"Well, that was an exciting morning. Eloise and I need a good scrub-up and a bite to eat, and then sadly, our little vacation must end before we wear out our welcome."

Prince was the only one to walk back to the house with enthusiasm.

Eloise was first in and out of the shower, packed her few belongings, including the box with the clay pipe, carefully wrapping it in her pajamas before placing it into her backpack. She left the harness brass sitting on the bedside table, running her fingers over it one last time. She took one last look out the window at the barn and yard.

Eloise then turned her back to the window. This house was cold and seemed to stay cold. Such an old house was never going to be energy efficient, even with updates. Eloise shivered. She was standing right where she had thought she had seen Louisa. Where she had heard Louisa speak. What had Louisa said to her? Something about betrayal and enemies and such. She had written it down and put the scrap of paper in her backpack.

Running away to Virginia was what she felt compelled to do. She thought she would receive a sign from the 18th century that would show her how to fix her massive screw-ups. Well, she *had* received all kinds of signs, hadn't she? Elaborate dreams, signs, and feelies. Salve for her bruised brain and bruised ego. But Eloise hadn't solved any problems, and in fact, may have only created emotional turmoil for her friend Dabs.

But she *was* on to something. She was. Eloise was someone who researched her history before taking her "flights of fancy."

She thought, "If you're going to have delusions, make them historically accurate ones!" Yeah, that was about right.

The thing is, she really did like Dabs. And Betsy had been a lifesaver. But surely, they both had her pegged as cracked. It didn't help when she described dreams as if she believed she was communing with the dead. But Louisa's journals *had* been just that. And she *was* connected to the place, somehow, however distantly. Eloise wanted to believe. She needed to believe.

Prince led the way down the elegant staircase. Eloise stopped on the landing to look toward Dab's study, imagining Priscilla, Louisa, and Aunt Bess sitting on the stairs to eavesdrop. That wasn't a dream. That had happened. Or something close to it. It was, after all, Louisa's journal, events seen through her eyes, as Betsy had reminded her.

Eloise dropped her backpack by the front door, did a little dance down the wide hall, that had served as the ballroom in some distant past. When she got to the kitchen, Dabs was there. The refrigerator door was open, and he was hauling out fixings for sandwiches.

"You can eat them here or pack them for the road."

Eloise had a moment of panic.

"Here! I hope you aren't sick of us, me, I mean."

Dabs smiled.

Eloise said, "That was upsetting. The angel and all that it means. I'm worried you're ready to see the last of us."

"Not even a little bit."

"You mean that?"

"Yes, really."

Then he put his hand on his forehead, "I can't believe I

haven't shown you the painting. In my bedroom. It sounds like a line, I know, I did tell you about it. Do you want to look?"

"Of course, I do."

Dabs motioned for Eloise to follow him.

The master bedroom was bigger than the upstairs bedrooms with a massive four poster bed that took up a lot of the space. One wall was mostly a massive fireplace. The walls had wood paneling with wainscoting, which made the whole room dark.

On the wall hung a rather small painting, and even with a light on the bottom, a light that Dabs now turned on, the picture was dark, the scene muddy.

Dabs said, "Unfortunately, it's coated with eons of smoke and grime from the fireplace."

Dabs had a flashlight handy. He flicked it on, and they leaned in for a close inspection.

The horse was easiest to see, white, alert, a dish to the face with flared looking nostrils, staring into the distance. It was more realistic and less stylized than the equestrian art of the age. The dog was large and black and shaggy.

Dabs shone the light on the dog in the painting, and then onto Prince, saying "Well, how about that? Big black shaggy dogs live in every age."

And then of course, was the rider. A woman. The face, sadly, obscured.

"Dabs! It's Louisa!"

He snorted, "Well, Sherlock Holmes, what makes you so confident it's Louisa?"

Eloise was getting excited, "That's her right leg. Her

right leg on the right side of the horse. Side-saddle both legs are on the left. How many women rode astride in her day?"

"Well, I'll be damned. You really are Sherlock Holmes. Or maybe I'm just stupid."

"You aren't stupid, Dabs."

"I am feeling especially dense today."

"It's not you, it's me. Corny line, but true. I make up stories, historically feasible ones. Sometimes I get lucky. Most of the time, "boom!" Shit explodes. I get exposed as a liar or delusional. I won't blame you if you need to cut me off. I'll try to leave you alone."

"Oh, for God's sake, Eloise. Don't be so dramatic. You're an Extreme Reader. You're an historian. You're intuitive. You have an amazing intellect. You're practically an archeologist. Of course, you'd be interested, or even obsessed with the journals, with Louisa, with the history of this place. Like me. Only better than me. But you just made yourself sound like one of those characters from Harry Potter who follow Voldemort."

Eloise laughed, "Finally, I get a contemporary reference from you! They were called Death Eaters, and no, I'm not that kind of crazy."

Eloise sat down suddenly on the edge of Dab's bed, put her elbows on her knees and gazed up at the painting.

Dabs knew she was formulating her thoughts and crossed his arms, watching her, waiting.

Eloise wondered how much she should say. Would she wreck it all?

Finally, she looked up at Dabs. "While I've been here,

I've been looking for signs, my brain on fire. And it's not the concussion. I've always loved fairy tales, and then historical romance novels. And when nothing in my life made sense, I looked for something magical to save me, looking for meaning in everything. Even the red birds. As if Louisa, and last night, Major Schmidt, as if they would have answers for me that would tell me what I need to do to keep Prince, to get Whiplash, to restore my friend's faith in me. My time here has been a lifeline to let my crazy brain and bruised ego rest in someone else's story. None of it fixes anything. I have to come back to the present day to untangle the mess I've made. I have to take what's coming. I have to steel myself."

Dabs said, "Do you want to tell me now, about that mess?"

"I guess you know what happened with Prince and Joe. It's too embarrassing to describe in detail. Pinky told me that I was keeping secrets from myself. I guess that's a kind way of telling me I was in denial. But that's Pinky. She's kind. It's just I hadn't been myself for a long time.

"My parents' divorce gutted me. I'll never understand it. At first, I blamed my mom. She sent Whiplash to Jock, for a list of bullshit reasons I knew were not true. I wanted to run away to Ireland. I felt like I needed to be with my horse and my dad. I knew Mom was sick, and I was willing to abandon her, to punish her. I hated hearing all the terrible things she said about Jock.

"But that's not why I made up a story about a Junior year abroad program in Ireland and a professor who was encouraging me to apply. None of that was true. What I could not admit was I wanted to bolt because I was watching her die, and no magical event was going to happen to save her. My love for my mom, watching her suffer, it was killing me. I did not think I could handle it. That's what I was hiding from myself."

Eloise sat up, looked at Dabs. He was still there, still listening. She continued, "Jock forbid my coming, of course. He said outright that he did not want me there, he wanted me to stay with mom. It seemed my dad didn't want to be my dad anymore. My mom got sicker and sicker. And I was terrified, like all the time.

"My animals, the ones that were mine, gone. The only home I had ever known had strangers living in it.

"Jock gets things to bend his way. I wanted things to bend my way for a change, like Jock, and I tried to bend them. Not by being honest, but by ..."

Dabs uncrossed his arms and sat down next to Eloise. "Not being honest."

"First it was the dog. He appeared like he was sent to me from heaven. Like in a story. And for real, he IS magical. He's a crime-fighting archeologist kind of magical dog. And then the journals. Magical. I'm studying Jefferson and I get to read a first-person account of the man? I became Louisa Roberts. I fell in love with Major Schmidt. And the lost dog flier, the one that was hanging on the wall, well, the owner, Joe, was in the photo too. He WAS Major Schmidt."

Eloise blurted out, "Good God, Dabs, I kissed Joe. A stranger!"

Dabs looked more confused than shocked.

"You think I'm being overly dramatic, but I *am* dangerous to myself and others."

Dabs was suppressing a smile, "It's too late for me to bar the door now."

"I hid the flier. I had to keep the dog."

"Okay, that's not good."

"So, when I hit my head, there I was, as Louisa, and there was Major Schmidt. The magic I had created had manifested. And I kissed him. Except it was JOE. Then I saw it was Joe. I said his name out loud, so that gave me away. Then I kind of passed out. It was a far better idea to pass out from pure embarrassment than own up to stuff. Maybe I was faking it. They did say I had a mild concussion."

Dabs put a hand on her knee. Then, he laughed. Then apologized. "I'm sorry for laughing. I realize this was painful for you both physically and emotionally, but give it some time and you'll laugh too."

Eloise stood up agitated. "Well, I can't keep passing out at critical moments. Actually, I'm feeling dizzy now."

Eloise sat back down, put her head down and took deep breaths.

She kept her head down but moaned, "They know the truth now. Doc, and Pinky. I'm not to be trusted. I have a whole list of people I can never see again, and I just added to the list. I don't think I can face any of them ever again."

"Yes, you can."

"I don't want to be a wounded bird, flapping around in the water tank, exhausted and about to drown, bedraggled and pitiful who needs rescuing with a horse's grain scoop."

Dabs scowled, "Huh? Did you just make that up?"

Eloise sniffed, "It was a pigeon. The point is, I don't want to be the crazy person who kisses strangers and whose only boyfriend is a face on a lost dog flier."

Dabs brightened up, was about to say something flirtatious, but could tell Eloise was about to bring her rant to a conclusion.

Eloise said, "I have a problem with truth. I have a problem with reality."

Dabs put an arm around her shoulders and pulled her into his side. "You were always up here." Dabs patted the air above his head. "Beyond my reach. A beautiful girl on a fiery red mare."

"That was Lulu. She's long gone."

Dabs said, "Consider that Betsy just made an excellent point that it takes someone with fresh eyes to see things clearly. You're looking from the inside out. But I see something very different looking from the outside."

Eloise's gaze seemed to be fixated on her feet.

Dabs continued, "Lulu Robertson is right here. I'm still that tall skinny kid who caught your red mare and handed her back to your beautiful mother. Life was more tender, fragile, and precious than we could know then. You and I have suffered some hard falls, harder than we ever took from our horses. But here we are. Somehow sitting side-by-side. And as far as your friends, you are doing them a terrible injustice."

"Are they still going to be my friends?"

"They know the whole story and yet, no one has disowned you. Um, unless there's more? You've killed someone? Insider trading? Stiffing a contractor?"

Eloise grimaced.

Dabs continued, "What Betsy did, bringing you all this way, staying here, marching around in the cold, wasn't done for someone she did not care about. You think Betsy would have turned up at my door if it hadn't been for you? She was taking care of you, Eloise."

"Because I was pitiful."

"Because you're worth it."

Eloise considered that Dabs was good, kind, and smart, and she noted too that he was handsome. Not like Joe. No long lashes and large soulful eyes. But handsome. She even decided in that moment that Dabs was not too old. Not at all. And he did not think her pitiful or crazy, wait, maybe he did, but if she was, he said she was "worth it." Her cowardly, dishonest, delusional self was still not a deal-killer?

That thought was, frankly, baffling.

Dabs tucked Eloise under his chin. "Eloise, you think I haven't made my share of messes. That I haven't had my share of crazy? But mistakes I've made brought me to where I am now. Back home. I'm staying here. And I'm going to keep after these journal transcriptions and that pile in the attic. I know you have to go back to Atlanta, to your friends, to your work, and especially to that red devil of a mare. But…"

Then Eloise did it again. Only this time, she knew who she was kissing. Although he seemed surprised, this time her kiss was returned.

Dabs responded so enthusiastically that it was Eloise who had to stop what she had started.

She pulled away, "I do have to go back. It terrifies me, but I think I'm ready."

"Do you have a plan?"

"No. But I am inspired by Louisa. I don't know why, but I believe she lived a long life, was given the gift of time to make things better, to right some wrongs as much as she could. I hope the remaining journals prove me right. I believe Major Schmidt stayed at Ivy Creek for Louisa, for Henry. He lived and she lived, and although Henry died before they did, he too lived a full life. This story, their story, well, it gives me comfort and courage."

Dabs said, "I hope you're right. But what about *your* story?"

Eloise paused, "I have to ask for mercy knowing I don't deserve it. I want to keep Prince. I want Whiplash. I want to keep riding Red and see Bev every day. But if I lose it all, I'll have to find the courage to go on. Mom would have wanted that. Jock too. He's been trying to say as much."

Dabs said, "When Whiplash put you on the ground countless times you let others catch her and help you back up. All those falls, in the end, came to something good. Whatever happens, let others help you this time too."

Eloise said, "That's true. Someone always caught her. Someone always helped me back into the saddle and encouraged me to keep going. And then I was off again at a gallop. Not pitiful. Strong."

Dabs smiled warmly, "And strangely, one time, Whiplash sought me out to help."

Eloise tipped her head, "And horses only run towards someone they deem trustworthy."

"You ran to me too."

"I did."

"Come back, Eloise."

At that moment a large hairy and wet chin was placed across her thigh. Dabs placed his hand on the dog's head, bright eyes, met bright eyes. He said, "And yes, God willing, you too Prince, you come back too."

* * *

Eloise and Betsy had made it several hours down the road when Dabs called. "Are you driving?"

"Betsy has the wheel at the moment."

"Put it on speakerphone, I've got something to share."

"Okay."

April 23, 1780

Father and I were reading late again, when I noticed he had not turned a page in some time. He was sitting up, but his eyes had closed. I knew I must wake him and send him to bed, but then thought, poor father should have a wife, not just a daughter, to gently guide him to bed.

He woke with a start. I asked him, softly, "Do you not miss having a wife?" He nodded. Then I asked, "Did you never think to marry again?" Father smiled and said, "Dare to bring in a new mistress to take precedence over Bess? Ha."

I did see his point. He said, "It's my children's turn."

416

I said, "Buck harangues me to marry, but he is the elder, he should do his duty first."

Father murmured ruefully, "It's not for want of trying. He cannot close the deal."

That was news to me.

Father continued, "I commiserated as I nearly failed to win your mother's hand. Old man Robertson was as tight-fisted and recalcitrant as they come. He thought Albemarle and Ivy Creek the back-of-beyond, and me not near good enough nor rich enough for his daughter."

"But mother chose you."

Father looked pleased, "She would have her choice and no other. Buck has not yet learned that he cannot have the daughter if the daughter will not have him."

Dabs said with excitement, "Eloise, do you know what this means? Louisa's mother was a Robertson, like you!"

Eloise had to take a moment to absorb the news.

She said, "Robertson. Like me! It means, oh my God, it means you and I might be related! That's too freaky."

"Eloise, we don't know for certain that I'm related to Louisa at all. But what we *do* know is that you are just as connected to this journal, to Louisa Roberts, to Ivy Creek, as I am, and maybe even more so."

After Eloise had hung up the phone, she looked over at Betsy. "I think you should let me drive, Betsy. I'm sure I'm fine."

Betsy glanced over at her. "Better than fine. You look the picture of health, in fact. Certainly not in the same state as you were on the trip up."

Eloise was quiet for a moment. She remembered what Dabs had said about Betsy, about all her friends. They had seen who she was, but they were still her friends. And it was almost beyond her understanding why that was.

She said, "Betsy, you saved me. You all saved me. The thing is, no one knows me like I know me, and I've come to believe I needed to keep it that way, because 'me' is damaged goods. I make crummy decisions and fabricate and prevaricate. And I screwed up again. I got caught. Like I've been caught before. But you, you dropped everything and came along on my bolt to Virginia. You stuck by me. Well, I'll never forget it. Just saying thank you seems so inadequate."

"Well dear, it's not. And you're not. And no one saved you but you. All anyone can do is go along for the ride. And I'm glad I did. What a ride it has been."

"Oh, Betsy. I may lose Prince. I may lose my job and who knows what else. Back in the day, on Whiplash, when I would have a fall on course, I understood that it's always the rider's fault, never the horse. I always knew it was me who had to change, get better, do better. But in those days, I had my mom and dad. And I thought that would never change. I only succeeded with Whiplash because of my dad and my mom."

"Well, they were there for you, for the ride, to dust you off, to comfort you, to give you guidance, but you still had to do the riding, right?"

"Yes."

"I assume there was plenty of pain involved in the process. Both physical and metaphorical?"

"Yes."

"What a grand metaphor for life. Eloise Robertson, you listen to me, no matter what, I think you are going to be just fine. You have friends, including one handsome Virginia Cavalier. You believe me?"

Eloise found she was smiling. And she didn't even feel dizzy, she said, "I do."

Acknowledgements

I have come to accept, as a rule, that all my endeavors will take longer, and cost more than they should. Writing this book and its companion, *Mercy Asked, Mercy Found* did nothing to dispel this belief. It's a very good thing that I began with outsized enthusiasm, because I needed it in spades to get over the finish line. But here I am, writing the acknowledgement page.

Reading and writing are solitary occupations. But to improve as a writer, one needs readers. I am lucky to have found an encouraging support team who helped make my story and me better.

I want to thank Christine Ranallo from PenPaperWrite for coaching me as I developed the concept for the story. Dr. Elizabeth Jacobs kindly read and commented on my first full draft. Fellow writer Susan Yaremko was my critique partner while I was composing, and Danielle Chiotti from The Manuscript Academy critiqued both volumes. A shout out to Marlene Butcher Whitaker's "Jeeter" who was one heck of a dog and an inspiration for Prince. Thank you to The Pharr Road Animal Hospital for hiring this English Major as a kennel maid all those many years ago.

And of course, the horses and riding students who continue to inspire me and keep me sane. A prayer of thanks to a certain red-headed horse in my past who provided many a "near-death experience" but was the ride of my life in a good way too!

I want to especially thank Deeds Publishing for continuing to believe in my ability as a writer and for producing beautiful books.

Like some of my characters in these two volumes, I could be called an "extreme reader." There is nothing I love more than assigning myself a "unit" of study and reading late into the night to tackle it. I could not have written these two books without reading a stack of non-fiction history books. I took Betsy's challenge and then some to read more than ten books on Thomas Jefferson as well as reading his own writings, public and private letters. Jefferson is a complex figure. Learning to appreciate his sublime achievements, while being honest about his extraordinary failings can be expanded to cover many other figures and historical events, as well applied to self-examination. It fit beautifully into the theme of my story. Jefferson wrote to his daughter Martha, "…and were we to love none who had imperfections this world would be a desert for our love."

My unit of study expanded. I wanted to understand the events of the American Revolution, especially as the war moved south. I wanted to know as much as I could about the Albemarle Barracks, about Tarleton's attempt to capture Jefferson. I wanted to understand how Cornwallis ended up trapped at Yorktown and was forced to surrender.

Of critical importance to me was to do justice to both

the enslaved people who lived near Monticello in the Virginia Piedmont, and those who were their enslavers. I wanted to get this right, even though my characters were fictional.

I began by reading the WPA Slave Narratives. These first-person accounts by (elderly) formerly enslaved Americans were collected during the late 1930's and early 1940's as part of The Federal Writers Project. I discovered a few had been recorded and these recordings can be found online. Fountain Hughes was especially interesting to me as he was the grandson of Wormley Hughes, who was owned by Thomas Jefferson. But I also listened to Laura Smiley and Harriet Smith's recorded interviews as well as others. To hear former slaves give first person testimony brings to mind the quote from Faulkner, "The past is never dead. It's not even past."

History is not dry facts. History is not distant or unreachable in understanding. History is in our DNA, in the faces you see, in the voices you hear. It is a long story with no end if we continue to speak and write and read and seek to understand.

—Karen McGoldrick

Karen McGoldrick rides and teaches dressage from her home base in Canton, Georgia. She is the author of the series, *The Dressage Chronicles.*

Karen earned her USDF bronze, silver, and gold medals on horses she trained herself. She is a USDF certified Instructor/Trainer, and earned her USDF "L" certificate, "with distinction." She is lucky enough to still have horses in her daily life.

Betwixt The Stirrup And The Ground, and *Mercy Asked, Mercy Found* (scheduled for release in first quarter 2024) feature new characters, but returns readers to a world filled with horses, dogs, and humor, with the addition this time of another one of her passions, American history.